I0594070

THE SECRET HOUR

EAGLE BROTHERHOOD SERIES

KAT LE VEQUE

OLIVERHEARTBOOKS

AUTHOR'S NOTE

They call themselves the Eagle Brotherhood.

We've all got 'that' group of friends. People we've bonded with that just 'get' you and you get them. Whether you bond over common interests, or a job, of even just mutual friends, we've all found that connection at one time or another.

Same with the Eagle Brotherhood.

It started with five Americans. They were young, brilliant, idealistic, and met during a semester abroad. When I first wrote this series, many years ago, it was originally called the American Heroes series. It was supposed to be about guys who knew each other as young men, but who went on to live their own lives and have their own adventures. Ordinary guys in extraordinary circumstances was how I described it. There were only five in the beginning, but somewhere along the line, we added two Brits as 'honorary' members. There are actually more books slated to be written, but I just haven't gotten around to it yet. One of the Eagle Brotherhood — Nash Aury — even has a sequel mostly written to his book, so this is really a series that has a lot of growth potential. And why not? It centers around men who are honorable, chivalric, and end up facing some really stressful and, in a few cases, dangerous situations. Some explainable, some not. That's the fun of it.

But it all had to start somewhere.

Each Eagle Brotherhood book starts out with the same "*How it began*" preface so you, as the reader, knows where these guys connect because they don't appear in each other's stories. It's a rather interesting connection, but one that opens up the hero of each tale — and eventually the heroine — to one heck of a story. These guys are connected to me as much as to each other.

They really are a true brotherhood.

I hope you enjoy the stories in this series because they were a labor of love to write. You don't have to read them in any particular order:

The Burning Hour
The Sunset Hour
The Secret Hour
The Unholy Hour
The Devil's Hour
The Killing Hour
The Ancient Hour

Happy reading,

AQUILA FRATRUM

Seven men.
Each with a story to tell.
Welcome to the world of the Eagle Brotherhood.

Years ago, five Americans on a semester abroad met at the home of their sponsor in Yorkshire, England. They were taking the same course at the University of York, including the son of their host. But it wasn't the course in International Law that bonded them. It was an incident from that time, something that happened on a dark and stormy night in an alley behind a bar in York called *The Calcaria.*

It is something that changed their perspectives forever.

These days, the men who once called themselves the *Aquila Fratrum* or the Eagle Brotherhood — a name based on the Americans who were military-based at that time — have gone forth in their lives. They are men in normal, everyday professions who succeed in extraordinary things. Their paths aren't smooth, and they aren't perfect, but they understand more than most that life is never about the smooth or the perfect. It is about the imperfect and the difficult. It's even about the unexplainable.

And, above all else, light overcomes the darkness.

Aquila Fratrum.

Ordinary men who have lived extraordinary circumstances.

And the women who love them.

HOW IT BEGAN
MORE THEN TWENTY YEARS AGO, THE CALCARIA, YORK

MICK MCCONNELL, PROPRIETOR

"Beck." A big man with a crown of auburn hair spoke with a drunken slur to his words. "Beck. *Seavington!*"

The blond Californian on the other side of the table, who had been half-lidded as he watched a group of women across the darkened room of the pub, jerked at the sound of his name as if he'd just been slapped.

"What?" he said, looking at the man with the auburn hair. "Christ, Phipps. Can't you just leave me alone for a minute?"

Archer Phipps struggled not to laugh. "Why?"

"Because you're breaking my powers of concentration, you ass."

That broke the table out in snorts of laughter. The man seated next to Beck, big and blond and with a mega-watt smile, put a hand on Beck's shoulder.

"What in the hell are you concentrating on?" he said, leaning over to see what Beck might be seeing. When he spied it, he gestured. "Over there?"

Beck full-on pointed to the women across the pub. "There."

"Those?"

"*Those.*"

"Well... what are you trying to do by staring at them? Just go talk to them."

Beck scowled at the man. "Because I'm trying to lure them with the power of suggestion, Trevor," he said. Then, he looked around the table and pointed. "It works. Colt over there has a laser stare. He doesn't even have to say anything — women know what he's thinking just by the expression on his face. Isn't that right, Sheridan?"

Colt Sheridan, clean-cut and square-jawed, waved an annoyed hand at the man he'd spent nearly every day with for the past six months. "Some of us don't have to be obvious," he said. "Look at Nash. All he has to do is give them one of those sexy, down-home expressions and they're falling all over themselves. I don't have anything on him."

Across the table, Nash Aury, the quiet and diplomatic sort with a Louisiana drawl, laughed softly. "It's all in the face," he said, gesturing to the big dimples in each cheek. "I don't have anything y'all don't have, but we don't have anything that Serreaux has, so maybe we should just give it up and let him take the lead."

The group looked over at Ethan Serreaux, a man with a French parents even though he was born in America. Dark-eyed and dark-haired, he looked like he'd just come off the pages of a men's magazine. When he saw that the entire table of semi-drunks was looking at him, he smiled lasciviously.

"*Belle fille,*" he said in his best Maurice Chevalier impression. "*Asseyez-vous sur mes genoux et dites-moi à quel point vous me voulez.*"

Everyone burst out laughing except for Beck, who slowly banged his forehead on the table. "You sound like Pepe Le Pew," he said. "Shut *up!*"

More laughter, most especially from Archer and the last man of their group, a giant of a figure who wasn't part of their academic group. Fox Henredon was in the process of obtaining his Ph.D. in Archaeology with an emphasis in Egyptology from Oxford. In fact, he'd come back a few months ago from a dig near Aswan and when he visited his best friend from grade school, Archer, he'd come across the Americans temporarily housed in Archer's pad. He'd gotten on so well with them that they'd made him an honorary member of their group. But not just the group — of their secret society, as well.

Aquila Fratrum.

The Eagle Brotherhood.

The whole secret group was really meant as a joke, but the basis of it — the honor, the patriotism — they took seriously. Three out of the five Americans had come from Annapolis and all five of them were majoring in International Law, hence the purpose of the semester abroad course. Archer was taking the same course, and he'd been the host house, and given that they were all within a few years of each other age-wise, they'd all bonded over common likes, common dislikes, and a passion for adventure.

It was a guy gang like no other.

But tonight, they were drinking to the group that would soon be separating. The course at the University of York was finished and the Americans would soon be heading back to their native lands, but promises of reciprocal visits had abound all evening. Nash, in particular, had invited everyone to New Orleans for the holidays because his family, having made their money in sugar, had a massive house that could accommodate everyone. Beck, Cord, and Colt had already committed to it, but Ethan had family obligations he needed to get out of. Archer was trying to figure out how to break the news to his parents, who were possessive of his time, while Fox was on the verge of committing. He'd never been to New Orleans and a street named after liquor intrigued him. As the Brotherhood planned their next gathering, Beck stood up from the table.

"I need to find the loo," he said, looking around. "Where is it? Back behind the bar?"

The problem was that he was drunker than the rest of them

and probably not in great shape to find anything, so Cord stood up next to him.

"Back in the corner," he said. "Come on, little brother."

He had Beck by the neck, pulling him back behind the bar where there was a dark corridor that led to bathrooms and the kitchen. The term 'little brother' was essentially referring to Beck's age because he happened to be the youngest out of their group. But he was also the toughest. Beck Seavington could out-fight anybody, Fox included, and Fox had participated in underground fight clubs during his earlier college days. He'd won money at it, too.

But Beck's fists were quite lethal.

The Navy wanted him that way.

Cord went with Beck so he wouldn't get into any trouble. Cord was an enormous man, having played football, and the rumor was that he was being scouted by the NFL. He wasn't a fighter by nature, but no one was going to test of man of that size. He'd just push the scrapper, Beck, in front of him, anyway, and let the career Navy man do the damage.

Every group had a scrapper.

It smelled like stale booze and bleach back here and the door to the men's room was locked. Beck rattled it but it remained fixed. With a heavy sigh, he looked at Cord.

"I can't wait," he muttered.

Cord tipped his head in the direction of the door to the alley out back, which was next to the kitchen door.

"Outside?" he said.

Beck nodded, which nearly threw him off balance, and charged through the back door. Cord followed him and they ended up in the dirty, damp alley behind the bar. It smelled worse out here, like garbage and animals. There were crates against the wall, broken down cardboard boxes, and little else. There were two ends to the alley, but they were standing closer to the end that dumped out onto the street where *The Calcaria* was located. Beck was looking for a discreet place to relieve himself when the back door smacked back on its hinges again, spilling forth the rest of their group.

"I think we're done with this place," Archer said, rubbing his eyes because the alcohol was messing with his vision. "There's another pub down the way called Valhalla. Let's go there."

Beck had found a spot behind some crates. "Are the women more proactive there?" he asked. "I mean, will they actually come up and talk to you? I don't think my mind control is working."

Archer grinned. "Do you seriously want a woman that approaches you?" he said. "The wooing of a woman is an art, Beck. You don't want some nervy woman up in your grill, do you?"

The others snorted in agreement. Ethan and Nash were by the back door, leaning back against the wall, as Colt went to stand next to Beck. Fox went to stand with Cord, maybe as a lookout since they really shouldn't be pissing in an alley, when three men suddenly appeared from what was a small walkway between buildings. It was dark, so no one really noticed, until one of the men walked up behind Colt and put a knife to the man's back.

Then, everything changed.

The drunken, happy mood was gone.

"Easy, big man," the man said. He was short, with a dirty jacket, but the knife he'd produced was quite large. "If you want to keep your kidney, you'll relax, mate."

Everyone froze — Ethan, Nash, Archer, Fox, Cord, Beck, and most of all, Colt. But his features never changed expression, even as he felt the prick of cold steel against his right kidney.

"If you're looking for money, you're too late," he said steadily. "We're coming out of the bar, not going into it. We've spent our money."

The man in the dirty jacket grunted as his friends also produced big knives. "Somehow, I doubt it," he said. "We were watching you inside. I think you're from money, so you've got more where that came from, Yank. I think all of you have more."

With that, his friends began to move. One of them was heading for Ethan while the other one was heading for Archer. The group, as a whole, instinctively started to back away from the men approaching, but Fox refused to budge. At seven inches over six feet, he had that luxury of being stubborn.

"You blokes really think you're going to rob guys who are twice your size?" he said incredulously. "You're either incredibly stupid or way too overconfident."

"I'll go with stupid," Cord muttered.

Fox quickly agreed with him. "Stupid, for sure," he said. "There are seven of us and three of you. You may be able to take out a couple of us, but there are five of us left who will break your fucking necks. Are you ready for that?"

That brought some pause to the man's companions, but the man in the dirty jacket poked Colt enough to draw blood.

"Give me your fucking money!" he hissed. "Another word and I'll cut a hole in this man big enough to stick my hand through!"

Colt didn't even flinch when the man jabbed him. He kept his right hand up while his left once reached into his pocket for his wallet. But as he was doing that, and the other two men with knives were advancing on Ethan and Archer, no one happened to be watching Cord.

And that would be their fatal mistake.

"*Quaere ferro scopum tuum,*" Cord suddenly mumbled. "*Oboedite mihi!*"

Inexplicably, the man holding the knife to Colt's back jerked. He jolted. His hand flew up and the big blade he'd been forcing on Colt flew up and into his own throat, straight back through so that the tip came out of the back of his neck. It went through him like a bullet. As he staggered back and fell to the ground, his friends were momentarily startled and that gave Cord the opportunity to turn against them.

"*In molles venter it ferrum,*" he growled, lifting a big fist as if to punch the men straight in the face. "*Utrumque vestrum!*"

The men screamed as the hands holding the knives came up and plunged the blades into their bellies as if they had a mind of their own. They went down as Ethan, Nash, Archer, Fox, Beck and Colt made haste to back up, away from what was evidently going on. No one knew what was happening and it was best to get clear considering knives were slashing all over the place.

At least, everyone but Cord backed up. He pointed a finger at the men who had just stabbed themselves in the belly.

"*Ferro ad carnem, ferrum ad os,*" he said in a low tone. "*Collum secari debet.*"

The men with knives in their bellies suddenly withdrew those knives and stabbed themselves in the neck, three or four times, until they could stab no more. They simply lay there and bled as Cord turned to his stunned group of friends.

"We need to get out of here," he said quietly. "Before the cops come. *Quickly.*"

No one moved. They stood there, eyes wide at what they'd just seen. Colt, who was the closest to Cord, grabbed him by the arm.

"What in the hell just happened?" he asked in awe. "What did you do?"

Cord looked back at the men bleeding out on the alley floor. "I protected us," he said simply. "We really need to go."

"Protected us *how?*" Fox was at Cord's side, his handsome face seriously. "What did we just see, Cord? Hypnosis of some kind?"

Cord scratched his head. "No," he said reluctantly, looking at the curious group. "Can we just get out of here, please?"

"Not until you explain," Fox said.

He was serious. No one was moving, not really. Exasperated, Cord sighed heavily. "Fine," he said. "I did it to save Colt's life. That guy was going to kill him."

Colt, who had blood running down the right side of his torso, stepped forward. "He probably was," he said. "Nobody is disputing that. But *what* did you do?"

Cord looked at his friend. "It's not something I really talk about," he said hesitantly. "I haven't... I haven't done that stuff since I was younger, but you all know I'm descended from Abigail Williams. When we all talked about our families and stuff, I told you guys that I was descended from one of the chief accusers of the Salem Witch Trails."

"You did," Colt said as his gaze moved to the men on the ground. "But what does that have to do with it? And done *what* stuff?"

Cord was clearly reluctant. "My dad likes to call us Casters," he said. "Abigail Williams was an accomplished witch and that trait is passed down in my family, like red hair or freckles. Only it's some kind of power we can summon. What you saw was a spell. I turned their knives against them."

"You're a witch?" Colt repeated in shock. "Seriously, Cord? Like — magic?"

Cord didn't answer. He just started walking, very quickly, and the others instinctively followed. They came to a walkway that led out onto the street and, nearly running, they headed up towards the main road.

"Yeah, like magic," Cord finally said as they came to the main avenue. "You saw it. I can't explain it more than that, but I wouldn't have done it if I thought we could have gotten out of that without Sheridan missing a kidney. Just... do yourself a favor. Forget you ever saw it."

"Wait," Ethan said as they began to walk, very quickly, towards the area with the car park. "We can't just leave. No matter what happened, or how it happened, we have to call the police."

"And tell them what?" Cord said. "That we got attacked and that I used a spell to turn the weapons against the guys who attacked us? They would think we were nuts."

As Ethan shook his head in disagreement, Archer grabbed him by the arm and pulled him along. "They would want to know who stabbed those guys," he said. "They'd take our fingerprints and find out that none of our fingerprints were on the weapons. How in the hell are we going to explain that?"

Ethan wasn't sure, but he didn't like running from a crime scene. "Guys, we can't leave," he said, trying to drag his feet. "We were witnesses to what happened. We have to..."

Cord suddenly came to a halt and grabbed Ethan by the shirt. "What do you think is going to happen?" he hissed. "Ethan, I don't want to run any more than you do, but I'm the one who killed those guys. That's the bottom line. And I'm not doing time for it and I'm not going to show the York Police how I turned those weapons against them, so forget it. We're not calling anyone. We're getting out of here and you are giving me your word that you'll never repeat what you saw. I need you to swear that to me."

Ethan could see how upset Cord was and he put up his hands in a gesture of surrender. "I swear that I'll never repeat it," he said. "Don't worry about that. But if anyone else saw us..."

"Who is going to see us?" Cord said, letting go of his shirt. "No one saw us. We're going to fly home tomorrow, anyway, and we'll be out of here. Done."

Ethan nodded, but he wasn't happy about it. Even if he wasn't happy, at least he understood. The entire group began walking again, very quickly, with the car park in sight. Beyond that, freedom.

Freedom from something they hoped wouldn't come back to haunt them.

Cord most of all.

"You... you really *did* that?" Beck finally said. He was still astonished by what he'd witnessed. "How in the hell did you learn how to cast spells?"

Cord school his head. "I told you," he said. "It's in my blood. But I don't like talking about it, so let's just drop it... okay?"

"But we saw it."

They had reached the car park by now and Cord came to an abrupt halt, facing the group. He was normally a congenial guy, but the event had him spooked.

"I know you guys saw it," he said. "But you need to swear that you will never repeat it. You will never tell anyone. Because if you do, I'm going to be in a shitload of trouble. How in the hell am I going to explain to anyone that I used witchcraft to kill some criminals?"

"But it was in self-defense," Ethan stressed. "No one is going to convict you, or any of us for that matter."

Cord's frustration bled through. "But we would have to explain *how* it happened," he said. "Don't you get it? One question would lead to another, questions you don't want to answer. Trust me."

Nash, who had been silent for the most part, put a hand on Cord's shoulder. "Cord, where I'm from, voodoo and witchcraft are part of the culture," he said quietly. "I've seen things I can't explain, so I believe what you're saying. I know what I saw. You have a gift, but it's a gift people don't understand. We've all witnessed something tonight that was... well, pretty damn amazing."

Cord registered some relief as he realized he had the support of Nash. The guy wasn't going to hound him. After a moment, he looked at the rest of the group. "You know, we've joked about calling ourselves the Eagle Brotherhood, but I think we really *are* a brotherhood now," he said. "We've experienced something that could have cost us our lives. It was small, but it happened. You saw something you shouldn't have seen because I did something I shouldn't have done. But to protect you guys... I'd do it again. I hope you know that."

"I feel like I owe my life to you," Colt said, reaching out to shake Cord's hand. "You were brave to do what you did, Cord, knowing... well, knowing that it wasn't something for all to see. But you did it and I'm grateful. I'll take an oath of silence on the Eagle Brotherhood if that's what it'll take. To protect you because you saved my life, I'll do anything. And if you ever need me, no matter where I am, I'll come. That's a promise."

More hands began shooting out, covering Colt and Cord's hands. It was a vow, a promise, not to discuss the event that bonded them more than a school or allied nations could. It was a bond that went deeper now because they harbored a secret. More than that, they had crossed into the realm of a brotherhood that would protect or kill for one another.

The true test of a brotherhood.

It was an oath that would take to their graves.

Wherever life would take them.

PROLOGUE

THE SANTA ANA winds had been strong the previous night and the sun rose to reveal a concrete and steel landscape that was scattered with downed trees and mounded leaves. But the sky of the new day was a brilliant blue, the temperature already on the rise. The San Gabriel Mountains, brown with dry brush, were stark and imposing against the clear sky.

Jack could remember the smog of the San Gabriel Valley when he was a kid, how the *Santana*, or Santa Ana, winds would blow away the brown layer of air and leave everything fresh and clear and brittle. Usually in the fall it would happen, inviting the brush fires that were so prevalent to the area. He could recall the home he used to live in, nestled right up against those dry, dry mountains.

Mother's last husband had been determined to have a home with an ocean view, even if that ocean was thirty miles away. The price Kevin had to pay for a view of Catalina on a clear day was the never-ending threat of a brush fire and more than once they had come close to losing everything. Jack still had visions of Kevin on the roof of the garage with a garden hose. But somehow, they always emerged unscathed.

Jack continued to stare at the mountains, recollecting. All of that, the fires of autumn as well as his childhood, seemed so long ago. He'd kind of pushed it all from his memory after Kevin had died at age forty-five of a heart attack. The man wasn't his biological father, but he was the only father Jack had ever really known and his death had left Jack shattered. Now, looking at the mountains seemed to bring those bittersweet memories around again like a never-ending merry-go-round.

Jack had been six years old when Mother had married Kevin. She had just moved back to the west coast after living in Maryland for a while. But Mother never really talked about those years she had spent in the east. Jack wasn't even sure if Kevin had known the details. He was a good man and maybe he'd just let it all slide, like Mother's secrets didn't matter to him.

Once, Jack had asked about his "real dad" when he was old enough to realize that Kevin wasn't the man who had given him life. Mother had turned white and stammered something he didn't understand. But when Jack got older, Mother told him, very matter-of-factly, that his biological father was a U.S. Senator who had died in a plane crash when Jack was four years old. She had stammered and wept through the story and Jack realized why his mother had been so reluctant to talk about that period in her life. His death had crushed her. At least, that was his impression.

Jack didn't recall his real father, nor did he have any real memories of life on the east coast. His only memories of his youth were of living in Pasadena with his mother and Kevin. He had grown up in a happy house with a couple of older brothers from mother's first marriage and a sister from her marriage to Kevin. Siblings who had grown up and moved away. They were heading to the west coast now as their mother lay dying, but that would take time. Jack wondered if they would make it at all. Out of the four siblings, Jack was the one who had always stayed close to his mother. There was a very strong bond between them.

A feeble cough roused Jack from his train of thought. He turned away from the window, turning to the sterile hospital bed upon which his mother lay. She was hooked up to one line that monitored her heart rate, oxygen saturation, respiration, and other vital information. It was all printed out on a screen above her head and Jack glanced up at the screen, noting that her life signs were weaker now than they had been an hour earlier. His heart sank but his mother's violet eyes fell on him and he forced a smile. He didn't want her to see how badly her illness was affecting him.

"So you're awake?" he asked softly as he moved to the bed. Taking his mother's tissue-paper thin hand into his palm, he kissed it. "Have a good nap?"

Mother didn't respond for a moment. Jack wondered if she even heard him. Then, she coughed again and closed her eyes. "Jack," she murmured. "What time is it?"

"Time for dinner. Are you hungry?"

Mother's head twitched weakly, trying to shake her head. "No."

"I'll go get Chinese take-out and sneak it in like I did last week. Sound good?"

"No."

"Pizza?"

"No."

Jack tried not to let his mood dampen. The woman could not afford to lose any more weight "You always did like a big, greasy burger. I'll run up the street and...."

"No." Mother's voice sounded strangely firm. The violet eyes opened and she was looking at him, her face still lovely in spite of her age and illness. Such a sweet, beautiful face. "What day is it?"

"Tuesday."

"It's a good day to die."

Jack tried not to show how bad that comment hurt him but he couldn't. Mother read his emotion and squeezed his hand in a surprising show of strength. "Don't grieve, Jack. There isn't time."

Jack met her eyes, then. "What do you mean?"

Mother held his gaze, memorizing every line of his strong-jawed face. "Exactly that," she whispered. When he looked away again, uncertainly, she squeezed his hand to force him to meet her eye. "Jack, the time has come. I think we must... talk."

Jack didn't like the tone of her voice. "About what?"

She didn't say anything for a moment. Then an eyebrow lifted. "You know," she said. "Just... things."

Jack shook his head. "What things?" Even as he said it, he knew exactly what she was talking about. But he wasn't sure he wanted to hear any more and he was about to divert the subject when Mother sighed heavily and began coughing. Even in this day and age, the marvels of medical science had yet to find a cure for cancer, and Mother's case was advanced. The doctors figured she had less than a few days to live, at best. The thought brought tears to Jack's eyes. He held her hand as she coughed, her body wracked with disease and a hint of anguish he couldn't begin to understand. When the spasms died and she lay gasping, her luminous eyes turned to him once again.

"Mom," he whispered, "you don't have to talk about anything. There isn't anything you have to explain to me."

Mother took a deep breath, struggling to form the words. "Yes, there is," she insisted. "You've ... you've got to know. And there isn't much time left."

Jack fought back the tears. He was a grown man, an FBI agent with a world of responsibility, but the sight of his dying mother made him feel like a four-year-old again. The woman, for so many years, had been his whole life. Even though he had a wife and kids now, still, his mother had a special place in his heart and like a clingy child, he didn't want to let her go.

"Mom," he said hoarsely. "I don't need to know anything. I've had a really good life and I've never wondered about the what-ifs or has-beens. It just doesn't matter, whatever you may feel necessary to say."

"I know," Mother said softly. "But it's right that you should know the truth. I... I've just never had the nerve to tell you."

Jack gazed down at his mother, his jaw ticking faintly. "Does it really matter? I know that my father was a U.S. Senator from Wyoming, Scott Dane. I also know he was killed in a plane crash more than forty years ago. What else matters?"

"A great deal."

He stared at her a moment before rising from the bed, shoving his hands into his pockets. His mother watched the gesture, something that hadn't changed since he was a kid. A sort of dejected, frustrated look.

"Look, Mom," he said, kicking at the wheels on her bed. "You've never wanted to talk about your life on the east coast. I know everything up until that point in time, and then there's a four year time gap that's like this big, mysterious void. I will admit that it used to bug me. When I was a kid, I used to imagine all sorts of things, like maybe you were a hooker or a spy. But now ... well, now I really don't care. If you want to keep that part of your life private, then that's your business."

"Did Hunter or Brody ever say anything?"

"Not a word. And I never asked."

Mother was smiling faintly. "You're far too accepting."

He grinned. "I've had to be."

She tried to shake a fist at him and he laughed; it was so much like Mother of old. But they both sobered, for the subject was too serious to take lightly. It was the first time in all of Jack's forty-six years that his mother had been willing to discuss her life in the east.

"Mom," he took his hands out of his pockets and leaned on the end of the bedrail. "You don't have to do this."

"Yes, I do," she said firmly. "Don't you want to know?"

He shrugged, lamely. "Know about what? Frankly, I don't care. You've already told me all I need to know."

She gazed at him, steadily. "Don't pretend to be so detached. There is far more to the story and you've been dying for years to ask me."

He didn't say anything. He stared at the floor, fidgeted with the end of the bed, until Mother finally put a stop to his twitching.

"Ask me something," she demanded. "Anything at all."

Jack snorted. "Christ, Mom...."

"Come on, just ask. You've always wanted to know. Can't you think of one single question?"

He pursed his lips, half in thought and half in irritation. He could see in her eyes that she wasn't going to let the subject go. All of these years and, now, she was almost desperate to talk about her secrets. "All right," he said softly. "I'll ask you something."

Mother lifted her hand. "Shoot."

She had meant to be flippant. Mother was a real character when she was feeling fit and it was a brief glimpse into her normal nature. But he couldn't respond to it; not now when she was dying and he was about to hear the mysteries of her life. Secrets she had lived with, hanging over her like a great, dark shadow. To finally discuss what she had hidden for decades was the supreme act of finality. She was dying, therefore, the need to relieve her conscience was strong. It all seemed to come back to this death thing again, like an endless circle, and Jack was torn between the excitement of finally hearing her truth and the grief of knowing why she was doing it.

"Okay, here goes." He kicked at the bed again as he summoned his courage. "Do ... do I look like my dad?"

The warm glimmer in Mother's eyes faded. "Why do you ask?"

He shrugged. "Because I've seen pictures of him and I don't think I look much like him."

"You look like my side of the family, you know that."

"Is that the truth, mom?"

It wasn't. But she had been telling him that for so long that she had almost convinced herself of the fact. But now, there was no longer any reason to lie to him. Jack was a grown man. He had a right to know. And she had a duty to tell him.

"No," she finally murmured. "It's not."

Jack's expression told her that he wasn't particularly surprised. Mother kept waiting for him to explode, but his features remained steady.

"Who was he?"

Mother continued to stare at him. Her eyes softened and her

cheeks seemed to pinken, the first color she'd had in weeks. Much to Jack's surprise, she actually smiled. Then she patted the mattress beside her and Jack sat down, laying his head on her shoulder like he used to when he was a boy. For a moment, the only sound that met his ears was the growling in his mother's chest. Then, the faint sound of her familiar, gentle voice.

He closed his eyes and listened.

ONE

WINTER WAS A HORRIBLE SEASON. Coming from Southern California, Casey Cleburne never really appreciated the true hell of winter's wrath. There were layers of clothes to wear and the threat of suffocating beneath all that wool. No one dressed like this in California unless they lived in the Sierras and then it was fun to bundle up because you knew that within a matter of hours you could be back at the beach sunning yourself and shaking off the chill. In California, you could have your choice of weather. But here, it was all one temperature – freezing. After twelve years, she should have been used to it, but she wasn't. She was a wimp.

The smell of exhaust was heavy in the air as she quickly covered the last hundred yards from the parking structure to the guard gate located at the north side employee entrance of the White House. It was stupid to have a car in D.C., she knew. Everyone took public transportation. But she had driven all the way from California in her Honda all those years ago and couldn't seem to part with having a car. These days, she had a big gas guzzler.

Running along the wet path that led towards the entrance, her Jimmy Choo pumps made sharp clicking noises along the pavement. At one point, she slipped and nearly lost her balance, but it didn't slow her pace. Directly in front of her was a large guard shed, painted a stark white, and a host of parka-clad security guards checking in the nine-to-five White House employees that worked in the West Wing.

"Hi, Stan," she said as she pushed her way inside the warm shack.

The African-American guard, a middle-aged man with bulging eyes, smiled at her as she displayed her identification. "Good morning, Ms. Cleburne. Have a nice day."

Casey flashed him a hurried smile, shoved her I.D. back into her purse, and pushed past the other employees in various stages of admittance. At the door leading toward the main building of the White House she came across a fellow employee, struggling with a scarf hooked into an earring.

Lisanne LeVine was in a panic. Her gold earring was twisting and the DKNY scarf wasn't faring much better. When she saw Casey, her pixieish face screwed up in desperation.

"Help, Casey," she moaned.

Casey shifted her briefcase and her purse, untangling the strings. She smiled at the tiny, dark-haired girl. "No damage, calm down," she said. "Your mother's scarf is safe."

Lisanne looked guilty and defiant at the same time. "She still doesn't know I took it from her when I was home for Christmas."

Casey snorted softly. "If she's anything like my mother, when she discovers that it's missing, she'll hunt you down like an animal."

Lisanne laughed like a delinquent kid. Either she didn't care about her mother's wrath or she was far enough away from home that she indulged a false sense of security. As the two women exited the guard shack and walked the path to the West Wing of the White House Administrative Offices, the wind picked up and whipped at them mercilessly. Casey pulled her coat tighter and grimaced.

"I can't stand this weather," she grumbled. "What in the hell was I thinking when I decided to move here?"

A strong gust of wind caught them just as a Marine guard

opened the door. Cold air and leaves followed them inside, faster than the Marine door guard could close the door. Debris scattered on the mat that had been placed on top of the plush, dark blue carpeting, adding to the pile of muck that had formed from countless employees entering and exiting. Casey stamped the damp leaves off her feet, the instant warmth of the corridor like a slap in the face.

"Thank you, Lord," she exclaimed softly, removing her gloves. "Let there be heat."

Lisanne was right behind her, removing the stolen scarf and pulling off her gloves. "You should have stayed on the coast." Her New York accent was strong. "Only hard-asses can take this weather."

Casey lifted a well-defined eyebrow "I can deal with the weather," she insisted. "But can a hard-ass take an earthquake?"

Lisanne shook her head, grinning. "Not on your life. I prefer my ground to stay still."

The door to the President's outer offices was wide open and already Casey could smell the cigar smoke, even at this time of the morning. The new President loved his cigars, at any time of day. Her jacket coming off, she marched through the lobby with Lisanne in tow, down the hall to the reception area, and greeted the Secret Service agent that sat to the left of the receptionist's desk.

The agent, an African-American with a Heisman Trophy physique, merely nodded his head. Lisanne, the receptionist, planted herself behind the huge mahogany desk and switched the night service off on the West Wing phone banks, which were already beginning to light up. Casey moved past the chaos of reception and continued on, heading for the door to her left that led into her own office. But she came to an abrupt halt when a stout woman with an expensive haircut blocked her path.

Casey almost bumped into the woman. "Good morning, Maggie," she said, pulling her camel-hair coat the rest of the way off. "What's up?"

Maggie Broom smiled. She was actually a very nice woman, middle-aged and built like a Russian factory worker. Her face was round and her teeth were a lovely shade of smoker's yellow. Casey had a difficult time looking at her when she smiled. She had to resist the urge to recommend a good dentist. Maggie was the assistant to the Chief of Staff, an efficient and no-nonsense woman.

"The President is in his office and he wants to see you immediately," she said. "Today is the day the new Special Agent in Charge takes over from Walt."

Casey pushed past Maggie and unloaded her coat on the hanger behind her door. "I know," she said, moving to her desk to dump her briefcase on the smooth, dark surface. With a quick glance at the day's agenda, she faced Maggie with her hands on her hips. "We've got a busy day, Mags. Can you handle my overflow? Russ has got several meetings lined up and I'll be taking minutes until my hand falls off."

Maggie nodded strongly. "The President has already asked that I take up your slack. There's an agenda for today's meeting with the Ways and Means Committee, and a ...."

Casey held up her hand. "I know the list, believe me." She sat down in her black leather chair, rolling it across the floor to where her three flat screen computers were lined neatly in a row. She soft-booted all three and watched as the monitors came online. Satisfied, she made sure the two fax machines were also online as the computer screen to the far right began to print out the returns from the New York Stock Exchange. Running a practiced eye over her electronic kingdom, she realized Maggie was still standing in her office.

Casey glanced at her. "Is there anything else?"

Maggie looked hesitant, unusual for the normally confident woman. After a moment of uncertainty, she simply shook her head and picked up the remote from the edge of the desk. Pushing the button, a panel in the wall opposite Casey's desk suddenly lifted, revealing three large plasma screens recessed into the wall. All three major news networks came on at another push of the button and Maggie set the remote back down.

She seemed solicitous but Casey wasn't paying too much attention. She was focused on her schedule for the day as her Outlook came online. Maggie lingered by the second desk in the office, the desk where the President's travel coordinator sat.

There was a doorway almost directly across from Casey's desk that led to a very small office where the President's Special Agent in Charge was positioned. It was empty, having been vacated yesterday by the man who had guarded the President since he began his election campaign two years ago. Maggie eyed the empty office and the empty travel desk, as if to confirm there was no one else around. Then she spoke.

"Have you ever met Colt Sheridan?"

"You mean the new Special Agent in Charge?" Casey shook her head. "No. Have you?"

"I've seen him in passing."

"Okay... so why do you want to know if I've met him?"

Maggie continued to look uncomfortable. Casey swore she even saw a hint of a blush.

"No reason," she replied, though it was a lie. "I just... well, I've heard about him and...."

Casey smiled. "Rumors?"

"About his reputation."

"Pretty intimidating stuff."

Maggie nodded. "But you ... you've never seen him?"

"No."

"Then you don't know anything personal about him?"

Casey was intrigued. Maggie was the consummate professional and not prone to be starstruck, by anyone. The woman had met many heads of state without batting an eye. So why did she seem so interested in a mere Secret Service agent?

"Like what, Mags?" her grin broadened suggestively. "Like ... if he's married?"

Maggie flushed a dark red. "Call me if you need me." She turned and left the office.

Casey watched her go, regretful that she had apparently offended the woman. She really hadn't meant to, but given Maggie's normally stiff nature it was hard to take her seriously- Maggie Broom inquiring about a *man*?

Still smiling, Casey turned back to her computer and decided she'd make up for her lack of tact by taking her friend to lunch. After everything was smoothed over, she'd probe her some more.

She hadn't been alone thirty seconds when Lisanne was in her office, waving a large white envelope in the air.

"This just came for the new Special Agent in Charge," she said, laying it on Casey's desk. "It came by Secret Service messenger with two escorts. Must be important."

Casey cocked an eyebrow, examining the exterior of the envelope. No name, no return address; usual Secret Service stuff. It was completely blank but stuffed full. She tossed it back on the desk and turned back to her computer.

"Just your usual spy propaganda," she commented.

Lisanne grinned, propping her skinny bottom on the edge of Casey's desk. "Haven't you heard about this guy? He's supposed to be some kind of James Bond."

Casey shook her head, her eyes reflecting the bright LCD computer screen as she logged on to the internet. "God, not you, too."

"What do you mean?"

"Maggie was just in here asking about him. Don't tell me you're starstruck, too."

Lisanne shook her head. "Not at all. But I'll admit his reputation is interesting."

Casey cracked a smile. "Ah, yes, Special Agent in Charge Colt Sheridan, a.k.a. 'The Antichrist'." She spun around in her chair, facing Lisanne. "Of course I've heard of him. It's hard not to. The guy has got a reputation out of a Robert Ludlum novel."

Lisanne nodded eagerly. "He'd been with Obama back in

Chicago, supervising the security arrangements of the former President. I hear Obama fought like hell to keep Sheridan with him."

Casey snorted. "Would you want to relinquish your best agent to the man who beat you in the Presidential elections?"

"Not really." Lisanne looked thoughtful. "More than likely, I'd pay the guy to off my opponent. Maybe...."

"Don't even joke about that." The African-American agent was standing in the doorway, his expression grim as he gazed at Lisanne. Rebuked, she slipped out of the office, leaving Casey alone with Mr. Humorless.

"She wasn't serious, Peter," she said, but Peter didn't look convinced so she changed the subject. "What can I do for you?"

He was still looking rather severe. He strolled into her office, casually. "Colt Sheridan is the finest agent in the Service. They don't come any better."

"I know," Casey nodded her head to placate the man. "Lisanne didn't mean to insinuate that he was an international assassin. Why do you have to be so damn serious?"

"They pay me to be serious." He crossed his arms, the material of his expensive suit straining against his muscular biceps. "And they pay you to be discreet. You know that talk like Lisanne's is discouraged, to say the least. And the fact that the President is sitting on the opposite side of that door...."

Casey rolled her eyes and put up a silencing hand. "Enough of the lecture, Agent Harrios. Is there a reason you've come to my office other than to eavesdrop on a private conversation?"

"I do, indeed, have a reason," he said crisply. "But I'm not finished lecturing yet. Didn't they teach you anything at the Pentagon about security and protocol?"

"Of course," she said impatiently. "I was the personal secretary to the Secretary of Defense, a position I worked myself in to less than six months after being hired for the pool, might I remind you. I've worked for politicians for the past twelve years before working my way in to the White House, so if you're thinking on rebuking me for my lack of responsibility, don't bother. I believe my employment record and my current position as personal assistant to the President of the United States speak for themselves."

Peter stared at her. Then, he broke out into a toothy grin as she succeeded in loosening his government-tight screws. "Mighty impressed with yourself, aren't you?"

"Aren't *you*?"

He laughed. "This room isn't big enough for the three of us – me, you, and your ego."

She broke down into snickers. "So tell me and my ego why it is you're in my office and then you can leave."

He sobered, eyeing the beautiful young woman with the striking violet eyes. She had caramel-colored hair, long and shiny with a fringe of bangs, a petite and shapely frame, and was a truly a fine female specimen in his opinion. Guys all over the West Wing called her a knockout, and she sincerely was. If he weren't already married, Peter might have found himself seriously interested because she was just that smart, funny and beautiful. She was the whole package.

"Special Agent in Charge Sheridan is expecting that package," he said. "If I were you, I'd deliver it to him immediately."

Casey's well-shaped eyebrows rose. "You mean The Antichrist? Don't tell me that he can't simply use his powers of evil to retrieve it." She put her fingers up to her temples. "Wait, I'm sending him a message. I'm telling The Antichrist that he will receive his package the very moment he walks into this office and not a second before. I'm not going out and hunt the man down."

The door to the President's office opened slightly; a figure lingered just beyond the door. But Casey didn't see or hear anything. She reached down and picked up the white envelope. Peter glanced up and saw the face. Immediately, he opened his mouth to speak but Casey's rambling cut him off.

"Wait!" she slapped the envelope against her forehead. "I'm not done. I'm telling The Antichrist that he better learn to work peacefully with the President's admin staff or I'll send him packing." She removed the envelope and fixed Peter in the eye. "I've heard through the grapevine that Colt Sheridan is a real jerk to work with. If he isn't intimidating the crap out of people, then he's being an ass. If that guy tries to disrupt my office, he'll be sorry. There's room for only one overlord in this administration and that's me."

The door to the President's office opened the rest of the way, silently. The white envelope in Casey's hand suddenly vanished.

"Thank you."

The voice was deep and smooth. Casey sat forward in her chair with a start, whirling around to the figure now standing in front of her desk. An enormous man in a crisp, dark suit stood there, fingering the envelope, and Casey's first reaction was to snatch it back.

"Give me that," she snapped, putting both hands on the envelope and yanking it from his grip. Glittering brown eyes gazed back at her steadily but she wasn't noticing their appraising manner; she was more focused on her outrage. "Who in the hell are you?"

"Casey, I'd like you to meet Special Agent in Charge Colt Sheridan." A trim, auburn-haired man emerged from the Oval Office. He was average in height, his handsome face lined with the tension of a strenuous life. President Russell Talbot fought off a grin as his personal assistant and new Special Agent in Charge got acquainted. "Special Agent Sheridan, I'd like you to meet my right-hand, Casey Cleburne. Don't let her size fool you. She's a tiger that I think you have, unfortunately, by the tail. I call her 'The General' and for good reason. You'd do well to remember that."

Colt simply nodded, his gaze riveted to Casey. She stared back at the man with the dark blond hair, stylishly cut. He was enormous, well over six feet tall, with shoulders as wide as the door frame. His handsome face looked as if it were carved from stone; square, angled, and unmoving. But the eyes that stared back at her were a deep, rich brown, liquid yet hard at the same time. It didn't make sense, this softness and solidity she was sensing from him. But maybe he was thinking the same thing about her, because he was appraising her the same way she was appraising him. Someone had to break first. Finally, almost sheepishly, Casey extended her hand.

"Pleasure," she said. "Welcome to the team."

His handshake was very firm, very warm. He had an enormous hand. He probably held on to her a moment longer than necessary, prompting Casey to yank her hand away because the warmth of his grip was unnerving.

"Thank you," he rumbled. Then he tipped his head in the direction of the white envelope, still clutched in her other hand. "Sorry I took it from you without permission. Can I have my envelope, please?"

Casey looked at the big, white package as if she had forgotten about it. Then she thrust it at him, almost hitting him in the jaw in her haste. He took a step back to avoid being smacked and collected the envelope as the President moved in between them, hands shoved casually into his pockets.

"To be honest, this is a better meeting than I had expected." Russ' dark eyes were glimmering with humor. "The last time a Sheridan and a Cleburne met, it was explosive to say the least."

Casey and Special Agent Sheridan were still locking gazes, still appraising, tearing their respective focuses off of each other to look at the President. Colt understood what the man was saying before Casey did. She was still struggling with her mortification.

"That's true, sir," Colt replied.

Casey was a little slower to come around. She cocked her head as she looked at him. "Sir?"

Talbot grinned as he tilted his head in Colt's direction. "Meet Philip Henry Sheridan the Fifth," he said. "His great-great-great granddaddy was Phil Sheridan, the great Civil War general for the United States of America, just like yours was General Patrick Cleburne, commander of the Army of Tennessee for the Confederate States of America. See where I'm going with this?"

Casey understood, then. With an expression of surprise, she turned to Colt as if now studying him through new eyes. Colt was doing the same thing, looking like he was fighting off a serious grin as their gazes locked. The granite-square jaw was twitching.

"Cleburne was probably the most underrated general in the Civil War," he commented, his gaze lingering on her. "I wasn't aware he had any descendants. As I recall, he never married."

Casey was quickly forgetting her embarrassment. "You know about him?"

Sheridan shrugged. "I grew up in a family that was all about history, for obvious reasons," he said. "I know a lot about the Civil War in general. I sort of had to."

Casey warmed to something they both had in common. She was eager to get beyond the situation of the big, white envelope.

"I totally understand," she replied honestly. "My mother was the same way. I knew about the history of the Confederacy before I knew American history in general. And, no, Patrick never married. He died before he could marry his fiancée, but years earlier he'd had a son with a freed slave woman in Arkansas. My family descends from that line."

Colt nodded in understanding. "Impressive."

Casey grinned. "Maybe so, but I'd say Phil Sheridan the Fifth is more notable. Our great-great-great grandfathers met a few times on the field of battle."

Stone-faced Colt finally cracked a smile, and what a smile it was; brilliant white, straight teeth and big dimples in both cheeks.

"A few," he agreed with the obvious. "Last time, I think Cleburne was pretty much a hero. It was at the Battle of Missionary Ridge, if I remember correctly. I'd have to read up on it to be sure."

Casey nodded. "You're right, it was. It was right before the Battle of Franklin where Patrick was killed."

Talbot interjected before he was forgotten completely. As much as he loved to listen to American history, living American history where it pertained to the descendants of two great Civil War generals, there were more pressing matters on the docket for the day. This conversation was going to have to wait.

"We're not going to have any North and South battles in this office, are we?" he wanted to know. "I don't want to come in here one morning and find the Confederate flag flying high and Sheridan hogtied in a closet."

Both Casey and Colt shook their heads. "No worries, sir," Casey laughed softly. "Besides, I think he's a little big to hogtie. He might give me a fight if I tried."

Colt grinned, simply nodding his head in a gentlemanly gesture. He was more the strong, silent type, never to be wrapped up in chatty conversation. It wasn't in his nature and it wasn't part of his job. A deeply introspective and intelligent man, he realized he wouldn't have been at all displeased with a lengthy conversation with Casey Cleburne. Something about that exquisite face and violet eyes made him wanted to open right up.

With a lingering glance at Casey, he followed the President back into the Oval Office. As the smile faded from her lips, Casey stared at the closed door for several long moments before turning to Peter. Her mortification was back.

"Oh, my God," she slapped her forehead. "Why didn't you tell me he was standing there? I looked like such an idiot!"

Peter was smirking. "Hell, you were on a roll. You really laid the law out for him."

She took her seat sullenly. "Shut up, Peter."

He started to laugh. "Oh, yeah, you told him. You let him know who's the boss around here."

She turned her back on him. "I've got work to do. Get out of here and quit bothering me."

Peter was still laughing as he walked to the door. "You know how to make a good first impression, don't you? I suspect Special Agent Sheridan will be eating out of your hand now."

She began to type, ignoring him. When he left the office, she paused, feeling sick to her stomach; not exactly a good beginning with someone she would be working closely with. The guy even had a desk across from her and they'd be staring at each other day in and day out like a couple of boxers waiting for the first one to throw a punch.

Casey sighed heavily. All she could do was apologize, hope time smoothed things over, and hope the new Special Agent in Charge didn't carry a grudge.

———

One of the first things Casey realized was that Colt Sheridan had piercing eyes. It wasn't so much the color; the brown was clear and normal enough. It was simply the way he looked at her that made her feel self-conscious, or guilty, even if she had no reason to feel that way. The man stared at her like he could read everything about her just in a fleeting glance. Casey passed him several times that morning as he milled around the West Wing and it came to the point where she could no longer look him in the eye when they met. She just put her head down and kept walking.

It got worse later that afternoon when the administrative assistant from Secret Service Washington office called to ask Casey if she could help her with the computer set-up in Sheridan's office. Casey had been in with the President and was preparing to go back into a meeting with the President and his National Security Advisor, and suggested that Maggie do the job. But the young secretary was insistent that Casey be the one, considering she knew the security protocols, and the computer programmer already working on the situation was having trouble with them. Begrudgingly, Casey sent Maggie into the meeting to take minutes while she focused on Sheridan's computer issues.

The young I.T. guy entered her office space a short time later bearing the computer meant for the Special Agent in Charge, going into the small, windowless office across from Casey's desk. It was more of a big alcove than an actual office, but the Special Agent in Charge of the President's detail had a desk there. The young man set the computer down on the desk and hooked everything up as Casey stood in the doorway, watching and waiting until she was needed.

"So I heard you met the new Special Agent in Charge."

The President's trip and conference coordinator, Chris Eckart, spoke from his desk next to Casey's. An efficient machine of a man with balding blond hair, he was a bit of a clown and anything coming out of his mouth was usually a joke or gossip. Casey glanced over her shoulder at him.

"Who told you that?" she asked. "Harrios?"

Chris was focused on whatever he was doing on the computer, grinning. "I've heard you get down and dirty with a lot of people but never the Secret Service," he said. "I wish I had been here."

Casey puckered her lips irritably and refocused on the I.T. tech as he finished up. "Stick around," she said drolly. "I'm sure there will be other opportunities for you to watch me make an ass out of myself."

As Eckart sat there and snickered, Casey entered the office and stood in front of the desk, suspecting the need for her knowledge was close at hand. She could see that the guy was struggling with something.

"What's the problem?" she asked.

The computer nerd spoke. "Actually, I've got it licked. It was some sort of problem in the autoexec.bat file, but I corrected it." He stopped, turning to look at her. "All that's left is for you to give the access code for Special Agent Sheridan and we're done."

Casey nodded as the programmer got up from the desk chair and left the office. As she came around the desk and took a seat in front of the computer, she noticed a figure sitting back in the corner. Sheridan had been tucked back away from the door, so much so that she hadn't even noticed him when she had been standing in the door jamb.

Like some surreal marble statue, he sat still and silent, his dark eyes missing nothing. Startled, not to mention embarrassed that he had heard her entire conversation with Chris, Casey's heart began to race.

"I didn't know you were in here," she said, feeling flustered. "I never saw you come in."

Colt sat forward in the chair, elbows resting on his knees. "You were in with the President when I came in earlier," he said, his dark eyes riveted to her. "Sorry if I startled you."

Casey wasn't sure what to say, so she simply nodded and returned her focus to the computer. She realized that Chris must have known that Sheridan had been seated in the office and he had set her up for a lovely little prank. Thank God she hadn't said more to incriminate herself in front of Sheridan. She made a mental note to kill Chris later.

"The package I received this morning contained my verified security clearance," Colt interrupted her thoughts. "You need to sign off on it and pass the protocol codes on to me."

He stood up from his chair, moving towards the desk. Casey looked up from the computer, watching the way he moved. It was like watching a panther stalk prey. She hoped she wasn't the prey... or maybe she did. Her heart began to race faster.

"I'll take a look at it and see exactly what you're entitled to," she said, hoping her nervousness wasn't obvious. "I would imagine you're entitled to everything your predecessor was, which isn't a whole heck of a lot."

The corner of his mouth twitched. "I realize that." He nodded his head in the direction of his desk; Casey saw the white tug-of-war envelope lying on the top. "You can sign off now while you're here."

Without looking at him again, because those eyes were really starting to unnerve her, she removed the contents of the envelope. It was much flatter than it had been earlier and Casey realized that the only item left was the security memo. Obviously, all of the cloak-and-dagger materials had been removed and she read the letter carefully, noting at the bottom of the page that she had been copied. She hadn't seen the copy yet, but she assumed it was probably in the afternoon's run of interoffice mail.

A quick stroke of the pen lying on Sheridan's desk cleared him for security access. But the white, wilted envelope continued to draw her attention and she suddenly felt the need to make some sort of apology for her actions of earlier in the day. Maybe it would help these feelings of anxiety she experienced every time she came near him; besides, he was staring at her again and her heart was pounding a mile a minute.

"Look," she began, rising from his chair. "I've got to apologize for the way I acted this morning. I suppose I was in a bad mood from the minute I walked in the office and, well, I'm not usually that cranky. Or smart-mouthed. Sorry."

He cocked an eyebrow. "Too bad. I thought we'd get along with you being a cranky smart-mouth and me being a jerk."

She cracked a grin, feeling her cheeks flush bright red. "I'm sorry about that, too. I guess 'jerk' wasn't the right word. More like...."

"Bastard? Hard-ass?" he said helpfully. "Or maybe a motherf...."

She put her hand up, quickly, to silence him. "No, no, none of those things." He actually smiled, broadly, and Casey began to feel giddy all over. "What I was going to say was demanding."

"Sure you were."

"I was," she insisted weakly. With him smiling so openly at her, it was difficult to maintain her gaze so she looked away, moving out from behind his desk and heading for the door. "Good luck with your computer, Mr. Sheridan."

She was almost out the door when he stopped her. "Wait a minute."

She paused, knowing her cheeks were still red and struggling not to appear too off balance. "What?"

He pointed toward his computer. "You didn't input my password yet."

The red cheeks deepened and she rolled her eyes. "Oh, right." *Please, God, let the floor open up and swallow me. Right about now would be a really good time.*

Sheridan stood back while Casey set him up for security clearance. Without another word, she displayed the code to him on the screen so he could memorize it and then she proceeded to erase it. Task complete, she headed for her own desk one last time. There was almost a desperate need to get away from him and regroup.

But he stopped her. "Ms. Cleburne?"

She paused, one foot out of the office as if it somehow made her feel safer. "Yes?"

His brown eyes were warm, glittering. For most of the day they had been piercing, appraising, but now they were almost soft. Casey instinctively took another step out of the office, away from him. She inched backward as he inched forward.

"Since we're going to be working in such close proximity, I'd be more comfortable if you'd call me Colt." His tone was grumbling, rumbling, incredibly soothing. "Special Agent Sheridan sounds so formal and Mr. Sheridan sounds like my father."

Casey couldn't remember feeling giddier or more uncomfortable, in her life. There was something about the way he was looking at her that made her want to run like hell.

"I know what you mean," she said, hoping the quiver in her voice wasn't apparent. "Ms. Cleburne is what my mother insisted on being called by her students. She was a married woman but she couldn't stand the title 'Mrs'. She even tried to keep her maiden name after my parents were married but my father said he'd divorce her if she did."

Sheridan grinned. "Sounds like your mother was a true feminist."

Casey snorted softly, feeling more at ease. "To the extreme," she agreed. "My dad wanted to name me Gwendolyn, after his mother, but my mom wanted to name me Morissey, which was her maiden name. They settled on Casey because my dad liked it and my mother didn't think it sounded too girly."

Sheridan's brown eyes moved up and down her body, very quickly, and Casey noticed. She also noticed that he was about to say something but thought better of it. He sort of nodded his head as if at a loss for words and politely turned away, but Casey caught the oddness of his manner. She didn't even know the guy, but for the first time all day, he seemed less than his usual confident self. The man had something on his mind.

"What were you going to say?" she asked, a smile on her lips.

He looked surprised. At least, he pretended to. "Me? Nothing. Just, uh... thanks for getting my computer set up."

Her grin broadened. Odd that the quaking in her limbs had eased now that she was warming to the conversation, and apparently in control of it by the look on Sheridan's face.

"I didn't do anything but give you access to certain files," she said. "But you, on the other hand, were going to comment about my name. What was it?"

He shook his head. "I wasn't going to. And even if I was, a comment like that could wrangle me a lawsuit, so I'll just keep my mouth shut." He grinned smugly.

Casey cast him a long glance. "Was it insulting?"

"Hardly. Well, at least, I don't think so. However, your mother might."

Her grin was flirtatious; she couldn't help herself. "Tell me. I promise I won't tell my mother."

He shook his head. "Not on your life, Ms. Cleburne."

"Colt?"

Now he paused, appearing slightly nervous. "What?"

She was perfectly calm, poised. "Call me Casey, please. Ms. Cleburne is my mother, the feminist."

Sheridan actually thought he might flush, though he didn't know why. Maybe it was the way she was looking at him. Christ, she was beautiful.

"Thanks," he said.

The corners of her mouth twitched as she turned and walked away. He watched her walk across the dark blue carpet into her own office until she sat behind her desk and out of his line of sight, cutting off his vision of a very beautiful woman.

She had long, straight hair and a heavy fringe of bangs that was sleek and sexy as hell, but it was her face that had him captivated.

He found her almond-shaped violet eyes and full lips incredibly stunning. Maybe this appointment would have unexpected perks and he realized that he wasn't disappointed to be sharing office space with her. It could be one of the better aspects of the job.

With the show over as Casey disappeared from his view, Colt took a seat in front of his computer, aware of a hint of perfume lingering in the air. It was a sweet, sensuous scent. He grinned as he sat back in his chair, inhaling the fragrance of Casey's perfume and thinking on what she was trying so hard to get him to say. He wouldn't tell her now, not when he didn't know her, but maybe someday when time and opportunity presented itself, he just might.

You certainly look girly to me.

TWO

ACROSS THE STREET from the Marriott Hotel adjacent to the Washington National Airport sat a dingy government building that was used for storage and miscellaneous office space. Once the building had housed the Maintenance and Operations Division for the State Department, but because of the constant noise coming out of the airport, the main body of the division had been moved in the mid 70s.

Pigeons nested on the window ledges, splattering the walls with white feces. The parking lot on the side of the building was unmaintained. The snow from the previous day had turned to a nasty rain, pelting the old building and staining the facade a dark, uneven gray, adding to the derelict ambience.

Cars passed to and fro, horns blaring as they traversed the Washington Bridge, when a black Audi suddenly turned into the old parking lot and made its way around the side of the building. There was an old rusty chain linked between concrete parking barriers that prevented the car from going any further, so it pulled to a slow stop and sat for a moment in the rain. Finally, the door opened.

A figure in an expensive black raincoat emerged, heading for the old building. There was a huge loading bay, covered by a slide-down panel that had been spray-painted with graffiti. It was dirty and worn, and the Masterlock that bolted it down looked as if it were several years old. The figure in the coat pulled out a key, unlocked the lock, and lifted the old panel. On well-oiled bearings, the door raised noiselessly and easily.

The man in the raincoat disappeared into the loading bay, closing the panel behind him and locking it from the inside. The interior of the building was dusty and unused as the man's expensive Kenneth Cole shoes crossed the concrete floor of the loading bay, weaving his way through a clutter of old boxes and equipment. He entered a loading elevator on the far side of the dock and shifted the old lever to the third floor. For the ramshackle appearance of the elevator, it moved silently and effortlessly and the man stepped off on the third level.

It was quiet up here, the noise of the street blocked out by thick walls of cement and steel. The man moved through a service corridor and into the main hall, tall and wide and empty. There were a few lights, illuminating his way as he walked down the hall. His steps were even, unhurried, as he reached a large polished door at the very end of the corridor. Without breaking his stride, he opened the door and stepped inside.

Suddenly, there was smoke. Thick, putrid cigar smoke from illegal Cuban cigars. It wouldn't have been so bad if everyone smoked the same brand, but there were varying tastes and preferences that created a halo of blue fog as thick as the air in Los Angeles on a smoggy summer day. The figure fought off the urge to cough, slowing his pace as he came into the room of cigar-smoking men.

The man in the coat didn't say a word. Eight men in expensive suits, nearly all the same color, sat in various positions around the room. The blinds on the long windows were drawn, streams of weak daylight filtering in through the smoke. There were banks of phones against the wall, a couple of state-of-the-art computers, but little else. Nothing else but old men smoking cigars, and one man with a bottle of Crown Royal that he apparently had no intention of sharing.

"Colt?" The selfish man with the half-empty bottle spoke, his voice old and brittle.

"You're late."

Sheridan held an even expression. "You realize that my schedule is very unpredictable. I came as soon as I could."

The old man took a sip of his Crown Royal as he mulled over the reply. "So," he decided not to make an issue out of the man's tardiness, "how was your first day with Russell Talbot?"

"Uneventful," Sheridan replied. "What did you expect?"

The man stopped sipping. Setting his drink down, he turned to the figure shrouded by milky blue tobacco smoke. "I expect you to do your job."

"My job is to protect the President."

"Remember who you're talking to, Colt."

Sheridan paused, shifted. "I'm well aware of my directive, Mr. Meade. And if you really believed that I would have a report to make to you after spending only twelve hours in Talbot's office, then you were mistaken. What you want will take a good deal of time to achieve."

Mr. Meade's gaze moved over the large figure, his eyes cold and calculating. He resumed his drink while his colleagues continued to smoke and listen. "We don't have much time, Colt. We've known for years that Russell Talbot was using his position as governor of New Mexico to conceal illegal drug smuggling. You're the closest agent we've managed to move in and it is imperative that you complete your mission."

Sheridan sighed. "I am fully aware of my mission," he stated. "But what Russ Talbot did was years ago, taking money from the Norte del Valle Cartel so that their planes could land in the deserts of Southern New Mexico. And from what I understand, the money wasn't for Talbot's personal gain – he had two kids with Cystic Fibrosis and all of the money went for either their treatment or as donations to the Cystic Fibrosis Foundation. For Christ's sake, the man had two dying children and couldn't afford the medical treatment. And now you want me to...."

"What he did was illegal, Mr. Sheridan." A man near the partially-covered windows spoke. He was in his mid-fifties, thin, and spoke with a heavy Boston accent. His entire manner reeked of arrogance, breeding. "The fact of the matter is that Russ Talbot took money from drug lords and used his position as governor of the state of New Mexico to allow drug shipments to come in and out of his state. For the fiscal years 1987 through 1999, we've traced over $900,000 in payments through banks in the Bahamas that are then placed in Swiss accounts, and the trail ends there."

The man moved away from the windows, the sickly glow of the yellow bulbs illuminating his grim face. "Sheridan, we've got a crook sitting in the White House. Doesn't that concern you?"

Sheridan's expression was steady. "He's no different from any other politician."

"Except now that he's in the Oval Office, the Norte del Valle Cartel is attempting to blackmail him into opening our southern border." Mr. Meade's voice was quiet, yet his words instantly silenced the room. "Colt, if we weren't positive that Talbot was in contact with these drug smugglers again, there wouldn't be a problem. For three years, the man allowed foreign drug traffickers to use his state as their own personal landing strip, but after 1999, the contact ends. If the ties remained severed, we wouldn't worry. A man has a right to a few secrets, even if he is the President of the United States. But the fact that he's renewed his ties with the Norte del Valle Cartel has us ... concerned."

Sheridan's expression was serious. "You think Talbot's going to succumb to their blackmail?"

Mr. Meade shrugged, smashing his cigar into the ashtray by his elbow. "If the most powerful drug organization in the world were threatening to reveal a relationship better left buried, wouldn't you do everything you could to stop them? Of course Talbot is back in contact with them, purely to prevent them from revealing his dealings with them. And in order to prevent them from squealing, he may have to give in to their demands."

"Open the border?"

"Exactly."

Sheridan sighed, slowly. "And you want me to track down any hint of a communication between Talbot and the cartel?"

"You're our best agent, Colt. Your family's heritage and work record speak for themselves. Your ancestor fought to preserve the United States of America and you're doing the same. We're depending on you."

Sheridan was silent a moment. Outside, the rain was coming down in sheets, pounding against the dirty windows. He listened to the rain, thinking.

"You sent me on basically the same mission with Clinton and Whitewater," he said quietly. "The man covered his tracks too damn good for me to discover anything. It was four years wasted – Clinton had people thwarting me at every turn. For every move I made, they countered me. They knew there was a plant close to Clinton, but they never discovered it was me. If I try the same route with Talbot, the CIA is going to put two and two together. They'll eventually figure out that I'm the plant."

Mr. Meade smiled faintly. "You worry too much, my boy. We've another agent in the President's office at your disposal, someone who's been there for years. In fact, he's a double agent for both us and the CIA. If the Agency gets too close, he'll send them on a wild goose chase like he did before. When your investigation of Clinton got too close to the truth and the Agency was frantic to find out who the mole was, Peter was excellent in foiling their efforts."

Sheridan nodded. "Harrios is a good man."

"Good and well paid. His directive is to merely hinder any and all investigations that threaten your mission. When the heat turns on, it's his job to cool it." Mr. Meade refilled his shot glass. "He doesn't know that you're the agent he's covering for, does he?"

"The emails I send him are encrypted. He doesn't have a clue."

"Good." Mr. Meade took a sip of his alcohol. Then he snorted softly, shaking his head as if suddenly finding humor in the situation. "It's insane, really. The CIA has agents in every corner of the White House, frantically running about like little ants, spying and counter-spying and making fools of themselves. They've so many turncoats that they don't even trust each other. And the other branches of the government, the State Department and the Department of Justice have their own agents, though they pretend otherwise. If I had to guess, I'd say one out of every three Secret Service agents are double agents for someone else. And then ... then there's us."

Sheridan shifted on his muscular legs; the Kenneth Cole shoes looked good but were beginning to pinch. "The branch of the government that no one will admit exists, yet we are stronger than the others could ever hope to be." He shifted again and began buttoning his raincoat. "No one will admit there is such a thing as The Core."

Mr. Meade cast him a long, beady glance. "Because we know more and do more than they could possibly imagine," he said softly. "They're afraid of us, Colt. We're like the fabled Minotaur, or the Loch Ness Monster. Elusive, omnipotent... and terrifying. We've access to files and laboratories and information that are beyond their realm of comprehension. We are, in fact, the government's worst nightmare because they have created something they can no longer control."

Sheridan didn't have a reply. He stood silently, his coat buttoned, listening to the driving rain pound the exterior of the old building. This meeting had gone the path of a thousand others, full of threats and arrogance and subterfuge. Sheridan had been a part of it for more years than he cared to admit, a tool for old men who controlled the country like a parasite controls a host. When he had been young, the spy business had been exciting and patriotic. But now, more often than not, it was a burden.

Finally, Mr. Meade set his glass down. "Don't contact us, Colt, we'll contact you," he said. Sheridan immediately turned for the door. "And Colt?"

Sheridan paused, his hand on the doorknob. Mr. Meade glanced at a couple of his colleagues before continuing, a sort of knowing glance passing between them. Sheridan didn't understand their expressions until finally Meade spoke.

"The secretary," he said. "She has access to all of Talbot's records. She might be a good place to start."

Sheridan's hand came away from the latch. Odd how a cold chill suddenly ran through him, like anger and defiance and, strangely, self-protection. "How did you know about her?"

"Harrios reports back to us on everything that happens in the President's office," Mr. Meade replied. "He said that Talbot's personal assistant and the new Special Agent in Charge met each other with a bang."

For the first time since his arrival, Sheridan showed some expression. Slowly, his eyebrows lifted. The urge to downplay the situation was overwhelming, though he could not understand why. "Bang? I'd say so. Hell, she made fun of me."

Mr. Meade looked at him, pointedly. "I would suggest you change her mind. She'd be a tremendous asset to your mission."

"Take advantage of her?"

"Use and abuse, Mr. Sheridan." Mr. Meade turned back to his drink. "Milk her for everything she's worth and move on."

Sheridan was silent a moment, pondering the insensitive directives of an insensitive man. But it was not his place to dispute him and he found it difficult to restrain himself. Wisely, he shifted the subject.

"If I do, in fact, discover communication between Talbot and the cartel, what then?" he wanted to know. "Are we really going to bust the President of the United States?"

Mr. Meade lifted his shoulders. "That remains to be seen."

"How?"

No one would give him an answer. It wasn't his business, anyway. He was an operative and nothing more. Sensing the conversation was over for the moment, he marched down to the loading bay and out into the pouring rain. By the time he got to his car, he realized he had ground his teeth so hard that he had bit his lip.

———

The night before had been sleepless, just like the three nights prior. Working on this damn proposal was finally taking its toll now that crunch time had arrived. It was Friday and the meeting with the new President was in an hour. As Senator Scott Dane sat in the back of his black Lincoln Town Car, it was difficult to keep his eyes open as he studied the finer points of the document one last time.

"Scott?" The man seated next to him elbowed him gently. "Wake up, sir. We're not done with this yet."

Scott took off his glasses, digging his knuckles into tired hazel eyes. "Damn," he hissed. "I don't think I've had more than 10 hours of sleep in the past four days."

His administrative aide grinned. "No time to sleep now," he said, handing the senator another stapled stack of papers. "You can sleep for a whole night when this is over with. But the Chairman of the Ways and Means committee had better know his stuff." He jabbed a finger at a highlighted paragraph on page two. "Take a look at that; Talbot's an environmental freak. You're asking for more funding to support the logging efforts in the Cibola National Forest. Don't forget that."

"I know, I know, Talbot's the former governor of New Mexico," Scott rubbed his eyes again and put his glasses back on, reading the information in front of him. He was in his late forties and was exceptionally handsome. His brown hair was perfectly groomed with flecks of gray and his face was tan with deep grooves carving through each cheek. He didn't look his age and took great pride in his top physical condition. He had a twelve-year-old son who looked just like him, a brilliant boy who was the center of his life.

After his wife, Carol, died ten years ago, it had only been Scott and Rob.

"What do you think?" Kurt asked when Scott had finished reading the paragraph.

The senator sighed, handing the paper back to his aide. "I think," he said, "that Talbot's going to rake me up one side and down the other. He isn't going to like this proposal in the least, but he's got to understand the potential revenues and job creation of this particular bill, especially for New Mexico and Colorado."

"Even at the expense of his beloved environment?"

"What's more important: feeding your family or starving with a view of the forest?"

"Talbot's going to say that without an environment, there won't be any families."

"Talbot needs to get a grip on reality. And the reality is, jobs are needed in that particular area. The Native Americans in the state of Arizona alone have a nearly 46.5% unemployment rate. So in order to preserve unused forest land, he'll let his former constituents starve." Kurt shrugged lamely and Scott shook his head with disgust. "Christ, Talbot knows better than that."

The White House came into view shortly thereafter. The rain had eased somewhat from a hellish torrent for most of the morning, but the streets were still running with water and the south lawn of the White House was unnaturally green against the contrast of the clouds. The Town Car pulled around to the north side of the White House to the West Wing entrance and Dane lithely climbed from the car. The senator moved very quickly, yet with a good deal of grace, and Kurt followed him, and a couple of White House aides, into the warm, stale building.

The aides, a man and a prim-looking woman, led the senator into a lobby that linked with a corridor. They took a couple of turns and ended up in another main corridor that led past the Roosevelt Room and on into the President's office. Dane almost ran the aides down with his naturally fast pace and it was an effort for the pair to keep ahead of him.

"You're the first to arrive, Senator," the woman said. "President Talbot is in his office and has asked for a short meeting with you before the others arrive."

"Fine," Dane replied shortly. He knew the layout of the administrative offices well, but this was the first time he had been here to see the new President. Most of the faces were different, as the staff changed from one President to the next. He had been quite familiar with Obama's people, as he had spent a good deal of time here battling for one thing or another.

They turned a sharp corner and the oval-shaped reception area of the Oval Office came into view. The aides led Senator Dane into the recently remodeled foyer, done in dark wood and vintage wallpaper. Dane began to unbutton his coat as one of the aides disappeared into the large office to the left of the reception room that connected with the President's office. Kurt was helping him from his coat and Scott was concentrating on what he was going to say to Talbot when he suddenly looked up and caught a glimpse of very pretty legs. Looking further, the legs were attached to a female form in a black suit that could only be described as magnificent. Gaze trailing up the torso, the head that topped the body possessed the most beautiful face he had ever seen. Sensuous violet eyes were gazing at him.

"Senator Dane?" The woman was extending a hand. Scott was so dumbfounded that he almost forgot to shake it. "I'm Casey Cleburne, President Talbot's personal assistant. If you'll follow me, please."

To the ends of the earth, doll, was Dane's first response, but he wisely bit his tongue. Instead, he found himself trailing after her, half in a daze, wondering why he felt as if he were sleepwalking. Like she had hypnotized him somehow. Sure, she was beautiful. But he knew a lot of beautiful women. Certainly, now was not the time to gape at one and especially not the President's secretary.

Christ, I'm rambling, he thought with distress. *I should be focused on my meeting, but I'm looking at a woman's rear-end and rambling about it.*

His hazy thoughts were abruptly cut short as Casey came to a sudden halt. Scott glanced up from her rear-end long enough to notice she was indicating a couch against the wall underneath three recessed T.V. screens.

"If you'll have a seat, the President will be with you in a moment," she said.

The televisions were going, all three of them, but she picked up the remote and turned them off as if she could read his mind. With all of the turmoil that was currently going through his brain, the last thing he needed was the added distraction of three separate news stations.

Dane took a seat, trying not to let his thoughts show and struggling to refocus. Kurt had his briefcase and he took it from the man, setting it on his lap and popping open the lid. Usually, Kurt would be helping him get organized. But a glance at his aide showed him to be focused on the lovely woman with the glorious hair as she took a seat behind her massive desk.

"How are you, Casey?" Kurt asked, ever-charming. "Long time, no see."

Casey smiled at the dashing-looking man. "It has been a long time," she agreed. "Still playing pool?"

Kurt nodded. "When I have time. How 'bout you?"

Dane couldn't believe that he was focusing on their conversation instead of the task before him. More than that, he could hardly refrain from jumping into the dialogue. *So Kurt knows her?* "You two know each other?" *Smooth, Dane, smooth!*

Kurt nodded. "We met a couple of years ago. Casey worked at the Pentagon when I was there and we used to pass each other in the hall all of the time."

"Pentagon?" Dane turned around, using the conversation as an excuse to look at her again. "What did you do over there?"

"I was Bill Perry's secretary, sir."

"The Secretary of Defense?"

"Yes, sir."

Dane tried not to stare at her too obviously as he spoke. "How'd you like it over there?"

She shrugged. "I like it here better. Too many military jarheads ... oh, I'm sorry, sir. I didn't mean ...."

He smiled, putting up a hand to stop her. "I was never a jarhead, Ms. Cleburne, merely a swabby. There's a difference."

Kurt was back in the conversation. "The Secretary of the Navy is more than just a sailor. He owns the whole damn fleet."

Dane glanced at him. "And four years was long enough for that nonsense. Then I moved on to bigger and better things."

"Being a senator?"

Dane turned his attention back to Casey. Christ, she was so lovely and sweet-sounding that it was difficult not to gawk at her. "Crazy, huh?"

She laughed. Even her laugh was beautiful. "Well, you must be doing something right. You have a tremendous reputation."

He dipped his head graciously. "Spoken like a true administrative aide. Always straddle both sides of the fence, Ms. Cleburne, and you can't go wrong."

She laughed again. "I wasn't straddling anything, Senator. I was simply speaking the truth. Your reputation is well-known and...." The intercom went off and she picked up the receiver. After a few short words, she hung up and rose from her chair. "The President will see you now."

Dane secured the lid of his briefcase and handed it to Kurt. Rising from the couch, he could smell Casey's perfume as she passed him en route to the door to the Oval Office. Opening the panel, she smiled and ushered the senator and his aide inside.

Scott was thankful that day for Kurt. The smile on Casey's face seemed to erase all of his memory and had he not had his aide present, he would have looked like a fool. Strange thing was he almost didn't care.

THREE

"COME ON, ZIP ME!"

"I'm ... trying!"

The zipper of the dress was stuck. It was an expensive and sexy confection, a sheath dress that ended mid-thigh, the material wall to wall sequins that made the dark gray dress shimmer with every move. It was tight, but it was meant to be, clinging to every curve now with an uncooperative zipper. Casey's twelve-year-old son, Hunter Cleburne Nantz, was trying desperately not to tear the fabric.

"What's it stuck on?" Casey demanded.

"A string," Hunter grunted. "Seriously, Mom, do I have to do this?"

"No," Casey said. "I can just go get the homeless guy down the street. I'm sure he'd be happy to do it, especially when I tell him he can have anything he wants out of your room as a reward."

Hunter made a face. He was an extremely handsome kid, blond with his mom's violet eyes, and tall for his age. He knew he didn't have a choice with this zipper thing, so he pulled gingerly at the zipper, the string, separating the two. Finally, the dress zipped with ease and Casey let out a pent-up sigh.

"Thank you," she turned to look at herself in the mirror as

Hunter made haste out of the bedroom door. Casey called after him. "Don't run off too fast. The money for the pizza guy is up here with me."

Hunter leapt back into the room, heading for the bed where Casey's purse was pulled apart as she switched her things to a smaller black clutch. Behind him came younger brother Brody, nine years of age and a blond hipster who carried his longboard with him everywhere he went. Even now, it was in the hallway as he rushed in on his brother's heels with the lure of money.

"Mom," he said when Hunter shoved him aside and took the twenty dollar bill on the bed. "Can Aiden and Jack come over later?"

Casey was putting on long, glimmering, dark gray earrings to match the dress. "Sure," she said, glancing at her son. "But don't make extra work for Aunt Riley. And clean up after yourselves, please?"

Hunter was already gone with the money and Brody nodded quickly, following his brother out of the room. As soon as they cleared the stylish bedroom with the big king-sized wrought iron canopy bed in the middle, a vibrant redhead entered the room, looking flustered.

"I almost tripped over that damn longboard," she hissed. "Brody is going to kill somebody with that thing someday."

Casey already pretty much knew that. She turned to her sister, younger by eleven months and three weeks, and held out her arms.

"How do I look?"

Riley Cleburne inspected her sister, eyeing the pale pearl-essence pantyhose and dark gray platform pumps. With her long caramel-colored hair, signature bangs, pale pink lips and dark eye shadow, the woman could stop traffic. She was stunning. The younger, pretty but slightly pudgy sister sighed.

"Like you always do," she said. "Great. So what's the occasion tonight? State dinner or simple cocktail party?"

Casey smoothed at the dress. "Cocktail party with the Ambassador of China and some other Chinese diplomats," she said. "It's

Russ' first official cocktail reception so it's a big deal. Are you sure I don't look too slutty?"

"Slutty enough that the Chinese will probably kidnap you and sell you into white slavery," Riley snorted, laughing when her sister couldn't decide if she was serious or not. "You look fine, Casey. Quit worrying."

"Are you sure?"

"I am." Riley plopped herself down on Casey's overstuffed bed. "So why don't you have a date?"

Casey shook her head. "You don't bring a date to a cocktail party at the White House."

"Different from Pentagon events, eh?"

"Just a little bit," Casey replied, looking at herself in the mirror one last time. "I'm still trying to get used to this. I had the Pentagon wired but the White House... it's a totally different animal."

"Regret taking the job?"

Casey shook her head. "Not at all," she grinned at her sister. "I control the man who controls the free world. Hey, you want to hear something funny?"

"What?"

"The new Special Agent in Charge took over today," she said, fussing with her new shoes. "Guess what his name is."

"Mickey Mouse."

"Very funny." Casey eyed her sister as she continued to mess with her right shoe. "His name is Philip Sheridan the Fifth."

Riley's eyes widened. "Seriously?"

"Seriously."

"Is he a descendent of the Phil Sheridan?"

"He sure is," Casey confirmed. "They call this guy The Antichrist because he's so intimidating, even the Secret Service guys are leery of him."

Riley chuckled. "Does he know you're a Cleburne?"

"He does. Weird that there are descendants from two great Civil War generals working in the President's office, eh?"

Riley shrugged. "As long as a Sheridan doesn't start anything with a Cleburne, there shouldn't be any problems."

Casey thought on the extraordinarily handsome agent. "I'll say one thing for him," she said frankly. "He's pretty damn cute. Maybe I wouldn't mind if he started something with me."

Riley giggled, watching her sister get comfortable in the new expensive shoes. As thoughts of the new Special Agent in Charge faded, she began to think of another time, back in their lives, when they were dressing up, preparing to attend an important event.

"Remember our prom?" she said. "Remember how I made my dress and it turned out all retarded, and Mom loaned me one of her dresses?"

Casey smiled. "How could I forget? You spilled Cold Duck all over the dress and ruined it. Mom was furious!"

They laughed, not at all concerned over their mother's anger. "I think she was angrier over the fact that we were drinking alcohol rather than the fact I ruined her dress," Riley said. Then, her smile faded. "I can hardly believe it's been seventeen years since we graduated. So much has happened, you know?"

Casey nodded. "I know. A marriage for you, a marriage for me, and then two divorces." She turned away from the mirror, focusing on the woman who had been her best friend her entire life. "And now look at us. I work for the President of the United States and you're an analyst at the Treasury Department. Remember when we planned to open a hair salon together?"

Riley snorted. "We didn't get far with that."

Casey shrugged. "Mostly because it would have been too boring. Who wants to brush hair ten hours a day?"

"Not me," Riley admitted. She rolled around on Casey's bed, sighing heavily. "So you're leaving me alone on a Friday night with my nephews. You suck."

Casey giggled as she went in search of her purse. "You'll survive. Just make sure they're in bed by eleven. Oh, and Brody is having Aiden and Jackson over, just so you know."

Riley waved her off; she knew the drill. She had lived with her sister for the past six years, ever since Casey divorced the Virginia State Trooper who couldn't seem to understand that when one was married, one does not see other women. Dennis Nantz was a nice enough guy, handsome, and had been good to his boys, but he'd never been very strong on the loyalty factor to his wife.

Casey had ten years of trying to change the man before finally giving up. Now, Dennis lived about fifty miles away and saw his boys about once a month. He was too busy doing his own thing and living the single life, which suited Casey just fine. She didn't want her boys to think their father's crazy social life habits were the norm. Because of that, she'd lived the relative life of a hermit. Her mention of the new Special Agent in Charge was the first time Riley had heard her sister talk about a man in years. Name and ancestors aside, Sheridan must have, indeed, been memorable.

Riley followed her sister down the stairs of the five-bedroom brick home in Falls Church that was in a quiet and family-oriented neighborhood. The boys had a pool in the backyard and friends all over the neighborhood. It was a little Mayberry-like. As Riley opened the front door to usher her sister out and allow two neighborhood boys entrance, she watched her sister walk out to her big Ford SUV and climb inside.

As Riley closed the door and yelled at the boys to turn the television down, she wondered if her sister would ever find the happiness in a relationship she so badly deserved. Casey had it all; looks, brains, personality, and a good job. She owned her own home and had two beautiful boys. But the experience with Dennis had left her with a bitter taste in her mouth when it came to men and although she'd had a couple of boyfriends in the past six years, the relationships had never come to fruition. The fear of a broken heart was holding Casey back.

Riley wondered if her sister would ever be able to let herself go and feel love again.

———

It was cold. Too cold for the wrap Casey had on, the relatively thin but glittery thing that matched the gray sequined dress so she was determined to wear it. She should have known better but she didn't want to ruin the look of the outfit, a fancy dress she rarely got to wear. Pride was her undoing. By the time she made the trip from the parking structure across the street to the White House grounds, she was turning shades of blue.

Teeth chattering, Casey entered the White House through a west side entrance from the West Wing and made her way to the Social Secretary's office near the map room on the ground floor. The secretary, an older woman with a severe school-marm look who had worked for four Presidents, took one look at Casey and nearly came apart.

"What's the matter with you!" she exclaimed softly. "Don't you know how to dress for this weather?"

Casey was shivering so violently that she could hardly talk. Carmen Hennderson pulled her into the small office, frantically looking around for something to wrap her in. But there was nothing to be found and, in desperation, she turned for the office door.

"I'm going to get you some tea," she said sternly. Then she shook her head. "Honestly, Casey, you should know better. A small wrap simply won't do in weather like this."

Casey nodded her head, twitching and quaking. "I-I know, but m-my heavy coat d-didn't look very good."

The older woman shook her head again, but it was without force. "You're going to catch your death."

Casey merely shrugged and Mrs. Hennderson left the office. Walking quickly toward the kitchens, she came into contact with three Secret Service agents dressed in sleek dark suits. She spoke to the first man she made eye contact with.

"You," she said pointedly. "I need you."

Sheridan lifted his eyebrows. "What for?"

Mrs. Hennderson pointed her finger in the direction she had come. "In the office adjacent to the foyer is a young lady in desperate need of your jacket. Silly girl, she's nearly frozen to death. Could you give her your coat until I return with some tea?"

Colt shook his head firmly. "Not me, but Peter ...."

Mrs. Henderson put up her hands in a hurried gesture. "I don't care who goes, but someone go help her." She marched away, quickly, muttering to herself. "If I've told Casey a hundred times, it's to bundle up in Washington. She runs around like she's still in California half the time."

Sheridan heard the name. Peter was already heading for the foyer but Colt stopped him. "I'll go," he said. "You two get up to the residence and tell the President I'll be there shortly."

Peter and the other agent nodded and then split off from Sheridan. Colt watched them mount the stairs before continuing into the small, cozy office.

Casey was sitting on the couch, a glittery gray wrap around her shoulders and quivering so hard that he could literally see the tremors. Sheridan rounded the couch and looked down at her, fists resting on his hips.

"Well, well, well," he said casually. "A human ice cube."

Casey looked up and he swore he saw a flash of pleasure cross her features. But it was quickly gone and she frowned. "What are you doing here?" she asked with quivering lips. "Shouldn't you be with Russ?"

He cocked an eyebrow. "That's where I was going until a panicked woman told me there was someone in her office, half-frozen. I came to help."

"I don't need help, thank you."

"Don't be stubborn. You're turning blue."

When Casey made a face and looked away, he sat his big frame on the couch beside her. Shocked at his suddenly closeness, Casey eyed him as he began unbuttoning his jacket.

"What are you going to do?" she asked warily.

He glanced down as he undid the last button. "I was going to give you my jacket, but I don't think that'll be enough." He opened the coat and then reached up to pull the cold wrap from her shoulders. "That thing isn't doing you any good."

Casey tried to snatch it back, but he tossed it behind the couch, up onto the desk. Before she could protest, he reached out and pulled her against his hard, searing torso.

Casey gasped as she came into contact with his heated tuxedo shirt. Her first instinct was to pull away from him and slap him in the face, but he wrapped the coat around them both and before she realized it, she was blissfully cozy and wildly content. Sheridan put out more heat than a furnace and as much as she tried to remain stiff and uncooperative in his arms, it wasn't long before her resistance gave way and she relaxed completely.

Colt felt her loosen up, slowly but surely, eventually collapsing against him. She went limp, like a rag doll, and he shifted, pulling her closer and wrapping the coat more tightly about her. She seemed to fit against him rather well. Strange thing was, neither one of them said a word the entire time. It was an odd silence but not uncomfortable. Colt actually thought she had fallen asleep, for she was utterly still and boneless. He tried not to think of how good she felt in his arms, but the truth was that she felt marvelous. He couldn't remember the last time he'd felt something like this.

"You can let me go now," her voice bubbled up, muffled against his chest. "I think I'm warm enough."

"Are you sure?"

"Pretty sure. Plus, I can't really breathe."

She certainly knew how to spoil a moment that could have potentially been pleasant, at least for him, anyway. He could see her point, however. He had her tightly wrapped up with her face in his chest. He almost refused to let her go but visions of her fists pelting his abdomen somehow cooled his determination. He opened his jacket and Casey pulled herself off his chest, her smoldering violet eyes gazing up at him.

"Feeling better?" he asked neutrally.

She nodded. "Now I'm sweating to death. You give off more heat than a furnace."

"It's all that testosterone."

"Or hot air."

He lifted an eyebrow. "I'm late for work and this is that thanks I get? I should have let you freeze."

She flashed him a taunting grin, one that had him captivated. But she stood up before they could explore any manner of flirtatious banter, straightening her skirt as she rose from the couch. Sheridan couldn't help but notice her magnificent figure as she smoothed her sexy little cocktail dress. No wonder the woman was cold because there wasn't much to it, but she looked absolutely delicious. He tried not to stare but couldn't quite manage it. When Casey caught him staring at her, she cocked an eyebrow.

"What?" she asked. "Is something wrong?"

Slightly embarrassed that he'd been caught checking her out, he shook his head. "Nothing's wrong."

"Oh," her gaze lingered on him a moment. "Sorry to have delayed you. You should probably get back to work."

"I'll wait if you'd like me to escort you upstairs."

She looked at him as if shocked by the suggestion, but after a moment, her expression eased and she shook her head. "The reception is in the Blue Room, but Russ is having us gather in the Diplomatic Room first."

Colt stood up, buttoning up his coat. "Then I'll escort you over there." He picked up her wrap and handed it to her. "Come on."

Casey took the wrap but she was hesitant about accepting his offer. "You really should hurry up to Russ," she told him. "It's not good for the new Special Agent in Charge to be late for his first official gig."

"I can drop you off at the Diplomatic Room and make it upstairs in less than a minute if you'll quit arguing with me."

Casey lifted her eyebrows at him as if outraged, but she ended up breaking out in a grin. Colt returned her smile, the dimples in his cheeks carving out deep canyons. A sweetly awkward moment followed as she giggled and he snorted, as if they weren't quite sure what more to say on the subject. Something was sparking between them although neither one of them could put a finger on it. In spite of their rough beginning, the seed of attraction had sprouted. Casey finally folded the wrap neatly over her left arm and held her clutch with her left hand.

"Okay," she swept her arm in the direction of the door. "Let's go."

"Ladies first."

She preceded him out of the office and into the warm corridor. Colt held out an elbow to her like a proper escort would and she laughed.

"We're not going to the prom," she said. "You don't have to offer me your arm."

He grinned and lowered the elbow. "I'm just trying to be a gentleman."

She laughed again, softly, and took his elbow with her free hand. "Okay," she replied. "I don't want you to think I'm ungracious. Escort away."

Colt's grin broadened as he settled in beside her, escorting her down the hall towards the Diplomatic Room, the former White House furnace room that had been transformed back in 1902 to a meeting and gathering room. As they approached, they could hear voices in the room and already, people were starting to spill out into the corridor. They were mostly Chinese diplomats and Colt studied the group as he approached. That was just habit with him.

More than that, he noticed that all of them were looking at Casey with great interest. He felt rather territorial of her, as if he was guarding his prize, but quickly realized he didn't have any more right to her than the rest of them. He just happened to be lucky enough to have her on his arm.

"All right," he took her hand off his elbow as they came close to the room entry. "Here's your stop."

He was holding her hand and Casey turned to him, a genuine smile on her lips. "Thanks for the escort," she said. "I'm not sure I would have made it here safely without you."

Colt cracked a lopsided smile. "The halls of the White House can be dangerous."

Casey nodded, realizing he was still holding her hand. She released her fingers but he didn't release his, prompting her to gently but firmly pull her hand from his grip.

"You'd better get going," she said. "Russ will be waiting."

Colt did nothing more than give her a smile and a nod, disappearing up the stairs to the left. Casey watched him go, thinking a lot of things at that moment, but mostly that she thought he was very handsome. She wasn't one to linger on a man but she found herself lingering on Sheridan. There was a lot to linger on.

Carmen Hennderson found her shortly thereafter, cup of tea in hand, but Casey didn't need the tea any longer. Still, she took it from the woman, sipping her tea while speaking with one of the lesser female Chinese diplomats who seemed to have a thing for Disneyland. Being a Southern California native, Casey was able to converse intelligently on the amusement park she had visited at least a couple of dozen times. She was also able to intelligently discuss the cache of Medieval coins recently found at a construction site in Anguo City, which impressed the young Chinese woman. Casey had been in politics a long time. She knew how to impress.

Russ appeared a short time later with his wife, Tracy, a vivacious woman with a fake tan and a loud laugh. Russ made the rounds to a few of the senior diplomats before directing everyone upstairs to the Blue Room, where alcohol and food were waiting. The entire group herded from the room, into the corridor beyond and up the stairs. Casey, the very last person in the room, set her tea cup down and followed. She kept looking up ahead as Russ led the group, pretending she wasn't looking for Colt when she knew damn well that she was. Feeling silly, as well as a little giddy, Casey joined the cocktail reception in the Blue Room.

The event dragged on into the night. The Chinese liked their liquor and they loosened up quite a bit as the wine flowed. Russ brought out a bottle of Amarone from his private reserve, a very fine Italian red wine, and shared it with the Chinese ambassador. It was enough to make him a bit tipsy, but only enough to make him hilarious. Casey worked the room, met aides and diplomats, and spoke of archaeology, commerce and, more than once, Disneyland. It was all very cocktail-y and very Washington-esque, but not once in all that time did she see Special Agent in Charge Sheridan again. He and the other Secret Service agents had made themselves scarce.

As the hour of midnight neared, the party was in full swing and Russ began making demands for music. Mrs. Hennderson phoned White House maintenance and two men brought in a compact Bose sound system and hooked it up in the adjoining Green Room. Soon, soft sounds of the Eagles were playing in the Green Room and half of the group had moved into the room, a few of them dancing. Someone had opened the doors that led out to the South Portico overlooking the south lawn just to let some air in. It was a very cold, but very clear night.

Casey had just finished up with another female aide, now alone for nearly the first time all night, and wishing she could get out of there. She was exhausted and the boys had soccer games the next day, so she would be up early with them. As she pulled out her lipstick to touch up her lips, a young Chinese aide approached her and wanted to dance. She graciously begged off but the man wouldn't be deterred. He spoke very good English and the more Casey declined, the more he insisted.

Finally, she resorted to lying, telling him that she had twisted her ankle and couldn't dance, but he still wouldn't leave her alone. He was, in fact, rather aggressive and kept trying to hold her hand or touch her in some way. When he went to get them both a drink, she slipped outside to the dark portico to hide.

It was a mistake. It was freezing outside and all she had was that little wrap to keep her warm. Still, it was better than being pursued by a drunk and amorous Chinese aide. She could hear everyone inside, having a good time, and she thought she might just slip out and go home. Russ probably wouldn't even remember if she said goodbye to him, anyway.

Wandering to the edge of the portico where the big staircase led down to the south lawn, she could hear a man's voice with a heavy Chinese accent calling her name. Desperate to get away from her suitor, she slipped down the stairs as silently as she could to hide from him.

Now, she was underneath the dark and damp portico, and it was as cold as a freezer. She inched out from underneath, peering up the stairs to see if the amorous Chinese man was still looking for her. She could hear voices, and music, but she didn't hear her name any longer. As she took another step out, thinking about heading over to the West Wing and then out to the parking structure, a hand grabbed her from behind.

Casey shrieked and tried to bolt as two hands suddenly grabbed her, trapping her. In the darkness, she could see a very large body and, after a moment, she recognized Sheridan's features in the darkness. Terror turned to relief.

"Oh, my God," she gasped, her hand over her chest to still her heart. "You scared me to death."

He grinned, his big, white teeth reflecting the weak light. "I saw you go out onto the portico," he said. "What are you doing down here?"

He was still holding on to her arms. His hands were blazingly hot against the frigid temperatures.

"Hiding from some Chinese guy who wants to dance with me," she said. "Your hands are so warm. I'm freezing down here."

Colt silently pulled off his suit jacket and slung it over her shoulders, pulling it tightly around her. Wrapped up in the wool coat, Casey succumbed to the heat with comfort and relief. It was heavenly. It was the second time in as many hours that Sheridan had come to her rescue.

"Do I need to defend your virtue?" he asked, watching her giggle. "Did he try anything?"

She shook her head. "No," she said. "He was just a little drunk. He wanted to dance. But he kept trying to grab me."

Colt grinned. "Can't blame a guy for trying."

"He's gross!"

"So what do you want me to do? Just say the word and I'll have him escorted out of here."

She laughed softly. "You'd better not," she said. "He's the son of somebody important and you'll just create an international incident. It would just be best if I left."

"Okay," he said, feeling the pangs of disappointment at the thought of her leaving. All evening, when he was supposed to be watching the President, he found himself watching her. She'd made the night far more pleasant. "I'll have someone walk you to your car."

She shook her head. "That's not necessary," she said. "I'm a big girl. My car is just across the street."

"Forget it," he said, more firmly. He lifted his right arm and spoke into a tiny microphone that was strung down his sleeve and ended in his hand. "This is Sheridan. Have Case meet me in the cross hall in five."

Someone came back with an affirmative. Even though Casey couldn't hear it, she heard his acknowledgement.

"Thanks," she said. "You really didn't have to do that. But I guess if something happened to me, you'd never hear the end of it."

His usually neutral expression came close to a scowl. "You're probably right. I'd get fired over some woman who insulted me when I first met her and then stole my coat and used me like a space heater."

Her mouth popped open in outrage, although there was humor to it. "So now you're insulting *me*?"

"You insulted me first."

She sighed sharply, lightly done. "You're right," she agreed impatiently. "I did. I've already apologized for it. What more can I do?"

Colt's brown eyes glimmered. "Do you really want to know?"

"Probably not, but tell me anyway."

"Dance with me."

Her outrage, her surprise, turned genuine. "What?"

He pointed a finger skyward, indicating the portico above them. "Hear the music? It's The Eagles singing 'The Best of My Love'."

Her eyebrows flew up. "You want me to *dance* with you? You've got to be crazy. You're on duty. If anyone saw us, you'd be in a hell of a lot of trouble."

The corners of his lips twitched. "You've got one minute."

He held up his hands as if to take her into his arms and dance with her. Casey just gawked at him. "Seriously?"

"Fifty-five seconds."

She eyed him; he was apparently dead serious and to tell the truth, the thought didn't repulse her. In fact, it was rather inviting. Sheridan was an extremely handsome man with a charming personality when he let himself bust out from the serious Secret Service agent persona. Casey felt herself relenting.

"So... if I do, you'll forgive me for insulting you earlier today?"

"I'll forgive you everything. It'll be a clean slate."

With a shrug, Casey took his jacket off and handed it back to him. Colt put the coat back on and then held his hands up again expectantly. Still eyeing him rather uncertainly, Casey placed her right hand in his left one and he pulled her against his firm, warm torso. His right arm snaked around her slender body.

Very quickly, Casey was in a very intimate position up against the man but she didn't say a word. She discovered that she liked it very much. There was something very magnetic about him and she allowed herself to submit, if even for just a brief moment. It had been a long time since she danced with someone handsome and attractive. As The Eagles sang overhead, drifting out into the night, Colt put his cheek against the top of her head and began to dance, very slowly and sweetly, with Casey wrapped up in his arms.

Fifty-five seconds passed in the blink of an eye. In spite of her initial reservation, Casey very nearly melted into the man, closing her eyes and losing track of time as he held her close and swayed in beat to the music. It seemed like they had been dancing just a few seconds when he spoke again.

"Time's up," he said hoarsely. "Are you really going to leave now?"

She started to laugh. "I am unless you want to stay down here and dance the rest of the night," she pulled back so she could gaze up into his handsome face. "If you don't, then I really am going to leave. Better that than fighting off a Chinese offensive for the duration of the party."

Colt looked down at her, thinking it had been a huge mistake to dance with her. He'd really only meant it as a joke, or maybe it hadn't been so much a joke as something he was just curious to do. He'd liked the feeling of her in his arms so much earlier when she was nearly frozen to death that he wanted to feel it again. This time was better than the first and he was loath to let her go.

"One more minute," he said, pulling her back against him.

Casey was grinning as he swallowed her up in his big embrace. "Why?"

"Because you're not completely forgiven yet. One more minute should do it."

She rolled her eyes, although not completely displeased. "Oh, brother," she muttered, her right cheek cuddled up against his chest. "You don't carry a grudge much, do you?"

"Depends."

"I can see that."

She snorted. He chuckled because she was. All in all, the next minute went more quickly than the first and when Colt finally released Casey, she nearly stumbled. She had been very relaxed and content in his embrace. He grinned at her as he offered her his elbow once more.

"Come on," he said. "If you're determined to go, let's get you out of here."

She took his elbow. "So we're doing the prom escort thing again?"

"Pretty much."

She giggled as she followed him out from underneath the portico and up the steps, feeling the warmth and seeing the glow from the rooms into the cold night. They'd taken a side entrance back into the White House, avoiding the rooms with the cocktail party, and Colt handed her over to a young, dark-haired agent in the big hallway that ran the length of the White House. With nothing more than a brief smile, he went back to his post as Casey followed the young Secret Service agent out into the night.

Thoughts of Colt Sheridan kept popping in to her mind all weekend.

Oh sweet darlin' you get the best of my love....

FOUR

CASEY WAS in the office bright and early Monday morning. She arrived at least an hour before she was scheduled to work, mostly because Russ had a meeting in the city with a company called GreenTopia, all part of the environmental bill that was heading for a vote in the next few weeks. Senator Dane was to be part of the meeting so Casey wanted to make sure the President was prepared for what would undoubtedly be discussed.

She had his black leather folio on her desk, neatly piling papers into it that he could study on his way over to the meeting. Ever since she had come into the office, she had been making copies and putting things in chronological order for Russ' review. Casey was a master at organization, which over the past six months as the President's personal assistant, had served her well. Russ hadn't known her to make a bad decision yet. He'd quickly come to trust her.

Dressed in a grayish-lavender dress with a matching sweater and spiky black pumps, her luscious hair was pulled back in a stylish ponytail, giving her a very high-end and sexy look without going overboard. Unfortunately, she'd been up with Brody most of the night, as the boy had a stomach bug, and Aunt Riley was taking him to the doctor that morning to have him checked out. There were lots of concealer covering up the dark circles beneath the violet eyes and, more than once, she had to stop herself from yawning. It was going to be a long day.

She finished the folio and moved on to the electronic wizardry she would bring with her as she followed Russ around – three cell phones, two iPads and one laptop would be part of her arsenal. As she fussed with one of the iPads, two of Russ' aides entered her office to wait for the President. Barbara Biel, a woman with a deep background in environmental and political science, and Jason Travis, a young man with connections who had a great political future, made small talk with Casey as she packed up for the day.

Her officemate, Chris, eventually wandered into the office and began to set up for the day, booting up computers and pulling out his Planner. He would be accompanying them on the outing as well, as the President's travel coordinator, so it was already shaping up to be a well-tended trip. More people came into the office area, which was too small to hold them all, as Russ eventually appeared.

Dressed in a blue suit, he greeted everyone amiably. Russ was fairly loud-spoken, with a wicked sense of humor when he got going, and the way he greeted people made each and every one of them feel as if the President was paying special attention to them. It was a gift he had, one that had helped get him elected, and by the time he reached Casey's desk, he smiled warmly at her.

"Well, General," he said amiably. "Are we all set for the day?"

Casey nodded, hands folded casually on her desk top. "All set, sir," she said. "We'll leave here in about an hour and it should take us about twenty minutes to get to GreenTopia. I'm bringing the agenda with me so you can study it in the car on the way over. You have a meeting right now with Barbara and Jason, so I'll let you know when it's time to leave."

Russ nodded confidently. "Thank you." Now that he knew what was going on with his morning, he waved his aides in. "Let's go have some coffee and shoot the breeze for a while."

Six aides, including Jason and Barbara, followed Russ into the Oval Office, clearing out Casey's small office area in a hurry. Setting aside everything she was to bring on the busy day ahead, she picked up the remote and turned on her three plasma screen televisions. CNN, MSNBC and the local Washington D.C. station popped up for their morning news run.

Eyes on the screen as CNN suddenly began to talk about the President's new environmental policy, she rounded the edge of her desk to hear the story a little better without blasting the sound. As she perched on the end of her desk, she happened to glance in the office across from her and saw that Sheridan was seated behind his desk.

She could only see part of his left shoulder and arm, but her heart began to pound. She'd thought about the man all weekend and, truthfully, she was looking forward to seeing him again today. It was the first time in her life she had wanted the weekend to end so she could go back to work. She wondered if his attitude towards her would be the same today as it had been on Friday, the stone-expression Secret Service agent who seemed to crack a smile only for her.

Leaning sideways, she eventually caught sight of the entire man sitting behind his desk, working on his computer. She watched him a moment, leaning off her desk, thinking that the man was more handsome than she remembered.

"Good morning," she called pleasantly.

It took Colt a moment to look up from his computer. He wasn't sure the greeting was meant for him but when he glanced up and saw Casey leaning sideways off her desk, smiling at him, he felt like his entire day just got better. He smiled in return.

"General Cleburne," he replied with a glimmer in his eye. "Good morning to you, ma'am."

She came off the desk, the television remote still in her hand. "I didn't see you come in."

Colt leaned back in his chair, watching her approach and feeling rather giddy at the sight of her. He didn't know if it was possible for the woman to become any more beautiful over the weekend, but it looked to him like she had. In the pretty lavender-gray dress and matching sweater that was sexy without being over the top, she was quite a sight.

"You were surrounded," he told her. "I slipped in under the radar."

She grinned, nodding in understanding. "I emailed the Secret Service the itinerary for this month about six weeks ago," she said. "I'm going to assume they passed it to you. Have you seen it?"

"Seen it and mapped it."

Mapping was a term used to strategize the President's movement outside of the Oval Office. Casey nodded to his statement.

"Good," she replied. "I emailed you the specific itinerary for the meeting early this morning. It was just finalized yesterday."

He nodded. "I got it," he said. "Thanks."

"Any questions?"

Colt paused. Christ, that was a loaded question with a myriad of answers. He gazed into her lovely face, her sweet jawline revealed with her hair pulled loosely away from her face, and all he could think of was the time he had spent over the weekend daydreaming about her.

He worked a fairly rigorous schedule, shadowing the President whenever the man made a move outside of the White House, which meant he'd spent the weekend at a luncheon on Saturday and golf on Sunday. He'd performed his job flawlessly, fully in control as the President's Special Agent in Charge, but the President's lovely assistant had repeatedly filled his thoughts. That dance to "The Best of My Love" had done something to him. An inherently lonely man and something of an introvert, things as small as that had meaning to him.

"Yes," he said after a moment. "I had the general rundown on the function of office personnel that were close to the President, but tell me how you fit into all of this other than organizing his life."

Casey leaned against the door jamb. "It depends," she said thoughtfully. "I generally go everywhere he goes unless it's a family vacation or something like that. The President decides where and when I go, but as his personal assistant, I pretty much shadow him, like you do."

Colt nodded, not at all displeased with the prospect of Casey Cleburne going everywhere he did. The new job just got better.

"I see," he replied. "We've got a trip back to New Mexico next week."

Casey nodded. "I know," she said. "My boys are jealous. They think I'm going to the Wild West."

Colt stared at her, his heart sinking a little. He had no right to feel that way, but he did. "I didn't know you were married."

She shook her head. "I'm not," she said. "But I've got a twelve-year-old and a nine-year-old, both of whom are interested in Wild West history. New Mexico sounds exotic to them."

Colt's smile was back as was, he realized, his relief. "Did you tell them it's no big deal?"

"They think I'm lying. They think I'm going to walk the streets of the old West and call out Black Bart."

He snorted but was interrupted from saying anything further when more people entered Casey's office. She pushed herself off the doorjamb, turning to a middle-aged man with carefully combed hair and an expensive overcoat, and extending her hand.

"Senator Dane," Casey said pleasantly. "I hear you're joining us this morning."

Scott smiled at Casey. "Yes, I am," he shook her soft hand and let it go. He couldn't help himself from gushing a little because she looked so lovely. "You're looking well this morning, Miss Cleburne. Kurt says to tell you hello."

Casey grinned as she headed over to the coffee service that was stationed on the wall between her desk and Eckart's. "He won't be joining you?" she asked.

Scott shook his head and began to peel off the heavy wool over-coat. "His kid is running a fever of one hundred and two," he said. "I told him to stay home. I don't want his germs."

Casey laughed softly and picked up a white ceramic mug. "Can I get you some coffee?"

Scott nodded. "Thanks. Black, please."

Casey poured a cup and handed it to him, smiling graciously when he thanked her. Then she stuck her head back into Colt's office where the man had gone back to work on his computer.

"Special Agent Sheridan?" she asked. "Can I get you some coffee?"

Colt already had a paper cup of coffee house coffee by his left hand. The computer monitor had apparently blocked her view of it, so he nodded.

"Thanks," he said. "Just a little creamer."

Casey flashed him a sweet smile and turned back for the coffee service. When her back was turned, he quickly dumped his coffee into the trash and covered it up with a few pieces of paper.

Colt watched her shapely backside as she poured him a cup of coffee. He happened to glance at Senator Dane, standing by the edge of her desk, and noticed that he wasn't the only one watching Casey. Senator Dane was zeroed in on her as well. Colt eyed the man he'd heard about but never met, realizing he didn't like the way he was looking at Casey. He couldn't put his finger on it but he knew, instinctively, that he didn't like it one bit.

Oblivious to the pair of men checking out the shape of her ass, Casey turned around with a full cup of coffee and went into Colt's office, extending the cup. He took it from her, their fingers brushing.

"Thanks, Angel," he said softly.

He sipped the coffee and set it down, pretending to busy himself with his computer. The truth was that he didn't want to look at her because he didn't want to see the expression on her face. He'd called her by a pet name because he'd wanted to, like it had just slipped out when the reality was that it hadn't. It was planned. He didn't look at her because he didn't want to see a negative reaction on her features. He wanted to keep doing it until she either told him to stop or told him that she liked it.

Casey watched the man go back to work, slipping from his office and going back to her desk. The term of endearment hadn't gone unnoticed by her. *Angel.* Maybe he called all the girls that, but somehow, given his straight demeanor and somewhat harsh reputation, she didn't think so. It was a strange thing, indeed, but not unwelcome. She kind of liked it but she knew that if anyone else had heard it, it might be construed as sexual harassment. She was sure Sheridan knew the same thing, which made the comment all the more puzzling.

Sheridan went back to work and Dane sat down on Casey's couch to do a few things on his smart phone before heading out. Casey kept busy, confused yet flattered by Sheridan's comment and unaware of Dane's discreet glances in her direction. She buzzed the President when it was time to depart and Russ soon emerged from his office with his aides in tow.

The Presidential limousine was waiting in front of the North portico as Colt, Peter, the young agent who had escorted Casey to her car on Friday night, Steven Case, and a few other agents began to move with the President outside. There were at least twelve to fifteen of them in any given movement, plus more following in chase cars. Casey was never really sure how many there were because they seemed to be everywhere. Colt and Peter led the way out of the office, taking the group from the Casey's office out through the lobby of the West Wing where the big black "beast", or Talbot's limousine, was already waiting.

The day was blustery and clear, dead leaves kicking across the driveway as Colt opened the passenger door for the President. Russ climbed in, followed by Barbara, Jason, Senator Dane, and, finally, Casey. Her arms were full of items, like a pack horse, and Colt watched her deftly juggle the mess as she climbed in last. He resisted the urge to offer to help her; that wasn't his job. Closing the door on the limousine, he signaled the other agents in the chase cars behind them, climbed into the front seat next to the limo driver, and off they went.

Pulling out onto Pennsylvania Avenue, they took 15th Street down to Constitution Avenue eastbound. There were helicopters in the air overhead and the D.C. police had the intersections blocked off for the Presidential motorcade. The people of Washington D.C. took such things in stride because it happened all of the time, so the traffic the President created didn't make too much difference. Once he was through the intersections, they were reopened and people went on with their lives.

Casey sat with her back to the front passenger seat of the limousine, directly across from Russ. She handed him his folio of papers, which he dutifully scanned. He seemed to be talking more than he was reading, which was normal for him. Casey waited until he was finished with the folio exchanging it for the President's iPad, which had his encrypted email on it, and Russ rifled through a few emails while he chatted with Senator Dane.

As the President went through emails and exchanged opinions on the strength of different teams in the National Football League, Casey turned her attention out of the window. The October landscape zinged past, the land still green even though the chill had been very strong over the past few weeks. She found herself thinking about Sheridan, seated behind her with a window and car bulkhead separating them, thinking once again about their Friday night together and their pleasant exchange this morning.

It wasn't realistic to think about him and she knew it. She'd known it from the start. She didn't know anything about the man personally, but what she did know was that office romances were discouraged. Not that she was hoping for anything with him, but he was certainly her type. The whole "The Antichrist" reputation notwithstanding, she found Colt Sheridan to be a charming and gorgeous man.

She heard rumor about how The Antichrist reputation got started, how Sheridan had worked for Clinton, Bush and Obama and how the man was always the first one on the line, shoving back crowds or restraining anyone who tried to get too close to the President. He scared the crap out of people and rightfully so; he was at least five or six inches over six feet with a big, muscular body. He was the Secret Service's muscle. He had been Obama's Special Agent in Charge the last two years of the man's term and now

Sheridan found himself heading up Talbot's forces. He was still very intimidating just by the way he carried himself, but she wasn't afraid of him. In fact, she rather liked him.

Russ finished with his email and handed her back the iPad, distracting her from her thoughts. As Casey took the iPad, she noticed that Senator Dane was watching her. She smiled pleasantly at the man before packing away the electronic device. When Talbot's cell phone rang, she answered it. Being that it was Mrs. Talbot, she handed the phone to Russ and listened to him calm his wife down because the family cat had escaped the confines of the White House and they were trying to track the feline down. Over next to Russ, Senator Dane snorted at the conversation, catching Casey's attention. When she grinned at him, because it truly was a hilarious conversation, he winked at her.

It was a rather bold gesture and Casey's genuine smile turned rather confused. She quickly turned her attention back to the window, watching the landscape go by and pushing aside the senator's rather saucy wink. She didn't even want to think about it so she pulled out the other iPad and busied herself with emails and other arrangements for the rest of the President's day. She didn't look at Senator Dane for the rest of the ride.

GreenTopia was in an old renovated building by RFK Stadium. There were press and police all over the place as the Presidential limousine pulled up to the front of the building, and Colt jumped out of the front seat, making sure his agents were in position before moving to open the car door. When he did, Russ emerged to a thunderous applause from the crowd and he waved, flashing the winning smile that had helped garner him an election. Barbara and Jason emerged after him, and then Senator Dane. Colt had already moved off with the President so Peter was left holding the door open for Casey. She emerged with one iPad and one cell phone, and followed the President's entourage inside.

It was the typical tour. Russ was shown great schematics of green projects in the giant two-storied lobby and then there was a host of photo opportunities. Two major news stations were in attendance and the cameras were rolling as Russ studied the schematics with interest and shook a few hands.

Casey stood back, watching the events unfold and catching a glimpse of Colt as he coordinated the security around the President. She found herself watching him more than anything else, the broad stretch of his shoulders and the handsome lines of his face. He was at least half a head taller than most of the people there so he wasn't hard to miss. His gaze, his focus, never left the President. He was a man on a mission.

Russ was supposed to have lunch at the Washington Hilton with a group of women's rights advocates so Casey kept a close eye on the clock. Russ was deep in conversation with the CEO of GreenTopia when Casey's cell phone went off. As she went to answer, she noticed that Jason's cell phone had gone off as well. He just happened to be standing a few feet from her and she saw him answer it. As they both answered their cell phones, Colt put his hand to his hear, listening to information being fed to him from the Secret Service coordinator in one of the chase cars. Casey didn't pay much attention to the simultaneous rings as she answered her phone.

"Casey," she heard Maggie's voice on the other end. "The Washington Hilton's on lockdown. Someone called in a bomb threat. Secret Service should be moving Russ back to the White House immediately and I...."

Casey swung around, phone still to her ear, to see Colt, Peter and the rest of the detail already very quickly herding the President towards the entrance. Everything was moving in fast motion.

"They're already moving him," she said, interrupting her. "I'll call you back in the car."

She hung up the phone and packed it away, moving for the main entry but realizing she was blocked by a substantial crowd, including news crews. She tried to push her way through, but there were just too many people. By the time she got to the front, the Presidential limousine and all of the chase vehicles, including the police, were tearing off across the parking lot.

Casey stood there, watching her ride disappear as the crowd around her disbursed.

———

"I get that you were trying to get me to safety," Russ was furious as he faced off against Colt. "But in doing so, you left half of my people behind. What about them?"

"Your aides aren't my concern, Mr. President," Colt replied steadily. "My job is to protect you and that was exactly what I was doing."

Russ wasn't satisfied in the least. "Casey and Barbara had to take a taxi back here," he spat. "Your job is to protect my office, and that means everyone."

"I have to disagree, Mr. President," said Colt's boss, Mark Miller, who was the head of the Presidential Protection Division. A trim, bald man, he had run over to the White House from his office when Peter Harrios had called to let him know that Colt was taking some serious heat from the GreenTopia incident. "The American people pay us to protect you, not your staff. I thought you understood that, sir."

Russ knew that, fundamentally. But he was still irate. "So you just leave them to fend for themselves in a crisis situation?" he wanted to know. "Look what happened to Jim Brady during the Reagan assassination attempt. I don't want one of my aides face down on the concrete with a bullet wound in the forehead."

"Jim Brady's injury had nothing to do with any perceived lack of Secret Service protection," Mark said quietly. "Although I understand your point, I have reviewed Special Agent Sheridan's actions today and have found nothing wrong with them. He did what he was supposed to do."

Casey had to shut the door to the Oval Office. She didn't want anyone else hearing Colt get reamed for how he handled the evacuation from GreenTopia. Mark was at least defending the man, but she felt badly for Colt getting in trouble his first few days on the job. Picking up the remote on her desk, she turned up the volume so no one could hear the raised voices.

"So," Chris was seated at his desk next to Casey's, trying to rearrange the President's schedule for the next couple of days. "Was it as bad as the President thinks it was?"

Casey shook her head, perched on the edge of her desk as she watched the news about the bomb threat at the Washington Hilton. "Of course not," she replied. "I took a taxi back. Big deal. I'm honestly not sure what Russ is so worked up about. Special Agent Sheridan certainly doesn't deserve to get his ass kicked like that."

Chris just wriggled his eyebrows and continued typing. Casey sat on the edge of her desk for a while before moving back to her seat and going through some emails. The Oval Office had grown oddly quiet and as she prepared an invitation for a private dinner with the President and some old friends during next week's trip to New Mexico, the door to the office suddenly opened and Mark Miller appeared. He smiled pleasantly at Casey as he walked through her office, followed by Special Agent Sheridan, who went right to his desk. Russ followed shortly, hands in his pockets as he approached Casey's desk.

"I'm going upstairs to have lunch with my wife," he told her. "I'll be back in a couple of hours."

"Have a good lunch," Casey smiled.

He nodded, looking rather pensive and solemn, as he left her office and headed over to the White House through the West Colonnade. Casey watched him go, noting that Chris was already packing up for lunch now that the President was gone. He slipped out after Russ did, leaving Casey alone and Colt in the next office. The sudden quiet was heavy and uncertain, at least for Casey. She felt very bad for Colt. Silently, she stood up and peered around the door of his office.

He was seated in front of his computer, typing. She came out from behind her desk and went to the doorway leading into his office.

"You're not typing your letter of resignation, are you?" she asked.

Colt glanced up from the screen. His gaze lingered on her a moment before motioning her in.

"Sit down," he said softly.

Casey did as she was asked, perching on the edge of the chair across from his desk. Colt folded his hands on his desk as he faced her.

"How long have you worked for the President?" he asked.

"Six months."

"Have you ever been a part of something like what happened back at GreenTopia?"

Casey shook her head. "No, not like that. Why?"

He sighed faintly, the brown eyes rather soft and glittery. "You know my job is to protect the President?"

"Of course I do."

"You know that I wouldn't have left you behind intentionally?"

Her brow furrowed. "It's no big deal," she assured him. "I took a taxi back. I'm a big girl."

He sat back in his chair, looking rather torn. "I'm sorry you had to do it," he said. "My primary concern was getting the President to safety and I'm so sorry you were left behind in the chaos."

She smiled at him. "Colt, I'm not upset about it in the least. You're taking this harder than I am and I'm sorry that Russ yelled at you for doing your job. He shouldn't have done that."

He just nodded, scratching at his head. "It's not the first time I've been yelled at and I'm sure it won't be the last. Are you sure you're okay?"

"I'm fine," she waved him off.

"Will you let me buy you lunch?"

She shrugged. "I think you'd better let me buy *you* lunch. You need somebody to be nice to you today."

He grinned. "You already have been."

"I haven't done anything except get you in trouble."

He laughed softly. "Tell you what," he said. "You can buy lunch but you let me buy dinner, okay?"

She cocked her head. "Dinner?"

"And drinks. Do you like sushi?"

She wrinkled her nose. "No way. I like a good steak."

His grin broadened in approval. "A girl after my own heart," he said. "I'm off at six. Where should I come and get you?"

Her smile cooled and she cocked her head, appearing somewhat thoughtful. "Are you asking me out on a date, Special Agent in Charge Sheridan?"

"And if I were?"

"If you were, then I'm not sure that's a good idea. As much as it pains me to say it, it's never a good idea to date someone you work with."

Colt studied her carefully. "Why would it pain you to say that?"

"Huh?" she wasn't sure what he meant, but then remembered how she had phrased her answer. "Well, because...because I guess I'd like to say yes but I'm not sure if it's appropriate."

He nodded in understanding, the brown eyes warm and liquid. "Let's talk about it over those sandwiches I was going to buy."

She grinned, reluctantly, and he took it as a signal to move forward. He waited while she collected her purse and took her outside into the breezy October sunshine. Casey thought they were heading to the White House mess but he ended up walking her down the driveway to Pennsylvania Avenue where they crossed the street to a sandwich shop about a block away. They got their sandwiches and sat by the sunny front window, watching the world pass by.

"Wow," Casey said, arranging her turkey sandwich. "This is such a treat. I usually just eat at my desk."

Colt had a big roast beef sandwich and he took a healthy bite. "I usually eat on the run."

Casey took a dainty bite, watching him chew. "I'll bet," she said. "How long have you been doing this crazy line of work?"

He grinned as he swallowed. "*Too* long," he took another bite. "Since I got out of the Marines. My first assignment was with Clinton in the last few months of his term and then I was assigned to Bush in 2001, right before the terrorist attacks in New York. I was with him in Florida when we received the news."

Casey was listening with interest as she ate her sandwich. "Where did you go to college?"

"United States Naval Academy," he told her. "I did coursework abroad, but mostly, my education was strictly Navy. Seriously, I had no choice. Everybody in my family up through my great-great grandfather was in the military. With a name like Philip Sheridan the Fifth, I never had a chance. It was military or my family would disown me."

Casey giggled. "So why do they call you Colt?"

It was his turn to grin. "Believe it or not, I was a skinny kid. My dad said I was all arms and legs, like a newborn colt. So they just started calling me 'the colt' and it stuck."

Casey continued to giggle. "I like it," she insisted. "So where are you from?"

"San Francisco," he told her. "My dad was born there. My parents live in the Gold Country."

Casey sipped at her soda. "That's God's country," she said wistfully. "I was born in Los Angeles and I can remember taking a few family trips up around there, seeing the old mining towns. It's gorgeous."

He watched her as he finished off one half of his sandwich. "Do you ever think you'll go back to California?"

She shook her head and looked down at her food. "Not now," she said. "I've been on the East Coast for twelve years and my boys were born here. Their life is here. Maybe I'll retire to California, but I don't see myself moving back there for quite some time."

He nodded and went to work on the second half of his sandwich. "Tell me about your kids," he said. "What do they like to do?"

She nibbled at her chips. "My oldest, Hunter, is as tall as I am and loves playing his guitar and playing baseball. Brody, my youngest, is kind of a beatnik in the making. He does everything but sleep with his damn skateboard, likes to goof off and play video games, but he's the best student out of the two. He gets straight 'As' without even trying. He's a lazy genius."

Colt grinned as he chewed his sandwich. "My brother and I were polar opposites, too. Ken was always in trouble as a kid, kind of a misfit, but he grew up to start his own company and become a very successful businessman. He recycles junk, makes a fortune, married a model and has four kids."

Casey smiled, finishing off her meal. "And you?" she asked. "Any kids?

He shook his head. "None," he said. "I was married years ago to my high school girlfriend, but that lasted about four years. We were divorced while I was on one of my Marine rotations. I haven't seen her since."

"Oh," Casey said softly. "I'm sorry about that."

He shrugged those enormous shoulders. "I'm not," he said. Then he glanced at her, noting her rather shocked expression. "I don't mean to sound callous, but she wasn't ready for marriage. I found out she'd been cheating like crazy when I was overseas, so I divorced her. I'm kind of thankful we didn't have any kids. I wouldn't want to put them through that."

Casey nodded in agreement, wrapping up what was left of her sandwich.

"Then we have something in common," she said quietly. "My ex-husband is a very nice man, but he didn't think a wedding ring should stop him from having relationships with other women. When the count got to six, I called it quits. That was enough for me."

Colt had finished his sandwich. He was staring at her as she spoke, shaking his head after a moment.

"No offense, but the guy's an idiot," he said quietly. "If I had you to come home to every night, all other women in the world would cease to exist for me. What a moron."

Casey was deeply flattered. It was such a sweet thing to say. With an enchantingly bashful smile, she took her eyes off of him long enough to look around for a trash can, mostly because she wasn't sure how to respond. He had managed to compliment her into silence. Colt saw her looking for a trash can and took her rubbish from her, using his very long arm to dump it in the nearest can.

"So," he said, folding his hands on the table and looking her squarely in the eye. "Let's talk about dinner tonight."

Casey fought off a grin, folding her hands just as he had folded his. She faced him just as squarely. "Yes. Let us."

"You wanted to know if I were asking you out on a date."

"Yes."

He thought carefully on his reply. "I am, probably more than anyone you'll ever meet, focused on appropriate behavior and protocol," he said quietly. "That's why I've gotten where I am so quickly. I know what's right, and what's wrong, and I don't make bad decisions. People's lives are in my hands and they depend on my judgment. So I am acutely aware of what is, and what is not, appropriate in any environment. That is, at least I thought I was until I met you."

Casey was watching him carefully. With his last sentence, her eyebrows rose. "What do you mean?"

He sighed faintly. Then, a big hand reached out and grasped the hands she had resting on the tabletop. His grip was very warm and very strong.

"This," he nodded his head in the direction of her their hands, "can be construed as sexual harassment."

She looked down at their hands. "I know."

"If it's unwelcome, you only need to tell me once. It will never happen again."

Casey was staring at his big hand as it covered hers. After a moment, she looked up at him. "Are you coming on to me?"

"Not unless you're receptive to it."

She gave him a half-grin. "That's a very politically correct answer."

He nodded, slowly, his dark eyes riveted to her. "The day we met, I knew I wanted to get to know you better. One look at you and... hell, I don't know. I'm not very good with words or really expressing how I'm feeling, so I probably shouldn't even be saying all of this to you. All I know is that when I look at you, I see something beyond the White House. I see the most beautiful woman I've ever seen and she's intelligent and funny and... oh, man, I'm doing it again. I shouldn't be saying all of this. I don't want to make you uncomfortable."

Casey pulled a hand free from his grasp, putting her soft fingers over his lips to silence him.

"You talk too much, you know that?" she murmured with a grin.

He nodded, somewhat miserably, with her fingers still over his mouth. Casey grinned and removed her hand.

"Listen to me," she said softly. "If I didn't want your attention, I would have slugged you when you put your coat around me in Carmen Hennderson's office or punched you in the face when you wanted to dance to The Eagles. But I didn't do either of those things, did I?"

He shook his head. "No."

"So I guess it must mean that I find you very attractive, also. In fact, I've thought a lot about you since I met you, mostly because I was hoping I hadn't given you a bad first impression."

He grinned. "You mean with the 'who the hell are you' question?"

She stiffened, although it was in good humor. "You deserved it, ripping that envelope out of my hand like you did."

He laughed softly. "I know, I'm sorry. It won't happen again."

"It had better not."

"So will you go out with me?"

Her violet eyes were glimmering at him. After a moment, she nodded. "I will," she said softly. "But we should probably keep it just between us. Not that I'm ashamed of it, but office romances are really frowned upon."

He nodded. "I agree completely. Not a word to anyone. Whatever happens between us is our business only. And along those lines, if we date a couple of times and decide we just want to be friends, then I promise that I'll be completely professionally with you at the office. No weirdness. I'll just consider you a friend made."

"Me, too."

"But I have to say at this point, if that happened, I'd be really disappointed."

She smiled. "So would I," she said softly. Then she looked thoughtful. "Let's say we go the other direction – let's say you and I go out a few times and get serious. We're crazy about each other, madly in love and all that. Just for hypothetical purposes, of course."

His face fell. "You don't think you could fall in love with me?"

She giggled. "Get serious," she scolded softly. "I'm trying to make a point. Let's say the entire terrorist nation launches an attack against Russ and I'm caught in the crossfire. You can only save one of us. Who do you save? The love of your life or the guy you're paid to take a bullet for?"

He lost his humor. He just sat there and stared at her, sitting back in his chair. When he spoke, he lowered his gaze.

"You're not going to like my answer."

Her humor faded. "It's okay," she said softly. "You *have* to save him, Colt. That's your job. I understand that."

He looked at her, almost sharply. "That wasn't going to be my answer."

Her smile left her completely. "Then that's why no one can know if you and I have a date or two," she whispered. "That very question could come up and if anyone thought your loyalty was more to me than to Russ, you'd suffer. The Secret Service would reassign you so fast that it would make your head spin, and you know it. They'd move you back to Chicago to be with Obama or somewhere else, and I'd never see you again."

"You wouldn't quit your job and move with me?"

Her smile was back. She couldn't tell if he was serious or not but just to be safe, she decided to treat the question as if he were teasing her. The alternative was much too scary and serious, at least at this early stage.

"That depends," she looked at her watch, noting the time. "If I had a big, fat rock on my finger, I'd have to, but like I said, my boys' lives are here and I don't think I'd want to uproot them for a fling."

"Trust me, you'd have a big, fat rock on your finger."

She laughed softly. "What makes you think I'd accept it? Besides, I'm not sure my dad would let me marry a Sheridan."

He grinned, glancing at his watch, also. Then he stood up. "We can talk about that tonight," he said, moving to pull her chair out. "What time do you get off work?"

She picked up her purse and began to move out of the sandwich shop. "That depends," she said. "If Russ doesn't need me, then I'll be off about four-thirty."

"I'm not off until six," he opened the door to the shop for her, stepping out behind her into the cool sunshine. "Give me your address and I'll come get you."

"How about if I just meet you somewhere? I live out in Falls Church."

He shrugged. "That's barely ten miles away," he said as they began to walk down the street. "But if you don't want me to pick you up, that's fine. Where do you want to go for dinner?"

She shrugged, her gaze moving out onto the street, the sidewalk, watching the world go by as she thought on his question. Before she could open her mouth, he took her right hand and tucked it into the crook of his left elbow. She looked at him, surprised.

"Why did you do that?" she asked.

He wouldn't look at her, the brown eyes scanning the landscape. "Because I figured you wouldn't let me hold your hand. This is the next best thing."

She laughed softly. "Are we going to the prom again?"

"Looks like it."

She continued to snort. "I'll have to let you go when we go around the corner. If anyone from the White House sees us, we'll have a lot of explaining to do."

"So just let me enjoy it for the next minute, will you?"

She squeezed his arm as they walked along. "Want to go to Charlie Palmer Steak House tonight?"

He nodded as he glanced over at her. "Sounds great."

She smiled up at him, aware she was walking very close to him with her arm looped through his. "Good," she said. "I'll be there at six-thirty barring any great world catastrophe."

He just nodded but there was a strange look on his face. Casey caught it. "What's wrong? Why do you look like that?"

He shrugged. They were nearing the intersection next to the White House so he took her hand off his elbow, kissed it, and let it go.

"I was trying to think of the last time I was out on a date and I really can't," he looked at her as they stopped to wait for the light. "I hope I remember how to behave."

Casey grinned, although she wasn't quite over the soft, warm kiss to her hand. Her heart was racing because of it.

"You'll do fine," she told him, stepping off the curb when the light turned green but noticing he wasn't following. "What's wrong?"

He remained up on the curb. "Nothing," he pointed to the West Wing in the distance. "You should probably walk in without me. I'll follow in a little while."

She understood, waving at him as she continued across the street and up onto the sidewalk on the other side. Colt watched her as she moved down the sidewalk and headed up to the guard shack near the West Wing. He found himself watching the way her gorgeous hair reflected the light, the shape of her legs in those sexy shoes, and realized that he had gotten himself in to a huge amount of trouble.

He was attracted to her more than he should have been and he couldn't help it. He didn't want to help it. Meade and the others were expecting him to get close to her and that was his goal, but he had no intention of using her and moving on. That was the last thing he wanted to do. Casey Cleburne was crossing lines with him and he couldn't stop any of it. Part of him felt sick about it but a greater part of him was giddy with joy. He hadn't felt such things in years. He was very much looking forward to their date that night.

Pulling his cell phone out of his pocket, he made a call.

FIVE

CASEY WAS FACED with a surprise when she walked back into her office.

An enormous bouquet of flowers were on her desk, the vase of cut crystal and flowers of gorgeous lilies, roses and gladiolas. The entire arrangement had to be three feet tall and when she entered her office, Maggie and Lisanne were there, smelling the flowers and admiring the beauty of the arrangement. They whirled on Casey when she entered.

"Look at this," Lisanne was excited. "Isn't it beautiful?"

Casey was a little taken aback. Startled, she inspected the massive arrangement with a good deal of curiosity. There was a big card stuck in a fancy holder and she plucked it out, looking at all of the flowers as she opened up the card.

"Good Lord," she hissed. "This thing must have set someone back a few hundred dollars."

"Who's it from?" Maggie wanted to know.

Casey finished opening the envelope and pulled out the card. It was a very pretty card and inside was a handwritten note:

Sorry you were left behind today.
Would dinner make up for it? I'd love to treat you to a night out.
Warmest regards, Scott Dane

Shocked, Casey quickly folded up the card as Maggie and Lisanne strained to see who had sent the flowers. Casey waved them off, shoving the card into her top desk drawer.

"Go back to work, ladies," she sat down in her chair. "I'm going to keep this a secret."

Maggie and Lisanne weren't about to let it go. "Casey, that's not fair," Lisanne whined. "Can we guess?"

"No."

"Please?"

"*No*," Casey was focusing on her computer. "I'm not going to tell you, so go back to work."

"The florist is the one near the Capitol Building," Chris said from his desk next to Casey. "Maybe it's from someone in the Senate."

Casey glared at him. "Zip it, Eckart," she commanded. "It's none of your business."

Chris snickered and went back to work. As Maggie and Lisanne pestered the tight-lipped Casey, Colt entered the office. He couldn't help but notice the massive flowers on Casey's desk but did nothing more than cock an eyebrow at the sight as he went into his office.

"Nice flowers," he commented.

Casey watched him, trying not to react. No doubt he was wondering who sent them and she was feeling some anxiety as a result. She really liked Colt and didn't want him to think she was a player with a string of boyfriends. She wasn't like that at all. She chased Lisanne and Maggie out of her office and went back to work, trying not to look at the massive flower arrangement on her desk. It really was beautiful, but she wasn't interested in dating the senator, not when Colt Sheridan had her attention. She definitely a one-man woman.

Russ came down from the family apartments around two thirty in the afternoon, passing Casey's desk and making a fuss over the flowers. He asked who had sent them but she coyly declined to tell him, causing the man to chuckle. Just as he was heading to his office, the uniformed Secret Service agent that was stationed in the lobby of the West Wing entered with another massive arrangement of flowers. Three dozen red roses were artfully positioned in another massive glass vase as the Secret Service agent sat them on Casey's desk next to the other arrangement. He looked at the two, nearly covering half her desk.

"Wow, Casey," he commented. "Is it your birthday?"

Casey was quickly growing mortified, even more so as Chris giggled over at his desk. She was ready to punch him right in his smug face. She stood up, inspecting the gorgeously perfect roses, before shaking her head.

"Somebody must feel sorry for me or something," she said, noting the card and pulling it from the holder. "Are these really for me?"

The uniformed Secret Service agent, a young man with an infectious grin, nodded. "They just came. Who are they from?"

Casey cocked an eyebrow at him. "None of your business," she said, sweeping her hand at him. "On your way, Anderson. Bye-bye. Get lost."

The young man backed out, a big grin on his face, as Russ came up to the desk, inspecting all of the flowers. "I'm surprised this doesn't happen more often," he said. "A beautiful, young, single woman ought to get flowers every day. Will you tell *me* who sent them?"

Casey gave him another bashful grin, the card in her hand. "I don't even know."

"Will you tell me when you do?"

"Probably not."

He snorted and turned back for the Oval Office. Sure that no one was looking over her shoulder, Casey opened up the small card that had come with the roses.

To the most beautiful girl I've ever seen.
Looking forward to dinner.

Casey couldn't help the grin on her face as she quietly folded the card and put it back in the envelope. That, too, went into the top drawer of her desk. Her heart was pounding and she just felt like smiling forever. She couldn't stop. As she turned back for her computer, Colt emerged from his office.

"So who are the roses from?" he asked casually.

Casey tried very hard not to sound giddy when answering him. Chris had a big mouth and big ears, and he would pick up on anything she said and spread it around.

"Somebody sweet and wonderful," she said honestly. "But don't ask for a name because I won't give it to you."

He cocked an eyebrow. "I've been trained in multiple interrogation techniques," he said. "I can make you talk."

She puckered her lips at his threat. "You'd better leave me alone," she said, "or I'll tell Mr. Roses and you'll be in a lot of trouble."

Colt cracked a smile. "Fine," he pretended to huff. "What about the other flowers? Did another Mr. Wonderful send those, too?"

The smile faded from Casey's face, her eyes riveted to his. "No," she said. "He's Mr. Unexpected. But I won't tell you his name, either, so don't ask."

Colt's smile broadened. "You're a popular girl," he said, watching her grin and lower her head, refocusing on her computer. "Actually, I need a few minutes with the President. Do I have to send you flowers in order to get on his schedule?"

She snorted. "Maybe," she looked at Russ' afternoon schedule. "How long do you need?"

"Fifteen minutes at the most."

Casey's attention lingered on the calendar. "He's got a few minutes now," she said. "Let me buzz him and see...."

Just as she went to hit the intercom, the President buzzed her instead. "Casey," he said. "Get Barbara and Jason in here. Find Paul Halferty as well. I want you all in here."

"Right away," Casey replied. Then she glanced up at Colt as she picked up the phone. "Looks like it's going to have to wait."

Colt nodded, watching her get to work. "It can."

He went back into his office, listening to Casey rally the troops. Within ten minutes, she was in the Oval Office with several aides and the National Security Advisor, Paul Halferty. As Colt returned his attention to the report he was writing from the incident that morning, he happened to see Casey's officemate, Chris, stand up from his chair and sneak his way over to Casey's desk. Colt glanced up without moving his head, seeing that Chris was going for the cards from the flowers in Casey's top drawer. The second Chris touched the drawer, Colt spoke.

"Do that and I'll break your fingers," he rumbled.

Startled, Chris looked at Colt with fear and defiance. "What are you talking about?"

Colt's head came up and he fixed Chris in the eye. "I'll repeat what I said - open that drawer and snoop and I'll break your fingers. Is that clear enough?"

Chris didn't reply. He just went back to his desk, quickly, and sat down. Colt returned his attention to his report, typing steadily until six o'clock. At that point, Chris left and so did nearly everyone else in the West Wing, but Colt didn't leave. He remained as long as the President remained, and as long as Casey remained. When the report was finished and the office was completely empty, he picked up the phone and pushed the line that was secure and encrypted. He had access to two.

He dialed a familiar number.

"Aury," the man on the other end said groggily.

Colt grinned. "Nash?" he said, keeping his voice down. "What in the hell are you doing sleeping in the middle of the day?"

Nash Aury chuckled sleepily. "Not usually, but I've been up all night," he said. "Did you call me just to harass me?"

"Not today," Colt said. "Any other time, I would, but not today. How's work going?"

"The usual," Nash said. "But things are good. How about you, Colt? Got any national secrets to spill?"

Colt snorted softly. "You think you're kidding," he said, lowering his voice even more. "But that's kind of why I'm calling you."

"Oh?" Nash said, as interested as he could be given how exhausted he was. "What's up?"

"This is confidential."

"Understood."

"Ever heard of the Norte del Valle Cartel?"

Nash thought for a moment. "I think so," he said. "Nasty outfit out of Sonora, right?"

"Yes," Colt said. "Given your position in law enforcement and the fact that Louisiana has Mexico to the south across the gulf, I thought you might have had some encounters with them."

Nash was the county sheriff for Ascencion Parish and the next police commissioner for the State of Louisiana. Some even though he was eyeing the governor's mansion, eventually, so he was a man in the know when it came to crime. Colt wanted to pick his brain a little.

"Not them specifically," Nash said. "I don't think they've made it to Baton Rouge yet. Why?"

Colt paused. "Just curious," he said. "Before you ask me again, you know I won't tell you, so let's talk about something else. How are the kids?"

"The *kids* are grown men," Nash reminded him. "They're doing great. You'd have some kids of your own if you ever got married."

"True enough."

"Anything new to report on that front?"

"Maybe," Colt said coyly. "You just never know."

"That's an interesting answer." Nash paused a moment before continuing. "Colt, you're not in trouble, are you? Because it's not like you to call me like this."

"No trouble," Colt assured him. "Since when do I have trouble?"

"Is it with the cartel you asked about?"

"No trouble, Nash. I promise."

"Because if there is... just say the word. I'm here for you. Whatever you need."

Colt sighed faintly. "I appreciate it," he said. "But you know if there is trouble, I'm not going to drag you into it."

"You're not dragging me into anything. We're brothers, remember?"

"Talked to any of the others lately?"

"I spoke with Ethan a few weeks ago," Nash said. "The man loves California and we'll never get him out of there."

"I don't blame him."

Nash paused again. "Colt, seriously," he said. "If you need my help, you just have to ask."

Colt was touched by the man's concern, but that was usual for Nash. He was a thoughtful individual. "I don't need your help," he said quietly. "But if I do – personally – I promise I'll ask. Okay?"

"I'll hold you to it," Nash said, but he didn't linger on the subject because he knew Colt wouldn't say more than he already had. "Any chance of you getting down my way sometime soon?"

"Not that I'm aware of," Colt said. "We've got a New Mexico trip coming up, but nothing more than that."

"You can always take a vacation and just come for a visit."

Colt chuckled. "Vacation?" he said sarcastically. "What's that?"

"No kidding."

"It's been great, Nash, but I've got to go. You take care."

"And you," Nash said. "I hope you'll..."

Nash faded off and Colt could hear the chatter of a police radio in the background. When Nash abruptly ended the call, Colt assumed that something critical needed his attention. That was par for the course with Nash. With the office silent once again, Colt ended up reading one of his security periodicals, waiting.

It was a silent, cold, and long wait.

Near eight o'clock, the door to the Oval Office finally opened and the President emerged. He was chatting with his National Security Advisor, heading for the corridor as Colt stood up from his desk. Russ caught sight of him.

"I'm going up to bed," he told him. "See you in the morning."

Colt nodded. "Yes, sir."

The President opened his mouth to continue his conversation with Halferty but ended up moving into Colt's office instead. He fixed the big agent in the eye.

"Look," he said quietly. "I just want to apologize for getting angry with you this morning. I know you were just doing your job."

"Yes, sir."

"I'm still kind of getting the hang of the way this works."

"Understandable, sir."

Russ was waiting for more of a statement but when none was forthcoming, he simply turned away and continued on with his National Security Advisor. The night shift of agents had already come on duty so Colt shut down his computer, watching the President's aides filter out of the office, waiting for Casey to come forth. She was the last one out, focused on the notebook in her hand. She didn't look up from the notebook as she wandered to her desk.

"It must be interesting," Colt said softly.

Startled, she looked up from the notebook, her eyes wide. "What in the world are you still doing here?" she asked. "I thought you went home hours ago."

His brow furrowed. "I don't leave until the President leaves," he said. "Besides, I have a dinner date and I had to wait for her."

Casey smiled, closing up the notebook. "I'm not going to get to these notes until tomorrow anyway," she said, glancing at the clock. "Wow, I didn't realize what time it was. Are you sure you want to eat this late?"

"I'm hungry. Aren't you?"

She nodded, moving around her desk to set the notebook down and shut down for the night. "I'm starving," she replied. "My stomach has been growling for the past two hours. I'm surprised you couldn't hear it through the walls."

He smiled, watching her as she shut her computer down and opened drawers to put things away. As Casey opened her top desk drawer to put her pens away, she noticed the two cards for the flowers lying on top of everything. She pulled them both out.

"Hmmmm," she took Colt's card and opened it, reading the words aloud. "'To the most beautiful girl I've ever seen. Looking forward to dinner'." She closed the card and smiled at him. "It doesn't look like my dad's handwriting."

Colt laughed softly. "I'm pretty sure it's not," he said, looking at the bigger of the two arrangements. "But I have to admit, I felt rather inadequate when I saw that monstrosity. Someone must like you a whole lot."

Casey handed him the second card. When he looked at it curiously, she put it in his hand. "Because I don't keep secrets."

"It's none of my business."

"I realize that," she said. "But I want to be completely honest and open. I don't hide things. I just want you to know that in no way, shape or form do I flirt or give out romantic signals to more than one man at a time. I'm not like that. These flowers were very unexpected and, truthfully, unwelcome. I'm not sure what to do about it."

Colt's gaze lingered on her a moment before taking the card and reading it. When he saw who had signed the card, he grunted softly and handed it back to her.

"I should have guessed," he said.

She looked at him, surprised. "Why do you say that?"

Colt scratched his head. "Because he was checking you out pretty seriously when he was here earlier today."

Casey put both cards in her purse and shut off her light. "I never encouraged the man," she insisted. "I only just met him a few days ago."

"You only just met *me* a few days ago."

She grinned as they left her office, walking the darkened

corridor towards the entrance. "Yes, I know," she said in a whisper. "But the difference is that I got to know you a little and I like you. I don't even know him."

"Maybe he's a nice guy."

She gave him a long look. "Are you telling me that I need to accept his invitation?"

He shook his head as they passed through the lobby. There were a couple of uniformed Secret Service agents there and he remained quiet until they went outside, into the cold night air. By the time they hit the driveway, he turned to her.

"Where are you parked?" he asked.

Casey pointed off to the west. "In the parking structure over there."

"Do you want to meet me over at Charlie Palmer?"

Her gaze lingered on him, the very handsome man in the moonlight. "No," she said after a moment. "I think I'll ride with you."

His lips twitched with a grin as he walked her across the street to another parking structure. It was cold but very well lit and they took the stairs up to the second level. Colt took her over to his beautiful, new, Audi A7, hitting the keyless entry and opening the passenger door for her. Impressed with the slick black car, Casey climbed in. Colt shut her door, walked around the back of the car, slid into the driver's seat, and pulled out of the parking stall.

"Nice car," she commented.

"Thanks," he replied. "I got it a couple of weeks ago."

Casey ran her hand along the side of the door, admiring it. "I drive a Ford SUV," she said. "I do so much driving with my boys and all of their gear that I need a bigger car. But I'd sure love one like this."

He smiled as they pulled out of the parking structure and onto 17th Street, heading south.

"You'd be getting flowers on a daily basis if you drove something like this around," he said, glancing at her. "And no, I don't want you to accept his dinner invitation but I don't have any say in the matter. If you want to have dinner with the senator, that's your choice."

She looked at him as they drove down the dark boulevard. She seriously considered his statement and the implications.

"I just want to make myself clear," she said softly. "I don't 'date'. I focus on one man at a time because I think to do anything else is kind of cheap. I'm not saying that you and I are exclusive, but as long as you and I are dating, even casually, I won't go out with anyone else. I think to do that shows a lack of respect for you and whatever relationship we're trying to build."

He was focused on the road as they turned the corner at E Street, heading east. "I can appreciate that," he said. "I think it's a very noble point of view. How would you feel if I went out with someone else?"

The mere suggestion made her feel sick to her stomach. She looked away, watching the scenery go by and wondering why she felt so sad and disappointed.

"That's up to you," she said softly. "You can do whatever you want and I won't judge you for it. It's not like I'm your girlfriend or anything."

"Would you like to be?"

She looked at him sharply. "I... I don't even know how to answer that."

He fought off a grin. "It's a pretty simple answer. It's either yes or no."

She couldn't tell if he was teasing her or testing her. She decided to fight back. "I think I would just like to eat dinner. I can't make any heavy decisions on an empty stomach."

Colt realized he was disappointed as they drove on to the steak house. He'd asked the question seriously but she hadn't taken it seriously.

"I'd like it if you were," he muttered.

They were at a stoplight. Casey had heard the softly uttered statement, laced with distress. She looked at him, intensely.

"Are you serious?"

He wouldn't look at her, sitting, waiting for the light to change. "I guess I was."

"Seriously?" she repeated. "Colt, you don't know the first thing about me. We haven't even kissed. How can you ask a question like that?"

Without another word, he reached over and cupped her face with one hand, planting a sweet and gentle kiss on her lips, one that quickly turned amorous once they got a taste of each other. One brief, wonderful taste was all they needed. Colt put both hands on her face and kissed her passionately, at least until the light turned green and the car behind him honked to get him moving. Somewhat dazed, he pulled away from the light, changing lanes because the steak house was up head on the left.

"After that kiss, I'm going to ask again," he said hoarsely, tasting her gloss on his lips, "Do you want to be my girlfriend?"

Truthfully, Casey was still recovering from that kiss as well. Her heart was pounding a mile a minute and she couldn't seem to catch her breath. The man had absolutely overwhelmed her and she struggled to keep a level head; otherwise, they'd end up in the back seat with their clothes off. Not that she wouldn't mind, but still....

"Can we eat first?" she panted. "Seriously. I need to... think."

He didn't say a word as he pulled into the underground parking structure for the steak house. He drove right past the valets, down to the second level, and pulled into a slot between two expensive new cars.

Turning the car off, he turned to Casey so swiftly that she hadn't time to react before his hands were on her face and he was kissing her again. It wasn't an aggressive kiss, but it was very passionate and very warm. Casey hadn't been with a man in a couple of years and she very quickly surrendered to Colt's lust. She had quite enough of her own.

Colt was practically in her seat, his big body looming over her, when he pulled the seat release and the back of the seat went slamming down against the back seat. His hands were on her face, her neck, before winding a big arm around her slender torso and pulling her against him.

Because of his size, it was awkward in the car, but he was making the best of it. He devoured her lips, her cheeks, her jaw and her neck. Casey had her arms around his head, giving off little gasps of passion as he suckled and kissed. Colt returned to her mouth, kissing her so furiously that she had to gasp for air when he suddenly pulled away.

"There," he whispered breathlessly. "Now we've had our first kiss. Will you at least think about being my girlfriend, now?"

She gazed up at him, rather overcome by everything. She licked her lips, still breathing heavily, tasting him on her flesh.

"Yes," she conceded. "I'll think about it. But you and I are going to get to know each other really well before either of us commits to something like that. I don't take it lightly and I hope you don't, either."

He shook his head, a big hand stroking her soft, pretty face. "I don't," he confirmed. "I have to be honest with you. My divorce was finalized fifteen years ago and in that time, I've only had one serious relationship. Doing what I do pretty much takes all of my time and attention. It's hard to maintain a relationship."

"Then why do you want one with me?"

He sighed faintly, shifting so he wasn't putting so much weight on her. "Because you're everything I've been waiting for and never thought I'd actually find," he whispered. "You've got this face... I can't even describe to you what I feel when I look at your face. It's like I'm seeing an angel. And you're funny, feisty and smart. I love that about you. I want to know everything about you and I want to hold it deep inside of me, like it's part of me. Damn, there I go, running off at the mouth again. I don't usually do that. I'm sorry if I'm freaking you out."

She was smiling at him by the time he was finished. Then, she lifted her head up and kissed him sweetly on the lips. Colt closed his eyes tightly as she kissed him, savoring it. It was the best kiss he'd ever had.

"You're so sweet," she cooed. "I want to get to know you, too. I'm so excited at the prospect."

He grinned and sat up, pulling her up with him. "Then let's go eat," he said. "We can get the process started. But I think I kissed off all of your lipstick. You may want to...."

He was motioning to his mouth and she pulled out a mirror and reapplied her pale mauve lipstick. He sat and watched her, acquainting himself with her on a more intimate level and loving it. He found women and their make up a very feminine and somewhat erotic ritual. It had been a long time since he'd been around it. When Casey was finished, she put her lipstick back in her purse and smiled at him.

"Let's go," she said.

Dinner was a sweet experience. Over shrimp and steak, they ran a variety of subjects around the table. Casey discovered that Colt had played football at Annapolis and had a passion for the Denver Broncos and the New England Patriots. He could converse intelligently on any subject she brought up, especially anything related to world events or politics from any nation.

He was extremely sharp, rather quiet, and overly observant. He was a man who saw detail, which didn't seem to be limited to her. He noticed her earrings, her hands and loved the shape of her mouth. Then someone would walk by the table, distract him, and he would devour every detail about that person. It had been an interesting experience for Casey, having dinner with a man who had an eye for minute detail, but she realized that it was his job to see detail. Her respect for him grew.

Colt, for his part, discovered a serious young lady with a quirky sense of humor, which he loved. She had a very level head on her shoulders and talked about her boys for about half of the meal, which made him laugh more than once as she told stories about Hunter duct-taping his brother to the basement wall or Brody trying to suffocate his brother because the kid stole something from him. Her boys seemed full of spit and vinegar, which reminded

Colt of him and his younger brother. It was hilarious and touching to listen to her.

Most of all, Colt was coming to see what a good, decent human being she was, as she volunteered at her boys' school and also volunteered with the local Meals On Wheels program and did charity work with the elderly. He admired that a great deal. She seemed like a loving, genuine woman who got screwed over by a man who didn't feel the need to stay loyal to her. Coming to know her as he was, it hurt him to know that had happened to her. It also made him more determined than ever not to obey Mr. Meade's directive to him; *use and abuse*. There was no way in hell he was going to follow that order.

Not this time.

The evening had managed to accomplish what they had hoped it would. They were able to come to understand each other a little better and from that, the seed of attraction took deep roots. It was close to midnight by the time he took her back to the parking structure across from the White House and took her directly to her big, black SUV parked on the third level. They had made small talk, almost awkwardly, like foreplay for the goodnight kiss that was sure to come.

After a minute or so of chit-chat, Colt had all he could take and kissed her so amorously that his head swam. Flushed, grinning, Casey stumbled out of his car and he followed, helping her into her car and following her out of the parking structure until she drove off in one direction and he went in the other.

It had been difficult to part from her but necessary, at least for the time being. Colt knew things would change soon because he wanted them to. He intended them to. He couldn't even think of Meade and the deep core of his objective hanging over his head; all he could seem to think of was Casey. He'd never expected this to happen, not in a million years, but happen it had. He had fallen for her.

He was a man in love.

SIX

THE PILOT of Air Force One had tried to avoid the storm, but it hadn't been enough. They were flying on the peripheral of a nasty storm front on their way to New Mexico that was covering most of the Midwest, bumping the plane around fairly roughly. Air Force One was the best built plane in the world, however, so Colt wasn't worried. He wasn't even moderately concerned. He sat in his chair in the Secret Service compartment of the plane, reading a book written by an ex-White House aide as the plane bumped and lurched over the clouds.

Peter came staggering into the compartment on his way back from the galley. He had two bottles of water in his hand, turning one over to Colt as he practically fell into his chair when the plane bounced. He strapped himself in and sighed heavily.

"Damn," he hissed. "Thank God we'll be landing in a little while."

Colt glanced up from his book. "This is nothing," he said. "When I was a Marine, we went on some plane rides that would give you nightmares for the rest of your life."

Peter snorted as he sipped his water. "I think most people on this plane would disagree with you," he pointed to the rear of the plane where the aides and press, including Casey, were seated. "There are a lot of miserable people back there."

Colt grinned, looking at his book. "Yeah?" he asked. "Anyone I know?"

Peter shrugged and held on as the plane hit a bad bump. "Most of them," he said. "The President's travel coordinator is still in the head. He's been there since this started. That guy's an ass, anyway, so I don't give a crap."

Colt snickered. "Me, either."

Peter grinned and took another drink. "Oh, and Casey," he said. "One of the stewards told me that she's a bad flyer, anyway. She's got a pillow over her face."

Colt lost his grin and looked up at him. "Where is she sitting?"

"Towards the front," Peter replied.

As casually as he could, Colt set his book down and unfastened his seatbelt. He staggered his way over to the corridor that ran the length of plane, peering down towards the press compartment to see if he could see Casey. He spied her immediately, right up in the front row against the window, slouched against the bulkhead with a pillow over her face. As he stood there, he felt a warm body come up beside him.

"See her?" Peter pointed.

Colt nodded vaguely. "Yeah," he muttered regretfully. "Poor kid. Did you see how she was?"

Peter shook his head. "No."

Colt left Peter and made his way down the corridor, bumping into the bulkhead as the plane rolled. The seat next to Casey was empty and he sat heavily, putting his hand on the pillow to gently pull it away.

"Hey," he said softly. "Are you okay?"

The pillow came down and the violet eyes looked at him. She had been crying steadily since the turbulence started, at least a good hour before, and her lovely face was red and wet. Colt was seized with sympathy.

"Oh, angel, I'm so sorry," he whispered. He unbuckled her

seatbelt and pulled her to her feet. "Come with me. Come sit with Peter and me."

Casey was sobbing softly, terrified. She clung to him as the plane bumped about and he pulled her into the Secret Service compartment with him. More than anything, he was trying not to look overly affectionate or comforting, but the poor woman really was terrified and he felt very badly. He took her to the far end of the compartment and sat her down by the window. He sat down next to her.

The plane lurched and she gasped, throwing her arms around him and burying her face in his chest. Colt looked at Peter, trying not to appear too shocked, but Peter merely looked sympathetic as well. Throwing caution to the wind, Colt put up the armrest between the seats, wrapped her up in his big arms, and settled back in the chair.

"No worries," he told her softly. "We're going to land in about forty minutes and this will all be over. Hell, I had this flight once from Bethesda to Paris across the Atlantic, and we caught the tail end of a hurricane. Talk about a bumpy flight. I had bruises for weeks after that."

She wept quietly as Colt kept up a steady stream of stories from his Marine days where he'd had more than his share of hairy helicopter rides. There were six Special Agents in the compartment, including Colt, and none of the agents had ever seen Sheridan utter more than a few words. Since his start as the Special Agent in Charge, Colt Sheridan had been an efficient and sometimes intimidating machine, but at that moment, they all saw something human in the man as he comforted a frightened woman. Perhaps "The Antichrist" wasn't so bad, after all. It was certainly something to watch.

Air Force One made it through the storm and had a rather hard landing at Albuquerque International Sunport. About thirty minutes before landing, Colt had tried to let Casey go so she could put on her seatbelt, but the descent was particularly rough and she wouldn't release him. Peter ended up belting her in as Colt held on to her all the way to the ground. Once the wheels were down, however, he needed to go into action so he forced her to let him go as the other agents rose from their seats to go collect their weapons.

"I've got to go," he cupped her face and forced her to look him in the eye. "Okay? You'll be okay now. We're down."

Casey wiped her nose with the back of her hand. "Oh, my God," she breathed. "I'm so embarrassed. I'm so sorry about this. I've just never been a very good flyer."

He smiled and stroked her cheeks with his thumbs before letting her go. "I really enjoyed it," he whispered. "Does that happen on every flight?"

She looked miserable. "If they're as bad as that one, it does."

He grinned. "Good," he said softly. "I get to hold you the whole time and have an excuse for it."

She smiled reluctantly and he turned around to see that he was alone in the compartment with her. He could hear the other agents in the next compartment collecting weapons. Sneaky, he stole a kiss before standing up.

"I'll see you later," he said softly. "Are you sure you're okay?"

She nodded, looking rather disgusted with herself. "I'm fine. Embarrassed, but fine."

He winked at her and left the compartment as the plane came to a slow crawl and began to taxi towards the terminal. Casey remained in the seat, exhausted, watching the world outside the window. When the plane finally came to a halt in preparation for the disembarking ceremony, she rose unsteadily and made her way back to her original seat to collect her things. She sat heavily as everyone around her chatted and prepared to disembark, feeling ashamed of her behavior but realizing that most everybody was scared through the bumpy flight. Taking out her compact, she went about fixing her face and erasing the signs of her meltdown.

She was sitting by a window and she saw when they brought out the giant rolling stairs and hooked them up against the fuselage of the aircraft. There were dozens of people below – cops, digni-taries and civilians waiting for Russ and Tracy to make an appearance. Casey was fixing her eye makeup when she noticed Colt making his way down the gangway and onto the tarmac.

He was talking into a radio, putting his sleek Ray-Bans on as he watched the Presidential motorcade being brought around from the C-17 Globemaster III that followed Air Force One both domestically and internationally. One thing that Casey had learned about Presidential travel was that the planes had back-up planes, the cars had back-up cars, and an entire world followed the President of the United States around as he traveled, whether it was across town or across the world.

There were at least six black Cadillac Escalades and one giant Cadillac limousine for the President. There were two dozen Secret Service agents spread out over the tarmac, including Colt at the base of the gangway. Airport personnel had brought out a big red carpet and about twenty feet of it was laid out at the bottom of the stairs. Casey finished with her face and went into one of the lavatories to fix her hair and take care of business. By the time she emerged, the President was already on the tarmac, shaking hands with the dignitaries who had shown up to greet him.

Casey went back to her seat to watch the ceremonies below. Russ and his wife shook hands and took pictures before heading into the limousine. The Secret Service detachment, including Colt, jumped into the chase cars to escort the President to his ranch near the Santo Domingo Pueblo about forty miles north of Albuquerque. The Apache Gap Ranch had been in Russ' family for generations, a working cattle ranch that his great-great-great grandfather had founded back in the 1860s. It was a beautiful spread in the mountains between Albuquerque and Santa Fe. Casey had been there once in six months. This trip was purely a family vacation even with the aides and press following. There was no real agenda intended.

After the President and the Secret Service took off, there was a charter bus waiting to take the rest of the entourage to the ranch. Because of the remote location, there weren't any hotels or resorts close by for lodging so temporary trailers had been set up like a campground near the ranch. It had been a nice drive up to the ranch, a brilliant afternoon in spite of the storm that had passed through, and Casey had calmed considerably as she sat with Chris Eckart and watched the high desert scenery pass by. They even saw two deer by the side of the road, nibbling wet winter grass.

The drive was over fairly quickly. As they were pulling onto the ranch property, Casey got a call from Russ himself and told her someone would be over to meet her where the trailers were located to drive her up to the ranch. She quickly found the small trailer she'd been assigned and dropped off her baggage. As soon as she emerged from the small but newer model trailer, a black Escalade was pulling up.

She went out to the car, seeing Colt behind the wheel. Without reacting, because she was sure that, somewhere, someone was watching, she jumped in with her arms full of iPads and her briefcase, and Colt pulled away back to the road.

"How are you feeling?" he asked as they headed towards the ranch house.

"Fine," she said. "Thanks again for... well, you know, helping me work through it. It was very sweet of you."

He glanced at her. "Don't think it's too sweet. I have an ulterior motive."

"What?"

"You still haven't agreed to be my girlfriend. I'm trying to score points."

She laughed softly. "You don't have to do that."

"Yes, I do."

She looked at him, putting her hand on his arm. "No, you don't," she said softly. "I'll be your girlfriend."

He stopped the car in the middle of the road and looked at her, surprised and pleased. "Really?"

She grinned. "Really."

He was fighting off a grin. "Wow," he said honestly. "I haven't had a girlfriend in so long I think I forgot what to do with her."

She laughed. "It's like riding a bike. It'll all come back to you."

"Do you think it'll come back to me at the Sunrise Springs Resort?"

She cocked her head curiously. "What's that?"

"It's the place I booked up the road for you and me. I was going to lure you there and force you to give me an answer."

She burst out laughing. "Are you serious?"

"Absolutely."

"How in the world were you going to manage that?" she wanted to know.

He began to drive again. "The President is on vacation for the next five days," he said. "The entire Secret Service detachment has a rotational forty-eight hours off, including me. I haven't had more than one consecutive day off in over a month, so I'm technically off for the next two days. I booked a room at the Inn at Sunrise Springs about ten miles from here with the intention of taking you with me."

She thought on that. "I'd love to go," she said, "but I'm not sure what to tell Russ. I certainly can't tell him that I'm going with you."

Colt suddenly turned the car around, a perfect spin that had the front wheels locking on the dirt road and the rear wheels spinning around 180 degrees. Casey held on to the overhead bar, shrieking with surprise and some delight, like an amusement park ride, as he took off back towards the cluster of trailers. He swung back around behind them, looking to see who was out and about to make sure he wasn't noticed, as he put the car in park. He held out his hand to her.

"Give me your key," he said.

Casey did as he asked, her brow furrowed. "What are you doing?"

"I'll be right back."

He climbed out of the rig and opened up her trailer, disappearing inside. Casey sat in the passenger seat of the black SUV, confused, wondering what he was doing in her trailer. After a minute or so, he came out bearing her luggage. Opening the door, he loaded it into the back of the car, shut the door, and climbed back into the driver's seat. Casey was more confused than ever.

"What did you do?" she asked. "Why did you bring my luggage out?"

He pulled out onto the main road and headed for the ranch once more. "Your toilet is broken," he said evenly. "The President will understand why you're going to stay at a resort ten miles to the east. You can be back to the compound in minutes if he needs you."

She stared at him, understanding what he'd done, and laughed softly. "You broke my toilet?"

"It was cheap, anyway."

She giggled and sat back in the passenger seat as they cruised along the dirt road towards the big spread of Apache Gap. The man apparently had an answer and a solution for everything.

It turned out that Russ needed help arranging an impromptu barbeque that weekend for some relatives, which Casey deftly handled. She and Tracy sat in the big family room and went over menus and other items while Casey got on the phone and on the internet, arranging for meat delivery and hiring a catering company from Albuquerque to do the cooking. When the party was arranged and the sun was setting, she happened to mention to Tracy that the toilet in her trailer was broken, which prompted Tracy to insist she stay at the ranch house.

Casey very politely declined, mentioning she'd heard that the Sunset Springs Resort was rather nice, and rather close, and she'd already made arrangements to stay there. Tracy wanted to stay there, too, because she wasn't thrilled with Russ' relatives, but Russ shut that idea down. Casey was pleased and surprised when Russ gave her the next couple of days off, telling her he'd call her if he needed her. He seemed to think he was going to sit around and drink for the next couple of days and not do any work, so she went right along with it. It was a vacation, after all, and he intended to take advantage of it.

Thrilled that she was now free for a couple of days as well, she packed up her stuff and called for a driver. She had no idea where

Colt was. He'd left her at the ranch's front door and disappeared, but she was mildly curious where the man was because he had her luggage. As the Secret Service night shift came on board and people began to shift around, Casey went outside to wait for the car that would take her back to her trailer, since she really had nowhere to go until Colt came around. As she stood out by the old-fashioned hitching post near the corner of the ranch house property, a red Jeep Wrangler pulled up. When she glanced inside, she saw Colt sitting in the driver's seat with street clothes on.

"Get in," he told her.

Casey opened the door and climbed in. "Are you crazy?" she hissed. "Someone might see us."

He had his sunglasses on in spite of the setting sun. He didn't say a word as he turned around and headed out of the compound.

"I'm your driver," he told her, quite logically. "I happen to be off as well so I'm giving you a lift to the hotel. There's nothing odd about that."

She sighed faintly, settling back in the seat. "If you say so."

He glanced at her as they headed towards the front gates and the checkpoint that harnessed the perimeter complex.

"You sound doubtful," he said.

She shrugged, looking up at the sky and its shades of red and sunset gold. "If you and I start associating with each other more than usual, people are going to think there's something going on. I just want to be careful, for your sake."

He slowed down as he came near the checkpoint with both Secret Service and local police. "Don't you worry about me," he said, eyeing the man in the distance who was preparing to approach the slowing car. "I can take care of myself. And I can take care of you, too."

She didn't reply as he pulled the Jeep to a halt and rolled down the window. The Secret Service agent approached and waved.

"Sheridan," he greeted, seeing Casey in the passenger seat. "Hi, Ms. Cleburne."

"The President is having me drop Ms. Cleburne off at the

resort up the road," Colt told the man. "I'm continuing on into Santa Fe. Harrios has my contact information and so does the shift supervisor, so don't hesitate to call if you need me. I also have a radio, so you can raise me on that if you need to. I'm taking a couple of days to breathe while the President is taking it easy."

The agent grinned. "I didn't think you did that kind of thing," he said. "I've only ever seen you on duty. Don't tell me you actually have a personal life?"

Sheridan wriggled his eyebrows. "I'm going to try."

"Good luck," the agent stepped back from the car and waved them on.

Casey remained silent as the Jeep pulled out onto the main highway and began to gain speed. Colt fussed with the radio, finding a station, before reaching over and taking her hand. She looked over at him, grinning.

"So now what?" she said. "Has it all started coming back to you now?"

He looked over at her. "What?"

"What you're supposed to do with a girlfriend?"

He grinned. "We're about to find out."

"Sounds either scary or intriguing."

He laughed. "I hope it's neither. I hope it's wonderful."

She clasped his big hand with both of her hands, gently caressing his big fingers. "So did you get two rooms or one room with two queen beds?"

He cast her a sidelong glance. "One room, king sized bed."

"I see," she fought off a grin, looking out of the window. "So you expect me to sleep with you?"

He grunted, trying not to grin. "A guy can hope."

"So this is all about sex?"

His humor left him. "No," he looked at her. "It's not that at all. It's about spending time with a woman I like a lot and want to get to know much, much better. We can sleep in the same bed and not have sex. I just want to spend time with you, Casey. This has never been about sex."

Her smile faded. "I believe you," she said softly. "I have to be honest and tell you that the past week has been one of the best weeks of my life. I've enjoyed getting to know you so much. I'm really touched and flattered that you would go to so much trouble to arrange something like this."

He lifted her hands, kissing them both, before lowering them into her lap. "No trouble at all," he said. "I wanted to. But I think you and I are going to have to steal time together when we can get it."

"No wasted opportunities."

"Exactly."

He pulled her hand back to his lips, kissing her fingers as they drove along the highway. Casey's heart was pounding with joy and anticipation for what was to come. Spending time alone with Colt was an unexpected treat and she found she was a little nervous as well. They'd never spent any length of time together. She hoped and prayed it strengthened whatever was growing between them.

The Inn at Sunrise Springs was upon them before they realized it. The sun was low on the horizon as they pulled in to valet, turning the Jeep over to be parked as Colt climbed out and went around to help Casey from the car. He took her hand, tucking it possessively into the crook of his elbow as they walked through the lobby, past registration, and out onto the grounds. Casey wondered why they hadn't checked in, or where her luggage was, until they came to one of the many casitas that dotted the property and he pulled out a digital key. Opening the door for her, Casey stepped in and found a wonderland.

There were dozens of candles, half-burned, and the smell of lemongrass was heavy in the air. The lights were dimmed as he took her by the shoulders and directed her into the dining area, where a glorious meal was set out. There was a bottle of champagne on ice and a huge bouquet of desert-like flowers on one of the plates. Casey stood there and gawked.

"Oh, my God," she gasped, looking at him. "What is all of this?"

He grinned. "I sort of remembered how to act with a girl-friend," he said. "I remembered they like to be treated nicely and that little romantic surprises mean a lot."

Casey pointed at the table, awed. "Is this where you disappeared to this afternoon while I was with Tracy?"

He nodded. "I checked in and got the ball rolling," he said. "How'd I do?"

Casey was literally speechless as her focus returned to the table. She moved forward, slowly, finally fingering the giant flower arrangement on her plate. Everything was so gorgeous and perfect. As Colt watched, she plopped down on the chair and started to tear up. He went down on a knee beside her.

"What's wrong?" he demanded softly. "Did I do too much? Not enough? Are you sorry you said you'd be my girlfriend?"

She started to giggle, wiping at the tears, and threw her arms around his neck. "I'm just so overwhelmed," she whispered. "This is the nicest thing anyone has ever done for me. I didn't know men like you still existed."

Colt wrapped her up in his big arms, holding her tightly. His face was in the side of her silky, caramel-colored hair.

"You deserve to be treated nicely," he assured her, kissing her head and pulling back to look at her. "I promise I will always treat you like you're the most important thing in the world. I'll buy you flowers every week and I'll do everything I can to make sure you feel special and loved."

Casey looked at him, shocked. "*Loved*?"

He smiled at her, a big hand stroking the side of her head. "If you think I'm just hanging out with you just to pass the time, think again," he said softly. "Everything I do has a purpose. Even you."

She wasn't following him. "What purpose?"

He cupped her face and kissed her lips, gently. "Let's eat dinner and then we'll talk about it," he whispered, rising to his feet. "Are you hungry?"

She nodded, looking to the table because he was starting to remove the metal heat covers.

"I didn't eat before we boarded the plane," she said, looking somewhat embarrassed. "I never do because I get motion sick on long flights."

He smiled as he put a plate of lobster and steak in front of her. "So what happens when we go to London on our honeymoon? That's a long flight, you know."

She laughed softly. "I didn't realize we had gone from being boyfriend and girlfriend to our honeymoon so quickly."

"I'm just testing the water."

She continued to giggle, watching him pop the champagne. "You don't waste any time, do you?"

"I can't afford to," he said, pouring two glasses of champagne. "Live for today because tomorrow, we may die."

Her smile faded. "That's pretty morbid."

"It's a famous quote," he put a glass of champagne in front of her. "But in my case, it happens to be true."

She knew what he meant. The man was essentially paid to take a bullet for the President. So she held up her glass to him, to toast.

"Here's to a long and healthy life, Special Agent in Charge Colt Sheridan," she said softly.

He held up his glass, clinking it gently against hers. His gaze never left her face. They sipped their champagne and he finally sat down, picking up his knife and fork as Casey cut her meat. She began to eat like someone was going to take her food away from her, shoving bread and steak into her mouth ravenously.

"Slow down, Angel," he admonished with a grin. "There's plenty."

She smiled, chewing. "Sorry," she said. "I didn't realize how hungry I was until I took the first bite."

He continued to grin, delving into his lobster. He took a bite, sighing with satisfaction. "This is really good," he said. "I didn't have lobster until I got out of college. Now it's one of my favorite things."

Casey was already halfway done with hers. "There's no lobster in San Francisco?"

His smile grew at her taunt. "Mom's from Montana," he said. "She couldn't stand seafood of any type. My brother and I grew up on meat and potatoes. When I was a kid, I would spend my summers on my grandparent's farm in Montana. I fed the animals, learned to drive a tractor, even learned to quilt. One summer, when I told my grandmother I was bored, she gave me an unfinished quilt and told me to finish it. I did and she entered it in the local county fair. I won third prize."

He was snorting and Casey started giggling. "That's impressive," she said. "I expect a quilt for Christmas, then."

He stuffed his mouth with steak. "My sewing days are over," he told her, watching her laugh. There was something so sweet and magical about the way she laughed. "Enough about me. Let's talk about you. Tell me everything about you from the time you graduated high school until now."

Casey continued to laugh. "Let's see," she pretended to think. "I got a scholarship from the Daughters of the Confederacy to the university of my choice, which happened to be Georgetown, where I proceeded to get my degree in American History. Imagine the horror of all those Southern women when Patrick Cleburne's descendent chose a Yankee college."

He laughed softly. "Imagine the horror of my parents when I applied to the Naval Academy and not West Point."

"So you understand," she pointed a knife at him for emphasis. "Anyway, I interned at the Pentagon and started working for the Secretary of Defense's office. It took me six months to work my way into the position of administrative assistant to the Secretary of Defense, a position I remained at for almost eleven years. I interviewed with the President when I was personally asked to by his Chief of Staff. Russ liked me and hired me the same day I interviewed."

Colt was listening to her with interest, chowing down on the steak fries. "Did you know much about him when you interviewed with him other than he was the new President?"

She nodded. "American History is my background, so I did a

lot of research on Russ before I even talked to him. I knew his background, how he lost two kids to Cystic Fibrosis, how he's a strong advocate for the environment and charitable causes. He's always doing fundraisers for childhood cancer and things like that because of the two kids he lost. I can't even imagine losing both of my kids. I don't know how he and Tracy keep themselves together."

Colt listened, thinking on Meade and his directive as Casey rattled on. He kept reliving the last conversation he had with the man, over and over in his head. He'd spent years of his life accomplishing directives from the shadowy group of men, proud of his achievements, knowing he was making his mark on the world in doing so. But now, he found himself struggling against what he was ordered to do and what he wanted to do. He had found the woman of his dreams, unexpectedly, and he didn't want to let that go, not ever. The situation had never weighed more heavily upon him than at this very moment.

"I can't imagine," he finally muttered, eating his vegetables. "Has the President ever talked to you about it?"

She shook her head, finished with her steak and her lobster and picking at her broccoli. "Only to point out the pictures of his boys on his desk and tell me their names," she slowed down her eating. "The oldest was James. He died when he was ten. The younger one was Sean and he died when he was only six. Russ said the boys spent most of their lives in hospitals receiving treatment. Russ even took them to France to try some kind of stem cell therapy that the Americans wouldn't do, but it only helped for a little while. I guess they had a particularly aggressive form of the disease. The boys died within nine months of each other."

Colt was staring at her. When she finished, he sighed heavily. "Wow," he exclaimed softly. "That's really sad."

Casey nodded, feeling depressed as she finished off her greens. "So I guess that's why I took the job," she said. "He's very much into kids and kids charities. He's huge on education. I like that passion for kids and I like working with him."

"Do you like working with the rest of us?"

She looked at him, grinning. "Well," she said reluctantly, teasing. "Most of the aides are okay. My officemate, Eckart, is a dweeb, but he has his moments. The Secret Service guys are a bit creepy, but I guess they're okay. I also love Maggie and Lisanne. Oh, and Jason, Russ' personal aide. He's been with Russ since his days as Governor of New Mexico. Jason's dad and Russ are best friends. Jason's a nice kid."

Colt made a mental note about Jason, the good-looking young aide who followed the President around everywhere he went. He hadn't paid much attention to him until now but he was thinking from this point forward, he needed to.

"Who's his dad?"

"Erik Travis," she was rattling on and he let her. "He's a director with the Department of the Interior. He oversees the Cibola National Forest and the Magdalena Ridge Observatory, among other things. The family owns a lot of land in Southern New Mexico down by the border."

Something was starting to make some sense to Colt. Like pieces of a puzzle, he was starting to see a pattern. Russ had connections with a director with the Department of the Interior, a man who, coincidentally, owned land in Southern New Mexico where the cartel drug drops were rumored to have taken place. The man's son was one of Russ' personal aides. He was learning a lot this evening.

Finishing off his plate, he pushed it aside and grabbed the bottle of champagne, filling up Casey's glass and topping off his own.

"So let's get back to you," he said. "You said you're from Los Angeles. Is that where you grew up?"

She nodded. "Yes," she clarified. "Well, actually, I was born and raised in Pasadena, right outside of Los Angeles. My parents still live in the same house I grew up in."

"Siblings?"

"A sister, Riley. She lives with me and the boys."

"What does she do?"

"She works for the Treasury Department."

"What's the situation with your ex-husband?"

"What do you mean?"

"Are you two close? Do you hate each other? Do I need to kill him?"

She grinned. "No, we're not close," she replied. "But we don't hate each other, either. I don't really give him much thought one way or the other. He likes living the single life and he only sees the boys about once a month, so I'm totally fine with that. Dennis isn't a bad guy; he's actually very nice. He's just one of those guys who should have never gotten married. It's not in his nature to stay faithful to one woman."

Colt was watching her with glittering eyes across the table. The candlelight gave his handsome face a surreal glow. "It's in mine," he said softly. "I intend to prove it."

She returned his smile, finishing her second glass of champagne and feeling buzzed. She had talked non-stop since they had arrived and, thanks to the alcohol, it was only going to get worse.

"I believe you," she said, holding up her glass as he poured her some more. "Can I ask you something?"

He put the bottle back in the ice. "Sure."

She eyed him for a moment. "Why do you want to date me?"

He lifted his eyebrows. "Because I like you."

"Why?"

He grinned. "Because you're gorgeous and funny and intelligent. Do I need any other reason?"

She cocked her head. "I don't know," she said. "I can't figure out if you have some other motivation."

He snorted. "Why would you say that?"

She shrugged and drained about half of her champagne. "I don't know," she said. "Maybe because you've been so attentive so quickly. I haven't even known you a week. I'm just not used to that kind of fast work."

"A woman as beautiful as you?" he asked, incredulous. "You must have men falling all over themselves for a chance to go out with you, and I know for a fact that Senator Dane wants to take you out. Why does it surprise you that I aggressively pursued you? I didn't want to miss out."

She smiled modestly. "You wouldn't have," she said. "I knew the moment you wrapped me up in your jacket in Carmen Hennderson's office that I was going to date you. If you hadn't pursued me, I was going to pursue you."

His smile broadened. "I'm flattered," he said. "But I have to say that I would have been a hell of an easy catch for you."

She laughed softly, draining the last of her champagne and feeling rather tipsy. "I'm going to make a confession."

"What?"

She got up from her chair and made her way over to him, planting herself in his lap. He pulled her close as she wrapped her arms around his neck. For the first time, they allowed themselves to feel the attraction, now in the privacy of the little *casitas* with no eyes watching, no protocols that were in danger of being violated. It was just the two of them with candlelight and champagne. It was romantic and sweet, on so many levels. Casey could feel herself letting go of any reservation she may have had. She was falling for Colt Sheridan and could no longer deny it.

"I have a secret," she whispered.

He could see she was slightly drunk simply by the way she was speaking. He fought off a grin. "What's that?"

She leaned close to him, her lips against his face near his left ear. "I haven't slept with anyone in four years."

His grin broke through. "I see," his mouth was by her ear and he kissed it softly. "I'm sure it will all come back to you."

"What about you?" she licked his earlobe, feeling him shudder. "When's the last time you had sex?"

It was difficult to think with her nibbling his earlobe. "Probably about the same as you," he confessed, quivering when she suckled his ear. "I had a girlfriend for about six months but...."

She cut him off by planting a powerful kiss on his lips, so much so that he was momentarily startled before responding strongly. He hadn't expected her to come on so strongly, but she had. Hands in her luxurious hair, he kissed her passionately, licking her lips until she opened her mouth for him. Casey pressed up against him, her arms around his head, kissing him so furiously that she ended up cutting her lip against her teeth. But the kisses were sweet and delicious, not sloppy. Every suckle, every lick, had a purpose. Before she realized it, she was up in Colt's arms and he was carrying her to the bedroom.

She was all wrapped around him as he carried her through the door, so much so that she didn't notice the candles and flower petals all over the room until he set her down on the bed. Then, she caught sight of the candles and the rose petals, and she pulled away from him, gasping again.

"Oh my," she breathed. "Look at this room. Did you do this, too?"

He nodded, already pulling off his button-down casual dress shirt. "Yes," he said, rather breathlessly. "I was going to run a bath, too, but I figured it would get cold. You may not even like baths. So I jazzed up this room a bit."

"You must have spent a fortune on candles."

"Bought every last one in the gift shop. The salesgirl was laughing at me."

She looked up at him, yanking on his t-shirt so hard that he lost his balance and fell down on top of her. She lay back on the bed, her arms around his neck, gazing at him in the soft glow of the candles.

"I'm not laughing," she whispered. "I think it's the sweetest thing anyone has ever done for me. I'm completely overwhelmed by it and by you. I think you're wonderful."

Colt's lips descended on hers, gently at first, but with increasing passion. The clothes began coming off; his t-shirt, her top, and finally both pairs of pants. Colt was down to his boxer briefs, his mouth on Casey's face, neck and shoulders. She had incredibly soft skin and he acquainted himself with the texture and taste, licking her cleavage and listening to her gasp. He hadn't yet tried to grope anything deeply personal, but his hands were glued to her ass. She had a great ass and he squeezed it gently through her silky panties.

Casey parted her legs and he slid in between them, still clad in briefs. She was stroking his body with her thighs, moving them up and down his hips. He had a magnificent chest; broad, muscular and smooth, and she ran her hands over it, becoming familiar with him, toying with his nipples. In fact, Colt had a magnificent body in general, like something out of the cover of a romance novel. He was built like a god with his soaring height and broad shoulders.

Casey's hand on Colt's chest seemed to push him over the edge because he reached around behind her and unhooked her bra, pulling it off and tossing it to the ground somewhere. Bare-chested, he took a moment just to look at her.

"God, you're beautiful," he whispered, gently kissing the top of her right breast. His mouth moved down towards the nipple. "You taste like flowers."

Casey arms were wrapped around his head as his mouth moved across her chest, finally capturing a warm nipple. She cried out softly as he suckled her hard, a hand coming up to fondle her soft, warm breasts. She was fairly well endowed, more than a handful for his big grip. Once Colt tasted a sweet nipple, he lost what was left of his self-control. He had to have all of her.

Colt pulled off her underwear and his own in one swift move. Then he was back on her, wedged between her legs, his mouth moving down her torso to her woman's center. He planted his face between her thighs, licking and suckling her as she gripped the headboard for support and tried not to scream.

He couldn't get enough, intoxicated by the taste and smell of her, finally lifting himself up and thrusting into her eager body as she peeled off a gentle cry. His mouth came down on hers, kissing her with all of the emotion and passion he was feeling, as he repeated thrust into her heated body.

Colt made love to Casey three times before midnight. She had such a beautiful body that he couldn't get enough of her, turning her onto her stomach to make love to her, onto her side with his arms around her, or on her back so he could look her in the eye.

She was responsive and aggressive, causing him to climax early twice because he simply couldn't help himself. She knew what she was doing with her fingers on his testicles or gently inserted into his anus. He had climaxed so hard the last time that he bit his tongue, tasting blood along with the pleasure. He'd never experienced anything like it.

They both fell asleep sometime after midnight but he was awakened in the very early morning hours by Casey as she gave him erotic oral sex. The woman had a magic mouth and he was absolute putty in her hands. They made love twice more after that before falling into an exhausted sleep sometime before the sun rose. Wrapped up in each other's arms, it was the most gratifying and peaceful sleep either one of them had ever had.

That night, things changed for both of them. The situation, once only gentle flirting, had gone from strong attraction to deeply serious all in a matter of hours.

SEVEN

COLT AWOKE to Casey's beautiful face.

She was sleeping curled up in his arms and when he opened his eyes, he could just see her forehead and part of her face. She was sound asleep and he very gently caressed her, thinking that this was the way he wanted to wake up every morning for the rest of his life. He didn't want to spend another night alone or another day without seeing her face, basking in her beauty and charm and wit. She was a part of him now like no one else had ever been. He couldn't even think of his Core directives, of any ulterior motives he might have for coming to know her. They didn't exist to him any longer. All that existed were his feelings, true and strong. He belonged to her completely.

The sun was peeking in from between the curtains as he very carefully disengaged himself and climbed out of bed. A glance at the clock showed that it was nearly eleven in the morning. Going to his suitcase, he quietly picked it up and carried it out of the bedroom, shutting the door carefully behind him.

Removing a pair of pajama bottoms from his suitcase, he pulled them on and sat down with his laptop. There were several emails for him and eleven messages on his cell phone. All of them were fairly benign but he responded anyway, with either a return email or a text. He didn't want to call anyone and chance waking Casey up when she heard his voice. Right now, he was pretty much in heaven with her sleeping in the other room, knowing that when she awoke, his would be the first face she saw.

He made one call to the resort concierge to make arrangements for a picnic and a horseback ride that afternoon, going out onto the patio to speak so there would be less chance of waking Casey. He thought it would be fun to get out onto the range, just the two of them and the New Mexico desert. He wanted to get to know her in a casual setting, away from Presidents and the circus that followed them around. Just a man and a woman, and nothing to distract them. After he hung up the phone with the concierge, he quietly called room service and ordered some breakfast.

He went back to work, doing some research on the internet for the President's trip to Argentina after the New Year when he heard the shower turn on in the bathroom. Setting the laptop aside, he poked his head inside the bedroom, seeing the bed empty and the bathroom door open. Going into the bathroom, he stuck his head in to see Casey standing with a towel in her hand, stark naked. When their eyes met, she grinned hugely.

"Ha!" she exclaimed softly. "It worked!"

His smile couldn't have been bigger. She looked sleepy, happy and adorable with her mussed hair and bright smile.

"What worked?" he asked.

She had the towel up in front of her, covering but not completely concealing, and it only served to make her more alluring. "I thought if I turned the shower on, you'd come running."

He stepped into the bathroom. "Why?"

Grinning, she dropped the towel and stepped into the big, tiled shower with the enormous shower head. As water pounded down on her head, saturating her beautiful hair, she crooked a finger at him.

Colt didn't need an explanation. He dropped his pajama bottoms and got in with her, wrapping his arms around her and listening to her giggle. As the warm water beat down on them, Colt and Casey lost themselves in a powerful kiss that only grew more powerful when he backed her up against the tile and began to do wicked things to her with his mouth. Then he turned her around, put her hands up on the wall, and made love to her as the shower blasted.

When their passion climaxed and cooled, Casey had him hold his hands open and she squirted shampoo into his open palms. Grinning, Colt washed her hair, delighting in running his fingers through the strands until she rinsed it off. Then she gave him her shower sponge with body wash on it and he took his task very seriously as he soaped her luscious body from head to toe. He was particularly interested in soaping her breasts, which aroused him tremendously and he ended up making love to her again, holding her up in his arms as she wrapped her legs around his waist. She was a petite woman as it was but against his size and strength, he could hold her aloft as they made love without any effort at all. In fact, it was one of the most arousing experiences of his life.

In all, the shower took about an hour, long enough so that room service came, knocked for several minutes, and then left breakfast on the doorstep. When they turned the water off and Casey went about drying off and putting on body lotion, Colt went to the door with a towel wrapped around his waist and collected their breakfast.

Casey went about putting on some makeup and drying her long hair. She could hear Colt banging around in the living area and she smiled as she listened to him, never more deliriously happy in her life. She'd spent years focused on her boys, giving all of her attention to them and none to herself and her own personal happiness because she figured the boys needed one parent who wasn't focused on the single life. While Dennis had a different woman every week, she had no one. But with the introduction of Colt, she was coming to realize what she'd been missing. She was also coming to realize she was in love.

Her smile faded as she looked at herself in the mirror, the awareness of her feelings for him shocking her somewhat. She'd only known him a week and already she was in love with the man. And why not? He was handsome as hell, tall and muscular, sweet and intelligent. He was the perfect storm of attributes and she had fallen hard. In truth, she was a little frightened but there was nothing she could do about it. She couldn't even summon the courage to protect herself.

Finishing with her makeup, she blow-dried her hair into her favored style of heavy bangs and long, sleek hair to her mid-back. It was an adorable style on her, one not missed by Colt when she came out into the living area dressed in purple yoga pants and a white tank top that emphasized her slender waist and lovely breasts. He was sitting on the couch, dressed in loose jeans and a casual pullover shirt, smiling at her when she emerged from the bedroom.

"Hello, Angel," he said softly, putting his laptop away. "Are you hungry?"

Casey nodded, went straight to him, and curled up on his lap. He held her happily, handing her half of a bagel while he ate the other half. He rubbed her back as she sat on his lap, munching the bagel.

"So what are the plans for today?" she asked, mouth full.

He had a mouthful as well. "What makes you think we're going to be doing anything other than this?"

She shrugged. "Because you don't seem like the kind of guy who can stay still for long."

He grinned. "You're coming to figure me out already," he said. "Actually, I do have something planned, but it's a surprise. Did you bring your jeans?"

She nodded eagerly. "I did."

"Then go get dressed."

She squealed with excitement and jumped up, putting the half-eaten bagel aside. "Are we going shopping?"

He cocked his eyebrow and shook his head slowly. "No, ma'am."

"Uh... sight-seeing?"

"In a sense."

"Am I going to be doing a lot of walking?"

"Sort of. Wear tennis shoes if you have them, or flat-soled boots. And bring a jacket."

She did a happy little dance and ran back into the bedroom, leaving him grinning in the living room. She had such a cute personality, one he was coming to love more and more. Shutting his laptop down, the one that he had been doing some research on major land owners in New Mexico with, he put it away in his briefcase. He could hear Casey banging around in the bedroom as he picked up his suitcase and wheeled it back into the bedroom.

"Can I get dressed in here with you?" he asked. "I've been doing all of my changing out in the living room."

She had her suitcase up on the bed, looking at him curiously. "Why did you do that? I didn't ask you to."

He shrugged, putting his suitcase up on the bed, also. "I pulled my luggage out there this morning so I wouldn't wake you up."

She watched him as he began to pull out a heavy plaid shirt. "Who in the world raised you to be so considerate? I've never met anyone so thoughtful."

He winked at her. "My grandmother was big on manners."

"The same one who made you learn how to quilt?"

"The same."

Casey grinned. "I think I'd like to meet her someday."

"You will."

With a lingering gaze on him, she returned to her suitcase. She pulled out her dark denim skinny jeans, an oversized lightweight sweater and a tank top for underneath it, and her tan, leather, knee-high boots with the heavy flat sole. Without a hint of embarrassment whatsoever, considering they had spent the past twelve hours stark naked, she pulled off her sweats and changed into her jeans and the big cream-colored sweater. The boots went on over the jeans, giving her a very casual and attractive look.

Colt watched her as he got dressed. He couldn't seem to take his eyes off her. He pulled off his casual pullover shirt and replaced it with a t-shirt and a heavier plaid shirt. He also put his big cowboy boots on. As Casey emerged from the bathroom where she had gone to collect her lip balm, she stopped to gawk at him.

"You look like the Marlboro Man," she said. "God, Colt, could you be any more of a hunk? Seriously?"

He laughed softly. "I don't know. Can I?"

She giggled and shook her head, going over to him and putting her arms around his neck. He scooped her up, her petite size against his big frame, and kissed her.

"You're the handsomest man I have ever seen," she admitted as he kissed her. "You make my heart jump every time I see you."

He grinned, flattered. "'Coming from the woman of my dreams, that's quite a compliment. Thank you."

"You're welcome," she kissed him one final time and let him go, looking around to make sure she had everything. "What else do I need?"

"A jacket," he reminded her, repacking his luggage and zipping it up.

"Oh, right," she said, digging into her suitcase and pulling out a lightweight, zipper front jacket with a fleecy inside. "Anything else?"

He thought a moment. "I don't think so," he said. "But no purse. Bring only what you can carry on you."

He expected an argument but was impressed when the worst she did was lift her eyebrows. "Hmmm," she put her hands on her hips, looking at her luggage and purse thoughtfully. "This is getting more mysterious by the moment. Should I bring money or a credit card?"

He fought off a grin. "No," he said. "You'll have nowhere to use them."

She puckered her lips, thinking. Then she went to her purse and pulled out her lip balm and sunglasses, sticking them both in her pocket. Then she looked at Colt and threw up her arms.

"I'm ready," she announced.

His smile broke through and he finished with his suitcase, grabbing his wallet, his keys and his sunglasses. He held out a hand to her.

"Come on, Angel," he said. "Let's go on an adventure."

Her smile vanished unnaturally fast as she took his hand. "It doesn't involve an airplane, does it?"

He laughed. "No," he replied. "I don't think I could get you on one."

"Swear it? No biplanes, prop planes or acrobatic planes?"

He continued to laugh. "I swear, no airplanes. No hot air balloons, either. I have a feeling you're a girl who likes to have her feet on the ground."

She nodded, relieved, and followed him to the door. "Sorry to be a party-pooper, but as you've seen, airplanes and I are mortal enemies."

"I promise I will never take you on anything that involves an airplane unless it has to do with a vacation or work."

"Thank you."

He pulled her out of the *casitas*, taking her through the rock garden, past the swimming pool and the eco-friendly garden, and into the main resort. He had her wait in the artsy Southwest-inspired lobby with its gold and green colors while he went to the concierge and had a few words with the woman. The concierge got on the phone as Colt came back to Casey and took her hand again.

"Come on," he encouraged.

Casey followed. She was just along for the ride, thrilled that the man thought enough of her to surprise her with an adventure. It had been such a very long time since something like that had happened. By the time they reached the front entrance, a couple of young men were leading two horses into the valet area. Grinning, Colt walked her up to the pretty palomino pony with the blond mane and tail.

"Can you ride?" he asked.

Casey was already stroking the horse's golden neck. "She's beautiful," she crooned. "Of course I can ride. I haven't ridden in years, but I can do it."

He went to help her mount, but she didn't need his help. She climbed right up and got comfortable in the saddle. Colt mounted the other horse, a big hairy half-draft breed that seemed to be quite lively, but Colt handled him with a confident hand. It was apparent he knew how to handle a horse. One of the young wranglers told Colt where to go, pointing off to the north, and Colt directed the big horse forward with Casey right behind him.

They were off on their adventure. Colt took the trail around the side of the resort that led down to a small riverbed surrounded by growth. They followed the trickle of water south until the riverbed forked off and they followed a small creek northwest for a couple of miles. Small talk bounced around between them as they enjoyed the scenery and each other. It was so peaceful and lovely, and Casey directed her horse up next to Colt's so they could ride side by side.

Birds were singing in the bushes and little creatures scooted in the underbrush. They came out of the canyon and onto a plateau that overlooked the Santa Fe, and they continued up the plateau until it leveled out. Once it leveled out, Casey dug her heels into the side of her horse and the animal took off at a canter. Colt kicked his beast forward, following.

Casey galloped across the flat of the plateau as her hair blew behind her like a banner, slowing when the plateau started to dip downward into an area thick with trees. They could smell the water. Casey eventually came to a halt and Colt pulled up beside her, eventually finding a small path down into the foliage.

Once down in the shade of the small trees, Colt dismounted and tied off his horse, going to Casey's horse and lifting her off. He tied off her horse as well, returning to his own mount and removing the saddlebags. Casey wandered over by the trickling creek, admiring the sounds and sights of nature. It was peaceful and beautiful as the sound of trickling water and birds filled the air. No politics, no craziness, only nature to keep them company. It was serenity at its best.

"When I was a kid, my parents used to take my sister and me to

Yosemite National Park," Casey said, her gaze moving over the foliage. "We used to hike all over the place. I loved it there. This kind of reminds me of it, the peacefulness of it."

He came over with the saddlebags, looking at what she was looking at. It was all so lovely and calm. Then he looked around for a patch of ground that was somewhat level and removed the saddlebags from his big shoulder. Digging around, he came out with a blanket, which he spread on the ground, and then he began pulling out containers of food. Casey looked over her shoulder from the creek, noticing what he was doing. She went to help.

"My goodness," she sank to her knees on the blanket. "What's all this?"

He grinned as he began opening up the containers. "I'm not sure," he said. "I told the concierge we wanted a picnic lunch, so your guess is as good as mine."

Casey began opening containers, too, discovering sandwiches and potato salad, cookies and fruit. There was also a bottle of white wine. Colt popped the cork and poured them a couple of glasses in the plastic cups provided. He handed her one of the glasses.

"To the best vacation I've ever had," he said softly, holding up his plastic glass.

She smiled, clinking her glass against his. "Thank you," she said sincerely. "That's really sweet. I hate to see it end."

He downed half his glass before handing her half of a pastrami sandwich. "Me, too," he said. "But we'll have more vacations like this, I promise."

Casey chewed on her sandwich, watching him as he devoured the other half. Now that she was coming to know the man on a deeper level, she wanted to know everything. He had been open and honest with her as far as she could tell, but there still seemed to be a hint of mystery about the man. It wasn't so much in his manner or in his words, but more a glimmer in his eyes. There was an intangible hint of intrigue. She wanted to know all about him.

"So tell me something," she said casually. "What's your goal in life, Colt? Do you have any big ambitions beyond the Secret Service?"

He swallowed the bite in his mouth. "I really like what I do," he said. "Someday, I think I'd like to run the agency. I think I have a pretty good shot at it."

She listened intently, eating grapes. "So that's it?" she asked. "No big dreams? You don't want to retire to the Adirondacks and raise goats? Or maybe have an art studio and make clay pots for retirement homes? What are your *dreams,* Colt?"

His chewing slowed as he thought on her question. "I don't really know," he said honestly. "I've never really had dreams, just goals. I've already met most of my goals. What are your dreams?"

She thought a moment, popping grapes into her mouth. "You won't laugh?"

"Of course not."

She smiled bashfully. "I've always wanted to have a racehorse rescue organization," she said. "I grew up near the Santa Anita racetrack in California. I've always loved racehorses and I used to know people who worked there. They told horror stories of what happened to racehorses after they could no longer race and owners got tired of them. So I want to buy a bunch of land in California and have a racehorse rescue, maybe just an animal rescue in general. I guess I want to save the animal world."

He was smiling at her by the time she was done. "My grand-parents have three thousand acres in Montana," he said. "I'm sure they'd be willing to turn over some of that acreage so you could have your horse rescue."

She smiled. "That would be great, but it's going to have to wait until the boys grow up and I retire. I have to earn a living between now and then."

He stretched out on the blanket, his hand ending up by her knee. He put a big hand on her leg, caressing her.

"I guess I do have a dream," he said softly. "I want to find a good woman and make a life with her, and maybe have a kid or two. I've got a responsibility to carry on the Sheridan name, you know. Somehow, someway, I have to pop out a Phil Sheridan the Sixth."

Casey laughed. "Good luck with that."

"You don't want to help me out?"

She continued to giggle. "Not at this moment, no."

"When?"

"I'm not sure."

He sat up, a grin on his face. "Don't you see? It'll work out perfectly. We can retire to Montana and have a horse ranch and a bunch of kids."

She was grinning dubiously at him. "What about the Secret Service? I thought you wanted to run the agency?"

"I'd give it all up for you."

Her smile left her and she gazed at him steadily. Then she just hung her head, picking at the grapes.

"I wouldn't want to see you do that," she said softly. "You have a great reputation and a great career in front of you. You've worked for it your whole life."

She was messing with the grapes, averting her eyes, anything to keep from looking at him. He sensed confusion and perhaps some sense of self-protection. He expected that. But what he told her was God's honest truth.

"Casey," he said softly. "Look at me, Angel."

She lifted her head after a moment, crossing her eyes at him and giving him a quirky smile. He laughed, moved closer to her, and rolled over so his head was on her lap. He gazed up into her beautiful face.

"I want you to think about something," he said quietly. "Imagine that after this vacation, I drop out of your life forever. How would you feel about that?"

Her expression darkened. "I'd hate it. I'd be miserable."

He smiled, reaching up to tuck a stray piece of hair behind her ear. "Me, too," he murmured. "I hate every single minute that I'm away from you. Even when I'm away from you, I'm thinking about you and when you're around me, it's like I can't focus on anything else. I guess what I'm trying to say is that I don't ever want to be without you. I want to be with you forever."

She gazed down at him, a soft hand on his cheek. "These past few days have been so amazing," she agreed softly. "I'd love it if the rest of our lives could be like this, but the reality is that it won't be. We'll go back to Washington and things will go back to the way they were."

He shook his head. "Not true," he said firmly. "We'll go back to Washington as a couple. I consider myself the luckiest man in the world to be able to work side by side with my girlfriend. It makes going to work such a pleasure. But I want it to be more than that."

"What do you mean?"

He sighed faintly. "I know you have your boys, and your sister, and your life back in Falls Church," he said softly. "I'm under no illusions that it's just you and you alone. I realize any decision would involve your family."

"What decision?"

He suddenly sat up and faced her. "I love you, Casey," he whispered. "I know I said that my job makes it difficult to have relationships, but I swear to God I'd give it all up for you. I want to come home to you every night, sleep with you every night, and go to the grocery store with you or fight about who's not putting the top back on the toothpaste with you. I don't care what we do or how we do it, as long as we do it together."

She stared at him with big eyes, shocked by his admission. She was speechless for a moment, gazing into his handsome, if not slightly apprehensive, face. Finally, she reached out and put a hand on his cheek. He held her hand tightly against his face, kissing her palm.

"Oh... Colt," she murmured. "I love you, too."

"You do?"

She nodded. "Of course I do," she whispered. "How could I not? You're so sweet and attentive and intelligent and kind. Of course I love you."

She pitched forward, throwing her arms around his neck. He

hugged her tightly, realizing he felt more complete and more content than he ever had in his life. He kissed the side of her head, her cheek, finally her sweet lips. He could taste her cherry lip balm on them.

"I want to marry you," he whispered. "I know you have your boys to think about so I'm not in any rush. We'll take what time we need to make the boys comfortable with the situation. You do what you feel is best."

She just stared at him, such hope and delight and fear in her eyes. "But... we've only known each other a week," she breathed. "How can you already know you want to marry me?"

"Because I do," he kissed her again. "You're what I've been waiting for my whole life, Casey Cleburne. You're in my heart and you'll be there forever."

She kissed him sweetly, her long hair all over her shoulders and on his arms. Colt kissed her passionately, finally just holding her against him like he was incapable of letting her go. He just wanted to hold her. But eventually, he let her go and between them, they finished off the bottle of wine and the rest of the food. Then they cuddled up on the blanket, talking about their plans for the next day. Casey wanted to go in to Santa Fe and see all of the art galleries, and he wanted to stay in their room and leave their clothes off. She giggled at him, knowing he wasn't entirely serious, even when he tried to undress her as she lay on the blanket.

Eventually, the sun began to set and they loaded everything back up into the saddlebags for the trek home. It was a beautiful day, growing cool as the sun set, and Casey bundled up in her jacket as she followed Colt back down the canyons and creek beds to the resort property. It was a shadowy and romantic trip. By the time they got back to the resort, the sun was almost down completely.

Turning the horses back over to the wranglers, they proceeded back to their *casitas*, preparing to change for dinner as Colt skimmed through his smart phone looking for good restaurants in Santa Fe. Casey got into the shower and as soon as he heard the water, he stripped off all of his clothing and joined her. They made love slowly and sweetly, Casey with her arms and legs wrapped around Colt as he held her aloft in his arms, her back against the tile of the shower.

They actually ended up using the shower for what it was intended at some point and he carried her out of the bathroom, damp and wrapped in a towel, and laid her down on the bed and covered her with his big, naked body. He was about to get busy with her again but Casey's cell phone alarm suddenly went off, interrupting their momentum.

"Oh, no," she groaned, arching her neck back to see her cell phone on the charger in the corner. "I haven't even looked at my messages since we left this morning. I probably should in case there's one from Russ."

He was nuzzling her damp neck. "He can wait ten seconds."

She giggled, pushing away from him and crawling across the bed because his body weight was on her. She flipped onto her stomach, still giggling as he lay on top of her, dragging at her, his mouth on her back, her buttocks and her thighs as she pulled herself across the bed and finally flipped off of it. Landing on her feet, she went over to the phone and pulled it off its charger, noticing she had six messages. As Colt crawled off the bed and surrounded her with his big body, his mouth on her shoulder, Casey managed to get the phone up to her ear and listen to her messages.

Colt didn't like the panic in her expression as she listened.

———

Tracy wanted to go to the airport with Casey but the Secret Service determined it would be too much of a security risk and a circus to allow her to go, so Russ, Peter and Colt determined who would be best suited to accompany Casey to the airport and fly with her back to Washington. She was distraught and no one wanted her going alone.

Brody Nantz had been riding his skateboard to a friend's house and had been hit by a car. Riley had called her sister repeatedly, trying to get a hold of her, but truly having no idea where Casey was. She'd eventually called Chris Eckart, who told her that her sister had gone into town to stay at a resort. Soon, everyone was looking for Casey, calling the Sunrise Springs Resort and leaving messages for her. Peter Harrios and Steven Case had even gone over to the resort looking for her but she was nowhere to be found. She wasn't even a registered guest, but Colt Sheridan was. He was nowhere to be found, either.

Brody was at Children's National Medical Center with a broken arm and a broken collarbone. Casey was nearly hysterical and he helped her pack up, driving back the ten miles to the Apache Gap compound so they could get her a flight out of Albuquerque back to Washington D.C.

Peter had met them at the compound entrance and told them that Chris Eckart had already gotten her a flight back to D.C. that left in seven hours. It was the first flight out they could get. So they took her to the ranch house where Russ and Tracy were, and the President and his wife comforted the young woman, remembering well what it was when a child was ill or injured. It brought back terrible memories.

While Tracy sat with Casey, Colt, Peter and Russ made the determination as to who should return with Casey and drive her to the hospital to see her son. Colt was struggling, very much wanting to go with her but knowing his duty was to the President. He was trying desperately to stay on an even keel as Russ and Peter discussed the logistics of it. He tried to say as little as possible, fearful that anything he said might sound too concerned or protective. He was in turmoil.

It was late in the evening when Russ finally chased Peter from his study, leaving him alone with Colt. Colt sat heavily on the big, leather chair in the room that was full of the feel of the Old West. Everything was leather, with Native American accents, and it smelled like cigars. Russ sat behind his antique desk, one his great grandfather had used, and regarded Colt over the soft glow of the desk lamp.

"So tell me what's on your mind, Colt," he said softly.

Colt looked up at him from his hands. "Sir?"

Russ shook his head. "I'm not as stupid as I look," he said with a grin. "Peter told me that they went to the resort looking for Casey but that she wasn't registered. You, however, were. You left this compound with her and you returned to the compound with her. If I was a betting man, I'd say that there's something going on between you two."

Colt's gaze was steady on him. "If that's true, it will, in no way, affect my job or my work. You are my priority, sir, and on the job, that will never change."

Russ nodded. "I believe you," he said. "I'm not condemning you. Hell, she's a beautiful woman. But I want to know the truth. I want to know what's going on around me."

Colt regarded the man for a moment. "What else did Peter tell you?"

"That was it," he said. "But he suspects there's something going on, too. The man isn't an idiot."

Colt digested that statement. It wasn't in his nature to be cagey and he was having a difficult time with what, or how much, to say. He finally shook his head.

"I've worked hard to be where I am, sir," he said. "I wouldn't do anything to jeopardize that."

Russ nodded. "I know," he got up out of his chair and went to the sideboard containing an array of alcohol bottles. Taking two glasses, he poured a measure of Wild Turkey into each one and handed one of the glasses to Colt. He lifted his glass. "You're the best of the best, Special Agent in Charge Sheridan. I know you wouldn't do anything to jeopardize your position and neither would I. I'm proud to have you. I'm proud to have Casey, too. Son, I'm not going to tell anyone and I'm not going to bust you, but I want to know the truth. Is there something going on between my Special Agent in Charge and my personal assistant?"

Colt couldn't deny a direct question. He couldn't lie about it. He realized he didn't want to. "Yes," he finally murmured.

"How much?"

"We're in love."

Russ' eyebrows lifted. "Really?" shocked, he sat down next to Colt. "But... you two just met and, I seem to recall, your introduction didn't go all that well. What changed?"

Colt tossed back the whisky; he found he needed it. "I don't know," he said honestly, setting the glass on Russ' desk. "One minute, she was calling me a jerk and the next minute, I was madly in love with her. I can't even tell you how it happened, only that it did. She's the most amazing, beautiful, intelligent and wonderful woman I've ever met. I'm crazy about her."

Russ was staring at him, his eyebrows still lifted. "Oh, my," he tried to get past his shock of the news, downing his drink. "Well, that certainly puts a spin on things."

Colt held up a hand for emphasis. "She doesn't want anyone to know because she's afraid that it will reflect badly on me and the trust I've worked to achieve," he said. "I'll tell you this much; this isn't an office fling. Casey and I are going to get married and if that means being reassigned, then so be it. But I have to tell you, I sure would hate to lose my job over this."

Russ' dark eyes regarded him carefully. "Would it be worth it?"

Slowly, Colt nodded. "Yes, sir. Without question."

Russ exhaled slowly and finished off his drink. He stood up and went back to the bar with both glasses in hand. "Well," he said after a moment, "I sincerely don't have a problem with it but Casey's right; you shouldn't spread it around. You need to keep it as low-key as possible during office hours. After hours, I don't care what you do."

"Then you'll keep our secret, sir?"

Russ poured two more drinks. "You bet," he said. "I'm kind of proud, you know. I brought the North and South together. Me and Mr. Lincoln, that is."

Colt gave him a lopsided smile, accepting the drink and

downing it in one swallow. "She's a wonderful woman," he said softly. "I hope my parents think so before I tell them she's a Cleburne."

Russ laughed softly as he reclaimed his seat again, watching the man's pensive movements and distant expression. The smile on his face faded.

"You should be the one flying back with her," he said. "She needs you."

Colt shook his head immediately. "My place is with you, sir."

Russ waved him off. "I've got forty Secret Service agents, Colt," he said. "Harrios can take over the detail. You need to fly back with Casey and make sure she's okay. I know what it's like to have a child in peril."

Colt looked up at the President, seeing that the man was downing his drink, gazing off into the dimness of the room as if reflecting on his boys that never got to grow up. It also made Colt think that this assignment for Mr. Meade was becoming more and more difficult. He liked Russ; he didn't want to cause the man's downfall. Torn, he got up himself and collected the bottle, pouring the President another shot before pouring himself one.

"I don't think I should, sir," Colt said softly. "People will... suspect. I know Peter will keep his mouth shut, but if he's observed us together, then others have. It could get back to Mark."

Russ glanced up at him. "You let me handle your boss," he said firmly. "I'll be flying home in a couple of days. I'm sending you back with Casey to prepare for my arrival. There's nothing strange about that."

Colt sighed sharply and down the third shot of whisky. He set the glass aside. "If you say so, sir," he said. "The truth is that I want to go with her very much."

"Then you will," Russ agreed. "Tell Eckart to make another reservation and tell him to put you both in Business Class. I'll talk to Casey myself in the morning before you both leave. But for now, why don't you two use the spare bedroom? She needs to try and get some sleep before she goes, poor woman."

Colt's eyebrows lifted. "You want us to *share* a bedroom?"

Russ grinned. "I'll have Tracy put her to bed and you can slip in after Peter and the boys clear the house. They're not in here when we go to bed, except on the perimeter."

Colt knew the protection detail and safety screen. He'd set it up himself, so he simply shrugged his shoulders at the President's assessment. After a moment, he held out his hand.

"Thank you, sir," he said sincerely. "I appreciate your discretion and your understanding."

Russ shook his hand firmly. "And I appreciate you and Casey, and everything you do to make my job easier," he replied. "I'm only as good as the people around me. You and Casey are two of the best. I don't want to lose either of you but I suspect, after what you just told me, if one of you leaves, the other one will, too. I don't want to chance it."

Colt felt as if they had reached an understanding, as if they shared something more now other than a work relationship. There was a deeper trust between them. Colt couldn't even think of Meade and his cronies at the moment; he just wanted to think of Casey and Russ, and of what decent people they were. He felt so very fortunate.

He stayed up late into the night, moving through the security zones, chatting with his agents and with Peter in particular. Peter had the ranch house perimeter, mainly the porch, so he and Colt stood on the big, wooden veranda, watching the sky with its blanket of stars and speaking of trivial things. It was a spectacular evening and they could hear the chipper of coyotes in the distance, giving the land a very cowboy-like feel.

Colt was slouched against one of the supports for the porch, gazing up at the sky as Peter stood on the ground below him, hands in his jacket pockets. He was looking at the corrals in the distance, listening to the horses nicker softly.

"Sorry to hear about Casey's boy," Peter said. "I hope he's okay."

Colt nodded. "He's got the best of care right now, so that has to be comforting," he replied. "I suppose she'll know more tomorrow when she gets home."

Peter nodded faintly, his gaze moving over the compound. "I'm sorry we couldn't find her sooner," he said. "We tried. We went all over the place looking for her."

Colt grunted softly. "Pete," he began. "It's okay; you don't have to beat around the bush. Yes, Casey was with me. We were together at the resort. You couldn't find her because we were out riding horses and having a picnic."

Peter didn't say anything. He continued to stare out into the night. "So... you two have a thing, I take it?"

Colt came down off the porch. "We're in love," he said softly. "I'm telling you this because I respect you and I suspect, after discussing this with the President, that you have already figured the situation out. But this doesn't go any further, understand? I'm telling you because you're my second-in-command and I won't keep secrets from you. Our lives may depend on it."

Peter nodded seriously. "I appreciate your honesty," he said. "Nobody is going to hear anything from me."

"Thanks."

"How does the President feel about it?"

"He's fine with it, provided we keep it quiet."

Peter grinned. "I do have to say that I'm surprised," he said. "I was there when you two first met. It wasn't exactly love at first sight."

Colt gave him a lopsided grin. "It was my fault," he said. "I shouldn't have grabbed the envelope out of her hand. She had every right to get pissed off."

"You're lucky she didn't smack you."

Colt wriggled his eyebrows. "No kidding."

"She's the 'Queen of Everything', you know. Even the President calls her 'General'."

"I know."

Peter's snickers held out a moment longer before he sobered. "So now what?"

"Nothing changes," Colt said. "Everything is status quo. But you know what's going on and I'm comfortable with that. I trust you to keep a lid on it."

Peter nodded. "You have my word," he said, eyeing him. "Can I ask you something?"

"Sure."

"Those flowers she got last week... were they both from you?"

"No."

"Was one from you?"

"Yes."

"Who sent the others?"

Colt looked at him, his lips twitching with a smile. "Senator Scott Dane," he enunciated the name softly but succinctly. "You'll keep that quiet, too. If that man makes a pass at her, I may have to kill him and bury the body."

Peter started laughing. "So why are you telling me?"

"I may need help."

Peter's laughter grew. "I suppose if I don't help, you might kill me and bury my body, too."

Colt just gave him a knowing grin and turned for the rear of the house. "Have a good evening, Special Agent Harrios," he said.

Peter watched him go, the smile fading from his face. Then he turned back around, focusing on landscape before him. His thoughts, however, were on Colt Sheridan and the man's confession.

Peter had been involved with Mr. Meade for eleven years. His father before him had worked for Meade, so he had fallen into the task like a family legacy. Most of his assignments were to simply observe and report, like this one. He'd never been given any real spy stuff to accomplish, so his work for them had always been easy to cover, easy to erase.

Although he promised Colt he wouldn't spread the word around that he and Casey were an item, he would make sure to tell Mr. Meade. Any alterations or changes around the President were to be reported, no matter how small. Sometimes the smallest details contributed to the biggest failures.

Meade would know about this latest change.

———

It was a burner phone. He always used burner phones, those disposable things that could be purchased at convenience stores with minutes pre-loaded on it.

Peter was too smart and too suspicious to purchase the phones locally, so he had family members from all over the States mail them to him. He asked for the phones for Christmas and Birthday gifts, giving everyone a sob story about how he was being stalked by an ex-girlfriend and she was unable to trace the pre-loaded phone numbers.

Therefore, he received the phones from his aunts, uncles, mother and cousins, and he had them from all over the country. Storing them in a safe deposit box that required a court order to open if anyone became suspicious, the box that contained the phones had an explosive device on it that, if the proper code wasn't input within fifteen seconds of opening the deposit box, would self-destruct using nitrates and gunpowder with an electronic ignition. It would blow up the box but not much else and make it look like one of the phones had combusted. It would be difficult to trace and even more difficult to prove because everything would be ash.

Peter was using one of those phones now as he called Mr. Meade from his post in New Mexico, guarding the perimeter of Russell Talbot's ranch. Sitting in an old Jeep with his Ray-Bans on, watching the golden sunset over the desert, he listened to Meade's greeting.

"It's Peter," he said as Meade identified himself.

Meade immediately warmed. "Peter," he repeated. "It's been awhile since we have heard from you."

"I haven't had much to report, sir."

"What do you have to report to me today?"

Peter kicked a foot up on to the dashboard of the Jeep. "Not too much, but I thought I'd better call in," he replied. "The President and his wife are on vacation and everything is fairly status quo except for Sheridan."

"What about him?"

Peter wriggled his eyebrows even though Meade couldn't see him. "It seems that he and Casey Cleburne have something going."

"Really?" Meade seemed pleased, although he didn't let on too much since Peter didn't know that Colt was a fellow Core agent. "How do you know?"

"Because he told me they're in love."

Meade chewed on the information, pondering and digesting it. He wondered how much truth there was to it or if it was Colt spinning yarn for the benefit of his colleagues.

"Interesting," he said. "Did he use those words?"

"He did."

"And there's nothing else of note around the President?"

"Nothing else. That was the only change."

"Then you'll call me when something else noteworthy happens," Meade replied. His calls were usually short because longer calls could be listened in on or traced. "Good evening, Special Agent Harrios."

The line went dead. Peter hung up the phone, shut it down, removed the SIM card and destroyed it. He put the phone back in his pocket to be thrown away at the next opportunity.

He'd earned his keep for the month.

EIGHT

LUCKILY, the flight from Albuquerque to Washington D.C. was smooth and uneventful. Colt and Casey sat in First Class, with Casey crying intermittently the entire way. Colt held her hand, trying to be of some comfort, as they counted off the three hour flight until they landed at Dulles International Airport. At one point, she climbed out of her seat and sat on his lap, curled up, her face in his neck as she sniffled softly. The flight attendants would pass by now and again, seeing that she was upset, and just left them alone. Colt held her for a good part of the flight, managing to get her back into her seat as they descended. Once on the ground, they were the first ones off the plane.

There was a Secret Service car waiting for them curbside after they collected their luggage. They loaded up their gear and climbed into the back of the Town Car as the driver headed for the White House so they could get their cars and continue on to Children's National Medical Center. Casey sat next to Colt, trying to compose herself, wishing he could hold her hand but knowing he wasn't going to because of the driver. Already, too many people knew about their relationship and there didn't need to be one more rumor to quash. She was okay with the President and his wife, but she wasn't okay with anyone else. So she sat with her hands in her lap, sniffling now and again, anxious to get to Brody. She called her sister to let her know they would be at the hospital shortly.

The driver dropped them off at the White House so they could get their vehicles. Both of them had parked in the structure across the street to the west and after the car left, Colt took Casey's luggage as well as his own and rolled them across the blustery street and up to the second floor where their vehicles were.

It was a cool day and the wind was whipping, even in the parking structure. As Casey unlocked her car, Colt opened her trunk and put her luggage in the back. His Audi was right next to hers and he put his suitcase in his trunk, slamming it just about the time Casey put her purse into the passenger seat of her car. He came between the cars, trapping her up against the driver's side of her vehicle.

She looked exhausted and pale, and he put his arms around her, hugging her tightly. Casey clung to him and the tears started to return but she fought them. His show of strength, comfort and compassion undid her.

"I'll follow you over there," he said. "Are you okay to drive?"

She nodded, struggling not to cry. "I'm fine."

He opened her door for her. "Get in," he told her, helping her into the car. He even reached in to start it because she hadn't managed to get that far yet. Then he looked at her. "I'll be right behind you, okay?"

She nodded, wiping at the tears that had managed to escape. "Thank you," she whispered.

He kissed her cheek and shut the door. Casey pulled her big Expedition out and Colt, as promised, followed close behind. Rain clouds were blowing in from the east as they made their way to the Children's National Medical Center on the grounds of George Washington University Hospital, about two miles from the White House.

As they pulled into the parking lot, it began to rain but Casey didn't stop to find her umbrella. Dressed in jeans, a casual top and a knee-length brown wool coat, she jumped out of her car with

Colt on her heels, walking very quickly through the growing rain until they reached the lobby of the hospital. By the time she hit the lobby, a red-haired woman ran up and grabbed her.

Colt could see it wasn't an unwelcome embrace. Casey and the woman hugged fiercely and Casey started crying again. The redhead had tissue in her hands and wiped Casey's face.

"He's going to be okay," she insisted. "He's just sore and he wants to go home."

Casey was back to sobbing. She held the tissue up to her mouth and nose as the redhead began to pull her towards the elevators.

"What happened?" she wept.

The redhead pushed the elevator button, realizing that the very big man who had followed Casey in from the parking lot was still following them. Riley wasn't sure if the man was with Casey or just happened to be going in their direction.

"He was going to Jackson's house and just wasn't paying attention," she told her sister. "The woman that hit him is a wreck. She's come to the hospital every day to bring him gifts and to make sure he's okay. She said he just jumped out in front of her."

The elevator door opened and Casey growled angrily as she stepped on with Colt behind her. "That's so typical of him," she said furiously. "He never looks where he's going. I swear, I'm going to kill him."

Riley wriggled his eyebrows. "He knows he's in trouble."

"Has Dennis been here?"

"He's with him right now."

Casey sniffled, wiping at her eyes, suddenly realizing that Colt was right beside her. "Oh, my gosh," she sighed, putting her hand on Colt's arm. "Riley, this is Colt Sheridan. Colt, this is my sister, Riley. Sorry I was so rude and didn't introduce you two right away."

Colt grinned at Riley. "No worries," he said. "I sort of figured out who she was. Nice to meet you, Riley."

Riley took a second look at the very big and very handsome man with his arm around her sister. She shook his extended hand.

"Nice to meet you, also," she said. Then, realization dawned. "*You're* Colt Sheridan?"

His grin broadened. "I see my reputation precedes me," he teased. "I'm famous with the Cleburne clan."

Riley grinned, already liking his sense of humor about their familial relations. "Maybe," she teased back, wondering what the man was doing with her sister and wondering why he had his arm around her. "You'd better watch out. We don't like your kind around here."

Colt laughed, looking at Casey. "Is that right?" he wanted to know. "You don't like my kind?"

Casey grinned, putting her head against his chest and wrapping her arms around his waist. "I like your kind just fine," she said, then looked at her sister. "You may as well know. Colt and I were married last week."

Riley's eyes nearly burst out of her skull. "What the *hell*?"

Casey giggled as Colt wrapped his big arms around her. "Just kidding," she said. "We're going to wait a little while before we unite the north and the south."

Riley just looked at the pair, realization dawning. It was very apparent from the affection going on between them. "So...," she pointed fingers. "You two...?"

Casey nodded. "Sorry I haven't really had time to tell you," she said. "Things have been kind of busy."

Riley went from surprised to stricken. "Lies!" she exclaimed softly as the elevator came to a halt. "You were home all last week and you never said a word!"

The doors open and Casey charged out. "That's because there wasn't anything to tell," she insisted. "It happened kind of fast."

Riley followed her sister out of the elevator with Colt tagging along behind the pair. "I'm going to kill you," Riley hissed at Casey. "I'm going to smash you to smithereens when I get the chance for springing this on me."

Casey pointed at Colt, a rather smug look on her face. "You

can't touch me," she said, "because he'll protect me. He can kill you twenty different ways and never leave a trace. So *there*."

Riley pretended she was angry when the truth was that she was thrilled. Deeply-protected Casey had apparently let herself feel something. Riley took another look at Colt Sheridan, a truly handsome and spectacular male specimen, and narrowed her eyes threateningly at him. He grinned, causing her to break down in a smile as she caught up with her sister to direct her to the right unit.

"He's over here," she said.

They ended up in a regular children's ward and not the ICU, a unit that was decorated with purple lions and pink monkeys. Brody Nantz had been moved out of ICU the night before and was in the very last room, his arm and shoulder casted, and a big bruise on his forehead. Casey walked into the room and suddenly, the brave young man turned into a weepy child. Casey went straight to her son, putting her arms around him as much as she was able. The kid looked like a mess with casts and tubes all over him.

"It's okay," she kissed his head. "I'm here. Everything's okay."

Brody was trying very hard to be brave, giving in to his mother's comfort. Casey pulled back to look him over, inspecting the wrappings and I.V.s.

"So I hear you have a broken arm and a broken collarbone," she said.

The handsome young man nodded. "That happened when I put my arm out to stop my fall," he said. "I heard the bones break."

Casey made a face of disgust. "Gross," she said, seriously inspecting his head, face, running a hand over his bruised forehead. "But you're okay?"

Brody nodded. "The doctor says I can go home in a couple of days."

Casey's smile faded. "Why a couple of days?"

"Because of the head injury."

Brody hadn't answered; the reply had come from behind. Casey turned to the sound of the voice, seeing Dennis Nantz rising from the chair against the wall. She hadn't noticed him when she came in. Blond, well built and very handsome, he smiled amiably at his ex-wife.

"Hi, Dennis," Casey said. "I didn't see you."

He grinned at her. The man had a devastating grin. "I know," he walked up on the bed, seeing Colt standing at the foot. He held out his hand.

"Hi," he introduced himself. "Dennis Nantz."

Colt shook the man's hand. He was a good-looking blond devil, seemingly gentle and friendly. That was the first impression Colt received from the man.

"Colt Sheridan," he replied. "It's nice to meet you."

Dennis acknowledged him pleasantly, turning back to his ex-wife. "Brody's helmet was destroyed in the accident," he said. "The doctor wants to keep him a couple of days just to make sure there are no issues."

Casey nodded with understanding, turning back to her son. "Is that what this big bruise is from?" She pointed to the kid's forehead.

Dennis walked up beside her, looking down at his son. "Yes," he replied. "But the helmet did its job; it saved his skull."

"But he's okay?"

"He's fine."

Casey was trying not to feel sick about it. Now that she knew the boy was out of danger and on the mend, she cocked her head reproachfully at her son.

"When you get out of here, we're going to have a long talk about skateboard safety, young man," she scolded lightly. "Seriously, Brody, you could have been killed. Do you have any idea what that would do to me?"

Brody made a face and tried to look away from her, but he ended up looking at Colt standing at the end of the bed. He pointed at him with his good arm.

"Who's the big dude?" he asked to distract his mother. "Did you bring him to punish me?"

Casey laughed in spite of herself, looking at Colt. Colt was grinning, too. "I'm with the Skateboard Police," he said. "I've come to put you in Skateboard Jail for doing something dumb on a skateboard and scaring your mother to death."

Brody cracked a grin. "No way. Really?"

Dennis and Riley were laughing as Casey, grinning, shook her head. "This is Colt Sheridan," she said. "He's the President's Special Agent in Charge. He's responsible for all of the Secret Service guys who protect the President. He escorted me back to Washington to make sure I got here safely."

"Oh." Brody looked Colt up and down, as impressed as a nine-year-old could be. Colt was a good deal bigger than his dad, who Brody once thought was the biggest guy he'd ever seen. "Do you really protect the President?"

Colt nodded. "I do."

"Do you carry a big gun?"

"Sometimes."

"Do you have one of those radios that's shoved down into your sleeve?" he lifted his good arm, gesturing. "I've seen the Secret Service guys talk into their sleeves."

Colt grinned. "I have a lot of radios," he said. "I've got one that's so small, I can pin it to my collar and no one will see it."

Brody looked interested. He was about to ask more questions when a nurse came into the room, looking around at all of the people.

"Looks like a party," she laughed, seeing a new face in Casey. "You must be Brody's mother."

Casey nodded. "I am," she replied. "How's my boy?"

The nurse looked over at the bruised young man. "Lucky," she said frankly. "The doctor will be in later, but Mr. Brody is very lucky. It could have been a lot worse."

"He's going to recover?"

"Completely, providing he stays clear of cars and skateboards."

Casey felt vastly better. The nurse reassured her that Brody would be fine and so did the doctor when he came by later that afternoon. Meanwhile, Casey planted herself in a chair next to her son and refused to leave, even when Colt tried to coax her to go out and get a little dinner with him. So Colt went with Dennis and Riley down to the hospital cafeteria, leaving Riley and Dennis down there to eat while he brought dinner up to Casey. He sat with her and Brody, eating sandwiches and coming to know a young man who was still convinced his mother was going to let him ride his skateboard after all of this. He was a very smart kid and very wily. Colt kind of liked that.

When visiting hours were ended, Casey was forced to leave but she did so under protest. Dennis had left just after dinner, so Riley and Colt escorted Casey down to the parking lot and made sure she got to her car, preventing her from pulling a stunt out of an "I Love Lucy" episode and sneaking back up to her son's room to spend the night with him.

Riley headed for home in her own car as Colt wrapped Casey up in his big arms and held her close.

"So now what?" she asked softly, her head against his chest. "Where are you going?"

He sighed faintly. "Not where I want to go."

"What do you mean?"

"I want to go home with you, Casey. I don't want to go to my empty townhouse. I want to go with you."

She looked up at him, putting her warm hands on his cheeks. "Then come over later," she said softly. "Go home, unpack, and come over later. I'll introduce you to Hunter. You can hang out with us for a while."

He smiled. "Are you sure?"

"Absolutely."

Pleased, he nodded. "Okay," he said. "But you need to tell me where you live. You never did tell me."

She laughed softly and pulled out one of her business cards from the glove box, writing her address on the reverse side.

"There," she said. "Now you can find me, anytime."

He kissed the address on the card and then bent down and kissed her lips. "What time?"

She lingered on the kiss. The man was a great kisser. "It's eight o'clock now," she said. "Come over any time you want. We'll be home."

"I'll drop my stuff off and head over."

"Okay."

Now that it was settled and he knew he'd be seeing her later, he hugged her tightly and kissed her again.

"I love you," he whispered.

She closed her eyes to the sweetness of the words, the first time he'd told her directly. "I love you, too," she murmured. "See you in a little bit."

"I'll be there."

When Colt still hadn't come by midnight, Casey called his cell phone but it went straight to voicemail. Concerned, and a little hurt, she left a nice message and went to bed.

———

The enormous house was dark except for a very small light near the downstairs entry. Exiting his Audi, Colt made his way to the very dark front porch of the mansion that had stood in the same spot since the Revolutionary War days. It was a great, cold expanse of brick and mortar, a testament to the wealth and glory of days gone by, and also to the sheer power that the Meade family had wielded for over one hundred and fifty years. Before he could lift a hand to knock, the door opened.

Mr. Meade stood in the archway. He didn't even say a word to Colt. he simply opened the door wider and admitted the man. Closing the door softly behind him, he silently led him into the room off the entry with the small light emitting the only warmth in the entire house.

It was a rich and luxurious room with a marble fireplace and great mahogany walls. It smelled of things old and timeless, and of tobacco that seeped from the very walls. Colt remained standing as

Mr. Meade reclaimed a chair next to the softly glowing lamp and a half-empty bottle of Glenfiddich.

"I am assuming you are bringing me good news," Meade said as he poured himself another glass of the amber-colored liquid.

Colt watched the man fuss with his ice cubes. "What do you mean?"

Meade looked at him, the dark eyes shrewd. "Colt, I didn't call you over here tonight to be toyed with," he said sharply. "Tell me of your progress with Talbot."

Colt shifted on his big legs. "No particular progress to report," he said. "You know that something like this is going to take time, establishing trust and...."

"Stop with your excuses," he snapped, cutting him off. "Tell me about Casey Cleburne. I understand you have a relationship with her now."

Colt tried not to react one way or the other; he didn't want Meade to capitalize on anything, good or bad.

"I was told to get to know her," he replied evenly. "I've done that."

"How well?"

"Well enough."

"Enough so that she's in love with you?"

Colt could feel himself getting defensive and very protective. He knew that Peter had told Meade what Colt had discussed with him, which underscored to Colt that he needed to be very careful with what he told Peter. As a Secret Service agent, Colt trusted him, but when it came to Meade, that was entirely another matter. Colt wasn't surprised, but he was displeased.

"That's the rumor," he said quietly. "Isn't that what you wanted?"

"Is it true?"

"That's she's in love with me?" Colt was very careful in his reply. He shrugged noncommittally. "We get along well. I've at least earned her attention. She's a beautiful woman."

Mr. Meade watched Colt, the man's body language, and

remained silent until the quiet grew oppressive. Finally, he sipped at his drink.

"Can you swear to me that your attention towards her is all business?" he asked.

Colt didn't want to lie to the man. If he did, everything he had worked for all of these years would be destroyed. His relationship with Mr. Meade was based solely on trust. But he was protective of his feelings, of Casey, and Meade was venturing in to the realm of the personal where he didn't belong. It had never happened before and it was a struggle for Colt not to lash out at the man.

"No," he said quietly.

"Then you are attracted to her?"

"I am."

"How strongly are you attracted to her?"

"Strongly enough."

Mr. Meade set his drink down, rather hard. "Tell me the truth, Colt," he commanded quietly. "Tell me what you're feeling for this woman so I at least know what we're dealing with."

Colt held steady. "No matter what I feel for her, it will not affect my mission or my goal. I will complete my assignment."

Meade wasn't buying it. His expression turned hard. "You were told to use her, not fall for her. Emotions will get in the way and we've worked too long and hard for this to fall apart at the end. Am I making myself clear?"

Colt considered all of the implications of that statement. Rather than argue with the man or stand his ground, he chose to remain silent on the matter. It would be better for him, and for Casey, if he did.

"You are."

"Good." Mr. Meade collected his drink again and took a healthy sip. "Now tell me about the President's trip to New Mexico. I want to hear everything and I also want to hear about any progress you've made with the President's financial records."

Colt had no choice but to give a full report, which ended up lasting most of the night. He never made it to Casey's house, nor did he give Meade the impression that he had better places to be. He was fearful, in the back of his mind, that Meade might lash out towards Casey somehow if he thought she was distracting Colt from his task. It was a fear he had, only because it had happened once before when The Core took measures against a certain young lady in Russia where Colt had been reassigned a few years back. Everyone thought it had been the Russian mafia that had assassinated her, but Colt knew better.

He knew exactly what happened to her. If the same thing happened to Casey, Colt couldn't live with himself.

———

Monday morning was rainy and cold. Casey woke up in the darkness, checking her phone and seeing that there were no messages from Colt. Feeling increasingly despondent, she got into the shower and cleaned up. As she was putting on her makeup with the television morning news on in the background, her cell phone rang. Putting down her mascara, she saw that it was Colt's number. She nearly dropped the phone trying to answer it in her haste.

"Hello?"

"Hi, Angel," he said softly. "I'm so sorry I didn't call or come over last night. Please don't be mad at me."

Her heart fluttered at the sound of his voice, like all was right in the world again. "I'm not mad," she said. "But I was concerned. Are you okay?"

"I'm fine," he assured her. "I got home, set my stuff down, and sat on the couch for a couple of minutes to take off my shoes, and ended up passing out. I didn't realize I was so exhausted. By the time I woke up, it was three in the morning. I've been up for a couple of hours but didn't want to call you too early. I'm so sorry."

She smiled. "That's okay," she said. "But you owe me breakfast."

"Gladly," he said. "I'll pick you up."

"I'm going in to the office," she said. "Just bring me a bagel and we'll call it even."

"I'm picking you up," he said again. "We'll get something to go, somewhere, and drive in together. Then I'll take you home."

She sighed, hesitant. "Honey, if we're trying to keep this quiet, that's not the way to go about it," she said softly. "I'm already freaked out enough that Russ knows. If people see us coming and going together, it's not going to take a genius to figure out that we're together."

"Too late," he said. "I'm already out in front of your house."

Casey jumped up and ran over to the window, facing the street. She could see his Audi parked on the curb below and she laughed softly. "Okay, you win," she said. "I still need to dry my hair and get dressed. Do you want to come in?"

"No," he said. "I'll sit out here and do some work. You take your time."

Casey hurried and finished her hair and got dressed. Riley was downstairs, bumping around in the kitchen, as Casey dropped her purse and briefcase off by the door. She headed into the kitchen.

"Hey," she said to her sister. "Where's Hunter?"

Riley was yawning over her cup of coffee. "Still in the shower," she said, noticing her sister was dressed in a dark purple suit that looked amazing with her coloring. "Are you heading to the hospital now?"

Casey shook her head as she pulled out the bread and went about making Hunter's lunch. "I'm going to go to the office first and then head over there," she said. "How about you?"

Riley yawned again. "I've been over there for two days straight," she said. "Now it's your turn."

Casey nodded. "Thank you," she said sincerely as she made a ham and cheese sandwich. "You get the Aunt of the Year award."

Riley waved her off, started out of the kitchen, and then stopped. "Hey," she looked at her sister. "Thanks a lot for blind-siding me with Sheridan. I'm seriously going to kick your ass for it when I'm not so tired."

Casey grinned. "Like I said, it just happened really fast," she said, glancing at her sister. "He's a keeper and I'm totally in love with the guy, so don't be too hard on me. This is serious."

Riley leaned against the door frame, mug in hand. "Really?" She lifted an eyebrow with interest. "How serious?"

"Serious enough. Let's just leave it at that for now."

"Are you going to marry him?"

"Maybe. Probably."

Riley exhaled slowly, struggling to adjust to the idea. It was shocking to say the least. "Wow," she said after a moment. "I just... *wow*. That's a lot to take in. You're not the kind to make rash decisions, Case. Why Sheridan? What's so special about him?"

Casey paused as she prepared Hunter's lunch. "Everything," she said quietly. "He's sweet, considerate, thoughtful... he's perfect. Just perfect."

Riley was forced to agree, at least from a physical standpoint. "Seriously, could that guy be any more handsome?" she wanted to know. "You have to date Mr. Perfect?"

Casey giggled. "He's pretty darn good looking," she agreed. "But he's more than that. He's got a good heart."

"I hope so." Riley turned around and headed for the stairs. "I'll see you later."

"Okay."

Casey finished with the sandwich and put chips and an apple in a brown sack for her oldest. Hunter wasn't long in coming, pounding down the stairs and hugging his mom when he came into the kitchen. The kid was a hugger. He poured himself some cereal, turning on cartoons as he told his mom about a book fair at the school that night. Casey promised she would attend with him because there were some books he wanted to buy. Kissing her son, she put on her coat and gathered her stuff by the front door, emerging out to the cold and cloudy day.

Colt saw her coming and unlocked the door. His car was nice and warm, the seats heated up, and he put his iPad away as she opened the door. He took her briefcase and purse, putting them in the back seat as she climbed in. She looked gorgeous and he leaned over, kissing her sweetly.

"Good morning, beautiful," he said softly. "How did you sleep?"

Casey shrugged. "Okay, considering I was worried that you hadn't called or shown up." She put up her hand to silence his additional apology. "That's just the way I roll. I get worried easily. It's the mother in me."

He smiled. "I'm going to say I'm sorry again," he replied. "I didn't mean to worry you."

"No harm." She returned his smile, drinking in the sleek sight of him in a dark suit and perfectly-combed hair. "You look pretty sharp this morning. Any reason?"

His smile grew. "I have to look good for my girlfriend because she's a total babe and I want to impress her," he said, watching her laugh. "Plus, the President flies in at thirteen hundred hours, so I'll be at the airport."

She nodded, putting her hand on his as he moved to put the car in gear. "I'm only going to be at the office for a few hours this morning," she said. "I'm going to spend the rest of the day with Brody. Unless you plan to drive me to the hospital, I should probably take my own car."

"When do you want to go to the hospital?"

"Probably about the same time you head over to Andrews Air Force Base to meet Air Force One."

"Then I'll take you over to the hospital."

"What if I want to leave? What if Brody is discharged and I can take him home?"

"Then you call me and I'll send a car over to get you. Or I'll come over myself. Either way, I'll take care of it."

It sounded simple enough. Shrugging, she sat back in the seat as he pulled away from the curb. He took her through her neighborhood and back to the freeway, heading on into the city. It was a nice ride, made better with just the two of them, holding hands and listening to satellite radio. Casey was just as happy as she could be as they finally entered the city and parked in their customary parking structure. Colt took her briefcase and she took her purse, and he lugged his stuff and her stuff across the street, detouring to go into the sandwich shop and get a couple of breakfast sandwiches. Then it was on to the White House.

Casey took her briefcase from him as they drew close to the property and he gave her a wink as they separated. She checked in through the guard shack at the north entrance and on into the West Wing while Colt went in another entrance. Since the President was out of the office, it was rather quiet at that early hour as Casey passed Lisanne's desk and then Maggie's, stopping to chat with her friends for a few minutes and letting them know how Brody was doing. Apparently, word got around about his injury and she was touched by all of the concern. Moving on into her office, she set her stuff down on her desk and was surprised to hear the sounds of typing coming from Sheridan's office.

Casey turned around to see Colt sitting behind his desk, working on his computer. Somehow, he had beat her into the office but she realized she had been talking to Maggie and Lisanne, which always took time. He would have had plenty of time to slip in and settle in.

"Good morning, Special Agent Sheridan," she said as she took her seat.

Colt glanced up from his computer. "Good morning," he replied, winking at her because no one could see them.

She grinned and sat down, booting up her computer and picking up the dead flower petals from the two enormous bouquets of flowers that still sat on her desk. She tossed them in the trash and tidied up a bit, putting the flowers behind her and starting the coffee machine.

Even though it was just the two of them in the small office space, neither one of them said a word as they went to work. People wandered in and out to see Casey all of the time, so Colt kept focused on his work, every so often glancing over to see who she was talking to or what she was doing. It was very difficult not to strike up a conversation with her but he didn't want anything to be overheard or, worse, the rumors she feared so much to get started. So he was content to watch her on occasion, hearing her voice on the phone and knowing she was only a few feet away from him. It was the best thing he could ask for.

Around mid-morning, Lisanne's voice came over Casey's intercom. "Casey?"

Casey was busy with some of the President's personal investment statements from boxes she had brought out of storage the week before, but she hit the intercom button. "Yes?"

"Senator Dane is here to see you. Can I send him back?"

Startled, Casey instinctively looked at Colt, who was gazing steadily at her. "Uh...," Casey stammered. "Sure."

The intercom went dead and Casey put the papers aside, going to stand in the doorway of Colt's office. He was still looking at her, a twinkle in his eye.

"What do I do?" she hissed.

He fought off a grin. "I don't know, but it's going to be interesting to watch."

She puckered her lips angrily at him, although it was without force. "You're a lot of help."

His grin broke through. "What do you want me to do?"

She shook her head. "Nothing," she said, turning away. "I'll figure it out."

He stood up and went to his office door, watching as she sat down. "I love you," he whispered. "Maybe that will help."

She broke into a reluctant smile, forcing it from her lips when she heard footsteps approach from the hall. Colt went back to his desk and sat down just about the time Scott Dane came through the door to Casey's office.

He was dressed in an expensive suit and expensive overcoat, his salt-and-pepper hair carefully combed. He smelled heavily of expensive aftershave as he came into the office, smiling at Casey.

"Good morning," he said. "Sorry to barge in on you like this."

Casey forced a smile, folding her hands neatly on the desktop. "No problem, Senator," she said. "It's always nice to see you."

Scott's smile grew. He had been carefully planning this moment since he sent the flowers last week, planning what he was going to say, what he was going to wear, how he was going to behave. He hadn't asked a woman out in almost twenty years, so he was nervous but hoped it didn't show. He'd asked his twelve-year-old son for advice but that had been a mistake; he wasn't sure bubble gum lip gloss and candy were going to work, not with a woman of Casey's star magnitude. He'd have to make his own way.

"Thanks," he said. "I was just on my way to the Capitol Building and thought I'd stop by."

Casey smiled pleasantly. "How can be of assistance?"

Scott could see, at least peripherally, that they were alone. "Is the President in?"

Casey shook her head. "No," she replied. "He's flying in to Andrews around noon. Do you need to meet with him?"

"No," Scott replied. "Wasn't he in New Mexico?"

"Yes."

"You didn't go with him?"

"I did," Casey nodded. "But a family emergency brought me back early."

"Oh," Scott looked concerned. "I hope everything is okay."

She nodded. "It's fine," she replied. "My son was in a skateboard accident, but he's going to be fine. Now, what can I do for you today?"

"I'm sorry to hear that. How old is your son?"

Casey could see that he wanted to talk, which irked her a little. She really didn't want to chat with the man, nice though he might be.

"He's nine," she replied. "Boys are tough, you know. They just bounce back. Anyway, I'm sure you're really busy this morning, Senator, so how can I help you?"

Scott could see she wasn't up for a big conversation, which disappointed him. He opened his mouth to speak but noticed his flowers on the back of her desk near the window. He also noticed a second arrangement of big red roses, wilting. His disappointment grew.

"Well," he scratched his neck in a somewhat nervous gesture. "I... well, I apologize if this is inappropriate. I'm certainly not trying to be. But, well, I offered to take you out to dinner when I sent those flowers and your very nice Thank You note didn't say anything about the dinner offer. I was just stopping by to see if we could make arrangements."

Casey was starting to feel sorry for him. It had obviously taken a good deal of courage to ask her and she appreciated that. She hated to shoot him down but there wasn't an alternative. She certainly wasn't going to go out with him.

"The flowers and the dinner invitation are very sweet," she said, standing up and coming out from behind her desk, "but I wanted to decline in person. I don't feel that something like that is appropriate in writing, so I'm glad you came by. As flattered as I am, I'm afraid I can't."

"Oh," Scott tried not to look too disappointed. "Okay... well, uh, I hope it's not something I said."

She smiled. "Of course not," she said quietly. "I'm seeing someone."

Realization dawned and although he was still very disappointed, Scott felt much relief at the fact that there was a solid reason behind her declining. It wasn't because she didn't find him an attractive prospect. His ego was intact.

"Oh," he said again, finally understanding everything. "In that case, I'm really sorry if I made you uncomfortable. That wasn't my intention. I had no idea you were seeing anyone."

Her smile broadened. "That's okay," she said. "I'm really flattered by your offer. If I wasn't already involved, I'm sure it would have been a different answer."

Scott wriggled his eyebrows. "Then I've never wanted to get rid of someone so badly in my entire life."

Casey laughed softly. "I don't know," she said warningly. "He'd be pretty difficult to get rid of."

Scott grinned, aware that there was no longer any reason for him to be there and starting to feel a bit awkward. He began to back out of her office.

"Well," he said. "I guess you can't blame a guy for trying."

"Of course not. Thank you for the consideration. I'm truly flattered."

He just grinned, still backing away. "Good luck, then."

"Thank you."

"If it doesn't work out, you'll let me know?"

She giggled. "Sure. But don't hold your breath."

His grin broadened and, with a short and embarrassed wave, left her office completely and disappeared down the hall. Casey stood there a moment, watching him go, until he disappeared around the corner. When she turned around, Colt was standing behind her. Their eyes met and he smiled.

"That was very classy, Ms. Cleburne," he said softly. "You are a woman of tact and kindness."

She crossed her arms, gazing up at him. "I just didn't want to hurt his feelings."

Colt shook his head. "I don't think you did," he said. "Thank God I didn't get that speech from you when I asked you out. I would have crawled into a corner and cried."

She grinned, turning back for her desk. "I'm almost finished here," she said. "Can you take me to the hospital in a little while?"

"Yes," he nodded, heading back for his desk. "I'll be ready to go in a minute."

Casey sat back down and starting filing her papers away. Colt was still standing up behind his desk, looking at the computer screen.

"Can you come here a moment?" he asked.

Casey looked up from her files. "What do you need?"

"I want to show you something."

Casey put her files away and stood up, going over to his desk. "What is it?"

He was still looking at the computer screen. "Come around here and I'll show you."

Obediently, she rounded the desk and went to stand next to him. The moment she did, he threw her into a bear hug and kissed her deeply. Shocked, Casey tried to pull away from him for about two seconds before giving in to his power and lust. Tongues tasted and plundered. Then, she put her hands on his chest and tried to push him away.

"Colt," she hissed. "Stop it. Let me go."

"Why?" his lips were on her cheek, her earlobe. "No one's around."

"Someone could walk in at any moment," she insisted, pushing at his chest as he nuzzled her neck. "Please, Colt. Let go."

He kissed her one last time before doing as she asked. Casey stepped away from him, straightening her skirt and wiping at her mussed lipstick. She frowned at him as he grinned.

"You know," she said, "for a man whose life depends on caution, you seem kind of reckless about this."

His smile didn't waver. "That's because I know the limits," he said. "No one is near your office. No one is even close. A five second kiss isn't going to hurt anything unless, of course, you don't want me to do it."

Her expression turned both soft and petulant, an odd combination. "I always want you to do it," she whispered. "I'm just scared to death we'll get caught."

He grinned and opened his desk drawer, pulling out his wallet, keys, cell phone and his radio.

"We're not going to get caught," he muttered, putting stuff in his pockets and collecting his iPad. He began to focus on the task at hand. "I will be at Andrews until Air Force One lands. After that, the President will be at the Hyatt Regency for a luncheon and photo op with the National Association of Farm Workers."

Casey was nodding before he finished his sentence. She knew the President's schedule intimately, as did Colt.

"I know," she said. "I sent him an email to let him know I'd be with Brody this afternoon, so he'll be winging this one without me. He's supposed to be home tonight, or at least there's nothing scheduled, and then tomorrow he's going to be talking to returning troops at Andrews."

Colt was nodding as she spoke, pulling on his suit coat. He fumbled with the collar but Casey came to the rescue and straightened it. "I know his schedule," he replied. "He's going to be in the office the rest of the week."

Casey nodded, turning around so she could go collect her purse. Colt came out of his office, putting his wallet in his pocket and looking at his smart phone to check the status of the President's flight.

"I will meet you over in front of the parking structure," he told her. "I'll see you over there in a few minutes, okay?"

She nodded, gazing up at him. "I'll be there. Just let me shut my computer off."

Colt winked at her and bugged out of the office. As he was heading down the corridor that led to the lobby, Scott Dane suddenly appeared from the lobby, heading back in the direction of the President's office. He nodded at Colt as he passed him and, as much as Colt wanted to turn around and follow him, he maintained his course and headed out of the West Wing. He did, however, slip around the side once he got outside to look in the windows to see where the man had gone.

He saw him talking to Casey.

NINE

COLT WAS WAITING for Casey in front of the parking structure when she crossed the street, arms heavy with purses and briefcases. He unlocked the door as she approached, taking her briefcase from her when she opened the door and handed it in. He put it in the back seat as she climbed in and closed the door. As she settled in, he pulled away from the curb.

"Are you going to be home tonight?" he asked as they pulled up to a red light.

She popped in her seatbelt. "One way or another," she replied. "I'm really hoping I can bring Brody home this afternoon. Hopefully I'll be hanging out with all of my boys tonight."

He looked over at her. "All of them?"

She smiled at him. "Aren't you coming over? You stood me up last night."

He suppressed a grin. "Am I invited?"

"I'd like you to meet Hunter."

He nodded. "Then I'd love to come," he said. "As soon as I'm done with Russ, I'll be over."

"Good," she said, settling back in the seat with a sigh as he took off from the red light. "Hey, did you see Senator Dane come back in? He came in right after you left."

Colt nodded. "I did," he said casually. "Did he come back to your office?"

She nodded. "He said he had a question about next week's environmental meeting with Director Marcia Woods from the Department of the Interior. He wanted to know if I had an agenda yet and I didn't. He could have just emailed me. I don't know why he had to come back."

Colt was careful in his reply; having seen Dane through the window of Casey's office, speaking with her, he seriously wondered if she was going to mention his reappearance. Not that he didn't trust her, but the truth was that no matter how crazy he was about her, he was just coming to know her. He wasn't going to say a word about Dane's return because he wanted to see how she would handle it, if she would tell him about it or if she would just keep it quiet. The fact that she brought it up spoke volumes to her honesty and he was deeply relieved and deeply impressed.

"He came back for the same reason I would have come back," he said quietly. "He wanted to see you again."

Casey sighed, looking over at Colt as the man took a left hand turn. "If he does it again, I'm going to have to say something," she said softly. "I'm not comfortable with him just dropping by like that."

Colt shrugged. "Be careful," he said. "He's a powerful senator. You don't want to make an enemy."

"I don't want to encourage him, either. That's disrespectful to me and to you."

He smiled. "Angel, don't worry about me," he said. "I know you can handle Dane. If it looks like he's stepping on my toes, I'll let him know. Don't worry about it."

She reached out and grasped the hand that rested on the gear knob. Colt held her hand tightly.

"You know, I was thinking something," she said as she looked out the window.

"What?"

"Thanksgiving is coming up in a couple of weeks. Do you already have plans?"

He shook his head. "I took a shift to let one of the guys with a family have the day off," he said. "I'll be working."

"Oh," her face fell. "I was... well, I was hoping you could spend it with us but you probably spend it with your parents, right?"

He looked over at her. "Not usually," he said. "I've worked Thanksgiving for the past six years to let those with families have the holiday off. I can't think of anywhere I'd rather spend the day than with you."

She smiled. "You'll have to fight Brody and Hunter for the turkey legs. They snatch them first."

He wriggled his eyebrows. "I'm a little bigger than they are," he said. "Maybe I can hold one of them off."

She giggled and clasped his big hand between both of hers, caressing his fingers. "What about Christmas?" she asked softly. "If you're not doing anything, you can come to my house."

He smiled at her. "I'm already there."

She smiled brightly and he brought her hand to his lips, kissing her soft fingers. They held hands in warm silence the rest of the way to the Children's National Medical Center, where Colt came up to Brody's room to see how the boy was doing. Brody was eating lunch, allowed a hamburger, which he thought was crappy, so Colt took fifteen minutes to drive down the street to a burger joint and bring the kid back a real burger. The gesture scored big points with both Mom and Brody.

But he did have to run, unfortunately. His men had already set up a security net at Andrews but he needed to get over there, so he bid Brody goodbye and pulled Casey out into the hallway with him, giving her a juicy kiss and words of love before departing for the elevators.

Casey watched him go, her heart swelling with adoration for the man. She still couldn't believe how the past couple of weeks had panned out for her. She felt like she was living a dream every single day, with Colt Sheridan right in the middle of it.

Life was good.

The doctor decided that Brody was well enough to go home, so Casey called her sister about an hour after Colt left because she knew he'd be in the middle of preparations for the President, whose plane was landing any minute. So she called her sister to come and take them home, and although Riley pretended she wasn't thrilled with the request, she was secretly glad she had an excuse to get out of work early.

The nurses were helping Brody get dressed to leave while Casey stood at the nurse's station and went over Brody's at-home care with the doctor. As she and the doctor reviewed the medication schedule for Brody for the next ten days, the television overhead was blaring frightening pictures. It was muted so there was no sound, but there were pictures of Air Force One, the President, men with guns and ambulances. Someone finally looked up, saw the chaos on CNN, and turned on the sound.

Casey could hear the faint chatter of the television but she wasn't paying attention until one of the nurses softly exclaimed "oh my God". Then the doctor casually looked up, noticing that most of the staff had come to a halt and was watching the television. Because he was looking up, Casey looked up. Then, she saw it.

"*Assassination Attempt*" blared across the bottom of the images. Casey's eyes widened as she demanded someone turn up the volume. Shocked, she listened to the rather breathless reporter talk about shots fired at Andrews Air Force Base, aimed at the President.

Shocked, she ran into Brody's room to grab her cell phone, calling Maggie. Maggie picked up on the fourth ring, rather upset, but she didn't know anything more than what the news said. No one seemed to, but the West Wing was in chaos and Casey told Maggie that she would be there shortly. Hanging up, Casey went to dial Colt's number but stopped herself, knowing the man would be extremely busy. Shaken, she went to call her sister to find out where the woman was when Riley suddenly walked into Brody's room.

"Hey!" Riley nearly shouted. "I heard on the news that....!"

"I know!" Casey cut her off. "I have to get to the White House. Give me your keys."

Riley plopped her car keys in her sister's hand as Casey rushed to Brody and kissed him. "Sorry, baby," she said. "I don't know when I'll be back, but I'll see you at home."

"Wait!" Riley grabbed her. "How are we supposed to get home?"

Casey was already running out of the door. "I'll send a Town Car or a taxi over," she called as she headed down the hallway. "Get Brody home and stay with him, please?"

Riley just nodded, waving her sister on as the woman jumped onto an elevator and disappeared. She felt some anxiety for her sister, for the situation in general, but she pushed that aside because Brody, who was very sensitive, was feeling some apprehension. She didn't want to the kid to worry.

Distracting him with talk of going home, her mind was nonetheless with her sister and the very frightening situation at hand.

Casey arrived at the White House in record time, parking her sister's car in the customary parking structure and practically running across the street to the West Wing. The White House was on heightened security as she was ushered through the north entrance. Still running in four inch heels, she raced into the lobby of the West Wing, which was full of uniformed Secret Service agents.

She recognized several of the men, agents she'd become familiar with over the months. The agent who had delivered flowers to her the previous week met her as she came to an exhausted halt.

"What happened?" Casey panted. "I came as fast as I could."

The young agent shook his head. "The cabinet is convening in a few minutes." He grabbed her arm and pulled her along. "They've been looking for you."

Casey trotted after the agent, down the twist of corridors to the cabinet room. The first person she saw was Vice President

Anthony Peck. At forty-nine years old, he was bespectacled and balding, but extremely sharp and amiable. He balanced out Russ' election ticket nicely with his Ivy League education and calm demeanor in contrast to Talbot's fast-talking cowboy image. Peck turned to Casey as soon as she came through the door.

"Casey," he stood up and went to her. "I'm glad you're here. We're going to need help."

Casey's heart was pounding from both anxiety and exertion. "Anything I can do, Mr. Vice President," she said. "What happened? Nobody had told me anything."

Peck sighed sharply. "It's coming to us in pieces, but from what we know so far, Russ was shot at by an airman we have yet to identify. He's stationed at Andrews and took six shots at Russ before he was subdued. He's in Secret Service custody right now."

"Oh, my God," Casey breathed. "Is Russ okay? Was anyone hurt?"

Peck nodded. "Russ wasn't hit, but Tracy was," he said. "So was the new Special Agent in Charge – what's his name – Sheridan? He was apparently hit when he threw Russ onto the ground and shielded him with his body. From what we heard, he was still able to get Russ into the Presidential limo and to safety. That's dedication."

Casey suddenly felt like she couldn't breathe. She grasped at a chair to steady herself, struggling against the explosive grief that was bubbling up inside of her.

"He... he was hit?" she swallowed, laboring to keep her composure. "Is it bad?"

Peck was distracted by more cabinet members entering the room. "Bad enough," he said. "We heard he was hit in the neck, but we don't know for sure. The President is at the hospital with Tracy and that's all we really know right now."

Casey was starting to feel woozy. "How bad is she?"

"She took one in the belly," Peck replied, now completely distracted by the cabinet members filling the chamber. "Gentlemen, take a seat. We need to get started."

As Casey struggled not to cry, Peck's cell phone suddenly rang. He looked at the caller ID and answered swiftly. "Russ," he said as he picked up. "How's Tracy?"

Everyone in the cabinet room seemed to freeze, knowing that the Vice President was speaking to the President. But Peck suddenly looked over at Casey as if she were the only one in the room.

"Okay, keep us posted," he said. "Casey? She's right here. Yes, I'll make sure. Okay. Just let me know what you want me to tell the press. We've called a press conference in a half hour. What? Sure. Okay, let me know."

Peck hung up the phone and pointed at Casey. "The President wants you at the hospital right now," he said. "He's sending a Secret Service car for you. Go out front and wait for it."

Casey didn't even question him. She just nodded her head and stumbled out of the room, heading for the lobby of the West Wing to wait for a car. She was trying so hard not to cry that she was starting to hyperventilate, but she saw Lisanne as she neared the lobby entry and tried to avoid her. It didn't work.

"Casey," the young girl ran up to her. "Did they tell you what happened?"

Casey nodded, swallowing the massive lump in her throat. "I'm heading to the hospital now," she said tightly. "I can't tell you what they told me, not until it's formally announced."

Lisanne was looking at her face, carefully. "Are you okay?"

Casey nodded, trying to breathe and calm down. "I'm fine," she lied. "It... it's just been a busy few days with Brody's accident and now this. I guess I'm just a little worked up."

Lisanne stroked her arm comfortingly. "I know," she said. "You call me if you need me to do anything for you, okay? They had me shut the switchboard down because it's going crazy."

Casey put her hand on Lisanne's arm. "There is something you can do for me," she said. "Brody is being discharged from the hospital but I took my sister's car. Can you please send a car over to the Children's National Medical Center to pick them up and then call Riley and let her know? Tell her I had to go to Walter Reed where the President is."

Lisanne nodded. "Sure," she said. "Anything else?"

Casey just shook her head and Lisanne fled. Casey came to a halt at the entrance to the West Wing, trembling as she waited for the Secret Service escort. The cloudy day turned to rain and still she stood there, wondering if Colt was dead or alive, trying not to let her anxiety overwhelm her. She was a bundle of nerves just waiting to pop. As she stood in the mist, waiting, a black Dodge Charger roared up.

Peter was behind the wheel. He rolled down the window, waving Casey over. "Get in," he told her.

Casey scooted to the car and opened the door, settling in and slamming the door closed. Peter peeled out of the driveway as she fastened her seatbelt.

"What happened?" she asked, hoping she didn't sound as shaken as she felt. "How are Colt and Tracy?"

Peter tore off onto Pennsylvania Avenue. "Tracy's in surgery," he said. "She took one right to the belly. It's just like they say; it all happened so fast that it was over before you realized it. Tracy was just talking to some people and suddenly, we hear this loud popping noise. She goes down and Colt and I jumped on the President and pushed him to the tarmac. As we're doing this, about ten agents rushed the gunman. He was just standing on the edge of the crowd like no big deal and after he got off six shots, he just dropped the gun. We jumped on him and I'm pretty sure we broke an arm."

Casey was looking at him, struggling with every ounce of strength she possessed not to burst into tears. "What about Colt?" she asked tightly.

Peter glanced at her as they tore at breakneck speed to Walter Reed Military Hospital.

"Well...," his voice softened up. "He did his job, Casey. He was the first one to get the President down on the ground, but he happened to be standing between the President and Tracy, so when she got hit first, he got it second. He's a pretty big target. His back was turned so he caught a bullet in his neck and, as he went to throw the President to the ground, he caught another bullet in the thigh. But it didn't stop him; he's bleeding all over the damn place and he still got up, picked the President up, and pretty much tossed him into the limo. They got Tracy in the car, too, and just took off for Walter Reed."

Casey turned to the window, unable to stop the tears. They streamed down her face as she tried to discreetly wipe them away. Peter knew she was crying and he knew why, feeling very sorry for her. He couldn't stay quiet any longer.

"Look, Casey," he lowered his voice. "I know that you and Colt... he told me what was going on between you two, so that's why the President sent me to get you. Colt won't go into surgery until he sees you. It's been about an hour since he was hit so we really need to get him fixed up, but he refuses. When the doctors tried to wheel him away, he grabbed one of the nurses around the neck and nearly strangled the guy."

By this time, Casey had turned around to look at him, a shocked expression on her face. "He *told* you?"

Peter nodded, sensing displeasure. "Don't be mad," he said quietly. "I'll take the secret to my grave, I promise. To tell you the truth, I pretty much figured it out anyway on that day we got the call about Brody and went looking for you. We figured out you were with Colt."

Casey wiped at the tears on her face, figuring there wasn't much she could do about it now. If Colt told Peter, then he must have had a good reason. She sighed heavily.

"How is he really?" she wanted to know, her voice soft and pleading. "What about the wound in his neck? Is it bad?"

He shook his head. "That one passed through without hitting anything vital," he said. "It's the one in his thigh they have to go in and remove. Any higher and it would have hit him in the ass... uh, I mean, his butt."

Peter didn't seem too distressed. In fact, he seemed to joke about it, which eased Casey's mind. She sighed again, wiping the last of her tears. "He has a cute butt."

Peter fought off a grin. "I wouldn't know."

Casey felt much better than she had since she first heard the news. Emotionally exhausted, she sat back against the car seat and remained quiet until they reached Walter Reed Military Hospital.

Walter Reed was a massive complex and considering the attempt on the President's life, it was now surrounded by Military Police as well as the Secret Service. Peter had to pass through two checkpoints before he was able to park the car. Still in the pretty purple suit that Colt had liked so much, a suit that had now seen a lot of activity during the day, Casey hurriedly followed Peter across the rain-soaked parking lot and into the main lobby of the hospital where they had to pass another Secret Service checkpoint. Once cleared, Peter took her up to the fourth floor.

There were more Secret Service agents when they got off the elevator and still more in the small waiting room to the left of the elevator banks. It smelled heavily of disinfectant as Casey and Peter went down the corridor and to a door that was just shy of the nurse's station that said "No Admittance". Peter knocked before pushing the door open.

Russ was inside the room with several advisors, glancing up to see Casey and Peter coming through the door. Russ jumped up and went to her.

"Mr. President," Casey reached out and took the hand he was extending at her. "How's Tracy?"

"She's going to be okay," he said, his voice trembling with obvious relief. "She wanted to know if the doctor could do a tummy tuck as she was going under anesthesia, so if she's thinking about feminine vanity, then she's going to be fine."

Casey smiled, squeezing his hand. "Thank God," she murmured. "Is she out of surgery yet?"

"They're finishing up now. They said there wasn't any real damage and she should be fine."

Casey nodded, whispering another pray of thanks. Then her thoughts turned to Colt. "How's Colt?"

Russ turned her around for the door. "Pete, take her to him. Last I heard, he was still waiting for her."

Peter nodded and took Casey by the hand, leading her from the small room into the clean, stark corridor that lead towards the east side of the wing. There was a secondary corridor that led off to the right and Peter hurriedly took her down that one to the second door on the left. A nurse was coming out of the door as Peter let the woman pass before pushing his way in.

Colt lay on a gurney in a small, windowless room, eyes closed and his big body lit up with I.V.s and monitors. There was a massive bandage around his neck and his right leg was elevated and prepped. As Peter remained at the door, Casey walked right up to the gurney and grasped Colt's right hand.

"Colt?" she said softly.

His dark eyes popped open and focused on her. Both hands, with I.V. needles sticking in them, came up to cup her face.

"Hi, Angel," he said, pulling her down to him. He kissed her sweetly and, feeling his tender touch, Casey broke down in tears. He shushed her softly. "No tears. I'm okay. I'm going to be fine."

Casey tried to speak but she couldn't seem to manage it. She held on to his big hand, struggling to wipe the tears from her face.

"You're sure?" she whispered.

"I am."

"Then you need to let them take you into surgery," she said, bending down to kiss him again with her salty lips. "Why did you wait for me?"

His dark eyes looked even more intense set within his pale face. "Because I wanted to see you first before they did anything," he whispered. "I wanted to tell you that I love you and that I'm sorry about this."

She ran her hand over his face, touching him tenderly. "Sorry about what?" she asked. "Colt, you need to let them take you into surgery. That would make me happy. Please don't be stubborn about it."

He kissed her hand. "I won't," he assured her. "I'll go. But I just had to see your face before I went."

Casey turned around to Peter and nodded her head, motioning out towards the nurse's station. Peter took that as a sign that Colt was ready for surgery and he quickly went in search of the nurse. As Peter fled, Casey returned her focus to Colt. Bending over him, she kissed his forehead, his cheek, and finally his lips.

"I love you," she whispered. "I'm so proud of what you did."

Colt closed his eyes as she kissed his nose and brow. "I got shot."

She grinned, caressing his rough cheek. "You were a hero. You saved the President."

He just grunted, closing his eyes as she stroked his forehead. It was a very gentle gesture, one that eased Colt tremendously. There was so much love and sweetness in her touch, her soft hand stroking his skin. He could have stayed like that forever, feeling the emotions in her touch.

Exhausted and injured, Colt let himself relax for the first time all day and began to doze. Casey kept caressing him, glancing up when a nurse in green surgical scrubs came around the other side of the bed with a syringe in her hand.

"So," she looked between Colt and Casey. "Can we finally get this bullet out of you, Special Agent in Charge Sheridan?"

Casey grinned at the way the woman said it. "Yes, you can," she answered for him. "I'm sorry if he's been a problem child."

The nurse laughed, looking at Colt. "Your wife says we can finally hack into you," she said, "so I'm going to listen to her and not you anymore. You're mine now, Sheridan."

Casey's grin faded, thinking how to tactfully explain she wasn't Colt's wife, but Colt opened his eyes and looked at the nurse.

"If my wife says you can cut me open, then let's do it," he said as the nurse took his I.V. line and plunged the contents of the syringe into it. "Casey's the boss."

The nurse disposed of the syringe in the biohazard bin. "Hmmm," she lifted an eyebrow. "You weren't that compliant when you came in here. She must have some magic powers over you. Had I known that, I would have gotten her over here faster."

Colt looked up at Casey, a faint smile on his lips. "Some kind of magic," he agreed softly, suddenly feeling very drowsy and realizing he was about to pass out from whatever medication the nurse had put in his I.V. "I love you. I'll see you when I wake up."

Casey squeezed his hand tightly. "I'll be right here," she promised, kissing his lips one last time. "I love you, too."

By the time she got the words out of her mouth, he was asleep. Casey continued to hold his hand, gazing down at his handsome face, as tears sprang to her eyes. She didn't know why she was crying, only that it had something to do with how close she came to losing him. She could have just as easily been standing in the morgue looking at his body. Just when she had found an utterly wonderful man, that happiness was threatened. The whole situation was just shattering.

The nurse was still standing next to the gurney, unplugging monitors and preparing to wheel him out of the room. The woman glanced up and saw tears popping from Casey's eyes, raining down on Colt's shoulder and arm.

"He'll be fine," the nurse said, her manner more gentle now. "He shouldn't be in surgery more than an hour at the most. The doctor will remove the bullet, repair any damage, and then take a look at the neck wound to make sure everything is intact. You can walk with me to the operatory if you'd like."

Casey could only nod. The lump in her throat prevented her from speaking. She was still holding Colt's hand when two more nurses came into the room to wheel Colt into surgery. As they moved Colt's bed out into the corridor, Casey walked beside him, his hand in hers, until they turned a corner and the surgery doors loomed in front of her. Squeezing Colt's hand, she kissed him one last time before the three nurses wheeled him in through the big, white double doors that led into surgery.

After that, there was nothing left to do but wait.

TEN
ONE WEEK LATER

"CONGRATULATIONS." Mr. Meade walked right into Colt's townhome the moment Colt opened the door. "How are you feeling?"

Colt eyed Mr. Meade. The elderly man was accompanied by his chauffer and bodyguard, an enormous Japanese man who had once been a sumo wrestler. The big man went everywhere with Meade but usually stayed in the car. However, he had accompanied him today and remained standing just inside the door as Colt moved stiffly back to his big, leather couch and sat gingerly, avoiding putting too much pressure on the thigh wound.

"I've been better," he grunted as he shifted around on the couch to find a comfortable position. "What do you mean by congratulations?"

Meade seemed rather warm and jovial today, an odd stance for the usually taciturn man. "Exactly that," he replied. "You've cemented the trust President Talbot has in you. Taking a bullet meant for the man was a brilliant way to do it."

Colt sighed heavily. "I didn't do it on purpose," he said. "It just happened that way."

"Then it was most fortuitous."

Colt didn't reply other than to look between Meade and his

bodyguard. "So why are you here?" he asked. "You don't normally make house calls. In fact, I can't remember you ever coming to my home."

Mr. Meade lifted his eyebrows as he sat across from Colt in a matching leather armchair.

"I knew you could not come to me and I didn't want to have this conversation on a traceable line," he said, his jovial mood fading. "This heroic injury could not have come at a better time. We must use it to our advantage."

"What do you mean?"

"Now that you have the President's trust, perhaps it will be easier to get closer to him."

Colt knew what he meant. He exhaled slowly and sat back against the couch.

"I've spent the better part of the past three weeks doing as much research as I can on the President and his financial dealings," he said softly. "My I.T. forensic contact has managed to crack the President's bank accounts for the past several years, at least as long as banking records have been made available online. He was able to trace deposits through an archived banking server that actually had stored microfiche. From 1987 through 1999, we've been able to trace over $900,000 in payments to *Swissbanc,* but not the source of the payments. They're simply listed as deposits. What I'd really like to do is get a hold of the President's printed bank statements from that time. They might tell us more."

Meade listened seriously. "So what are you going to do?"

Colt looked thoughtful. "I need to find out if the President keeps records that far back," he said. "Somehow, someway, I need to found out what kind of financial files the man keeps."

"What about Ms. Cleburne?" Meade wanted to know. "As his personal assistant, she should have access to those things or at least know something about them."

Colt nodded, fighting off the extreme protectiveness he felt every time Mr. Meade brought Casey into the conversation.

"I'm sure she does," he replied, "but that conversation will have to take place at the appropriate time. I'm not going to bring it up or just throw it out there. Timing is everything."

Mr. Meade's old, dark eyes held his gaze appraisingly. "Has she been of any help to you?"

Colt shook his head. "Not as much as I'd hoped," he said. "She's only been his assistant for six months and, unfortunately, doesn't have a deep history with him. But I don't think it's a dead end. I'm working on it."

Mr. Meade gazed at him a moment longer, hard eyes growing harder, until finally looking away and standing up. If he didn't believe Colt, he didn't say so, but Colt knew the suspicion was there. *He's protecting her,* he thought.

"See that you do," Mr. Meade said as he moved for the door. "We will have another conversation like this soon and I will expect progress."

"I'll do my best."

When the door closed behind Mr. Meade and his bodyguard, Colt just sat there and closed his eyes, his jaw ticking, feeling increasingly sickened by his meetings with Meade. It was increasingly difficult for him to perform, to do what he was tasked with. He didn't want to betray Casey and he didn't want to lose her, not now when she was the center of his world.

He was a man deeply torn.

———

"Good morning, Special Agent Sheridan," Chris Eckart seemed unusually social. "You don't look like a man who got shot last week. Welcome back."

Casey glanced up casually from her desk as Colt entered her office, trying to stay as neutral as possible, but her heart leapt at the sight of him. He looked healthy, handsome and whole in his sharp dark suit. Colt glanced at Chris but his focus was drawn to Casey.

"Thanks," he said, his eyes on Casey. "Hi, Casey."

She couldn't help but smile at him. "Welcome back."

"Thank you. It's good to be back."

"How are you feeling?"

"Fine," he said. "Still a little sore, but fine."

"Good to hear. We were worried about you."

It was such a show the two of them put on, like they were just seeing each other for the first time in ages when the truth was that they had only seen each other minutes before. As had been their routine almost since they had met, Colt came by her house early in the morning to take her to work, waiting a nominal amount of time for her to enter the West Wing before making his approach.

Colt had been released from the hospital the day after the shooting. He'd gone home for a few days to recuperate and Casey had spent her time between Colt and Brody, nursing the walking wounded as best she could. Colt thought it would be easier on her if he just went to her house, but Casey wasn't sure how her boys would feel about a big stranger recuperating from a bullet wound in her bed. More than that, Hunter hadn't even met the man yet. So, he stayed at his house and saw her at lunch time and in the evening when she got off of work. She would bring him dinner, sit with him for a little while, and then head home to tend to her children. It was a crazy pace but he found himself looking to those few brief moments with her as the highlight of his day.

Four days after the shooting, Colt refused to stay down any longer. His neck was sore, as was his right shoulder, and his right thigh was sore, but it certainly wasn't anything that would keep him out of action.

After his run-in with Mr. Meade, he felt a strong need to get back to work so he spent the subsequent weekend at the White House, working with his boss and the Secret Service analysts to determine what had gone wrong with the security net and why events happened as they did. The assassination attempt against Russ Talbot was the lead story of every news channel all over the world, still, and the American public was still freaked out about it.

Colt had been commended from the start for his quick and selfless actions, and there were rumors that he was going to be awarded a Congressional Medal of Honor for his heroic actions. He was becoming the poster boy for the dedication and bravery of the Secret Service and over the weekend, one of the media outlets had gotten a hold of his photograph, which was now being splashed around by the news people. The public wanted to learn more about the handsome and courageous Special Agent in Charge, Colt Sheridan. His name and family history were now media fodder. Everybody was coming to know the great-great-great grandson of the great Civil War general Philip Sheridan.

But it was something that Colt was very uncomfortable with. He had the only adoring public he needed in Casey, and for the past three nights, he had come to her house well after the boys had gone to sleep and then left before they got up. He wasn't getting a whole lot of sleep but he was having the time of his life. He would drive over around midnight and slip in, making love until the early hours and then get a few hours of sleep before slipping out before dawn.

Yesterday, Riley had been awake very early and had bumped into him as he had come downstairs. All she did was grin and shake her head, and he grinned sheepishly as he slipped past her. Casey had gotten an earful from her sister later on.

Colt went to his desk and booted up his computer, removed his suit jacket gingerly because the movement hurt his neck, and laid it over the back of his guest chair. He sat down at his desk and prepared to go through the dozens of emails he had stacked up and waiting for him. Casey had taken his smart phone away while he had been recuperating and had refused to let him do any work. He had to negotiate to get it back. The result was that he had over a week's worth of emails waiting for him and he began to plow through them.

The morning was normal enough. Casey was going over speaking engagement arrangements for the President in Hawai'i that were a couple of months off, listening to Chris argue on the phone with someone about something she wasn't even paying attention to. She was paying more attention to Colt in the next office, listening to him type. They never sent emails to each other for fear of being hacked or being discovered by the I.T. Department and they only texted very rarely for the same reasons. Even though he was sitting in the next room, she missed talking to him. It was increasingly difficult to concentrate.

Toward mid-morning, Casey's intercom buzzed and Lisanne was on the other end. An envelope had been delivered for the President from the Pentagon, so Casey stood up from her chair and stretched her stiff muscles. She was dressed in a beautiful sheath dress in a chocolate brown with nude pumps that made her legs look great. Colt had picked the dress out for her that morning because he liked the color and when she stood up from her desk, he caught a glimpse of her in the sexy dress that was both professional and alluring. She wore it like a goddess.

"Would you like some coffee, Special Agent Sheridan?" She paused by his office door. "I'm going down to the mess."

Colt glanced up from his computer screen. "If it's not too much trouble."

She shook her head. "Of course not," she said. "We have to take care of the man who saved the President."

They grinned at each other before she turned away, her smile vanishing as she looked at Chris.

"Do you want any coffee?" she demanded.

Chris looked at her fearfully. "No," he said. "You'll just spit in it, anyway."

Casey couldn't help but laugh at him as she left the office and made her way down the corridor towards the lobby area. As soon as she hit the lobby, Maggie was there standing next to Lisanne's desk. Casey walked up on the pair, smiling.

"Hey, hey," she said softly. "What's new, ladies?"

Lisanne handed Casey the envelope. "Wow, Case," she said, looking the woman up and down in the empire-waist brown dress. "You look great. Why are you so happy this morning?"

Casey shrugged, looking at the special delivery envelope. "Life's good," she said simply. "How was your weekend?"

"Good," she said. "How was yours?"

"Wonderful."

"How's Brody?"

"Better. He's already crying for a new skateboard."

Lisanne nodded. She seemed to be glancing at Maggie a lot, so much so that Casey looked at the woman as well. Stout, matronly Maggie was looking at Lisanne, the desk, the wall, or anything else she could manage to behold. Anything other than Casey. Casey's brow furrowed as she looked at the older woman.

"What's the matter, Mags?" she asked.

Maggie was still looking away. "Nothing."

Casey sensed something was up. She leaned against Lisanne's desk. "Uh... I don't think so," she said quietly. "What's wrong? What's going on?"

Maggie's dour face was stiff. "I guess we should be asking you that."

"What do you mean?"

Maggie looked at her, then. "Nothing," she said, turning her back on her. "I need to go back to work."

Casey frowned and went after her. She caught the woman just as she was entering her office area.

"Maggie," she grabbed her by the arm. "What's wrong? Why are you upset?"

Maggie was so angry that she had a white ring around her tight lips. She pulled her arm from Casey's grip. In spite of her anger, she started to talk.

"I thought you were my friend," she hissed. "I thought you were honest with me."

Casey was confused. "What in the hell are you talking about?"

Maggie was beginning to quiver. "You knew I...," she faltered and started again. "Everybody is talking about the fact that Colt Sheridan is married."

Casey's eyebrows flew up. "Married?" she repeated. "What *are* you talking about?"

Maggie took a step back from her, crossing her arms angrily.

"Someone at the hospital said he's married," she said. "His wife's name is Casey."

Casey felt as if she'd been struck. She took a step back from Maggie, startled, looking at the woman with shock and some chagrin. "Where in the hell did you hear that?" she demanded.

Maggie was more hurt than angry. "I heard some of the Secret Service guys talking this morning in the lobby when I came in," she said. "They were talking about Sheridan's heroism and about his wife who came to see him when he was shot. A nurse said her name was Casey and people said they say *you* at the hospital. Is it a coincidence?"

Casey just looked at her, wondering how in the world she was going to get out of this one. People saw her arrive at the hospital and people saw Peter escort her back to see Colt. She was so upset at the time that she hadn't really thought about being discreet. It should have occurred to her but it hadn't. Now, what she had feared was coming to pass. The rumors were starting.

"You know I'm not married," she finally said. "Next time, if you have a problem with me, come talk to me like an adult and don't act like a jilted teenager. Maybe you don't think I'm honest, but you just lost some of my respect for giving in to rumors and gossip."

She turned around and walked away, shaken and upset, returning to her office and planting herself heavily behind her desk as she threw the overnight envelope onto the surface. She didn't say a word to Chris, or to Colt. She just went right back to work, or at least she pretended to. Chris noticed she didn't have any coffee in her hands.

"Casey, where's the coffee?" he asked.

Casey paused and looked around as if realizing she had forgotten something. Then she just shook her head.

"I don't need any," she said, resuming typing.

Chris cocked an eyebrow. "What about Special Agent Sheridan?"

She faltered again. "Caffeine slows healing. He doesn't need any, either."

"But...?"

"Shut up."

Chris promptly did just that, although he had made it his mission in life to harass Casey every chance he had. Still, just by her demeanor he could tell she wasn't taking his teasing very well. She'd had a hard week with her kid and all, so he decided to leave her alone. At least, for now.

Colt had heard the exchange and the tone of her voice, concerned. It wasn't like her to snap or slam things around, so he casually stood up and went to his office entry. Casey was focused on her computer.

"So... did they run out of coffee?" he asked.

She paused and looked up at him. "Sorry," she said, although she didn't sound like she meant it. "I got sidetracked. If you really want me to, I'll go get you some."

Colt shook his head. "No worries," he was already heading out of the office. "I can get my own. I'm not a complete invalid yet."

He walked out and Casey returned to her computer, feeling worse and worse. The truth was that if there really were rumors going around, he would hear them sooner or later. So would Russ and everyone else, and the dynamics of the situation would change. She was scared to death he would be reassigned, but after what just happened with the attempt on the President, maybe not. Maybe he had proven his worth and they would leave him where he did the most good.

As she sat there and messed with her email, her cell phone buzzed. She had a text message and she picked up the phone, seeing that it was from Colt.

Lafayette Square now.

Casually, she set the phone back down and continued messing with her email. Then, she opened up the overnight envelope on her desk, pulled out the contents, and went into the Oval Office to put them on the President's desk. Coming out of his office and closing the door, she went back to her computer, locked it, and picked up her cell phone.

"I'll be back," she said.

Chris didn't look up or acknowledge her. Only when she was out of earshot did he roll his eyes and grunt. "Go take some Midol or something," he muttered.

Casey didn't hear him. She passed through the lobby, past Lisanne's empty desk, and out of the main entrance of the West Wing. She had her I.D. badge on as she went past the guard entry and took the gate out onto Pennsylvania Avenue. Crossing the street, she headed into Lafayette Square under gray and threatening skies.

Colt was waiting for her by the statue in the middle of the park. He saw her coming and went to meet her.

"What's wrong?" he asked quietly.

She looked frustrated and teary as she tried to reply. "Maggie said she heard some of the uniformed Secret Service guys talking about you," she said. "They said that someone at the hospital said that your wife came to visit you and that your wife's name is Casey."

He sighed slowly, calmly digesting the information. "Well," he said after a moment. "There were a lot of people there that day. People that know you saw you there and I'm sure someone saw you when you went to visit me."

"Maggie said a nurse said your wife came to visit. Now she's pissed off because she thinks... oh, it doesn't matter what she thinks. What are we going to do?"

"What does Maggie think?"

Casey crossed her arms, cocking her head at him. "She's been hot on you since you started," she replied. "I think she wanted to date you and now with these rumors, she thinks I betrayed her."

Colt just lifted his eyebrows thoughtfully. "Angel, even if you didn't exist, there's no amount of money or persuasion that could convince me to date Maggie Broom, so don't let her guilt-trip you into thinking she even had a chance. She didn't."

"That's mean."

"That's a fact."

Her expression darkened but she refrained from verbally sparring with him. She just looked away, watching the cold pigeons hobble around a few feet away. Colt took a step closer to her and crossed his big arms.

"What, exactly, are you upset about?" he asked softly.

She shrugged, still watching the pigeons. "Everyone is going to find out."

"So what?"

She looked at him then, shocked. "So *what*?" she repeated. "We talked about this in the beginning, Colt. Office romances are discouraged to say the least and...."

"This isn't an office romance," he cut her off. "It's not a fling or a thing or casual sex or anything else like that. I love you and you love me, and you're mine forever. The President knows and Peter knows. We can't stop the gossip, so are we going to deny it instead? Are we going to lie to people and carry on in secret like we're ashamed of each other? I don't want to do that anymore. We can come out in the open and still conduct ourselves with self-control and dignity. We can be two people in love who happened to work together."

She just stared at him. "Are you serious?"

"Yes," he said firmly. "Why do you have a problem with that?"

She shook her head. "I didn't say I did." She was starting to soften up. "But I'm terrified that your bosses are going to reassign you. Colt, I don't want you to go anywhere. Things are so good right now and I just don't want anything to mess it up."

He put his arms around her, in public, and held her close. Casey let him, wrapping her arms around his waist and laying her head on his chest.

"I'm *not* going to get reassigned," he comforted. "I don't care if anyone knows that you and I are together. It makes me so proud to have your love, Casey. It's the best thing that has ever happened to me."

She looked up at him, smiling. His calmness with the situation eased her considerably and, if she thought about it, she felt the same way he did. She was so proud to be with him.

"Me, too," she whispered. "So... what do we do?"

He shrugged. "As much as I want to, I'm not going to go around shouting it, but if anyone asks, I won't deny it."

She sighed heavily and squared her shoulders. "Okay," she agreed. "Me, too."

"One more question."

"What?"

"You never have given me an answer about marrying me. I want to marry you and have a life with you. Do you think we can talk about that?"

Her eyes widened. "Right now?"

"Why not?"

She thought about that. Then, she pulled out of his embrace but she took his hands in hers. "Okay," she said softly. "Of course I'll marry you. I just thought you already knew that."

"I wanted to hear it from you."

"So now you have."

"And I don't want to wait forever."

She cocked her head. "What did you have in mind?"

He shrugged, squeezed her hand, and began walking back towards the White House. "I liked calling you my wife in front of that nurse," he admitted. "I'd be happy if we did it tomorrow or in six months, but I don't want to wait for years. I don't think I could take it."

Casey loved the feeling of holding his hand in public. It was sweet and liberating. "Come over tonight and meet Hunter," she looked up at him. "You still haven't met him."

"That's because every time I come over, he's asleep."

She grinned. "Well, come for dinner if you can. The sooner the boys start getting accustomed to you, the sooner we can take the next step. I don't want to do anything unless they're comfortable with it."

"I understand."

She smiled at him as they reached Pennsylvania Avenue and crossed the street. The second they reached the White House grounds, he let go of her hand and they continued onto the property. They reached the West Wing and Colt opened the door for her as they walked in together. It was the first time they had ever entered the West Wing together, which was something of a milestone. Colt stopped to talk to the uniformed Secret Service agents at the desk as Casey continued to the complex of offices.

Maggie's office was to the right when she came into the lobby area. After a moment's deliberation, Casey went into Maggie's office to find the woman behind her desk going over some reports. Maggie glanced up, saw Casey, and pulled her glasses off.

"Casey, I'm sorry," she said before Casey could open her mouth. "You're right. I listened to gossip and I'm so sorry. I shouldn't have. Please don't be angry with me."

Casey went around the woman's desk and hugged her. "I'm sorry, too," she said. "I shouldn't have been so harsh about it. I guess... I guess you just caught me off guard."

Maggie was holding on to Casey's hands. "It was wrong and I'm sorry."

Casey shushed her. "Listen to me," she said quietly. "The rumor you heard was wrong, but only slightly. I'm not Colt's wife yet but I will be. It all happened so fast... we love each other, Mags. Colt is the most wonderful, brilliant and sweet man in the whole world and I love him to death. I know you had a thing for him and it was never my intention to betray you or hurt you. It just sort of happened. So, the rumors are mostly true. I'm just sorry if you feel hurt by all of it. I never meant to hurt you."

Maggie stared at her for a moment before breaking into a weak smile. "Like I really ever had a chance," she said softly. Then she hugged her. "I wish you all the best, you know that. I'm so happy for you."

Casey smiled timidly. "Really?"

"Really."

"Thank you. That means a lot. But I would appreciate it if you didn't spread it around. We're trying to keep it as low-key as possible."

"Sure."

Casey touched the woman's hand one last time before leaving her office, emerging into the lobby about the time Colt was passing through. He very nearly ran her down as he came around a corner and she yelped as he bumped into her.

With a grin, Colt grabbed Casey to keep her from toppling over on her towering high heels but she returned his smile and waved him off, regaining her balance.

"Holy Cow, Sheridan," she exclaimed softly. "Working with you is hazardous."

He cocked an eyebrow. "No more hazardous than those three foot tall heels you wear."

"Leave my heels alone. If you insult them, you insult me."

He fought off a grin. "Not an insult, Ms. Cleburne, but a statement of fact."

"Don't you like them?"

He cocked an eyebrow, looking at her legs rather seductively. "Ask me that again tonight when we're alone," he whispered.

She just grinned as they headed back to their offices. Casey preceded him into the office area and went straight to her desk, shoving aside one of the two or three storage boxes partially shoved under her desk so she could sit. She went right to the box on the top and resumed where she had left off before all of the excitement of the morning. As Eckart yelled at someone on the phone again, Colt paused by her desk to see what she was doing.

"What are you working so hard on?" he asked. "I saw you pull out these boxes last week. Looks like you're moving."

She grinned. "Russ has me fishing out some records," she said. "He's trying to establish a history of donations to one of his charities, so I've been going through all of his bank and financial records since last week. Some of this stuff goes back ten or fifteen years even, when he was the governor of New Mexico."

"Audit?"

She nodded. "Exactly. The President's tax and bank records have to be transparent, even before he was President."

Colt simply nodded and went back to his desk. But he was seized with the possibilities; *bank records that went back fifteen years*. It was the golden opportunity he had been waiting for, to do what he had been positioned there to do. He was feeling the pressure from Meade, something he tried to push out of his mind, but something he couldn't seem to shake. Meade said a lot of things. Meade meant a lot of things. But Colt was extremely protective over Casey, feeling torn like he had never felt in his life.

The morning went on and Russ came into the office sometime close to noon. His time in the office was infrequent because of Tracy's recovery, and even now, he looked weary and beaten. Casey looked up from the stacks of files on her desk.

"Mr. President," she greeted pleasantly. "How's Tracy?"

Russ paused by her desk. "Being released from the hospital later today," he said, rather positively. "She's able to walk and eat, so that's a good sign. And speaking of good signs...."

He turned for Colt's office, seeing the man inside at his desk. He walked in and sat down in Colt's guest chair.

"You don't look any worse for the wear," he said to Colt. "How are you feeling?"

Colt folded his hands on the desktop. "Fine, Mr. President," he assured him. "Ready to get back to work."

Russ lifted an eyebrow. "No lingering effects?"

Colt shrugged. "A little soreness, but nothing I can't handle, sir."

"How does Casey feel about you being back to work so soon?"

Colt glanced over the President's shoulder where he caught a glimpse of Casey, looking at him from her position at the end of her desk. He smiled weakly.

"She knows I feel fine," he lowered his voice so Eckart wouldn't hear him. "She supports my return to work."

That seemed to be good enough for Russ, better than a doctor's release. "I know she'll keep an eye on you," he said, standing up. His gaze lingered on Colt a moment. "If I didn't thank you for what you did, then please accept my deepest gratitude. You saved my life, Colt. I'll never forget that."

Colt nodded humbly. "I did my job, sir. But you're welcome."

Russ nodded in acknowledgement, shoved his hands in his pockets, and made his way towards the Oval Office. He seemed pensive and weary, trying to cover up a man who was emotionally exhausted. As much as the country, if not the world, liked to look at him as being the most powerful man on the planet, the truth was that he was human just like everyone else. As much as he didn't want to admit it, the attempted assassination had him rattled. It reminded him that he was, indeed, mortal.

"Casey, can you join me?" he asked as he passed her desk. "I have a lot of things I need to go over."

Without a word, Casey got up, collected her steno pad, and followed him into the Oval Office. Colt caught her eye as she was rounding her desk and she winked at him before disappearing. He smiled to himself, pretending to go back to work when, in fact, he was calculating his next move. And it all depended on Eckart.

As expected, the moment the President disappeared into his office, Eckart grabbed his wallet and his keys and bolted for the exit. Colt sat there quietly and answered a few emails as if completely focused on his work. He gave Eckart a good five minutes before he moved into action.

Rising from his chair, he went out of his office and into Casey and Chris' office, going to the doorway that led to the main hall and making a mental note of what he could see and hear. Since it was lunch, most people were leaving or at their desks, so he slipped back into his office and collected his smart phone.

With extreme quiet, he went to the office door that led into the Oval Office and listened carefully. He couldn't hear anything, which wasn't unusual given the soundproofing of the office, but sometimes snippets of loud conversation could be heard. It was dead silent. With stealth, he made his way to Casey's desk and visually inspected the three boxes she had sitting out at her feet. Peering closer, he noticed they were very carefully labeled and organized by color and year, and he quickly found 1997 and 1998. Taking a tissue from the box off of Casey's desk, he pulled out the big pressboard folders that contained bank statements. Flipping it open to January 1997, he took out his smart phone and started taking pictures of the statements.

He moved quickly and quietly, moving swiftly through 1997 and then on to 1998. He wouldn't stop to read anything now. He would do that later at home where he could go over everything carefully. He finished twenty four statements in under five minutes, so he decided to do 1996, as well as a file of medical records. In seven minutes and fourteen seconds, he had photographed three years of bank statements from New Mexico State Bank. Swiftly putting the file back where he found it, he pulled out investment folder statements for three different investment firms and quickly photographed those as well.

It took him a little under twenty-five minutes to photograph the entire storage box from 1996 through 1998. He was starting to think that if Russ was particularly clever, he wouldn't find a thing in these statements alluding to big deposits from South American banks. So far, with all of his contacts, Colt hadn't been able to find hide nor hair of anyone with any suspicion or inkling of the President's previous cartel connections, except....

He put the files back very carefully, made sure nothing else was out of place, and then returned to his desk. He pulled out his iPad and began to run searches on Russ' years as governor and the one article from a reporter with the Albuquerque Press that had intimated Russ Talbot's connection to the cartel. It had only been one article, something that had been printed twelve years ago, but nothing more was ever done about it because Russ lost his children right about that time. No one is going to write horrible things about a man who had just lost his two children to a disease.

The conspiracy theory of Russ Talbot and the Colombians had been quashed. Perhaps that's where he would glean more information because there certainly wasn't anything in the obvious places from what he could see. He would have to dig deeper.

Colt was still on his iPad when Casey emerged from Russ' office ten minutes later. He glanced up as she sat down at her desk, seeing her moving around as she pushed boxes aside and began typing on her computer. He locked the iPad and came out of his office.

"Hey," he said softly. "Want to grab some lunch?"

She stopped typing and smiled at him. "I'd love to, but I have to get a memo out for the President," she said. "Can I order us some lunch or do you want to go out?"

He returned her smile. "I want to be wherever you are," he said. "If you're going to eat here, so am I."

She sighed dreamily. "You're so sweet," she told him. "Do you want a roast beef sandwich?"

"Sure."

"How are you feeling?"

"Fine."

"Are you sure? You're not too tired?"

He just grinned. "I'm fine, Angel. Don't worry so much."

She winked at him as she picked up the phone to order some sandwiches. Colt was just turning back for his office when the President buzzed him and asked him to come into the Oval Office. He turned on his heel and marched back to the President's office, but not before reaching out and touching Casey's hair as he passed by. Still on the phone, she smiled at him as he continued on into the Oval Office.

Later that day, after downloading all of the images to his iPad, Colt's phone conveniently vanished.

No records, no trace, no suspicion. He bought a new one after work.

ELEVEN

HUNTER NANTZ HAD his mother's violet eyes and his father's blond good looks. While Brody was very friendly to the enormous Secret Service agent, Hunter wasn't so amiable. He was polite but seemed wary of the man, even through dinner. Colt tried to engage him in conversation a couple of times but it was clear that Hunter didn't want to talk to him. When the meal was over, Hunter fled to his room and shut the door.

Riley had plans that night so she left Casey to the dishes. Colt helped Casey in the kitchen, bringing her dirty dishes to put in the dishwasher and even wiping off the table for her. Brody, still the walking wounded with the cast on his arm, had an excuse not to help with the dishes as he sat in the family room and played video games. Colt could see the kid killing aliens from his post in the kitchen.

"You're a good cook," he told Casey. "That meatball and spinach soup was amazing. Where'd you learn to cook like that?"

Casey smiled up at him as she put the leftovers away. "My mother is a great cook," she said. "I guess I just carry on the tradition."

"Does your sister cook?"

Casey nodded as she closed the refrigerator door. "She does, and very well," she said. "You don't happen to have a single friend she can cook for, do you?"

He grinned. "I've got a few good friends, a group from my college days, but they're spread out all over the place," he said. "I really don't have many friends in D.C. Hell, I didn't have many friends growing up, either."

"Why not?"

He shrugged, leaning back against the kitchen counter with his big arms crossed over his chest. "I don't know," he said. "I was always kind of a big, quiet kid. Because I was so big, kids were scared of me so they stayed away. The more they stayed away, the more introverted I became. By the time I reached high school, I just had a couple of good friends and that was it. College was a little different because it was more of a level playing field, but growing up... not many friends at all."

Casey moved close to him, reaching up to run her fingers gently through the hair at his temple. "You're so sweet and grounded," she said. "You should have hundreds of friends. I can't believe you keep to yourself so much."

He eyed Brody as he reached out and put an arm around her waist, pulling her a little closer to him. "I think it was a self-perpetuating problem," he said. "People are scared of me so they stay away. Therefore, I keep to myself and do my own thing. It's no big deal. But I was captain of the football team in college and voted Best Couple."

She giggled. "With whom?"

Again, he shrugged. "My ex-wife was a cheerleader and we were voted Best Couple in one of those stupid student polls my senior year. She was really outgoing, very popular, so I just kind of followed along on her coattails."

Casey was still grinning. "Well, the title was well deserved," she told him. "But where did this 'Antichrist' nickname come from? Do you know I heard that term tossed around for three days before I ever knew your name?"

It was his turn to grin. "Oh, *that*," he said as he pulled her a little closer. "Look at me. I'm six feet five-and-a-half inches and around two hundred and seventy pounds. On my first assignment with Clinton, some guy was reaching to shake the President's hand but he had something in his palm. I couldn't quite see it because of the way he was holding it, kind of hidden-like, but it was just large enough to be a weapon, so I reached out and grabbed his arm. Turns out I busted it in three places. The guy was just trying to hand Clinton a pen in a box. But the broken arm was only the first of many."

Casey's eyebrows lifted. "You broke more arms?"

He nodded. "It happened with Clinton four times," he said. "Arms, wrists, people grabbing for the President and me stopping them. Finally, the Special Agent in Charge just started sending me out at the head of every detail, like a bodyguard protecting a rock star. I'd shove people back, restrain overzealous reporters, things like that. My reputation got around and when people saw me coming, they'd just scatter. Someone once said 'here comes the Antichrist' and it just kind of stuck."

She sighed heavily, shaking her head reproachfully. "You're better than that," she said. "You don't deserve that kind of reputation."

He didn't stop grinning. "It's gotten me a long way. I'd rather have people afraid of me than thinking they can run me over."

She found herself pulled into his embrace, gazing up at his handsome face. "I'm not afraid of you."

He winked at her. "I can see you're the one person I can't intimidate."

"Do you really want to?"

His features softened as he gazed into her beautiful face. "No," he said softly. "But I think I may intimidate Hunter a little."

Casey gave him a squeeze. "Give him time," she said softly. "He's very protective of his mom and, to tell you the truth, the only real experience he has with men around his mother is his father, and all he's seen of that is hurt. I've never once brought a date or a boyfriend home. Just give him time."

Colt nodded in understanding. "I want to make an effort with him but I don't want him to think I'm coming on too strong. What would you suggest?"

Casey cocked her head, thinking. Then she cast a long glance at Brody, battling aliens over in the family room. A twinkle came to her eye.

"Do you play video games?"

He shrugged. "Not really," he said, seeing where her attention was. "But I guess I can learn."

Casey grinned. "Come on."

Colt found himself seated on the couch next to a nine-year-old who was more than happy to explain to him the finer points of alien kill zones. Colt picked up the game fairly quickly, and he and Brody spent an hour very loudly killing off aliens as part of a colonial Marine force. Since Colt had spent time in the Marines, he was very much at home with the game and actually started to enjoy it. Casey sat on the couch beside him, her hand casually rubbing his back as he played. She loved the way he was bonding with Brody, showing interest in what interested him. As she watched, she fell more deeply in love with the man. She just couldn't help it.

As the battle went into the second hour of play, it got louder. Brody and Colt were becoming comrades-in-arms and Brody was having a great time. There were lots of "watch your back, dude!" or "behind you" from the players as they helped each other navigate the alien bombardment. As Casey sat back on the couch next to Colt, glass of wine in one hand and the other hand on Colt's back, Hunter suddenly appeared in the doorway.

Casey caught a glimpse of her oldest as he hovered in the door jamb. She glanced over at the boy.

"Hey, Hunt," she said casually. "Want to play?"

Hunter remained in the doorway, his eyes on the television. "I dunno," he shrugged, moving around the couch and giving the players a wide berth as he came to sit on his mother's opposite side. He plopped down next to her. "I could hear it all the way upstairs."

Casey knew that. It was for that reason that she had Brody and

Colt play the game. She shifted her wine glass to the other hand and wrapped an arm around her eldest.

"Grandma and Grandpa are flying in tomorrow for Thanksgiving," she hugged the boy. "Is your room all cleaned up for them?"

Hunter groaned. "Why do they have to sleep in my room?" he wanted to know. "Why can't they have Brody's room?"

Casey was patient. "They're not sleeping in your room," she said. "Aunt Riley is. Grandma and Grandpa are sleeping in her room."

"But I don't want to sleep in Brody's room," Hunter whined. "He snores."

"Then wear earplugs."

"Can I just sleep on the couch?"

Colt just finished a brutal kill by splashing alien guts all over the screen. As the game recalculated, he looked at Hunter and Casey.

"When I was about Hunter's age, my grandparents came out from Montana one year to spend Christmas with us," he said. "Mind you, I've got a younger brother and at that time in our lives, we had a real love/hate relationship. I was supposed to sleep in Kennedy's room and absolutely hated the idea because not only did he snore, but he just had one bed and I was expected to sleep with him in it. He kicked and thrashed around, so I really wasn't looking forward to it. Anyway, I concocted this elaborate plan so when we went to bed on Christmas Eve, I made a big deal about sleeping in the backyard in my Boy Scout tent so we could watch for Santa Claus. Ken got sucked into it, and we went outside, got into the sleeping bags, and waited for Santa."

Casey was grinning at him. "What happened?"

Colt cocked an eyebrow. "Now, mind you, I'm about eight, so I knew damn well there was no Santa, but Ken didn't yet. He was kind of on the cusp of getting too old to believe. Well, Ken falls asleep and I bailed from the tent, went inside, locked up all the doors, and got into his bed. I think it must have been the middle of the night when Ken woke up because it was freezing and realized I wasn't there. He tried to get into the house but I'd locked all the doors. He's so little that he's afraid to go walking around to the front of the house where the master bedroom and our parents slept, so he stands in the backyard and throws rocks at his bedroom window because he knew I was in there. He ended up busting the window and we both got in trouble. I didn't get my Christmas presents until New Year's."

Casey laughed softly and even Hunter grinned. Colt could see he had the boy's attention. "Do you have a tent or a dog house you could get your brother into?" he asked Hunter.

"Hey!" Brody turned to him, grinning. "I thought you were on my side."

Colt laughed at the kid. "Just kidding," he said. "If your brother kicks you out, just head over to my place. I've got a sixty-inch plasma screen that would make killing aliens feel like the real thing."

Brody was interested. "Really?" he asked, then looked at his mother. "Mom, can I stay with Colt while Grandma and Grandpa are here?"

Casey smiled at her youngest over the rim of her wineglass. "I don't think so," she replied. "Grandma and Grandpa will be disappointed if they don't get to see you. You need to stay here."

Disappointed, Brody turned to Colt. "Do you have any kids?"

Colt shook his head. "No," he replied. "No kids. Just a younger brother, three nephews and a niece."

"Oh." Brody's mind was recalculating like the game. "Are you sure you don't want a kid for Thanksgiving? I'll volunteer."

Colt grinned as Casey shushed her boy. "Actually, I have to work," he said. "Maybe I'll see you for leftovers."

"Why are you working?" Brody wanted to know. "My mom has the day off and you work with her. Isn't everyone taking the day off?"

Colt shrugged and sat back against the couch. "My job is a little different from your mom's. I don't follow a normal work schedule."

"You got shot." Hunter was suddenly in the conversation, completely off the subject. His violet eyes were intense on Colt. "My mom said you were a hero."

Colt looked at the young boy, with fine features like his mother. "I did my job," he replied modestly. "I'm paid to protect the President and that's what I did."

"Did it hurt?" Brody wanted to know.

Colt gave the kid a half-grin. "I didn't even feel it."

"Seriously?" Brody was awed.

Casey shook her head, interrupting. "Of course he felt it," she sounded like she was scolding both Colt and Brody. "He got shot, for heaven's sake. He could have been killed."

As Colt put his hand on her knee to soothe her, Hunter moved onto the floor next to his brother so he could see Colt a little better.

"Do you wear a vest?" he wanted to know. "My dad does."

Colt lifted an eyebrow, glancing at Casey. "What does your dad do?"

"He's a state trooper."

"Oh." Colt hadn't known that. He focused on Hunter's question. "Yes, I wear a vest."

"Mom said you got shot in the neck and in the leg."

"Everywhere the vest didn't cover."

"Were you scared?"

Colt's smile was back. "I wasn't thinking about being scared," he said honestly. "I was just thinking about making sure the President was safe."

"Oh." Hunter pondered that. He seemed to be warming to Colt in just the slightest way, a good sign. "How did you get to be in the Secret Service?"

"I applied when I got out of the Marine Corps."

"What did you do in the Marines?"

Colt shifted on the couch and ended up leaning against Casey, who casually put her hand on his left thigh.

"I was with the 3rd Light Armored Infantry division in charge of the 2nd Weapons Platoon," he replied. "When I graduated from the Naval Academy, I was stationed in Somalia for a while before moving to Iraq. We saw a lot of action there. I was in the Marines until I joined the Secret Service, and my first assignment was Clinton's last year in office."

Both Hunter and Brody were all ears. "Did you kill a lot of people in Iraq?" Brody wanted to know.

Before Casey could scold him, Colt answered. "You know," he said evenly, thoughtfully. "I think a lot of people think that's all we did, go in and kill Iraqis, but that's not what we did at all. For the most part, the Iraqi people were very gracious and kind to us. I made some good friends over there. I also lost some good friends over there. The bad guys, Saddam Hussein's guys, would take kids your age and make them fight. That was a problem. If I saw a kid your age coming at me with a gun, I knew he meant to kill me. So what am I going to do? Not defend myself because a kid with a gun is trying to kill me? Things like that still haunt me."

By this time, the boys were very serious, as was Casey. "Did you kill some kids?" Brody asked.

Colt took a long, slow breath. "If I'd had any other choice, I wouldn't have," he said softly. "One kid put a bullet in my gut. He was about seven years old. As I lay on the ground, his fifteen-year-old sister tried to put a bullet in my brain. It was the worst thing I'd ever seen. There's an old saying that war is hell. It really is. I know, because I lived it."

Casey squeezed his leg. "Whoa," she murmured, smiling at him when he looked at her. "That's pretty heavy stuff for a nine-year-old and a twelve-year-old."

Colt looked at her. "Why?" he wasn't arguing with her but it was a legitimate question. "You let them play video games where they're smearing alien guts and brains all over the screen. You don't think that's pretty heavy stuff, too?"

Her smile faded. "It's just a game."

He lifted his eyebrows at her but refrained from saying anything more. He could already see that it was something they weren't going to agree on and he didn't want to spar with her. He returned his focus to the boys.

"I like doing what I do," he told them, diverting the subject somewhat because he could see that Casey wasn't thrilled with his topic of choice. "Have you guys thought about what you want to do when you grow up?"

Brody shrugged, and turned back to the television with his controller. "I want to do Black Ops."

Colt shook his head regretfully. "No, you don't. You really don't."

Hunter jumped in, taking the other controller. "I want to be a state trooper like my dad."

"That's a good goal," Colt agreed.

The conversation died as the boys returned to the alien-killing game. Colt sat back on the couch with Casey, discreetly gathering her fingers off his thigh and holding her hand when the boys weren't looking. She leaned against him, snuggling, as they watched the boys protect the world from alien invaders. She ended up handing him her half-full glass of wine, which he finished off, all the while cuddling with her. It was as heavenly and satisfying as he could have imagined. It made him want it forever.

Hunter Nantz wasn't so standoffish with Colt the next time he met up with him.

———

Nick and Janice Cleburne flew in two days before Thanksgiving to spend the holiday with their two children and two grandchildren. Because of her work schedule, Casey didn't see them a whole lot but the boys did, hanging out with their grandparents as their mother and aunt worked. She didn't get a chance to introduce them to Colt at all because he was tied up with the President for those two days, which in hindsight, was probably best considering Casey hadn't been able to talk to her parents about Colt and break them in a little. She wanted to give them plenty of time to get used to the idea of a Sheridan in the family.

Because of this, Colt didn't come over late at night like he usually did. He didn't want to chance running into the parents. He went home after he was finished with his shift but he couldn't sleep, not without Casey in his arms, so he would sit up and work until the early morning hours.

He spent all of one night organizing the images he took of the President's bank statements and emailing the woman who wrote the article about Talbot's alleged cartel connections. He'd been so swept up with Casey and her boys that he hadn't done anything with the images or the newspaper reporter. If he was going to keep Meade and the old boys off his back, he was going to have to do what he had been assigned to do, but he was increasingly reluctant to do it. He was just going through the motions. He wanted out.

But it wasn't meant to be, at least not right away. The woman who wrote the article back in the late nineties about Talbot's cartel connections emailed him the day before Thanksgiving, and on his lunch break he called the woman with a disposable cell phone he'd purchased in Alexandria. He gave her a phony story about how he was from the Washington Post and that he wanted more information on the article she had written.

The woman, Katy Ross, was reluctant at first but ended up agreeing to meet with him. The only time she could do it was on Thanksgiving Day because she now lived in Hawai'i and this was her only day in New Mexico with her family before returning home. Colt made some swift arrangements to cover his shift on Thanksgiving Day and agreed to fly to Albuquerque to talk to her. She wouldn't do it any other way; not by phone and nothing in writing. It was face to face or nothing.

Thanksgiving Day, he was up well before dawn. His flight didn't leave until nine in the morning, which would have him in Albuquerque at ten o'clock given the time difference. He would meet Katy at the airport and had two hours with her until his flight departed back for D.C. He'd get back home around six in the evening, plenty of time for him to head over to see Casey.

He went to the gym down the street and worked out for about an hour, emerging from the gym to see that it was still dark, although the eastern sky was just starting to turn shades of pink. As he made his way up the street back to his townhome, his cell phone went off in his gym bag and he unzipped it, pulling the phone out of a pocket. The caller I.D. was Casey.

"Hi, Angel," he answered as fast as he could. "What are you doing up so early?"

"I've been up for a while," she sounded sleepy. "It would seem that I just can't sleep anymore if you're not next to me."

He grinned. "I've been thinking the same thing," he said softly. "I miss you so much."

"I miss you, too," she whispered. "Can you have breakfast with me?"

He glanced at his watch. "Sure," he replied. "It'll have to be quick, but as long as I get to see you, I'm fine with that. It'll be the best part of my day."

"Then I'll come to you since I know you need to get to work," she said. "Is there someplace close to you?"

He could see his townhome down the street. "There's a café about three blocks from my house," he said. "It's on P Street NW near Dupont Circle."

"What's it called?"

"The D.C. Café."

"I'm on my way."

He smiled. "Good," he said softly. "I love you. I'll see you over there."

They hung up and he hurried back to his townhome for a quick shower and a change of clothes. In less than twenty minutes, he was showered and dressed, heading over to the café only to see that it was closed. Being Thanksgiving Day, he wasn't surprised. It should have occurred to him. When he saw Casey's big, black

SUV pull up behind him and park, he got out of his car and went back to her.

Casey was already climbing out and they came together on the dawn-hued street, sharing a very passionate kiss. Colt hugged her so tightly that he was sure he was breaking bones.

"Hi, Angel," he whispered into her hair. "God, I've missed you."

Casey clung to him. "I don't like this," she confessed. "I don't like it when I don't get to see you very much. I feel so lost."

He cupped her face in his big hands, kissing her cheeks, her lips. "I don't want to do this anymore," he whispered between kisses. "Tell your parents about us or I will. I'm not going to spend another night away from you."

She stared at him. Then she started giggling. "My dad might not take it too well."

"I don't give a damn."

She continued to laugh. "I'll tell him today," she promised, returning his kisses. "You can come over tonight when you're finished with your shift."

"Swear?"

"I swear."

He smiled at her for the first time. "Good," he stopped kissing and hugging her long enough to point to the café. "They're closed for Thanksgiving. Have any other ideas?"

She turned to look at him. "We can go back to your place. If you have eggs and coffee, I'll make us some breakfast."

His smile grew. "I don't think I do, but we can swing by somewhere and get some."

They did, at a convenience store down the street. Casey followed Colt to his townhome, a place she had become familiar with while he had been recovering from his bullet wounds. It was a two-story brownstone built at the turn of the last century and absolutely beautiful. The townhome had one bedroom, one bath, but was very big and roomy, and sparingly decorated because a bachelor lived there. There was a couch, a giant flat screen television, and a gigantic bed that was neatly made. It looked like it had never been slept in.

He also had a very nice kitchen with granite countertops and new fixtures, but very few pots and pans. As Casey got organized to make their breakfast, Colt began to remove his clothing.

"Sorry I don't have much in the kitchen," he said. "I don't cook at all."

Casey grinned as she put the frying pan on the stove. "I think I've cooked on this stove more than you have and I've only done it twice."

He laughed softly, pulling off his tie and throwing it over the dining room chair. "This is a kitchen meant for you and only you. I'll never let anyone else cook here, ever."

"You'd better not."

They grinned at each other as she beat at the eggs, paying attention to what she was doing and not noticing that he had taken off his dress shirt and white t-shirt. As she prepared the eggs for the frying pan, Colt stripped off his pants, shoes, socks and briefs. Just as Casey was preparing to put the eggs in the pan, he walked up behind her, stark naked, and put his arms around her.

"I don't want to eat," he murmured, kissing her ear. "I just want you."

Wrapped up in his enormous embrace, Casey put her hands back to feel for him and realized her hands were meeting with bare flesh. In fact, she could feel his arousal on the small of her back. Without another word, she turned in his arms and lifted her mouth to him for a kiss. Mouths fused, Colt managed to turn off the burner as he picked her up and carried her into his bedroom. The eggs were forgotten in the bowl.

As dawn broke, Casey's clothes came off and Colt nursed hungrily at her breasts as she tried to pull her jeans off. He eventually let go of her long enough to help her disrobe, but he was back on her the moment she was nude, his big body covering hers, his hands stroking her. Casey was so highly aroused that by the time he thrust into her, she was already climaxing and Colt made love to her as the sun rose, feeling her multiple orgasms before taking his own.

Fulfilled, content, and utterly in love, he kissed her sweetly as their passion cooled, touching her soft skin and luxurious hair, so completely happy for the first time in his life. But as he kissed her neck, he caught sight of the clock from the corner of his eye. He stopped kissing her and sighed heavily.

"Damn," he whispered. "I'm going to be late if I don't get out of here."

Casey had her arms around his neck, craning her head back to look at the clock. It was almost seven in the morning. She lightly slapped his tight bare buttocks.

"Get up," she told him. "You can't be late."

He was back to nuzzling her neck and sucking on her earlobe. "I don't want to leave," he murmured. "I want to stay here with you."

She smacked his butt again, harder. "You can't," she said. "Get up, Sheridan. Duty calls."

He was still on top of her, his big face looming above hers. "I know," he muttered. "But... I love you, Casey. I love you so much. I don't ever want this moment to end."

She reached up, stroking his face. "Me, either," she whispered. "I love you, too."

He gazed at her a moment longer before kissing her, very sweetly, on the lips. Then he pushed himself off of her and climbed off the bed. As he went into the other room for his clothes, Casey got out of bed and found hers. She pulled on her underwear and her jeans, finally her long sleeved t-shirt. As she wandered into the dining area outside of the bedroom on the hunt for her shoes, she noticed that Colt was already completely dressed. All he was doing was fussing with his dark tie. Casey found her shoes, slipped them on, and went to stand in front of him. She ran a hand down his finely tailored arm.

"Nice suit," she commented. "In fact, you always dress extremely well. You must spend a fortune on clothes."

He grinned. "What else do I have to spend it on?" he wanted to know. "I don't have a wife or kids – yet – so my money is spent on me. Clothes reflect the man and in my position, it's important to project a certain image. So I wear Armani suits and Kenneth Cole shoes."

"And you look fabulous," she agreed, then looked at him wistfully. "I'm going to miss you today."

Still fixing his tie, he bent over and kissed her. "I'll miss you, too," he said softly. "But I'll see you tonight, I promise."

She smiled at him, watching him finish with his tie and pull on his expensive overcoat. Pulling on her own coat, she collected her purse and followed him out of the house. When they got down to the street, he wrapped his arms around her and kissed her again. After a long, sweet hug, he took her hand and led her around to the driver's side of her car. Casey unlocked it and he opened the door.

"Get in," he told her.

She climbed in, kissing him yet again. "Love you," she said. "Have a good day."

He couldn't seem to stop touching her face or kissing her soft lips. He couldn't seem to make himself pull away from her.

"You, too," he murmured against her lips. "I'll see you tonight, I promise."

She smiled at him as he closed her door and went back to his car, parked behind her. Casey pulled away from the curb, watching him in her rear-view mirror as he made a u-turn and went in the other direction. As she drove away, she lifted her hands, smelling him on her flesh, and her heart fluttered wildly. She never knew it was possible to love someone so much, without reserve or fear. All of the love stories that had ever been written couldn't do justice to what she felt for Colt or what he meant to her. She felt like the most fortunate woman on the planet.

Not surprisingly, Nick Cleburne didn't take the news of a Sheridan in their midst too well.

———

The West Wing was fairly empty of people at two o'clock on Thanksgiving Day. Casey entered through the main entrance, greeting the uniformed Secret Service officer at the desk. Dressed in a form-fitting suede jacket with fleecy white trim, skinny jeans and sexy knee-high leather boots with a spiked heel, she looked delicious with her luscious hair pulled back in a stylish pony tail and a big picnic basket in her hands. Even the uniformed officer gave her a second look as she walked past him. *Casey Cleburne is one fine lady,* he thought, eyeing her with appreciation.

Heading back to her office, she was surprised to see Chris Eckart at his desk. She was also a little disappointed. Peering into Colt's office, she noticed it was empty.

"Where is everybody?" she asked, setting the picnic basket on her desk.

Chris was in jeans and an old shirt, working on his computer. "The President went to church at noon. They're eating now up in the family apartments. What are you doing here?"

Casey didn't want to ask him if he knew where Colt was but her mere presence here was awkward now. She sat down at her desk and put the basket on the floor behind her.

"I came to work on a couple of things now that it's so quiet and everyone is occupied," she lied. "What are *you* doing here?"

Chris shrugged, his eyes glued to the computer screen. "I don't have any family around here," he said. "I came to clean up some files and get some work done. Actually, I'm glad you're here. I want to show you something."

Casey really didn't have any patience for him but she dutifully stood up and went over to his desk. "What?"

He turned one of his two monitors in her direction. He began pointing at the screen, which just looked like a picture of the corner of his desk.

"I have a webcam on my desk so when I'm away, I can see if anyone has been screwing with my stuff," he told her.

Casey fought off a smile. "Isn't that a little paranoid?"

He grunted. "No," he replied frankly. "Last year, I found that a couple of aides had been messing with my computer, logging on and getting on to porn websites and stuff. They were trying to get me fired but it backfired on them, those bastards, so I've always had this webcam taking shots of my desk. It's come in handy."

Casey did grin, then. "Okay, so you got the last laugh," she pointed at the screen. "What do you want to show me?"

He clicked on what was apparently a video and all she could see was his desk, his computer area, and then she noticed that her desk was in the shot. It was mostly the bottom part of her desk, from about the desktop down, and it only mostly showed the underside of her desk. Still, she could clearly see the storage boxes that contained the President's old bank statements. Suddenly, someone sat in her chair and began pulling out files from the storage boxes. Casey's eyes widened.

"Hey," she pointed at the screen. "Who's that?"

Chris held up a finger. "Wait for it."

They did, for about a minute. Then the suited figure bent over enough so that the head was in the shot, in profile, and Chris paused the recording. Casey's eyes widened even more when she realized who it was.

"Sheridan?" she breathed in disbelief.

Chris nodded. "Exactly what I said." He rolled the recording and they could both see Colt digging through the boxes and pulling out files. "Why would he be at your desk rummaging through files?"

Because of the angle of the camera, they couldn't see what he was doing once he pulled the files out, but he very rapidly went through all three boxes, pulling out files, replacing them, and pulling out more. Casey was confused more than anything but along with that confusion, she was beginning to feel sick. Why would he be going through file boxes containing Russ' old bank and investment statements? What could he possibly be looking for? The more she watched, the more upset she became because she realized it went on for quite some time. He never touched her desk drawers as far as she could see and he never moved to her file cabinets, but he was very interested in old records. Great angst began to swamp her but she fought it. She didn't want to show any real reaction in front of Chris.

"How long is this recording?" she asked him, realizing her voice was trembling.

"About twenty-five minutes," he said. "What's he doing?"

Casey's mind was whirling and she struggled to give him an answer, any answer, that wouldn't have him running off and telling someone. She didn't want any of this getting around.

"I... I, uh, asked him to help me with a project," she moved away from the monitor; she couldn't look at it anymore. "That must be what he's looking for."

"What project?" Chris wanted to know.

"None of your business," she snapped. "It's something for the President. Where is Sheridan, anyway? Have you seen him around?"

Chris shook his head. "He's not working today."

Casey froze at her desk, her heart suddenly leaping into her throat. "I thought he was scheduled."

Chris was messing around with his monitor. "Harrios has the detail today. Sheridan is off."

"Are you sure?"

"Positive. Harrios told me when he was down here earlier in Sheridan's office."

"Oh." Casey was ready to burst into tears right at that moment. She had to get out of there before she made a fool of herself, so she grabbed a couple of folders off her desk and crammed them into the picnic basket to pretend that she had what she had come for. "Well, I'd better get home. I guess I'll see you on Monday."

Chris looked up as she made a break for the office door. "What do you want me to do with this recording?"

Casey paused in the doorway. Everything about her was trembling and it was a struggle for her to remain calm as she answered him. She wanted to erupt but she fought it.

"Just erase it," she said as steadily as she could. "I'm not worried about it since he was... um, helping me... with a project...."

Chris just shrugged and went back to his computer as Casey very quickly headed out of the West Wing. She couldn't even think at the moment. She was beginning to feel like the biggest fool in the world and the mere thought that Colt had been playing her had her shattered as she had never been shattered in her life. She was cracking and pieces of her were bleeding out all over the place, leaving a trail of heartbreak. She practically ran to her car and tossed the picnic basket in the back, slamming her car door and turning the key as the painful tears came.

Body wracking sobs hit her. She couldn't drive. She couldn't see. All she could feel was betrayal. *He had lied to her.* He wasn't working at all. Turning off the car, she climbed into the back seat and wept until she could weep no more. As the sun set over the capital of the United States of America, Casey passed out from sheer exhaustion in the back seat of her car.

When her cell phone rang around six thirty in the evening and she saw that it was Colt, she threw the phone over the side of the parking structure.

———

"I don't even know why I agreed to talk to you," the woman said. "Last time this subject came up, I think someone tried to kill me."

Colt was sitting in the Southwest Grille in Isleta Pueblo, New Mexico, about ten miles south of Albuquerque's International Sunport. The town was a little dusty, and the Grille was more of a dive than an actual restaurant, but it was the only place Katy would meet him. In jeans, cowboy boots, a big cowboy hat and dark sunglasses, Colt didn't look anything like his usual self as he sat in the booth opposite the hesitant woman. He was a reporter from the Washington Post and that's all she needed to know.

"I read your article," he avoided the assassination comment. "Thanks for taking the time to talk with me about it. I won't keep you long, I promise, but I'm doing some research for an article of my own and I want to know how you came across all of this information on Talbot."

Katy was a small woman with a bob haircut, looking a little bit like the old silent screen star Louise Brooks with the shape of her face against the haircut. She was clearly uncomfortable with the subject matter.

"Look," she lowered her voice seriously. "I'm just a journalist. I don't have any political ambitions. All I wanted was the truth, and the truth is that my photographer friend took pictures of Russell Talbot at a private airstrip near Socorro meeting with guys who flew in on a plane registered in Bogota, Colombia."

Colt listened with interest. "That's what your article said," he replied. "But I want to know what makes you think that plane was part of the Colombian drug cartel and why you think President Talbot was involved with them?"

Katy looked around to make sure no one was listening. "You're sure you weren't followed?"

"I wasn't followed. Just tell me what you know."

She sighed heavily. "I was a freelance reporter back then," she said quietly. "My photographer friend – he was my boyfriend at the time – was an amateur astronomer and he used to do a lot of hiking back in the mountains near Magdalena Ridge. One day, he's up in the foothills and sees this plane fly in. There were trucks there to meet the plane and he saw them offloading packages and loading them into the trucks. He saw it twice more on his hikes up there. Then, he started taking pictures with a telephoto lens because he thought they might be smugglers and he wanted to turn them over to the cops."

"Did he?"

Katy shook her head. "One day, we got to examining the pictures," she said. "I had a friend at the Department of Motor Vehicles and asked her to run some of the license plates on the trucks. Turns out they were registered to Erik Travis, who's a huge supporter of Russ Talbot. He also owns the land that the planes were landing on and I think his son now works for the President. Anyway, one day I decided to go with my boyfriend on his hike and we saw another plane land so we began taking pictures. When we developed them, we saw Russ Talbot as plain as day driving one of the trucks. After I wrote the article of my suspicions, some men came to our house, tore the place up, broke the cameras, and destroyed all of the film they could get their hands on. They told us that if we didn't forget what we saw then they'd burn the place down over our heads and make it look like an accident. I didn't believe them until they beat my boyfriend up so badly that he had to have surgery."

Colt sighed. "Did they ever identify themselves?"

Katy shook her head, edgy with the bad memories. "Never," she said quietly. "But I saw Russ Talbot on television a few weeks later and one of those men was on television with him, like his bodyguard or something. Whoever they were worked for Russ when he was governor of New Mexico."

Colt pondered the information, pausing when the waitress brought them a couple of Cokes. When the waitress wandered away, he leaned forward onto the table with his hands folded thoughtfully.

"So you believe, based on what you saw, that then-Governor Russell Talbot was allowing drug smugglers to land their planes in the New Mexico desert?"

Katy nodded firmly. "Yessir," she replied. "I saw it with my own eyes."

"Do you remember the time period?"

"I saw it myself in September of 1998," she said. "My boyfriend saw it several more times prior to that. Russell Talbot is crooked, Mr. Sheridan, and that's the truth."

Colt sat back in the booth, scratching his scalp beneath the big cowboy hat. After a moment, he took the glasses off and set them on the tabletop, wiping the sweat from around his eyes and digesting everything he'd been told. It only confirmed what they'd already heard.

"It's too bad all of the photos were destroyed," he said regretfully. "I would have liked to have seen them."

"What would you do with them if you *did* see them?"

Colt wriggled his eyebrows. "Use them."

"For what?"

"For whatever I had to do. Maybe my article will succeed where yours didn't."

He took a sip of his cola. As he did, Katy dug into her backpack and pulled forth a wrinkled, white envelope, setting it on the table between them. It was worn and dirty, and Colt eyed it.

"What's that?" he asked.

For the first time since they met, Katy seemed to loosen up. A faint smile came to her red-hued lips.

"They didn't get everything," she whispered. "Good luck."

TWELVE

IT WAS ALMOST eleven o'clock at night when Riley's cell phone rang. The number was restricted but she answered it anyway.

"Hello?" she practically shouted.

There was a long pause on the other end of the line. "Riley?" It was a deep male voice. "This is Colt Sheridan. Is Casey there?"

"No!" Riley was in a panic. "She left around two this afternoon and we can't find her. She hasn't called or anything."

Standing in his living room, Colt's worst fears were confirmed. He'd spent the past five hours calling Casey's cell phone every five minutes, but it went straight to voicemail. He'd finally called a guy he knew who worked for Verizon and was able to get Riley's number, but now her panic was feeding his. He felt like he couldn't breathe.

"Where did she say she was going?" he asked with more calm than he felt, moving to find his coat.

"She didn't," Riley sounded as if she was verging on tears. "She kept saying how bad she felt that you were working today, so she made some turkey sandwiches and took off. I assumed she was going to find you. She didn't find you?"

Colt's stomach dropped to his knees. "Did she say she was going to the White House?"

"No," Riley was losing her battle against tears. "But she kept talking about you and how it wasn't fair that you didn't get any turkey. When I asked her where she was going, she grinned and was really cagey about it, you know? I think she was going to surprise you with some turkey. Oh, my God... are you saying she never made it to the White House?"

Colt's heart was thumping so strongly against his chest that he felt faint. He couldn't remember ever feeling such terror, grasping the closet door for support as he tried to pull out his coat.

"Did you call the cops?" he demanded.

"Yes," Riley replied. "They won't take a Missing Persons report until it's been twenty-four hours. She'll be dead in twenty-four hours!"

"Like hell," he growled. "Riley, listen to me. I'm going to go look for her, okay? I've got more resources at my disposal than the cops do. I'm going to find her. You said that you think she went to the White House?"

"I think she was going to surprise you with turkey because you had to work."

Colt managed to get his coat on one arm, swearing softly as he thought of Casey going to the White House when he wasn't even there. He struggled to pull his thoughts together.

"I'll start there," he said. "You stay home and call me if she calls you, okay?"

"Okay," Riley agreed, feeling vastly better now that Colt Sheridan was on the hunt for Casey. "I'll let you know right away if she calls."

"Thanks," he said, grabbing his keys. "I'll call you in a bit."

He hung up and bolted from his townhome, out to the garage where his car was. He peeled down his driveway, throwing the car into gear once he hit the street and tearing off towards the White House.

His first thought was to hit their parking garage to see if her car was there. He didn't know where else to start. As he blew through red lights and raced to the neighborhood surrounding the White

House, he struggled with all of the panic he was feeling; panic for Casey's safety, panic that she may have discovered he had lied to her about working on Thanksgiving, wondering what in the hell he was going to tell her. God, he hated himself for having been put in this position but he hated Meade more. He hated that old man for giving the orders, for forcing the directives. But the truth was that Colt had no one to blame but himself. He was responsible for his own actions.

Up until the past few weeks, his career had been perfect. No slip ups, not even a minor mistake. Everything had been as it should be. But the introduction of Casey Cleburne had changed everything and suddenly, he wasn't thinking of his career anymore or the secret directives he'd been tasked with. He'd only been thinking of her and of this wonderful life he'd never known to exist. He wanted nothing more than to settle down with her and have a few children, watching them grown, taking them to soccer games or putting Band-Aids on scraped knees. It's what he wanted most in the world but he didn't realize that until recently. Casey had changed his whole life.

He swung around a corner and the parking garage loomed off to his left. He drove up to the ticket box and swiped his card, waiting impatiently while the arm lifted. Then he tore up the ramp, heading to the third level and immediately seeing Casey's SUV by the staircase on the far end. He gunned it across the garage, squealing to a halt next to her car. Throwing his vehicle in park, he bailed out of the still-running car and ran to Casey's driver's side window.

The front seats were empty and he couldn't help the panicked little gasp that escaped his lips. But in the darkness, he could see her purse in the passenger seat and he'd never felt so much dread in his entire life. He tried to open the door but it was locked. Just as he tried the door to the back seat, he saw movement in the darkness. Something was moving in the car and as he strained to see, he could make out a pair of legs with boots. Someone was lying in the back seat.

"Casey!" he shouted, pounding on the window. "Angel, open the door!"

She didn't move. Seized with terror, Colt ran back to his car, popped the trunk, and emerged with a tire iron. Racing to the driver's window, he smashed through it with one powerful swing.

Inside the car, he could hear a scream. Reaching in through the broken glass, he unlocked the doors. Tossing the tire iron aside, he threw open the back door about the time Casey was sitting up. Her face was extremely pale, makeup smeared all over her cheeks. She looked like hell and Colt stood in the open door, his expression wide and frightened.

"Angel, what happened?" he demanded softly. "Why are you here? Everyone is worried about you."

Casey just stared at him. As he watched, her features dissolved into tears and she suddenly turned away from him, huddling up in a ball against the opposite door as if cowering from him. He climbed inside and she screamed at him.

"No," she shouted. "Don't come in here. Leave me alone!"

He was sitting behind the driver's seat, watching her with big eyes. His heart was pounding so hard in his chest that he seriously thought it might break. He was frightened and confused.

"Casey, what's wrong?" he begged softly. "Please tell me; what happened?"

Casey was collapsed against the opposite door, sobbing her heart out. "Oh, my God," she wept. "How... how could you do this to me?"

His breathing began to quicken. "Do what?" he pleaded. "What did I do?"

She wept to the point of hysteria. "You... you lied to me," she gasped. "You said you were working today but you weren't. I came to bring you turkey because I felt sorry for you and you were nowhere to be found. You lied to me."

Colt's jaw ticked as he closed his eyes, feeling sick and ashamed. He went to open his mouth and say something, anything, but Casey whirled on him. Despondent, she was full of venom.

"Chris has video of you going through the boxes at my desk," she hissed, "Boxes that contain Russ' personal financial information. You went through the records, all of them. Why? What were you doing, Colt? You had no reason on God's good earth to be digging through those boxes, but you were. Why? What else have you been lying to me about?"

Shocked at the accusation, Colt struggled to recover. He thought he'd been so careful about everything, knowing security placement and every detail of the office, but it never occurred to him that there was a camera, somewhere, that he had missed. *Damn!*

"Angel, listen to me," he begged hoarsely. "It's not what you think. It's not...."

"Don't call me that," she screamed at him. "I'm not your angel. I'm just someone you slept with and lied to. God knows why. I never did anything to hurt you, Colt, not one goddamn thing, but you still lied to me and told me you loved me. Why did you do it? Why did you treat me like that?"

She was hysterical and for good reason. He didn't blame her in the least. So he just sat there, listening to her cry, feeling like the lowest form of human life.

As he pondered the situation, he found himself weighing what was more important - Meade's directive or Casey's love. It took him about two seconds to realize that it was Casey. It was all about Casey. He couldn't live without her. Therefore, he had to trust her. He had to trust her and pray it didn't backfire on him.

"Casey," he said softly, calmly. "I'll tell you what's going on, but you need to slow down. I know you're upset, Angel, but please calm down. It's important."

"Who is she?" she acted like she hadn't heard him. "Just tell me who it is. Who were you with today?"

He didn't say anything. He just sat there, listening to her weep, hoping she would cry herself out and begin to calm down so they could carry on a rational conversation. As it was, she was far gone

with devastation and he didn't want their conversation to deterio-
rate into a shouting match, saying things they didn't mean just to
be hurtful. So he sat and waited.

Casey cried until there was nothing left. Then she went
through a series of dry heaves, absolutely distraught and exhausted.
Colt watched her, painfully, feeling horrible and disgusted with
himself to have caused her such agony. After what seemed like
ages, she stopped weeping and gagging, and just sat huddled up
against the door. Her eyes were closed and she was breathing in
swift little pants. The storm had passed for the time being.

"Casey, I want you to listen to me," Colt finally said, his voice
soft with emotion. "Angel, there *is* no one else. There has never
been anyone else. There has only been you and there will only ever
be you until I die. I love you and only you, I swear."

Casey's eyes slowly opened. Colt could see it. She was staring
at the floor of the car as she spoke. "Then where were you today?"

"In New Mexico."

The information didn't register for a moment. Then, she
blinked as if suddenly understanding him and she lifted her head,
fixing him with her dark-circled eyes.

"New *Mexico*?" she repeated. "What in the world were you
doing there?"

He gazed at her steadily. "Casey, I swear I will tell you the
absolute truth about everything. It's your choice whether or not
you believe me, but everything I'm about to tell you is God's honest
truth. Do you understand me?"

She was sitting up by this point, gazing steadily at him. She
looked so very tired.

"Why did you lie to me?" she asked, her voice soft and hoarse.

He sighed faintly. "If there had been another way, I wouldn't
have. I had no choice."

She wasn't buying it. He could tell. She shook her head and
averted her gaze and, feeling rather desperate, he continued.

"I know you're upset," he said softly. "You have every right to be. I deserve the screaming and the distrust. But what I'm about to tell you can't leave your lips or my life might be in jeopardy. Are you with me so far?"

She nodded her head, barely, and he quickly continued before he lost his audience.

"My family name stands for something, just like yours does," he explained. "My dad was in the army, as was my grandfather, and on back. When I graduated from the Naval Academy, my dad started talking to me about some really weird stuff. He started telling me stories that sounded like they came out of a James Bond movie, spies and secret weapons and crazy people wanting to take over the world. I thought it was just my dad making up stories but I came to find out that those stories my dad told were about him. *He* did all of that crazy stuff. I didn't believe him but my mother confirmed it. My dad did more stuff during the Cold War to keep the United States safe than you can possibly imagine."

Casey was looking at him again, all braced up against the door still. She looked like she was recoiling from him and he didn't like that feeling one bit.

"Anyway," he went on, "when I graduated from the Naval Academy, my dad took me to meet up with some of the people he had been working for. The meeting was so cloak and dagger that it was unbelievable, but I became acquainted with a covert branch of the Central Intelligence Agency with unlimited resources and power. This group has access to files and laboratories and information that are beyond the realm of comprehension. It's a super-secret domain of the CIA that grew into something they can no longer control, and it's something as far-reaching as you can imagine."

Casey was listening to him seriously, torn between disbelief and curiosity. "Really?"

"Really."

"Who are they?"

"They call themselves The Core."

"I've never heard of them."

He snorted softly. "No, you wouldn't have," he murmured. "To mention their name anywhere inside the walls of Washington D.C. is pretty much a death sentence. Anyone who knows about them, and openly speaks about them, is dealt with. They're *that* powerful."

Casey was calming somewhat but along with the calm, she was starting to feel some apprehension. "So why are you telling me?"

"It's where the term 'Antichrist' came from. Those who first called me that are dead. Those who continue to call me that don't have any idea how I really got the name."

Fear was creeping into her veins. "Colt, now you're scaring me."

He smiled gently at her. "I'm not trying to, Angel. I'm just trying to explain everything to you so you understand that I haven't been deliberately lying to you and I certainly haven't been cheating on you."

"Go on."

He shifted in the car seat so he could move closer to her. She was still pressed up against the passenger door. Carefully, he put a hand on her booted food. He just wanted to touch her.

"Because of my dad, I was recruited into this group," he said softly. "I've been doing their dirty work for over twelve years, spying, counter-spying, taking care of problems when they arise, and doing the occasional snuff job."

Her eyes widened. "You *what*?"

He could see she was getting upset again and he stroked her booted foot. "Black Ops," he whispered. "That career that Brody seems to want. Trust me when I tell you he doesn't want it."

Her eyes were filling with tears again. "You're an assassin?"

He sighed heavily and hung his head, gripping her foot. "I'm a lot of things," he confirmed, lifting his head to look her in the eye. "I've done it all, Casey. These people have connections like you can't believe. When I got out of the Marines, they got me a fairly well-placed job with the CIA, where I ended up ratting out a high-placed official who had been selling secrets to Venezuela. When the Venezuelans sent agents to dust this guy, I had to take care of the entire cell. It was... messy. Then, I was moved into the Secret Service to get close to Clinton during Whitewater. I was the one who provided enough information to convict Clinton's business partners in the fraudulent scheme and also enough evidence to convince the man who succeeded Clinton as the governor of Arkansas. The Core wanted to nail Clinton himself but I was never able to get enough evidence on him."

Casey's tears had faded as she listened to him. "So... you're a spy?"

He shrugged. "Kind of," he said. "I was with Obama for several years because the man is linked with Chicago politics and, as we all know, crooked as hell. But we could never get anything tangible so for a while, they moved me into arms dealing. I was in Russia for a year or so shadowing Putin. That guy's crazy-crooked. He runs that entire country like his own private Mafia gang."

She was becoming more interested in what he was saying. "Do you speak Russian?"

He nodded faintly. "*Eu vorbesc foarte fluent si daca poti sa ma inteleaga, atunci stii cit te iubesc.*"

"What did you just say?"

"That I love you very much."

The wariness returned to her expression. "Then tell me why you were going through Russ' files and why you lied to me about today."

He sighed. "With everything that I've told you, you should probably see a pattern in my presence."

She cocked her head as she thought on his statement. Then it occurred to her. "Are you spying on Russ?" she asked, shocked.

He didn't say anything for a moment. Then, he reached out his hand to her. She gazed at his open palm a moment before shaking her head.

"Not until you tell me everything."

Pain flickered across his expression and he lowered his hand. "Casey, angel, you need to understand that if anyone knows who I really am or what I really do, I won't live to see the sunrise," he said softly. "If I tell you everything, my life is literally in your hands. Fellow Core agents don't even know each other for the most part. It's too dangerous if we do. There are a lot of people who would like to see me dead. So what I tell you can never, ever be repeated. Do you understand?"

She nodded seriously and he continued. "Russ Talbot took money from Colombian drug lords and used his position as governor of the state of New Mexico to allow drug shipments to come in and out of his state," he whispered. "From 1987 through 1999, we've been able to trace over $900,000 in payments to Swiss bank accounts. It's my job to find the source of those payments because we have information that the Colombians are putting pressure on Talbot again, now that he's President, to open up the borders again to allow for drug shipments. It's our understanding that Talbot is being blackmailed. The Colombians are threatening to make their relationship with the President public knowledge if Talbot doesn't comply."

Casey gazed at him, confused and in disbelief. "But...," she shook her head. "That can't be. There must be some mistake."

Colt shook his head. "It's our assumption that he needed the money for his boys' treatment," he said softly. "Remember how he told you that he took his boys to France to try alternative treatment for their Cystic Fibrosis? He couldn't have afforded that on an ordinary governor's salary. He took money from the Colombians to finance the medical treatments."

Casey's jaw dropped. "If that's true, then you can't blame the man," she insisted. "He had two dying kids. He'd do anything to save them. Maybe you don't understand that because you don't have any children, but believe me when I tell you that you would do anything and everything to save your children."

"Even illegal activities?"

"Even that," she fired back. "Colt, if I were dying and you needed money to save my life, what would you do?"

His dark eyes were intense. "Anything I had to do. I'd beg, borrow, buy or kill to save you."

She believed him implicitly. "So maybe you understand what Russ went through to save his boys. Are you going to punish him for it?"

Colt shook his head slowly. "That's not my call, Angel. If it were up to me, I'd leave him alone. I've grown to like the man. But my job is to either find a trail leading to Talbot or exonerate him somehow, because if the Colombians really are on to him, that just made my job as the Special Agent in Charge about a thousand times more dangerous. They'll take Talbot out and anyone who gets in their way."

Her fear was back. "Then you were going through those files to find something."

He nodded slowly. "You made it easy. They were sitting right out in the open."

She thought on that a moment. Then, she hung her head. "Did you get close to me just to see what I could tell you?" she asked softly. "I haven't known Russ that long, you know. I can't be much help to you."

He couldn't help it. He reached out and grasped her hand, holding it tightly when she tried to pull it away. He leaned forward, kissing her fingers sweetly.

"I will be honest with you," he whispered. "My directive was to use whoever I could to accomplish my task. You were perfect, as the personal assistant to the President. I was encouraged to get close to you. What I didn't anticipate was falling so hard for you. Casey. Whatever you may think of me, please know that everything I told you about my feelings was God's truth. I love you more than anything. I would never knowingly hurt you and if I lied to you, it was to protect you. I didn't anticipate you in the least and I have never in my life had such feelings for anyone, so if I stumble while trying to navigate these unfamiliar waters, then please know how sorry I am. I fell in love with you and I wasn't supposed to."

She was watching his hand as he held on to hers, tears trickling down her cheeks. "Why did you go to New Mexico?"

He kissed her fingers again, with painful sweetness. "Because I needed to speak with the reporter who initially broke the story about Talbot allowing drug smugglers to land planes in Southern New Mexico. The woman has had her life threatened and wouldn't talk to me over the phone. I had to go find her."

She looked up at him, her lower lip trembling and tears spilling out of her eyes. "Swear it?"

He nodded fervently, kissing her hand. "I swear on my life, Casey. I wasn't cheating on you in any way, shape or form. I would never do that to you, not ever. I love you deeply and would never disrespect you that way."

She sniffled and wiped at her eyes. Then she pulled her hand out of his grip and he watched her as she fumbled with a big basket at her feet. She opened the lid and drew forth something wrapped up in a plastic bag.

"I made you some turkey sandwiches because I felt so sorry for you," she said, pulling forth a big, fat sandwich from the plastic bag. "I don't know if they're any good still, but they should be if you want one."

The thoughtful, sweet gesture touched him deeply. But it also made him feel that much worse, hurting this woman who was so wonderful and unselfish. He took the sandwich and took a huge bite. It was delicious with cranberry sauce and mayonnaise.

"It's wonderful," he said, his mouth full. "You were very sweet to bring it to me."

She wouldn't look him in the eye. She was still wiping tears off her cheeks. He swallowed the bite in his mouth.

"Please tell me what you're feeling," he whispered.

She shrugged. "I don't really know," she replied, lifting her eyes to his. "What you've told me is terrifying, Colt. I'm scared to death. Maybe I shouldn't believe you but I do. I don't think you'd lie to me about something as serious as all of this, but it really makes me confused."

"Why?"

"Because I don't know how to act now that I know the truth.

Do I help you find something to convict Russ? Do I not? What do I do?"

He lowered the sandwich. "You just do your job and don't worry about me, okay? You have nothing to do with me or what I do."

She fell silent, looking at the sandwich in his hand, the floor of the car, the seat back; anything but Colt's face. He watched her, concerned, hoping that their relationship hadn't been irrevocably damaged by all of this. If it was, he would do whatever it took to right it. He wasn't going to give up. Just as he was pondering his next question to her, she suddenly looked up at him.

"The truth is that I love you and if I have to choose loyalty between you or the President, I would choose you," she reached out and took his hand, holding it in her soft, warm grasp. "I don't want you to sink Russ. He's a good man who did what he had to do to try and save the lives of his children. If the Colombians are really after him, then I want to help him. *You* can help him, Colt, if you can find out the truth behind all of this. I believe you can do it because I believe you're a great man. I knew of your reputation before I even met you, so I know you're a very great man. I'll help you however I can so you can get to the bottom of this. If you need something, just ask. You don't have to go through my files when I'm not looking. I'll give you what you need."

Colt could feel the conversation taking a turn, becoming some-thing hopeful and warm. He wasn't sure it would ever reach this point and he realized there was a lump in his throat. "I love you so much," he whispered. "I'm so sorry for all of this."

She smiled. "I love you, too. I always will."

Colt put the half-eaten sandwich back in the basket and pulled her into his arms. Casey collapsed against him, her arms around his neck as she burst into quiet tears again. Colt held her tightly, his eyes filling with a lake of tears, unable to blink them away. He was still shaken up having come so close to losing her. Not a praying man, he found himself giving thanks.

Trembling, he pulled back to look at her, cupping her face

between his two enormous hands. He just looked at her, studying her, thinking of how much he loved her.

"We will get through this," he whispered hoarsely. "I swear to you, we will survive."

She nodded, her eyes wet with tears. "Just promise me one thing."

"Anything."

"No more lies. No matter how scared you are, or how terrible it is, never lie to me again. Promise?"

"I do."

"I believe you."

He stared at her moment longer before pulling her close. As he held her tightly with one arm, he pulled out his cell phone with the other and dialed Riley's number. With Casey cradled against him, he had to pull the phone away from his ear when Riley answered on the second ring, practically screaming into the phone.

"Riley, it's Colt," he said, his tone soft with emotion. "I have her. She's fine. I'm taking her back to my place tonight so she can get some sleep."

On the other end of the line, Riley was freaking out. "What happened?" she wanted to know. "Where was she?"

Casey could hear her sister yelling. Before Colt could answer, she took the phone from him and put it to her ear.

"Hey," she said to her sister. "It's a long story, Ry. Tell mom and dad I'm fine, and tell the boys I'm fine. I'll see you guys tomorrow, okay? I need to spend a little time with Colt."

Riley was flabbergasted. "So that's it?" she demanded. "We're freaking out all day and this is the only explanation we get?"

Casey sighed, feeling very exhausted and short on patience. "Honey, I'll talk to you tomorrow, okay?" She sounded firm. "I'm fine and everything is okay. Cut me a little slack, will you? Just back off."

"Okay, okay," Riley backed down, but she wasn't happy about it. "You're sure that you're okay?"

"I'm sure."

"Okay, then. I'll see you tomorrow."

Casey hung up the phone and handed it back to Colt. He climbed out of the back of her car and took her with him. Casey stood up, stretching out her stiff muscles, looking at her broken driver's side window. Colt could see where her attention was.

"Sorry," he grunted. "I'll call the Auto club tomorrow and see about getting it fixed."

Casey didn't say anything about it. She didn't have the energy. Colt reached into the car and collected her purse and the picnic basket, taking them in one hand and Casey in the other over to his still-running car. He packed everything in, including his girlfriend, and took off back down the parking structure.

Casey was silent as they drove the couple of miles to his brownstone. He pulled up the dark driveway and into the dark garage, taking the picnic basket, the purse and Casey out, in that order, and bringing everything upstairs to his townhome. It was dark inside as he opened the door and ushered Casey in, flipping on the foyer light and setting her purse and the picnic basket down just inside the door.

Casey just stood there and yawned as Colt moved into the townhome, flipping on lights as he went.

"Come on, Angel," he paused by his bedroom door, turning to look at her as he pulled his jacket off. "Let's go to bed."

She followed him, groggy, into the bedroom, where he began pulling off his clothing. Casey sat down on the bed and pulled off her suede jacket, her boots, and then the rest of her clothing piece by piece. Colt was standing in his closet, hanging up his coat and pants, emerging from the closet to find Casey already in bed. She was burrowed under the covers, eyes already closed, and he flipped off the lights and removed his briefs, getting into bed next to her.

He pulled her into his big, warm embrace and she snuggled down against him. Colt didn't say a word. He just held her, stroking her back and gazing off into the darkness, wondering how things were going to be from now on. He'd told her things that the best interrogators in the world couldn't wrest from his lips. He doubted she really understood the seriousness of what he'd told her, but she would come to understand it in the days to come. He would make sure of it. Right now, however, she was safe in his arms and that was all he really cared about. The rest he could deal with when the time came.

"Colt?"

Casey's soft voice floated up between them and he pulled away from her a little so he could look down at her, snuggled against his chest.

"What, Angel?"

"Is your life really in danger with this work you do?"

"Yes."

"Will they try to kill me, too?"

"Nobody is going to kill you. Don't worry about that."

"But I'm really scared for you."

"Don't be scared," he said softly, "but understand just how serious this is. You know something about me that only a handful of people know. I trust you to keep that knowledge safe."

She sighed faintly, gazing up into his handsome face. "Will our life ever be normal?" she asked softly. "You want to get married but I'll be terrified for you every second. I'm not sure if I can live with that kind of fear day and night."

He stroked her back, his dark eyes serious. "I've been thinking about that," he murmured. "This is going to be my last task for them. I want to settle down with you and raise a family like any other normal human being. I'm not going to do this kind of thing anymore. I'm done with it."

"Would you have been done with it had you not met me?"

"No. You've changed my life completely, Casey. You make me want to be a better man."

That brought a smile to her pale lips. "That's such a sweet thing to say," she whispered. "I love you so much."

He kissed her forehead and pulled her back against him, holding her close. "Go to sleep," he whispered. "You've had a busy day."

Casey closed her eyes, lulled by his warm body and deep voice. "Do you work tomorrow?"

He sighed with contentment, closing his eyes. "If you're off, I'm off."

"I'm off."

"Then I wonder what we can do with a day off?"

Eyes closed, Casey grinned. She had a pretty good idea.

THIRTEEN

"THESE PICTURES ARE PERFECT," Mr. Meade said with satisfaction. "This is exactly what we've been looking for. This is direct evidence of Russ Talbot allowing the drug cartel to land their shipments in the New Mexico desert."

"They're pictures of the President and men in the desert with an airplane," Colt pointed out. "There's no way to prove those men are drug cartel or that Talbot is doing anything illegal. They're just pictures."

Mr. Meade was still looking at the photographs, spread out across his two hundred-year-old oak desk. He was fixated on them.

"We have these photographs," he looked up at Colt. "We have the bank statement records. We have all the pieces to the puzzle and they tell the story."

Colt cocked an eyebrow. "What we don't have is the sources of the big deposits to Swissbanc and an eyewitness," he said. "Katy Ross saw what she saw from afar. She wasn't present. She didn't hear what was said and she doesn't have inside knowledge of any of those transactions she took pictures of. It's purely circumstantial and you know it."

"It's enough to start an investigation."

"An investigation that's going to drag Talbot through the mud, whereupon, I suspect, he'll be acquitted." He went for the bottle of Glenfiddich even though it hadn't been offered to him; he found he needed it. "When you assigned this to me, it was to find irrefutable evidence. These puzzle pieces make for a good story but it's not solid proof. However, I think I did find something, something I didn't mention before."

Meade was interested. "What is that?"

Colt sat heavily in one of the old wingback chairs that lined Mr. Meade's library. The ancient leather creaked under his weight.

"When I took all of those photographs of his financial records, there were other records mixed in," he said quietly. "Do you recall? There was a file of medical bills from that time for treatment for his children."

"And?"

"And, I spent all night, one night, adding up what he'd spent for treatments over the years," he replied. "It came to a little less than three hundred thousand dollars. Then I added up what he donated to the National Cystic Fibrosis Foundation between 1987 and 1999, and that totaled up to around six hundred thousand dollars. Do you see where I'm going with this?"

Mr. Meade was silent a moment, thinking. "I believe I do," he said after a moment. "The deposits into *Swissbanc* totaled around nine hundred thousand."

"Yes."

"If you add up what Talbot spent on treatment for his boys against what he donated to charity, the amount is about the same."

"Exactly."

Mr. Meade's eyebrows rose. "He spent all of the money he received from the Colombians on treatment and charities?"

"It looks that way."

"If we did convene a grand jury, they would dig in to that link and, I suspect, come up with the truth."

Colt didn't reply. He sighed deeply, looking at his drink, perhaps pondering where all of this had brought them. Mr. Meade was watching him.

"You disagree?"

Colt shrugged. "I told you this before. I'm simply finding it difficult to convict a man for doing everything he could to try and save the lives of his two boys. Who's to say that in a similar position, I wouldn't do the same thing?"

Mr. Meade's gaze lingered on Colt a moment before looking back to the photographs spread out over his desk.

"This is no time to develop a heart and soul, Colt," he said quietly. "You have a job to do."

"And I'm doing it."

"Dispense with the sympathy or this will crumble."

"I'm not showing sympathy. I'm simply voicing my opinion."

Meade looked up from the photographs. "Ms. Cleburne has two boys, doesn't she?"

Colt's dark eyes turned to him, hardness evident. "She does."

Meade could see he had to be careful with how he presented his thoughts. Colt was always very edgy when discussing Casey Cleburne, although he tried to hide it. Mr. Meade had known him too long not to see the change come over him. He was very much attached to her.

"She has served her purpose," he said quietly. "Perhaps it is time to move on."

Colt had suspected that directive was going to come down one of these days but found he was ill prepared for it. He struggled not to become emotional or enraged.

"I'm not moving on from her," he said softly.

"Why not?"

"Because I love her."

Mr. Meade sighed heavily as confirmation came of what he already knew. "I fear she's clouding your judgement, Colt."

"She's not clouding anything. I can and will keep her separate from my task, so don't worry about it."

"But I do worry," Meade insisted. "I've known you for many years, Colt, and I've only known you to get emotional one other time."

"Leave Katja out of this."

It was a threat. Colt had reached his limit and now, the threats were coming. Meade's gaze lingered on him a moment before lowering his head back to the photographs.

"I will contact you another time," he said, pretending to busy himself with the images. "You may go."

Colt got up out of the chair and left without another word. By the time he hit the driveway outside, he was trembling. All he could think about was getting back to Casey and forgetting the rotting old man stuffed up in the old coffin of a house. He had to get the smell and image out of his mind.

Mr. Meade heard Colt's car tear off down the driveway. As the sound faded away, he picked up the phone and made a single call.

Peter picked up on the second ring.

———

Christmastime in Washington was a magical time. It had snowed heavily the day before Christmas, so they had been blessed with a winter wonderland on Christmas Day. It had almost been enough to offset Casey's disapproval at the completely cool new skateboard that Colt got Brody for Christmas and the sporty new bike he got for Hunter. There was much joy for the young men of the Cleburne household on Christmas morning.

Shocked at the awesome gifts from their mom's boyfriend, the boys were willing recruits to Team Colt for the holidays. Casey hadn't really had the heart to chastise Colt about the controversial skateboard, given the fact that he'd never had kids to buy presents for other than his niece and nephews. He had really enjoyed doing it and it helped bond him with her sons, so Casey's disapproval vanished completely by the time they were eating Christmas Eve dinner.

It was snowing heavily outside as Casey brought the beautiful crown roast to the dining room table. Riley had charge of the mashed potatoes while the boys had charge of the vegetables. Colt was the bartender, making sure everyone got something to drink. The fire in the fireplace crackled softly as Casey dimmed the lights and lit the candles, making everything beautiful and glowing. It was a festive winter's eve. Colt held out Casey's chair for her as everyone took their seats around her dining room table.

Once everyone was seated, Casey looked around at her little family, feeling more happiness than she could express. There was a completeness to it now with Colt's presence. He made the circle full. Casey smiled at Colt as she spoke.

"It's a little tradition around here on Christmas Day dinner to tell everyone what you're thankful for," she said. "My parents started the tradition and I've carried it on with my kids. Now that you're at our table, you have to tell us what you're thankful for, too."

Colt grinned at her. Dressed in jeans and a gray pullover sweater, he looked dreamy, like he had just walked off the pages of a men's magazine. Casey hadn't been able to take her eyes off him for most of the day. He lifted his big shoulders.

"Fair enough," he said. "For the price of a meal, I'll do it."

She laughed softly. "Good," she said, looking around the table. "I guess I'll start. I'm really thankful for my family, for the good things in my life, and for Colt. I'm so glad he's been able to share the holidays with us."

Riley just grinned, looking between Colt and her sister and seeing how much in love they were. It was really good to see.

"I'm thankful for all of this snow," she said. "Hunter?"

Hunter looked around the table, thinking. "I'm thankful that I have my bedroom back because Gramma and Grampa are gone. But I'm really thankful for my new bike. I hope I get to ride it when all of this snow goes away. Thanks again, Colt."

Everyone giggled as Colt acknowledged the gratitude. Then the attention turned to Brody. Ever the performer, he stood up and held up his water glass as if he were toasting.

"I'm thankful for my mother," he announced, his gaze moving from Casey to Riley. "And for Aunt Riley and for Colt because if he hadn't given me my new skateboard, I'd probably be fifty years old by the time I got another one. If anyone else had given it to me, my mom would have made me give it back, so thank you, Colt, for the 'board. You have the power, dude."

Casey shook her head reproachfully at her son, grinning, as the table burst out in laughter. Colt had really come to like Brody over the past several weeks, the wily kid with the heart of gold. He was a sly one and definitely knew how to work his mother. When Brody took a bow and sat back down, all eyes turned to Colt. His smile faded and he cleared his throat softly.

"Well," he began, his eyes moving over the Cleburne Clan. "I think the last time a Sheridan met up with a Cleburne, it didn't go so well. I've got to tell you, when I took on my new job a couple of months ago, never in my wildest dreams did I expect to meet someone like Casey Cleburne. I could never have imagined my life to turn out the way it has since then and to tell you the truth, I still wake up in the morning and pinch myself. It's like a dream. So I guess I'm thankful to all of you for not only accepting a Sheridan into your home, but into your family as well. I'm thankful that you four have always made me feel so welcome. I've never had that before."

Casey reached over and grasped his hand, squeezing it. "We're thankful for you, too."

Thinking the "thankful" speeches were over, the boys began to grab at the mashed potatoes but Colt stopped them. "Hang on," he said, looking at the two young men. "There's something more I want to say. As you all have probably figured out, I'm pretty crazy about your mother. I love her very much. In fact, I kind of fell in love with all of you in a sense, so when I thought about proposing to your mother, I realized I had to do it to the whole family because she comes with a sister and two sons. Therefore, I'd like to ask your permission to ask your mother to marry me."

The boys looked surprised, grinning, glancing at each other and at Riley, who was starting to tear up. Brody was the first one to nod his head.

"Sure," he said, wondering why both his mother and aunt were starting to cry. "Are you going to live here with us?"

"If you'll have me."

They were looking at Hunter, who was sitting back in his seat, looking at his mother. The initial smile on his face at Colt's question was fading. "Mom?" he asked. "Why are you crying? Don't you want to marry him?"

Casey wiped at her eyes. "Yes, I do, very much," she sniffed. "I'm just really happy."

Hunter thought on that a moment, pondering the times in the past when he had seen his mother cry that hadn't been under happy circumstances. He didn't like it in the least. Then he looked at Colt.

"Do you swear you won't make her cry?" he nearly demanded.

Colt's eyebrows lifted as he pointed to Casey. "I can't," he said. "She's crying now."

Hunter shook his head. "I don't mean that," he said, suddenly growing somber. "My dad made her cry a lot and I don't want you to make her cry like that. You need to swear that you'll make her happy."

Colt grew very serious. "I swear, Hunter. I swear with all my heart."

Hunter gazed at him a moment longer, a sort of affirming stare, before looking at his mother again.

"I'm okay with it, then," he said. "But he'd better do what he promised."

It was a threat and Colt took it seriously. He knew that Hunter was just being protective of his mother and he respected that.

"I'll make you proud, Hunt," he murmured, looking at Casey. "Now, there's just one thing left."

She was wiping the moisture away from her eyes. "What?"

Colt suddenly stood up from his chair and before Casey realized what he was doing, he was down on one knee beside her. He pulled something out of his jeans pocket and Casey could see it was a small box. A ring box. Her heart began to pound as he reached out and took her hand.

"Casey Catherine Cleburne," his dark eyes were glimmering at her. "I loved you from nearly the first moment I met you. You're a sweet, intelligent, compassionate and beautiful woman, and I would be deeply honored to be your husband. Will you please marry me?"

Casey was back to happy tears again as she nodded her head, throwing her arms around his neck and nearly sending him off balance.

"Yes," she whispered, pulling back to kiss him sweetly. "I'll marry you. I love you so much."

Riley began clapping and cheering, so the boys followed suit. As Colt opened the box to show her the three carat solitaire he'd purchased for her, Brody clanged his knife against his water glass.

"Can we eat now?" he demanded.

Casey burst into laughter as Colt put the gorgeous platinum and diamond ring on her left ring finger.

"Yes, eat," she shook her head at the boy, turning to admire the brilliant ring. "Brody, you sure know how to spoil a beautiful moment."

Colt stood up, kissing her hand and kissing her again on her lips before taking his seat. "He didn't spoil anything," he said, reaching for the big carving knife to cut up the crown roast. "Everything is still perfect."

The meal had an extra spark of joy as they devoured the delicious food. The boys plowed through it and then wanted to go out in the backyard to play in the snow. Casey turned on the flood lights, illuminating the winter wonderland outside, as she and Colt and Riley remained at the table, drinking wine and talking, as the boys tried to build a snowman outside in the dark. A couple of neighbor kids joined them and soon, there were about eight kids in the backyard all trying to build a big snowman as the powdery snow continued to fall.

As the evening deepened, Riley took care of the dishes and

sent Colt and Casey to the living room with the fireplace. Alone in the dark room with only the firelight for company, they sat on the couch and snuggled, listening to Riley washing dishes in the kitchen and the kids outside playing. Colt had his arms around Casey, his face in the side of her head, as she watched the snow fall outside of the living room window.

"Do you like your ring?" he whispered.

She admired the diamond again. "Absolutely," she said. "It's gorgeous."

"Good," he kissed her ear. "It took me weeks to pick that thing out. I kept changing my mind."

"You did a good job. It's perfect."

He sighed faintly, turning his head to watch the snow fall, also. "Perfect enough that you'll forgive me for giving Brody a skateboard?"

She giggled. "Probably, but it's going to take a few days for that one to wear off. I should have slugged you right then and there."

He grinned, nuzzling her cheek. "It's like riding a horse. He's got to get back on the board sometime. Might as well do it now, while he's still young. You know you're never going to get him away from a skateboard completely."

"I know. But did you have to buy him such an expensive one?"

"Yes."

"Why?"

"Because I wanted to."

She grunted and shook her head. "You're impossible."

He grinned. "No, I'm not," he said, suddenly moving off the couch and pulling her to her feet, "but I've got one more trick up my sleeve."

Curious, she cocked her head. "What do you mean?"

He pulled her towards the front door. "Come take a look."

"Take a look at what?"

He opened the front door and pointed to the curb. "At that."

Casey peered out of the front door, across the snowy front lawn, to a car parked on the curb. She couldn't see it very well until suddenly, the lights and the engine turned on. Somewhat confused, she looked at Colt to see that he was holding up a wireless ignition remote.

"Merry Christmas," he said softly. "It's your new Cadillac SUV."

Casey's jaw dropped. "*What?*"

She was suddenly running outside towards the curb with Colt behind her. There was so much snow that it was difficult to see the pearl-colored Cadillac crossover SUV that was sleek, sexy and beautiful. She started jumping up and down.

"For me?" she squealed.

He laughed softly and handed her the keys. "For you, Angel. I'm sick of worrying about you in that eight-year-old Ford. Now you have a brand new, beautiful car to drive the boys around in."

Casey could hardly believe it. Shrieking with joy, she ran around to the driver's side and jumped into the luxurious tan interior. It had every feature known to man, including video monitors in the back seat, heated and air-conditioned front seats, and a glove box that doubled as a refrigerator. She was giddy with joy.

"Oh, my God," she gasped as she inspected the space-age interior. "This is amazing. I can't believe you got this for me!"

Colt was bending down, looking into the driver's door. "Do you like it?"

She jumped out of the driver's seat and bashed him on the chin with her head as she threw her arms around his neck.

"I love it," she hugged him tightly. "Thank you so much. This is such a thoughtful gift."

Colt held her snuggly, snow falling on their eyelashes as they shared a sweet kiss. "I can't believe you didn't notice this thing parked outside all day," he said. "I had it brought over this morning."

Casey shrugged. "I guess I just wasn't paying attention," she said. "Seriously, Colt, this is such a sweet thing to do. I love it."

He was smiling broadly. "I'm glad," he said softly "So I guess you got the best present of all."

Her smile faded as she gazed into his handsome face. She suddenly grew very serious. "Maybe not," she murmured. "As good as this is, I have a better one for you."

His eyebrows lifted. "Really? What?"

She shook her head. "You can't open it now."

"Why not?"

"Because you've got to wait until summer."

"Why do I have to wait?"

"Because that's when the baby is due."

At first, it didn't register. It took Colt several long seconds to process what she had said. Then, the dark eyes widened.

"Baby?" he repeated. "What baby?"

She tried to gauge his reaction. "*Our* baby," she said softly. "I saw the doctor a couple of days ago. We're going to have a baby in August."

His mouth popped open. "Oh, my God," he hissed. "Are you serious?"

She couldn't figure out if he was happy or upset about it. "Yes," she said, suddenly stricken by the look on his face. "Oh, God... you're not happy about this, are you?"

He was still in a state of shock. He shook his head and then he quickly nodded, wrapping her up in such a hug that she could hardly breathe.

"I'm happy," he insisted, sounding breathless. "I'm just... shocked. Shocked as hell."

"Is that a good thing or a bad thing?"

He let go of her, taking a moment just to stare at her as the snow fell softly and silently around them. Casey had never seen such an expression on his face. It was as if the control he held so dear and the composure he was so practiced with was suddenly gone. His face was full of naked emotion.

"It's a great thing," he finally whispered, the dark eyes fixed on her. "It's the greatest thing in the world. I can't... I can't even...."

He threw his arms around her again and held her tightly. Then he let her go so swiftly that she nearly fell over. She was dressed in black pants and an oversized cream-colored sweater, and he put his hands on her still-flat belly.

"Are you sure?" he hissed.

Increasingly certain that he wasn't horrified by the situation, she smiled. "Very sure. Doctors don't lie about this kind of thing."

"How...?" he still had his hands on her torso as he looked at her. "How do you know? When did you know?"

Her violet eyes were twinkling. "I've suspected for a few weeks," she said. "I haven't had my period since you and I first slept together. It's been about six or seven weeks. So I went to the doctor a couple of days ago and he did a blood test."

"And it was positive?"

"It was."

He slapped a hand over his mouth, absolutely overcome with giddy surprise. Now that the shock was wearing off, he was starting to feel utter and complete joy. He wrapped her up in his arms one more time, holding her reverently.

"Oh, my God," he breathed again, rocking her sweetly. "I can't believe this. We're going to have a baby."

"Merry Christmas."

He burst into soft snorts of laughter. "No kidding," he chuckled. "This is the best Christmas I've ever had."

She pulled away from him this time, looking him in the eye. "Really?"

"Swear to God."

"So you're happy about this?"

"I... I can't even describe how happy I am. I'm beyond happy. I'm about ready to start shouting this all over the neighborhood."

She giggled, putting her hand over his mouth. "Not before we tell the boys," she said. "We're really going to have to treat this carefully, you know. How can I tell them not to go get some girl pregnant when this has happened to us?"

He shrugged. "Maybe we'll just get married in the next few weeks and that'll solve the problem," he said. "They don't have to know this baby was conceived before we got married."

She cocked an eyebrow at him. "They can count, you know. They'll eventually figure it out."

"When they do, we'll explain it. There's no shame in two adults loving each other enough to have a baby."

As always, he had a plan and he was decisive about it. Colt Sheridan was always the man in control and in charge, even with something like this. Feeling satisfied with how to handle it with the boys, a smile crept onto Casey's lips and she put her hands on his cheeks, grinning broadly when he hugged her tightly.

"I have to tell you, I'm really happy about this," she said softly. "I was kind of scared at first, but not anymore. This is such a blessing."

He kissed her forehead. "Absolutely," he agreed, kissing her nose. "Angel, your nose is freezing. Let's go inside, okay?"

She pulled away from him, shaking her head. "I want to drive my car."

He had her by the arm, pulling her out of the car. "It's too snowy," he told her. "You can drive it tomorrow."

"No!" she put on good act of a whiney little kid, gripping the steering wheel as he tried to pull her out. "I want to drive it!"

He was chuckling as he tried to pull her out but she kept putting up her feet and pushing him away. "Come out of there," he told her.

"No!" she squealed, giggling. "I want to drive my new car!"

He had her by both feet but she was holding on to the steering wheel with a death grip. He started laughing so hard that he couldn't get a good grip on her as Hunter, Brody and Riley suddenly came through the front door, seeing Colt and Casey squabbling over a new car. The boys descended on the car, trying to sweep the snow off of it to get a better look.

"Mom's got a new car?" Brody was thrilled. "This is really cool!"

"It's your mom's Christmas gift from me," Colt let go of Casey's feet as Brody tried to climb on his mother in the driver's side.

"This is awesome!" Brody was excited as he threw open the back door. "It's got a video panel!"

Hunter slid in from the other side and Colt could see that he wasn't going to be able to get any of them out of the car any time soon. So he let Casey drive the car around the block, very carefully, just so she could say she drove her new present. He sat in the front seat, listening to their excitement, and it made him smile. He was really looking forward to spending the rest of his life with the Cleburne Clan, all of them, and the more he thought about the new baby, the more excited he became. All of his life was spread out before him like a paradise he never knew existed.

Later that night, Colt called his parents on Skype to tell them the good news and they got a good look at Casey for the first time. Phil and Susie Sheridan were thrilled to meet their future daughter-in-law and thrilled beyond words about the new baby. Finally, their oldest son, the over-achiever in every sense of the word, was finding peace with himself and with what seemed to be a very good woman. He was getting married and having children. They couldn't have been happier.

When they went to bed that night, Colt held Casey in his arms, listening to her gentle breathing and watching the snow as it continued to fall outside the window. He couldn't put the moment into words, never knowing it was possible to love something as much as he loved her. When she shifted in her sleep, he put his big hand on her naked belly, imagining the son she would bear with her beautiful soul and his good looks. It was enough to bring tears to his eyes.

When he finally fell asleep, it was with happy dreams of the future.

FOURTEEN

CASEY WAS LOOKING A LITTLE PALE. Colt could see her from his office as she moved more slowly than usual. She was filing and he could watch her discreetly from his position in front of his computer, his gaze moving up her luscious body, thinking of all of the wicked things he would do to her once they were alone that night. But the more prevalent thought was of the baby she carried and how she hadn't been feeling so well the past several days. Even as Colt prepared to escort the President to a local middle school for the event of President's Day, he found his focus heavily on Casey. He was worried about her. He'd never been around a pregnant woman in his life, so this was all new territory for him.

Nine o'clock in the morning rolled around and the President and his aides were meeting with the door to the Oval Office open. There was a lively conversation going on inside. It was coming time to leave for the school, however, so Colt stood up from his desk, collected his radio and notified his detail, and moved out of his office. Chris Eckart was on the phone, as usual, not paying any attention to those around him as Colt went to Casey's desk and quietly thumped on it a couple of times. She turned around from her files, smiling wanly when she saw him.

His expression was gentle. "I'll be with the President until early afternoon," he said softly. "Will you be okay?"

She nodded. "I'm fine."

He didn't say anymore, although he wanted to. He winked at her and went to go stand outside of Russ's office, waiting for the man to finish with his aides. Peter and Steven Case joined him a few minutes later, as did a couple of other special agents, and they all stood outside of Russ' office. Casey wasn't paying much attention to them, with a headache and nausea, so she put her filing aside for the moment because she really needed to sit down. She was looking forward to Russ leaving so she could have a few quiet hours with him gone.

As she collected her herbal tea and took a few timid sips, the President finally emerged from his office and passed in front her desk with his brigade of Secret Service agents, Colt included. There were four aides trailing after him as well. Casey looked up from her tea as Russ paused by her desk.

"Come along with me, Casey," he told her. "We can do some work in the car on the way over."

Grossly disappointed that she was being called into service, Casey dutifully picked up her leather folio with the notepad and pens inside, her iPad, grabbed her purse, and trailed after the President and his aides. By the time she hit the entrance to the West Wing, she felt like she was going to vomit.

The Secret Service had cleared up the West Wing driveway area and only the Presidential limo and six big, black Chevrolet Escalades for the Secret Service were parked in the drive. As the aides disbursed and the Secret Service agents began to filter towards various vehicles, Casey followed the President to the limousine. She glanced up at Colt as the man opened the door for the President and his Chief of Staff. As Casey waited for the men to climb in and get comfortable, Colt caught her attention.

"Are you going to make it?" he whispered.

She gave him a weak smile. "Do I look that bad?"

"You look beautiful," he murmured. "But I can see you don't feel well."

She rolled her eyes as she moved to get into the car. "I feel like shit."

He fought off a grin as she climbed into the car and he closed the door behind her. Engaging his radio, he gave the word to the detail and the black cars with their black windows and state-of-the-art weaponry began to move out.

Casey was sitting with her back to the front passenger seat, trying not to get sick as the car pulled out onto Pennsylvania Avenue. It was increasingly difficult, however, and she finally put her hand to her mouth to hold back the gas and rolling nausea. Russ was chatting with his Chief of Staff, finally turning to Casey and noticing the woman was extremely pale. She also had her hand over her mouth. He leaned forward and peered more closely at her.

"Casey?" he asked. "Are you all right?"

Startled that the attention was on her, Casey looked at the President and tried to toughen up but she couldn't seem to manage it.

"I... I'll be okay," she said.

"You don't look okay."

"I think I must have the flu or something."

Russ was genuinely concerned. "Why didn't you say something?" he demanded without force. "We'll take you back to the White House and I want you to go home."

She shook her head. "No, really," she said weakly, trying to change the subject. "I'll be okay. What did you want to work on?"

The President hit the intercom to the front seat. "Sheridan?" he said. "Did you know that Casey was sick?"

Colt, sitting in the front passenger seat in his dark suit and dark glasses, turned around to look through the glass compartment divider as he answered.

"Yes sir, I did," he replied.

Russ was outraged. "And you let her come to work?"

They could hear him sigh. "She seems to think she can work through it, sir."

"Ridiculous," Russ snapped. "She needs to go home. Turn around. We're taking her back to the White House."

Colt was looking at the back of Casey's head because of where she was sitting. "Casey, do you want to go home?"

She lifted her shoulders reluctantly; she hated to admit defeat. "I'm thinking about it."

That prompted Colt to get on the radio. Russ looked confused as to what the man was doing until, less than a minute later, Colt got back on the intercom.

"At the next stoplight, Harrios is going to come forward in the chase car and take her back," he said.

Satisfied, Russ sat back and continued his conversation with this Chief of Staff while Casey struggled not to become ill. She was horrified at the thought of puking in the Presidential limousine. They'd never stop teasing her about that. When the convoy came to a halt at the next stoplight, Colt bailed out of the front seat and opened up the back door. As Casey climbed out, she noticed he was carrying a nasty-looking short-barrel AK-47 in his left hand while opening the door with his right. As she looked up at him, a black Dodge Charger roared up and screeched to a halt.

"Peter will take you back," he told her softly. "I'll call you later. Love you."

She smiled weakly at him because it was all she could muster and got into the car with Peter. The car sat and idled as the light turned green and the Presidential procession took off again. Then Peter hung a right and headed towards the river. Casey couldn't even think of being disappointed that she wouldn't be where Colt was that morning. She was thinking about her lurching stomach. As they made the turn east to head down Independence Avenue, she turned to Peter.

"Colt drove me to work this morning," she said. "Can you just take me home?"

Peter was focused on the road ahead. "Where do you live?"

"Falls Church."

"We'll head that way. Do you want to stop and get something to make you feel better?"

She sighed faintly. "I'd love something to drink."

Peter didn't say anything more. He continued along until they found a liquor store and then he pulled into the parking lot. Casey climbed out of the car, wearily, and went inside. When she emerged a few minutes later, she had a small brown bag in her hand. She climbed back in the car, put her seatbelt on, and Peter pulled back out onto the street and continued east.

As Peter took the onramp to the Custis Memorial Parkway, he saw that she was crunching heavily on something. He glanced over at her.

"What are you eating?" he asked. "It sounds like rocks."

Casey looked over at him, her mouth full. "Pork rinds," she said. "They're really salty and that's about all I feel like eating."

"Oh," Peter focused forward. "What else do you have in that bag?"

Casey opened up the bag and looked inside. "Peanuts, a big dill pickle, bologna, and chocolate milk."

"*What?*" he looked at her, making a face. "What in the hell are you eating?"

He was half-grinning and she started laughing. "Whatever I feel like," she said.

He made another face and looked back at the road. "That's really disgusting. That's just going to make you sicker."

Casey crunched on her pork rinds, watching him drive. She knew Colt trusted the man so she didn't feel too strange sharing their news with him. Besides, he would probably figure it out eventually.

"Not really," she said softly. "It's kind of like pickles and ice cream. Pregnant women eat weird stuff. You just never know what's going to settle your stomach."

Peter's eyes widened and he glanced at her again. "Oh, my God," he hissed. "You're pregnant?"

"Yes."

His jaw popped open. "Colt...?

She laughed. "I hope he's the father. Either that, or there's something in the water around my house."

Peter's open mouth turned into a laughing one. "Seriously?" he said. "Congratulations. That's really great news. Does the President know?"

"No," she shook her head. "Not yet. I didn't want to throw that on him just yet but if I keep feeling like this, I'm going to have to. I'll be sitting at my desk eating pork rinds, peanuts, bacon and chocolate milk, and he's going to wonder what in the hell is the matter with me."

Peter was snorting. "No joke," he agreed. "How does Colt feel about this?"

She smiled at him. "He's thrilled," she said sincerely. "He's over the moon about it. He's already picked out names."

Peter laughed. "You don't have a choice, Casey," he said. "If it's a boy, it has to be Phil Sheridan the –what is it? – the twenty-fifth or something like that?"

She nodded with resignation. "I know," she said. "If it's a girl, he wants to name her Addy, after his grandmother, Adelaide. He's already made these decisions, like I have no say in the matter."

Peter just grinned, knowing that was more than likely true. Colt Sheridan was a take-charge kind of guy.

"Then it's your fault for hooking up with him," he said.

She nodded, a smile on her lips. "I know. But I kind of like him, so that's okay."

"So... when are you two getting married?"

"Soon. Maybe Valentine's Day. It's only a month off."

"You'd better plan ahead if you're going to do it then."

"I realize that. We talk about it all the time but I can't make up my mind where I want to get married."

"Hasn't he decided that, too?"

She laughed and shook her head. "I won't let him. I told him this is one decision I'm going to make on my own."

Peter's smile faded as they continued along the expressway. He was thinking of the perfection of the moment, of the prime situation he had found himself in. He'd thought of it the moment she got into the car. Meade had told him he needed to get a hold of Casey. Now he had her where he wanted her, like some crazy stroke of luck. He picked up his cell phone as they drove along, dialed, and put it to his ear.

Casey wasn't paying much attention to what Peter was doing. She was crunching on her peanuts now, feeling much better than she had earlier. When he hung up the phone, she pointed ahead.

"I'm at the next off-ramp," she told him.

Peter didn't say anything. They drove right past the off-ramp. Casey, with peanuts in her mouth, turned to look at him.

"That was my exit," she said, not particularly upset. "You can get off at the next one."

Peter was looking straight ahead. "We're going to take a slight detour."

She still wasn't particularly upset or particularly concerned. "Where?"

"You'll see."

Since she was feeling much better with the introduction of salty food, she didn't really care. She had no reason to feel uncertainty or fear. So she sat back and crunched her food, peeling the bologna into strips and sucking it down, then drinking most of the chocolate milk in just a few swallows. By the time she was satisfied and her stomach was somewhat settled, she realized that they were pretty far out of town and continuing to head east. She looked curiously at Peter.

"Where in the hell are we going?" she asked.

His eyes were still forward. "It's not too much farther."

"*Where* is not too much farther?"

Peter didn't reply and Casey sighed heavily. "Peter, I'm really not feeling all that great," she said. "Today is not the day for a road trip."

Peter suddenly took the off ramp onto Highway 50 to the east of Dulles International Airport and headed into the heavily wooded and rolling hills of Virginia's horse country.

"It'll just be a few minutes," he said patiently. "Sit back and relax. It's a beautiful day."

Casey just shook her head and rolled her eyes. "Did Colt put you up to this?" she asked. "He knows I don't feel well. I just want to go home and go to bed."

"Just another couple of minutes."

Casey gave up. She sat back in the seat and pulled out her bag of goodies, now crunching in the dill pickle. The truth was that it really was a lovely day and the winter-kissed land was covered with a layer of melting snow. Since they were in horse country, every so often they'd drive by a field of furry horses, out in the cold and enjoying the weak sunshine. Casey was just starting to kick back and doze when Peter suddenly slowed down and took a left into a pair of big stone and iron gates. He pulled up to the intercom and said his name when someone answered. The giant gates lurched open and Casey sat up, suddenly interested in their surroundings.

"What is this place?" she asked.

Peter pulled down the half-mile long gravel driveway, pointing to the big mansion looming ahead.

"Have you ever seen anything like this?" he asked.

Casey shook her head, focusing on the massive French Colonial brick mansion lying directly ahead. It looked very old, with massive columns supporting a big white portico. The driveway wound through paddocks with big white fences, keeping horses corralled in finely kept fields. Her attention was diverted when they pulled alongside a fat, hairy mare and her little colt, munching grass along the fence line. Casey poked Peter on the arm.

"Stop," she demanded. "I want to see the baby!"

He pulled to a stop and she opened the door, climbing out of the warm car into the chilly air so she could go up to the fence and pet the little horse. She grinned as the colt, no more than a couple of weeks old, nibbled curiously at her fingers while his mother crunched winter grass.

"Hey!" Peter yelled at her. "It's cold out there. Get back in the car!"

Giving the little horse a final little scratch, she jumped back in the car and slammed the door. Peter resumed their progression down the gravel drive, taking the roundabout driveway and ending up in front of the big, white portico of the home with its massive Doric columns. Peter put the car in park and turned it off, bailing out of the car before Casey could ask him any questions. As Peter went around to open her door, a small man in an expensive suit and bright white hair emerged from the front door.

Casey climbed out of the car to find the man standing in front of her. Even at her average height, she was still taller than he was. He immediately extended a hand to her.

"Ms. Cleburne?" he greeted. "I'm Victor Meade. It's such a pleasure to meet you. I've heard so much about you."

Casey shook the man's hand. "That's nice of you to say," she said, looking around. "Uh... it's nice to meet you, also."

"Thank you."

"Your home is lovely."

"Thank you, again." Meade didn't let go of her hand; he continued to stare at her, pulling her apart, digesting her. "I had heard you were beautiful but I had no idea just how beautiful you really were," he said, almost wistfully. "Colt is a very lucky man."

Casey fixed him in the eye. "You know Colt?"

"Very well. I know his father, too."

Casey was growing more confused by the moment. She glanced at Peter before looking back at Meade. "Uh...," she began, "I don't mean to be rude, but I'm not really clear as to why I'm here."

Meade held her hand as he led her up the steps and into the house. "I've wanted to meet you for the longest time," he said, avoiding answering her statement. As they passed through the enormous front doors, he pointed at it. "So you like my home? Those doors are original to the house. You'll see how heavy they are. They don't make doors like that anymore."

Casey couldn't help but notice that no one would tell her why she was here. She wasn't frightened in the least but she was annoyed. It was a struggle to remain pleasant.

"When was the house built?" she asked simply to be polite.

"1767," Meade replied. "Well, at least parts of it were. My family has owned this home for two hundred and forty five years. We even owned the property that Dulles Airport is sitting on."

"Impressive." Casey looked around the giant two-story entry with new interest. "I noticed your horses out in the paddocks. They're beautiful."

Meade smiled at her. "We breed Thoroughbreds," he told her. "The finest. Do you like horses?"

"Love them."

"Good girl," he patted the hand he was still holding and began leading her into another part of the house. "Are you hungry?"

Casey instinctively put a hand to her stomach. "Not really," she admitted. "Thank you, though."

Meade had pulled her into a room off the entry, an enormous room of books and leather and antiques, smelling heavily of tobacco. He indicated a fat leather chair for her to sit in, one that happened to be positioned in front of the gently snapping fire. Casey glanced back at Peter, with great confusion on her face, as she sat down. The fire felt good on her legs.

Meade went to the sterling coffee service that was sitting on the gigantic antique desk. He picked up a fine china cup. "Coffee, Ms. Cleburne?"

She shook her head. "No, thank you."

Meade poured a cup for himself and took the chair across from Casey. He was smiling as he looked at her.

"You really are beautiful," he complimented. "Poised, lovely, intelligent and graceful. Now I see why Colt is so smitten. I don't blame him."

Casey fixed him in the eye. "Can you please tell me why I'm here?"

Meade sipped his coffee. "It would be my pleasure," he said. "This all must be very confusing."

"And annoying."

Meade grinned as he began his speech. "Ms. Cleburne," he said, his voice softening. "You are part of the great American elite. Your ancestor was a great Civil War general."

"Yes, he was."

"So was mine," Meade said. "In fact, I have great generals on both sides of my family. On my father's side, we descend from the great Civil War general George Meade. On my mother's side, my grandmother was the granddaughter of U.S. Grant."

Casey's eyebrows lifted. "Wow," she said. "That's quite a pedigree."

Meade nodded. "It is," he agreed. "But with great heritage comes great responsibility. I'm sure you are aware of that."

She shrugged. "In a sense," she said. "I've always been very proud of my heritage but unlike you, I didn't have great bloodlines on both sides. I would imagine much more was expected from you than could have ever been expected from me."

Meade's grin returned. "Well said," he replied. "Colt bears a great heritage, also. Phil Sheridan is inarguably one of the greatest generals the American army has ever seen. Colt very proudly carries on that heritage in that he is a flawless and brave decision-maker. He is the most courageous and resourceful man I have ever met and it has been a sincere privilege to work with him."

"Where did you work with him?" Casey asked.

"I still work with him," Meade said quietly. "I am assuming he told you that he works for another entity in addition to the Secret Service."

Casey felt as if she had been hit in the gut. Shocked, she struggled not to react. *There are a lot of people who want to see me dead.* It was all she could think of at the moment. She didn't want to betray Colt or give him away. More than that, it occurred to her that Peter must be in on this as well since he brought her to

Meade's front door. Peter was a part of something, although she couldn't guess what. She was beginning to get very frightened.

"What do you mean?" she was trying so very hard not to blow anything.

Meade sipped at his coffee, glancing at Peter, who was standing behind Casey. "Colt Sheridan is a spy, Ms. Cleburne," he said frankly. "Although I suspect he has already told you, I admire your determination not to betray him. I understand. Colt is one of the very best I have ever seen and he works in ways that normal men cannot. His assignments are always flawlessly executed, which is why we put him so close to Russ Talbot. You are President Talbot's personal assistant, are you not? It was Colt's job to get close to you. I understand he has performed that assignment flawlessly as well."

Casey's blood ran cold. The man was speaking smugly and that infuriated her. Shaken, and not particularly well, she began to tremble.

"Colt and I love each other," she said, hoping she wasn't divulging anything too critical. Still, she didn't really care if she was or not. "He's a wonderful man and we're very much in love. Now, I would appreciate it if you would come to the purpose of this visit. I'm not feeling particularly well and need to go home."

Meade seemed concerned. "I'm so sorry," he said sincerely. "I didn't know you weren't well. Perhaps you should lie down for a while?"

Casey shook her head. "Please tell me why I am here so I can go home."

Meade could see she was trying very hard to be brave. He respected that.

"Of course," he said. "You are here because I need to emphasize to Colt how important it is for him to finish his assignment with Talbot. Apparently, you are seriously distracting him from that task. Colt needs to understand that nothing can distract him from what he must finish."

Casey's quivering was growing worse. She was starting to feel nauseous again. Knowing what she did about Colt's mission from what he had told her, she was feeling increasingly frightened by the old man's words. She cleared her throat softly.

"May I have some water, please?" she asked.

Meade was immediately up, going to a sideboard near his desk that contained various phials of alcohol and water. He took a cut crystal glass and poured a measure of water into it. When he turned to drop a couple of ice cubes into it, he opened a small box that looked like a snuff container and took a pinch of white powder and put it in Casey's glass. Dropping the ice cubes in it mixed up the powder so it was undetectable. Then he turned around and quickly moved to Casey with the glass of water.

"Here you are," he said, almost gently. "I'm very sorry you're not feeling well."

She drank almost the entire glass, licking her lips. "I'll be okay," she waved him off. "Can you please come to the point of my visit?"

Meade reclaimed his seat. "Men in love are strange creatures," he said quietly. "It tends to blind them to all else. When we told Colt to get close to you, we had no idea that he would cross the line and fall in love with you. Colt has gotten close to many people in the course of his duties, some of them women. He's even slept with some of them to gain his wants. But something happened when he slept with you – would you care to elaborate on why you are so different from the rest?"

Casey was outraged. "Absolutely not," she snapped. "You've got a hell of a lot of nerve asking me that question, and you've got a hell of a lot of nerve bringing me here without my permission." She stood up and whirled on Peter, standing a few feet away. "And you – what's your deal with all of this? Does Colt know you've taken me here?"

Peter put up his hands to calm her. "Casey, it's okay," he insisted softly. "Sit back down. I'll get you out of here in a little bit."

"Actually, you won't," Meade looked at Peter as if daring him to contradict him. "You're going to be my guest for the time being,

Ms. Cleburne. I think it will be very enlightening for the both of us."

"Bullshit," Casey snarled, backing away from the old man and from Peter. "I'm getting out of here if I have to walk. I'm not staying here any longer and I'll charge you both with kidnapping if you try to keep me here. I'm going home and Colt is going to hear about this."

Meade stood up as Peter tried to calm Casey down. "Casey, please," he begged softly. "It's not all bad. Mr. Meade is just trying to figure out how best to solve the issue."

Casey wouldn't let him get near her. She kept backing away but as she did so, she realized she was feeling very woozy. It was difficult to keep her balance and a strange, lightheadedness filled her.

"There is no issue, Special Agent Harrios," she hissed. "You're in a hell of a lot of trouble if you don't... if you don't...."

She suddenly tipped backwards and Peter leapt forward to grab her, but he couldn't catch her before she hit her head on the bookshelf. She went out like a light as Peter caught her, preventing her from banging her head on the floor. Peter pulled her up his arms, distress on his face. As he stood up with the limp woman against his chest, he turned to Meade.

"That was a hard knock," he said. "I'm taking her to the hospital."

Meade shook his head. "She'll be okay. Take her upstairs, third door on the left."

"She knocked herself out when she fell backwards," Peter said, concerned. It was the first time he had ever stood up to Mr. Meade. "She needs to see a doctor."

Meade waved him off. "Don't go getting a conscience, Harrios," he said. "Colt did and now he's in trouble. Take her upstairs and put her to bed. She'll be fine once the drug wears off."

Peter looked at him, disgust and shock on his face. "What drug?"

"The one I put in her water. Rohypnol. You know – the date rape drug."

Peter's eyebrows lifted. "You gave her *that*?" his disgust was evident. "If you just put it in her water, it wouldn't have taken effect so quickly. She knocked herself out when she tripped and hit her head. She needs a hospital."

"Put her to bed," Meade's expression was deadly serious. "I'll look out for her this afternoon. You go tell Colt that I want to speak with him. Immediately."

Peter's jaw ticked as he turned for the stairs. He took Casey up to the lavish second floor, down to the bedroom that Meade had indicated. The old man was following him and Peter entered the very pretty bedroom with its massive canopy bed, laying Casey carefully on the mattress. Meade, in an oddly fatherly gesture, took a quilt neatly folded in the closet and put it over her. All bundled up on the big, fluffy bed, Peter stood over her a moment, hands on his hips, knowing Colt was going to kill him for this.

"Go," Meade told him. "Bring Colt back here immediately."

Peter headed for the door, angry and disgusted. "Don't give her any more drugs," he told him. "She's pregnant."

Meade registered great surprise, turning to look at Casey as Peter quit the room. "Pregnant?" he repeated to himself. "Interesting. Very interesting."

————

When Casey woke up, it was dark in the room. She had no idea where she was and she blinked her eyes a couple of times, thinking she was dreaming. She could see a very big canopy over her head and a bedroom she didn't recognize. It was so dark in the room that she really couldn't make out any detail, but she was both very puzzled and very scared. Uneasiness crept over her. When she shifted slightly on the bed, a big head suddenly loomed over her in the darkness.

"Angel?" It was Colt. "Are you awake?"

Casey had no idea why she burst into tears, but she did. She sat up and threw her arm around Colt, her nausea returning full-bore. He held her tightly, his big hand on her head, stroking her beautiful hair.

"It's okay," he whispered soothingly. "I'm here. Everything's okay."

Casey was sobbing, her head on his shoulder. "I... I don't remember...," she choked. "What happened? Where am I?"

Colt was rocking her gently. "You're at Chase Hollow," he explained. "You don't remember how you got here?"

"I don't know," she wept. "What's Chase Hollow?"

Colt wasn't sure how to answer. "It's a historic home outside of Middleburg," he replied. He knew she had passed out and hit her head. He also knew about the Rohypnol. He was struggling with every ounce of self-control not to lose his temper again, like he had earlier. There was still carnage downstairs. "Peter brought you here. Do you remember that?"

Casey had stopped her painful sobbing and now lay against him with her head on his shoulder, feeling safe with his big arms around her. She wasn't so frightened anymore now that he was here and was able to calm her tears somewhat. She struggled to clear her mind.

"I remember a little," she said, her voice hoarse and her nose sniffly. "He brought me out to meet some guy who introduced himself as Victor Meade. But... I don't remember a whole lot after that."

Colt stroked her back and hugged her gently. "It's okay," he whispered, kissing the side of her head. "I don't want you to worry about anything. I'll take you home."

She pulled back to look at him, pale-faced and red-eyed. "Why am I even here?" she wanted to know. "Peter never did tell me why he brought me here."

"And he probably can't now," a voice came from the bedroom door and they both turned to see Mr. Meade standing in the doorway. He smiled weakly and flipped on the lights. "Colt saw to that. Last I saw of Peter, he was heading to the emergency room."

Casey was disoriented, nauseous and scared as she watched Mr. Meade enter the bedroom. She looked at Colt with a mixture of curiosity and shock. "What did you do?"

Colt's jaw ticked and he glanced at Meade, making sure to keep his arms around Casey as if protecting her from the powerful old man.

"A lot less than what he deserved," he muttered.

"Colt," Casey's forced him to look at her. "What did you do to Peter?"

"He beat him soundly," Meade replied as he approached the bed. "I sent Peter to retrieve Colt from the White House. Colt went peacefully enough but when they reached Peter's car and Peter told him the details of the summons, your lover beat the man within an inch of his life, threw him in the trunk of his own car, and drove him over here. I had to call an ambulance to take him to the hospital."

Casey's eyes widened at Colt. "You did that to Peter?"

Colt wouldn't answer her. He was looking at Meade. "He's lucky I let him live," he growled. "If anyone else touches Casey again, I swear to God that I'll make sure it's their last day on earth."

Meade wasn't intimidated. In fact, he nodded. "I believe you completely."

"That includes you."

Meade smiled as if he found something very funny. "I know."

Colt's dark eyes lingered on the man a moment before turning back to Casey and burying his face in the side of her head. It was as if he just wanted to reassure himself that she was okay, using the scent of her to calm his nerves. It was like a drug to him, soothing and centering him. Meade watched with some astonishment.

"I had heard how devoted you were to her," he said softly. "But seeing you with her now hardly did that rumor justice. Tell me something, Colt – do you remember how to breathe without her?

Sleep without her? Function without her? That is a very real possibility, my friend, unless you and I come to an agreement."

Casey could feel Colt tense against her. His grip tightened as he pulled his face from the crook of her neck. Then he turned to Meade with as much hatred as Casey had ever seen. He was seething with it.

"You saw what happened to Peter," he rumbled. "If you so much as touch a hair on Casey's head, I'll make you wish you'd never been born. Let me be more specific. I'll systematically pick off The Core members one at a time until there are no more idiotic old men left to kill. If you threaten her, you threaten me, and I will protect what is mine. Is this in any way unclear to you?"

Meade didn't back down. He could see where this was heading and he sighed faintly. "Truthfully, I know you'll do exactly as you say," he nodded thoughtfully. "I know what kind of a weapon you are, Colt. I've seen you in action. But here is the problem as I see it – I want you to focus on your assignment. You want to focus on Casey. How shall we solve this problem amicably?"

Colt still held Casey tightly. "Leave her alone," he growled. "Leave her alone and put her and her family out of your mind. Have I ever failed you?"

"No."

"I'm not in any danger of breaking that record, but if you push me, you'll be sorry you did. I have no reason to turn on you or ignore my responsibilities, but involving Casey as you have, you won't give me any choice. I'll protect her to the death and I'll kill anyone who gets in my way. Is that really what you want?"

Meade eased somewhat. "Of course not," he said honestly. "But you have a job to do."

"And I'll do it. Just leave her out of it."

Meade stood at the foot of the bed, pondering the situation and his choices. The situation was critical enough that he felt he needed to stake his claim. His wants were more important than Colt's emotions. He sighed again, looking at Casey as she was huddled in Colt's embrace. He could see the love between the pair, so the reports he had been given were not untrue. If anything, they didn't do the attachment justice. He was beginning to feel some uncertainty, but that was all. The ability to feel compassion had died in him long ago.

"I will leave her out of it, providing you accomplish what you are supposed to," he said quietly, moving for the door. "Enough said tonight, Colt. Take her home. But don't think to betray me or there will be serious consequences. I can get to her any place, anywhere, and you'll never know until it's too late. I will say no more."

He left the room, leaving Colt and Casey in a tight embrace on the bed. Casey's gaze lingered on the doorway before turning to Colt.

"He's going to kill me if you don't find something to convict Russ, isn't he?" she whispered.

Colt just shook his head. Then he pulled her into such a tight embrace that Casey could scarcely breathe.

"Let's go home," he murmured. "Do you feel all right to travel?"

"I'm fine. I just want to get the hell out of here."

Colt stood up from the bed and carefully pulled her to her feet. She was a bit wobbly so he ended up sweeping her into his arms and carrying her down to the black Dodge Charger down in the driveway.

Meade wasn't anywhere to be found as they crossed the dark gravel path to the car. Colt put her down when they reached the car, hitting the unlock on the remote and carefully helping her into the car. As they drove away in the darkness, Casey couldn't help but wonder if she wasn't going to end up back here at some point if Colt didn't do what he was supposed to do.

He was supposed to ruin a President.

————

The office was dimly lit at this late hour, but Scott had been on a conference call with members of the Ways and Means Committee for a couple of hours, well after the closing bell and people went home for the night. As he finished up some notes on the call, he heard someone banging around in the outer office. It didn't take long before a familiar face made an appearance.

"Hello, Senator," Kurt gave him a wave as he leaned in the door. "You're here awfully late."

Distracted from his notes, Scott sighed heavily and leaned back in his chair. "So are you," he said, rubbing his tired eyes. "Don't you have a life?"

Kurt laughed softly. "If you don't have one, *I* don't have one."

Scott grinned, glancing at the clock. "I'd like to get home to see my son before he goes to bed," he commented. "The kid is growing up right before my eyes."

Kurt stepped into the office, nodding. "Kids grow fast."

Scott rubbed his eyes again. "He looks so much like his mother now, it's really eerie. He sounds like her, too. He's been complaining so much lately about being an only child that he sounds like his mother did after he was born. Carol wanted more kids right away but it just didn't happen. Now it looks like I'm going to have to marry someone with kids already so Robby will have someone to grow up with. And I suppose it would be nice to come home to someone every night."

Kurt watched Scott a moment as he wrestled with that very sentiment. He knew exactly what the man was driving at; he was probably the only one other than Scott who did. The man had been hung up on Casey Cleburne for weeks but she had made it clear she wasn't interested. The talk of remarriage, of coming home to someone every night, wasn't new. Kurt had been hearing it for weeks.

Casey's lack of interest hadn't deterred Scott, however. He still talked about her and made attempts to go to the White House on pointless visits, always making contact with her somehow while he was there. Kurt thought it was rather sad to watch, the man going on fool's errands. He lingered near the senator's desk, his hands in his pockets. He felt deeply sorry for the man.

"I heard something today that might interest you," he said softly.

"What's that?"

Kurt wasn't quite sure how to say it without coming right out and telling him. There was no gentle way to couch the rumor.

"Word at the West Wing is that Casey is dating the new Special Agent in Charge," he said. "It's all anyone can talk about."

Scott looked at him, the wheels of thought churning behind the dark hazel eyes. He cocked his head thoughtfully. "Sheridan?"

"The new guy. The big guy."

Recognition dawned. "*That* guy?" Scott seemed incredulous. "Not The Antichrist?"

"That's what people are saying."

Scott looked as if he were seriously mulling over the possibility. After a moment, he lowered his gaze. "She said she was seeing someone," he muttered. "It never occurred to me that it was... so she's seeing Sheridan, huh?"

"You never heard that rumor?"

"Never. Not a word."

Kurt didn't sense depression from the man at all. If anything, he sensed a challenge. It was in his tone, in his demeanor.

"He's a big, mean guy, Senator," he said casually, thinking that perhaps he should discourage whatever Scott might be thinking. "You've heard all about him, right? Why he's called The Antichrist?"

Scott looked at his young aide. "I've heard about him," he agreed. Then he began to mutter, more to himself than to Kurt. "She shouldn't be with someone like that. Not him."

"Maybe you need to let her decide, sir."

It was apparent that Scott was thinking long and hard about Casey Cleburne and the big Secret Service agent. Kurt could see that. But what he didn't know was that Scott knew more about Sheridan than he let on. He'd known for a while, things that most people in Washington could only guess at. Scott had inside knowledge of the man and his workings. He was shocked to realize that The Antichrist was his rival for Casey's affections.

He hustled Kurt out of his office, pretending he was leaving, too. But when Kurt finally vacated and Scott turned off the lights to continue the ruse, he went back into his office in the dark and picked up the phone. Using a secure line and dialing a number that wasn't written anywhere, or recorded anywhere, he listened as it rang five times. Someone picked it up on the sixth.

"Hello?"

Scott sat back down in his chair, the moonlight from the mild Washington night streaming in through the windows.

"Hello, Victor," he said softly, leaning back in his plump leather chair. "It's Scott."

FIFTEEN

CASEY'S INTERCOM had been ringing steadily for the past several seconds but she hadn't taken the time to pick it up. A glance showed it to be Lisanne but she didn't have the time to spare to talk to the woman. Russ was waiting for an agenda for his first meeting of the morning and she was running late.

It had been her fault, really. She and Colt had driven to work together, parking in their usual spot in the parking structure, but once Colt had put it in park and turned off the engine, he had grabbed her before she could get out of the car. He'd gotten rather amorous with her and, being weak to the man's charms, she had let him. They both needed the comfort and reassurance after what had happened with Mr. Meade. Casey's skirt had ended up bunched up around her waist as his fingers had worked her into a couple of climaxes. It had been sweet, thrilling and erotic. The car windows were all steamed up by the time they were finished and they'd both had to run to get to the office on time.

Colt had gone straight into a meeting with his boss in a smaller conference room while Casey, her legs like spaghetti and her heart still fluttering, had tried to focus on work. As she finished up the last of Russ' agenda and the intercom went off like crazy, a figure in an expensive overcoat entered her office space.

Casey glanced up, rather startled to realize it was Scott Dane. He smiled at her and she mustered up the strength to smile back.

"Good morning, Senator," she said pleasantly. "How can I help you this morning?"

He glanced at his watch. "I'm a little early for my meeting with the President. I hope that's okay."

Casey's brow furrowed as she looked at the President's schedule for the day.

"I'm sorry, but I don't seem to see you on his schedule," she said. Then she started looking at the next day. "There you are; you're a day early."

Scott wriggled his eyebrows. "Wow," he pretended to be very forgetful. "Are you sure? Isn't it Wednesday?"

"Thursday."

He shook his head. "And I rushed all the way over here," he said with feigned disgust. "I'm getting forgetful in my old age, I guess."

Casey just smiled pleasantly. "We'll be happy to see you tomorrow."

Scott nodded. Then he shrugged, glancing over at the coffee service behind Casey's desk. "Do you mind if I have a cup of coffee before I head back out into the world?"

Casey was already getting out of her chair. "Of course not," she said. "You take it black, right?"

Scott smiled, watching her as she moved to pour him some coffee. She was dressed in a gorgeous lavender suit that looked spectacular on her figure.

"Right," he said. "I'm flattered you remembered."

She simply smiled as she handed him the coffee and regained her seat. Scott sat down in her guest chair, very close to her desk, and Casey struggled not to become unnerved by his proximity. She found herself wishing Colt would come back from his meeting quickly.

"I haven't seen you in a while," Scott said casually, leaning back and sipping his coffee. "How have you been?"

Casey's forced smile was becoming something of a habit. "Well, thanks," she said. "And you?"

"Very well, thank you," he replied. "How were your holidays?"

Casey was anxious to get him out and get back to work, and it was a struggle not to sound rude.

"Good, thank you."

"Did you spend it with your family?"

"My parents flew out from California."

"Nice," he commented, eyeing her as she tried to refocus on the paperwork in front of her. "Was Santa good to you?"

She nodded. "He brought me a new car."

Scott's smile grew. "Very nice," he said. "You must have been a very good girl this year."

She just smiled, because she knew she should, and refocused on her paperwork. Scott watched her, sensing the conversation was dying, until he happened to glance at her left hand and saw the big ring on her finger. His heart sank but the fight didn't go out of him, not yet. Engagements could be broken.

"It looks like he brought you something else, too," he said quietly.

When Casey looked up, having no idea what he was talking about, he gestured to her left hand. Casey looked at the ring a moment.

"That wasn't from Santa," she said rather matter of factly.

She hoped he would take the hint and leave well enough alone, but he didn't. He continued to sip his coffee, watching her, making her uncomfortable with his unwelcome attention.

"Congratulations," he said, his voice low. "Sheridan, isn't it?"

She glanced up at him. There was no use in denying it since he'd obviously heard the rumors. In fact, maybe the knowledge that she was dating big, bad Sheridan would force him to give up.

"Yes," she replied.

He nodded faintly, his gaze moving back to the ring as her hand perched on the computer keyboard. "I've heard," he said. "I'm just... well, as long as you're happy."

"I am."

"I hope so. You're taking a big risk, you know."

He was starting to piss her off. Casey stopped typing and looked at him squarely. If he wanted to push the subject, then she was going to push him back.

"I suppose I should ask what you mean by that comment, but the truth is that I don't really care," she spoke in a low, even tone. "Look, Senator, I told you when you first sent me those flowers that I was flattered, and I was. I told you I was seeing someone. A true gentleman would have left well enough alone, but instead, you keep pushing the subject of my personal life. Please let me make this very clear – it's none of your business. I appreciate your interest but I am with someone else, someone I'm going to marry, and that's all there is to it. All you're succeeding in doing is making me mad, so I'd really appreciate it if you would stop bringing up my personal life. It's absolutely none of your business."

Scott could see that he'd upset her and he was frankly surprised by her reaction. In all of the contact he'd ever had with her, she'd always been exceedingly polite and pleasant. Now he'd roused her anger. He scrambled to make up for offending her.

"I'm sorry," he was no longer casual or cocky; he was repentant. "I didn't mean to upset you. It's just that... Casey, I'd be lying if I said I wasn't concerned about it."

Her jaw started to tick. "I don't know why," she said. "I am absolutely no concern of yours, so please just... drop it."

He sighed faintly and set the coffee down. "Okay, I will," he said. "But on the condition you hear me out. Just listen to what I have to say and I promise I'll drop the subject forever. Please?"

Frustrated, Casey just waved a sharp hand at him and turned back to her computer. Scott wasn't sure if that gesture was the go-ahead, but he did anyway. He just started talking.

"Casey, I'm sorry if I'm pestering you," he said in a low, soft voice. "It's just... well, I told you this before, but I think you're the most beautiful, intelligent and sweet woman I've ever met. I guess

I'm not used to not getting what I want, and it's tough to fight down matters of the heart."

Casey didn't say anything. She just kept typing. Scott continued. "I heard that your mystery boyfriend was Sheridan," he continued. "Casey, I just can't let this go without saying something. You know that guy has a bad reputation. He's mean, he's rough, and there's something very shady about him. Do you know that his last girlfriend was murdered?"

Casey stopped typing and looked at him. "Seriously?" she shook her head with disgust. "That's the best you can do?"

"I'm deadly serious," Scott insisted quietly. "A few years ago he was working on an assignment in Russia and he got a woman killed. From what I was told, her father was the head of one of the most powerful factions of the Russian Mafia and rumor had it that Colt was trying to infiltrate the faction and they got wise to him. They tried to kill him with a car bomb but the girl got it, instead. Bad elements seem to follow Sheridan around and I couldn't live with it if something happened to you because of him. Don't you have children? What if something happened to your children because of him? You need to get away from him, for your family's sake."

Casey was off-balance and furious, trying to shake him off but she only grew more frustrated. She remembered Colt mentioning he'd had a girlfriend a few years ago but he had never elaborated on her. Maybe there was a reason he hadn't. Casey's patience snapped and she smacked her hands on the desktop to get Scott to stop talking.

"Enough," she hissed. "You're not going to force me to change my mind about him no matter what you say, so I'd appreciate it if you'd just shut the hell up. I don't want to hear your slander anymore, okay? It's not working. Colt and I are going to get married and that's the end of it."

Scott sat back in the chair, eyeing her. She was very angry. He could see it, but he hoped that at least some of what he said was getting through to her. It was the truth, a very self-serving truth.

He'd gotten all of it from the horse's mouth, and Victor Meade had been more than willing to talk about it.

Before he could reply, the door to the Oval Office opened and men began pouring out into the hall. His private time with Casey had ended. With a lingering glance at Casey, who was gazing back at him with enormous hostility, Scott stood up from her guest chair and quit the office without another word.

People moved past Casey's desk, leaving the Oval Office, as she struggled to shake off the conversation with Scott and finish up the President's agenda. She realized, as she went back to typing, that her hands were shaking. *She* was shaking, mostly because some of what he said had her thinking.

Damn him!

———

When Colt emerged from his meeting with Mark Miller, the official story was that Special Agent Harrios was taking a few days off to recover from an accident. At least, that was what Colt had relayed to the President. The truth of the matter was something very different.

As Casey sat at her desk and typed minutes from the President's meeting with his National Security Advisor, she was trying very hard to focus on her job. After her run-in with Senator Dane, she realized, to her horror, that she was seriously starting to re-think everything. Scott may have been hell-bent on breaking her and Colt up, but some of what he said had made sense. Like it or not, it had, and coupled with the run-in with Mr. Meade, suddenly, things in her life were not so rosy. Things were getting scary.

The result of her fear was that she had been distant to Colt. She barely acknowledged him when he came out of his meeting with Mark Miller and really hadn't spoken to him all morning. As the day advanced, so did her sense of disquiet. Perhaps she really *was* in danger and putting her family in danger because she was being foolish. If Colt's last girlfriend really was murdered like Scott said, then maybe she needed to re-think her position. So many thoughts were rolling around in her head that they were making her crazy, but she kept it bottled up inside, not sure how to deal with it. All she knew was that she was terrified.

As Casey wrestled with her emotions, Colt sat in his office, watching her, increasingly concerned with her behavior. Usually, she would look at him, wink at him, or give him a little smile once in a while. He lived for those moments. But this morning, she had deliberately kept her eyes off of him. As the clock neared noon and the President went upstairs for lunch with his wife, Colt collected his car keys and went to Casey's desk.

She had her head down, going through a file folder of paperwork. Chris was sitting at his desk next to hers, in a rare moment of not being on the phone, but Colt didn't give the man a second glance. Usually he was careful around Eckart because the man was a gossip, but not today. He was beyond caring about that. He thumped quietly on Casey's desk to get her attention.

She looked up at him without even a hint of a smile on her lips. "What can I do for you, Colt?"

She said it with such defeat in her voice. He held out his hand to her. "Come with me," he said softly. "Let's get some lunch."

"I'm not really hungry."

He just held out his hand. "Please," he begged softly. "We'll get something fast."

Casey almost refused him again but she really didn't have the energy to dispute him. She felt so dull and sick inside. Silently, she collected her purse and her coat, and followed him out of the office.

They walked out of the West Wing in silence, side by side, into the cool late January air. Casey pulled on her coat as he held her purse, buttoning it up against chill. Colt eyed the coat as he handed her back her purse.

"We need to get you a heavy coat," he said. "You still wear those lightweight things. I thought you would have learned your lesson by now."

She shrugged, her head down, watching the pavement as they walked. "I like this coat."

Colt sighed heavily and came to a halt at the end of the White House driveway along Pennsylvania Avenue. He faced Casey seriously.

"I can't take this anymore," he said quietly. "There's obviously a lot on your mind and I would appreciate it if we can discuss it like adults. I don't do well in a relationship with a lack of communication. I'm not sure what I did to deserve the silent treatment."

She looked at him and, after a moment, shrugged weakly. "I... I don't even know where to start," she said softly. "That whole thing a couple of days ago just really shook me up. I just don't know where to start with what I'm feeling. I'm still trying to figure it out."

He put his hands in his pockets. "Angel, I know you're shook up. *I'm* shook up. But I told you before; we'll get through this but I really need your trust. I don't like it when you give me the cold shoulder, even if it's because you're afraid or confused. You need to talk to me about it so we can work it out."

She looked at her shoes again. "I keep thinking about my family," she admitted. "I look at Hunter and Brody and I'm scared to death for them. Mr. Meade said he could get me anytime, anywhere. What if he goes after my boys? And what about this baby I'm carrying? Is it fair to bring this baby into a situation like this?"

His eyes widened and the hands came out of his pockets. "What do you mean?"

She put her hand on her belly, tried to speak, but ended up bursting into quiet tears. Colt quickly, gently, took her by the elbow and began to walk her across the street just to get her away from the pedestrian traffic. They continued on into the cold, busy confines Lafayette Park so they could have some privacy. Colt put his arm around her shoulders as he led her into a section of the park less traveled.

"Angel," he said softly. "I know you're upset and I'm very sorry that all of this has happened. What can I do to make you feel better? What can I do to help?"

She wiped at her eyes but the tears kept coming. "I'm just so scared, Colt," she whispered. "I'm scared for my boys and for Riley and for this baby."

"You don't have to be."

She looked up at him, a flash of anger in the violet eyes. "Of course I have to be," she said. "By being with you, I'm putting them all in danger. If you and I break up, they'll be safe. I don't want to put them in danger but I don't want to break up with you. What kind of mother does that make me that I would put you before the safety of my own children?"

She was rightfully miserable and he put his hands on her arms to pull her close, but she slapped at his hands and pulled away. She didn't want his comfort. Colt's expression was wrought with pain and disappointment as she refused to let him console her.

"Angel, you're a wonderful mother," he insisted softly. "You're going to be a wonderful mother for our baby. I'm so lucky that my child is going to have you as his mother. How can I convince you that the boys and our baby will be safe? Nothing is going to happen to them or to you."

She looked up at him with her watery eyes. "You told me you had a girlfriend four years ago," she wept. "What you didn't tell me was that she was murdered. Why, Colt? What happened to her? Did you promise you'd keep her safe, too, and you weren't able to?"

He stared at her, stunned. "Who in the hell told you that?"

She could see that he was reeling. "It doesn't matter," she said. "What happened to her? You promised that you wouldn't keep secrets from me but you have. Tell me the truth."

His palms began to sweat and his heart began to thump against his rib cage, feeling cornered and angry. "Well," he said hoarsely, "I guess if you can't be honest and tell me who told you, I can't be honest with you and tell you what happened."

He turned away from her and started walking back towards the White House. It was the hardest thing he'd ever had to do but, much like her, he was dealing with unfamiliar emotion these days. Casey keeping a secret from him was like a stab to the heart. He wasn't sure how to deal with it other than to get away from her for the moment. But he hadn't taken five steps when he heard her calling after him.

"Colt!" she cried. "I'm sorry. I'm so sorry!"

He came to a halt and turned around about the time she crashed into him. He was so glad she had come after him because, if he was honest with himself, he really didn't know if he would have been able to make it another few feet without turning around and begging for her forgiveness and understanding. Gratefully, he wrapped his arms around her and she broke down into fresh tears.

"I'm sorry," she wept into his coat. "I wasn't trying to be... I'm just so scared. Maybe you're used to this kind of stuff, but I'm not. I'm scared to death every minute of every day and all I can think about is protecting my children and saving you. I feel like I'm going crazy."

He shushed her softly. "It's okay," he kissed her damp cheeks. "You're not crazy."

"Yes, I am. And I'm hormonal."

He grinned. "Okay, so you're hormonal."

"And... and *crazy*!"

He laughed softly. "Angel, you're *not* crazy," he insisted, wiping the moisture off her cheeks. "But you do need to be honest with me and tell me who told you about Katja."

She gazed up at him with her big, wet eyes. "Senator Dane," she whispered. "I saw him this morning when you were in your meeting with Mark. He just started talking to me about stuff and next thing I know, you're the topic of conversation and he's telling me that your last girlfriend was killed."

Colt's features tightened. "I underestimated him," he muttered after a moment. "I thought he would give up when you politely rejected him, but I guess not. The man has done his homework on me."

"He knew I was dating you."

He cocked an eyebrow at her. "It's not like we've been keeping it a secret. Word gets around."

She wiped at her nose. "Did he lie, then?"

Colt wriggled his eyebrows. "No," he said honestly. "But what he told you was fairly confidential information. I'd like to know how he got it."

She was starting to feel scared again. "You said yourself he's a powerful senator. I'm sure he has his ways of getting what he wants."

"That's apparent," he appeared thoughtful for a moment as he gently caressed her arms. "Yes, she was murdered, but the case was never solved. Given the fact that her father was a Russian arms dealer, it's not surprising she was killed. We'll never know who did it."

She was listening seriously. "Did you meet her while you were in Russia?"

"Yes."

"Did you love her?"

His dark eyes glimmered at her. "Yes," he said honestly. "But it can't measure up to what I feel for you."

She smiled at him, the first time she had done so in over a day. "I'm sorry she was killed," she said softly. "That must have hurt."

"It did, but it pales in comparison to the hurt I feel whenever we have a disagreement or are at odds. I just can't handle it when we have conflict, Casey. It just destroys me."

"I'm sorry," she whispered, reaching up to caress his cheek. "I'm not handling all of this very well. I'll try harder."

He kissed her forehead and then her lips. "You're doing fine," he told her. "But no more holding back, please. If you're upset, I need for you to talk to me about it. Don't shut me out. All right?"

She nodded, looking rather sheepish. "I guess... well, I guess my only real experience with communication in a serious relationship was with Dennis, and he just didn't like to talk about anything. He would just joke his way through it and avoid the reality of a problem, so I learned to just deal with things myself.

I'm sorry. I'm still learning with you. It's only right that we communicate completely."

He cupped her face with his big hands and kissed her. "Tell me the truth," he whispered. "Did Dane come on to you?"

She shook her head. "I would tell you if he did, but he really didn't. He was never suggestive. He just seemed to have a lot of information about you."

Colt thought on that a moment, dropping his hands from her face and taking her hand as they headed out of the park. "He's done his reconnaissance," he said. "He knows his enemy."

"You're not his enemy."

He cocked an eyebrow at her. "Angel, the only reason he would tell you those things is to drive you away from me. I am absolutely his enemy. I have what he wants."

She put her arm around his waist. "Well, he's not going to get me," she said firmly. "I belong to you."

He kissed her forehead as they neared Pennsylvania Avenue. "I'm glad to hear that," he murmured. "But I will admit, I have been thinking very seriously about our run-in with Meade. Scott Dane aside, Meade's the real issue right now and I think I'm going to do something very drastic to counter-punch him."

"Oh, my God," Casey breathed, clutching a hand to her stomach. "I don't like the sound of that at all. Colt, whatever you do, please be careful. I don't want to raise this baby on my own. I'd rather have you alive and on the run than a dead hero."

He gave her a squeeze. "You won't have to do anything alone, I promise," he said softly. "But whatever I do, I want you to understand that it's what I feel is right. I want you to support me no matter what."

"I will. You know that."

Colt did. He took her over to their favorite sandwich shop to get some lunch before they headed back to the White House. Not surprisingly, Casey wasn't very hungry.

Neither was he. He knew what he had to do.

It was mid-afternoon in the West Wing, a surprisingly quiet afternoon that saw Russ working on a speech with Jason Travis, and nearly everyone else just going about their business. Usually, there was a sense of bustle, but not today. It was actually rather calm, an odd peace that wasn't entirely comforting. It was like the calm before the storm and there was always a storm.

Casey sat at her desk, discreetly munching on salty peanuts as she went through some plans for Tracy Talbot's birthday in April. The President wanted to have a theme party and Casey was trying to nail down a country-western theme with the help of one of Washington's most popular party planners.

Colt was back over at his desk. She could hear him alternately typing and on the phone to someone in the Presidential detail. As she put her peanuts away, she caught movement out of the corner of her eye and turned to see Colt standing next to her desk.

"Can I have some of the President's time the afternoon?" he asked quietly.

Casey nodded as she glanced at his schedule. "He should be done with Jason soon," she looked up at him. "How much time do you need?"

"A half hour at most."

"I'll make it happen. You can go in when Jason is finished."

He winked at her and went back to his desk. Casey went back to her work, losing track of time until the door to the Oval Office suddenly opened and Russ and Jason came through. The young aide had some re-writing to do and he slipped out as Russ wandered up to Casey's desk and sat heavily in her guest chair. He kicked out his feet and leaned back against the cushions.

"Whew," he grunted. "I was never any good as a writer. I'm much better speaking off the cuff. I can never stick to a prepared speech."

Casey put her work aside, grinning at the President. "Don't go too far off the prepared speech. You'll freak everybody out."

Russ snorted. "It's good to give 'em a scare once in a while," he yawned and scratched his head. "Is the day over yet, General?"

Casey shook her head. "Not yet," she said. "Special Agent in Charge Sheridan needs a few moments of your time."

Russ laced his fingers behind his head, leaning back as he turned to look into Colt's office. "Sheridan?" he called.

Colt could only see the President's legs from where he sat. He came out from behind his desk and stood in the doorway. "Mr. President," he greeted.

Russ was casually looking up at the man. "Good God, you're tall," he grunted. "Is your brother as tall as you are?"

Colt shook his head. "He's taller, sir," he replied. "He's an inch taller than I am and about eighty pounds lighter."

"Hmmm," the President looked him up and down before rising wearily to his feet. "You Sheridan boys are a big bunch. As I recall, General Phil Sheridan was a short guy."

Colt nodded. "He was," he replied, "but my mother's grandfather was six feet six inches. We don't get our height from the Sheridan side of the family, only our brains."

The President chuckled. "Well, come on, then. Let's go shoot the breeze."

Colt turned to Casey as the President made his way back to the Oval Office. "Will you join us, please?"

Rather surprised at the request, Casey grabbed her steno pad and followed. As she entered the yellow and deep blue Oval Office with the big antique Resolute Desk near the windows, Colt closed the door softly behind her.

Russ had already moved to sit on one of the two blue couches in the room, both of them facing each other and Colt indicated for Casey to sit on the couch opposite the President. He sat down beside her.

"Thank you for seeing me on such short notice," Colt said. "I know your time is valuable, so I won't waste it. I have a situation on my hands and I need your help, Mr. President."

Russ looked at him seriously. "I'm sorry to hear that," he said. "What's going on?"

Colt drew in a long, thoughtful breath, organizing his thoughts. "Mr. President, as you know, I have served four Presidents including you. I take my work very seriously."

Russ nodded. "You're the best, Colt. I'm proud to have you."

"Thank you," Colt replied sincerely. "I hope that there is a level of trust between us that supersedes the roles of your office and my position. I hope there is a level of trust that is man to man."

Again, Russ nodded, his gaze moving to Casey. "You know there is," he said quietly. "You entrusted me with a very big secret, once. I kept it. You also saved my life. I will never forget that and, as I said before, I owe you. I am deeply indebted to you."

Colt remained quiet a moment. When he spoke, his tone was very low and soft. "What I am about to tell you must not leave this room. If it does, we're all in jeopardy."

Casey was prepared to take notes but suddenly, she froze with her pen poised just above the paper. Shocked, she looked at Colt, having a vague idea as to why he had called this meeting. The truth was that she was more than afraid. She sat there, wide-eyed, as Russ leaned forward, his expression grave.

"Of course, Colt," he said. "What is it?"

Colt deliberately looked at Casey, who was still looking at him with apprehension. He reached out and put his hand on her knee before turning to look at the President.

"I have a big problem," his voice was so quiet it was nearly a whisper. "Actually, all three of us have a big problem. I need your help, Mr. President, otherwise, Casey is facing a lot of danger."

Russ's brow furrowed. "Danger?" he repeated, looking at Casey. "Why? What in the hell is going on?"

Casey wrapped her fingers around Colt's hand to reassure him that she was with him, that he had her support. He squeezed her hand before continuing.

"Mr. President, have you ever heard of The Core?" Colt asked quietly.

Russ stared at him. Then, he sat back on the couch, evidently mulling over the question. After a few moments of silence, he slowly nodded.

"I think so," he said quietly. "I seem to remember hearing about them when I was a senator and sat on the Intelligence Committee. They're a division of the CIA, aren't they?"

Colt half-nodded, half-shrugged. "In a sense," he replied. "They were created by the CIA after World War II as a super-secret division that could operate under the radar of normal CIA activities. No accountability, no consequences. They're funded through a communications line item in the defense budget because of the international implications of their work."

The President nodded. "I seem to recall that," he said. "I also seem to recall that The Core is more a rogue element than anything else, full of assassins, double-agents and spies."

"I am an agent for The Core."

Russ didn't react other than to nod his head faintly. "I see," he said, his voice low. "You realize that by telling me that, I can have you removed from my detail."

Colt nodded. "I know," he said honestly, "but you won't, not when I tell you everything."

"What is everything?"

"I was sent to destroy your presidency."

Russ did react, then. His eyebrows lifted. "Is that so? And just how are you going to do that?"

Colt's dark eyes were intense. "My father was an agent for The Core during the Cold War, which is how I was recruited," he said quietly. "I went to work for them straight out of the Marine Corps and my first assignment was to get close to Clinton during White-water. I was the one who provided enough information to convict Clinton's business partners in the fraudulent scheme and also enough evidence to convict the man who succeeded Clinton as the governor of Arkansas. I was with Obama and Bush for the same reasons, to keep an eye on them. It was my job to seek out corruption and destroy careers if necessary, but it was more complicated than that. I've taken out rogue operatives, enemy operatives, turned double-agent myself, and a host of other things I won't go into, but suffice it to say that I know your dirty secrets, Mr. President. So does The Core."

By this time, Russ was pale. "Know what?" he demanded.

Colt didn't pull any punches. "Nine hundred thousand dollars worth of bribes from the Colombian Drug Cartel to allow them to land their drug planes in the deserts of New Mexico," he said. "We have witnesses. I've seen your financial records. There's enough evidence to bring you down, Mr. President."

Russ was sweating. "I don't know what you're talking about."

Colt lifted an eyebrow. "I hope you do," he said. His tone was non-threatening, more friend to friend. "Here's the gist of the situation, Mr. President. I was sent to gather information on your Colombian drug dealings. When I first started this position, my task was clear cut. I was directed to use Casey to my advantage in order to accomplish my mission, but therein lies the problem. I fell in love with Casey. I love her more than anything. When you found out about it, you were gracious and kind. You kept our secret. Meanwhile, I did my job and discovered quite a bit about you, at least enough to begin an inquest. But simultaneously, I also came to know you. I like you, Mr. President, when my personal feelings should not be entering into this at all. The Core has discovered this because there are other Core agents in the West Wing. Now, The Core is threatening Casey if I don't complete my mission."

Russ was listening to him, trying not to appear shaken when the truth was that he was very shaken. He knew what The Core was capable of; everyone in Washington did. They were the Black Ops of politics, the dirty and deadly little secret that no one wanted to talk about. God help them all with The Core around.

"So what do you want from me?" Russ' voice was hoarse with emotion.

Colt looked at Casey, squeezing her hand again before turning back to the President.

"If you remove me from my post, they'll just put someone else here, someone who doesn't have any emotional investment in all of this, and you'll go down," he said softly. "I promised Casey that I would help you, not hurt you, and that's what I'm going to try to do. The Core has caught wind that the Colombians are rearing their ugly head again and trying to blackmail you into opening more borders for their drug shipments by threatening to tell the world about your connections to them back in the nineties. Is this true?"

Russ' hand was shaking as he moved to wipe the sweat off his upper lip. "If you know so much, then you probably already know the answer to that."

"I need to hear it from you."

Russ sighed deeply, sitting forward on the couch with his elbows on his knees. He was looking at his hands. "I'm not sure why," he said. "Anything I say will be incriminating."

Colt watched the man struggle. "Look," he lowered his voice. "I'm trying to help you, Mr. President. I know you're shook up about this and I understand. But you have to understand that I'm doing all of this for Casey; not you, not the United States of America, not The Core, but for Casey. They've already tried to kidnap her to force me into turning evidence against you and I'm afraid if they try again, I won't be able to protect her. If you give me information on the drug lord who's blackmailing you, maybe I can stop it. If I stop it, The Core won't have any reason to go after you because the threat of you reopening the borders to the Colombians will be ended. Sure, you took all of that money and we can trace some of the deposits, but I also noticed on your tax returns from the late nineties that you donated almost six hundred thousand dollar to the National Cystic Fibrosis Foundation. Of the nine hundred thousand that you took from the Colombians, what didn't go to pay for treatment for your kids went to the CF Foundation. You didn't keep the money for yourself. It was to help your boys and kids like them. Even if it was illegal, it wasn't selfish. You did it to save your children. I just can't condemn you for that."

Russ was staring at him, his expression ashen and morose. "That's a compassionate statement coming from a man whose reputation doesn't include that trait."

"Will you tell me the truth?"

Russ sighed heavily. "It's not that easy, Colt."

"Yes, it is."

"You have no idea what...."

Colt cut him off. "Don't do it for me. Do it for Casey. Please, I'm begging you."

Russ lifted his gaze, looking at Casey's teary-eyed expression. Emotions rippled across his face, those of remorse and fear and resistance. "We can put her in a safe location until we can get this sorted out," he said. "She'll be...."

"She's pregnant," Colt cut him off again, almost desperately. "I need to protect my family, Mr. President. As you did everything you could to save yours, including illegal bribes, you need to help me save mine. Please, sir, I'm begging you."

Casey broke down into soft tears, hanging her head. Russ watched her, feeling sick and sad. He had always feared those moments of weakness when he was determined to save his family would come back to haunt him one day, and they had. He was cornered. But he was also a champion and the greater part of him wanted to help Casey and her unborn child. He couldn't stand by and watch bad things happen. More than that, Colt promised to end his Colombian nightmare once and for all. Perhaps Colt Sheridan would save his life one more time. After a moment, he exhaled heavily and sat back on the couch.

"Okay," he finally whispered. "I'll tell you everything. What do you want to know?"

Everything The Core had ever wanted to know about President Russell Talbot was revealed. What the best intelligence in the world couldn't completely gather, the threat against Casey Cleburne was able to discover in a little under an hour.

———

"He told me everything," Colt said quietly.

They were in Mr. Meade's study, once again keeping company with the smell of tobacco and priceless antiques. Meade looked up from his ancient desk, a surprised expression on his features.

"What...?" he actually stammered. "Who? Talbot?"

"Yes."

"He told you *everything*?"

"Everything we ever wanted to know. I know it all."

Mr. Meade was astonished, so much so that his wrinkled, old mouth actually popped open, then swiftly closed. As he sat there looking shocked, a semblance of a smile spread over his face.

"What, *exactly*, did he tell you?" he wanted to know.

Colt was exhausted and edgy, sitting heavily in one of the many luxurious leather chairs in the room. He could still hardly believe it himself, the course of his conversation with the President.

"He allowed the Norte del Valle drug cartel to land on Erik Travis' land south of Magdalena Ridge in New Mexico to bring cocaine shipments into the United States during his tenure as governor of New Mexico," he said quietly. "And, yes, he accepted almost nine hundred thousand dollars in bribes from Gael Rodriguez Noestra, the head of the cartel, for that privilege. It was as we suspected – what he didn't use to try to keep his boys alive, he donated to the Cystic Fibrosis Foundation. He never kept a penny of it. As he says, he did what he had to do to keep his boys alive and he'd do it again if he had to do it all over again. But that's not the problem."

"What's the problem?"

"Noestra is back," Colt lowered his voice. "Talbot confirmed the rumors that we'd been told. Now that he's President, Noestra wants carte blanche in landing his drug planes on Federal lands or he's threatening to tell everyone what Talbot did for him as governor of New Mexico. More than that, he threatened Tracy Talbot."

Meade looked surprised. "The First Lady?"

"That shooting at Andrews Air Force Base was no accident. That airman was aiming for Tracy. It was a warning."

Meade carefully digested the information. "You know this for certain?"

"The President told me himself although that airman hasn't confessed to it. Still, investigations into his bank accounts showed a deposit of fifty thousand dollars the day before the assassination attempt. I think it's pretty clear. The cartel hired him to shoot Tracy to force Talbot into agreeing to their demands."

After a moment of thoughtful silence, Meade got up out of his chair and began to pace his study, a room where generations of Meades had made critical decisions that affected the path of the nation. He paused by the big fireplace with its carved marble mantel, gazing up at a portrait of General George Gordon Meade. He had his great-great-grandfather's big, puppy-dog eyes, and he had his cunning brain. What he didn't have was his heart. The man completely lacked compassion.

"So now we move," he turned to Colt. "We tell Talbot that he can resign his office or we go public with the information. We tell him that...."

Colt shook his head, cutting him off. "No, we don't," he said firmly. "Mr. Meade, I've worked for you for a lot of years. I've always taken my directives without question and I have executed every task, no matter how dirty, flawlessly. But this time, you're going to listen to me on this. It's important."

Meade wasn't offended. In fact, he was rather curious. He leaned back against the hearth. "Go on."

Colt stood up from the chair. "The problem isn't Talbot," he said. "It's the Colombians. If we boil all this down, they're the root cause of all of this. Russ Talbot did what any father would do to save his children. I can't fault him for it. The man's not crooked by nature and I've been around him enough to know. He's intelligent, handles himself well, has an excellent approval rating, and is getting things accomplished in Congress. Haven't you been paying attention?"

Meade nodded slowly. "I have."

"Do you disagree that he's been an excellent President?"

"I do not. He's been one of the better ones when it comes to policy and decisions."

"So why remove the man from office because he did something, albeit illegal, to save his children? Do we really want to see Anthony Peck as president?"

Mr. Meade shrugged. "He's not nearly the caliber that Talbot is, but he'll do."

"Maybe he will, but that doesn't solve the root of the problem. I have a better idea."

"What?"

Colt began to walk slowly towards Mr. Meade as he spoke. "I don't want to see Talbot thrown out of office and into jail because of what he did fifteen years ago to save his children," he said quietly. "I like the man. I think he's good for the country. So I will make you this proposal."

"I'm listening."

"I will go to Colombia and take care of Noestra. I'll wipe the man from this earth. That will eliminate the problem of the cartel blackmailing Talbot because with Noestra gone, that entire organization will fall into chaos. Everyone will be vying for a chance to lead it. Noestra's the head and if we cut it off, the group will be ineffective. But if I do this, it will be with a concrete understanding between you and me."

"What's that?"

"That The Core leaves Talbot alone, that you leave Casey alone, for good, and that this will be my last mission for The Core. I want out after this. I'm finished."

Mr. Meade scratched his cheek thoughtfully before reaching on to the mantel and flipping open the humidor that carried his beloved Cuban cigars. He lit one up as he thought on Colt's proposal, mulling over all angles as he was so capable of doing.

"I don't want to lose you, Colt," he finally said. "You're the best we have but I will be honest when I say that I had a feeling it would be coming to this."

"I want to marry Casey and raise a family. I don't want to do this covert stuff any longer. It's time for me to grow up and move on."

Meade puffed on the cigar. "You realize that it will not be an easy thing to assassinate Noestra. You may not make it back."

"I am aware. But if I do succeed, my provisions stand."

"If you succeed, then they will."

"Then you agree?"

Meade didn't say anything for a moment. He puffed on his cigar, thoughtfully, but Colt could sense his indecision. It wasn't like Meade to give in or give up. But he had been known to compromise. Perhaps that's what he viewed this as. Colt could only hope.

"I do," Meade finally said. "You've always accomplished everything you set out to do. I've never had to worry about you. But you're distracted now with Ms. Cleburne and that diminishes your effectiveness for our cause. I can see that she's not a passing fancy so I am resigned to her presence in your life. Little did I know when I told you to get close to her that you would get closer than I anticipated. It's my fault, really. I told you to do it and you did."

Colt wasn't sure what to say to that. "I just can't make my work for The Core my life anymore," he said quietly. "I was very content to do that while I was single and unattached, but now... I realize there's something more for me and I want it."

Meade didn't really understand but he nodded anyway. "There are others who can eventually take over for you. I will admit I'm sorry to see our association coming to an end."

Colt was surprised by the sentiment. He'd never known Meade to show any emotion that wasn't either self-serving or manipulative. To be honest, the display put him on guard.

"I'll take care of this," he said after a moment. "But you leave Casey alone. Are we clear?"

"We are. But if you don't make it back...."

Colt didn't like the sound of that. "Go ahead, what if I don't make it back?"

Meade blew pale gray smoke into the air before speaking. "Talbot goes down and there isn't a damn thing you can do about it."

Colt didn't say anymore. He quit the study, desperate to get home. Home to Casey.

———

Colt was standing in the kitchen talking to Casey after dinner until Brody came in and rammed him with a runaway skateboard. Grinning, Colt fell over the counter, pretending to be wounded, as Brody made a grab for the skateboard and a quick escape. Colt grabbed it, too, quick as a flash, and yanked on it.

Brody fell forward and Colt put him in a headlock, rubbing his knuckles against the top of Brody's blond head. Trapped, the kid alternately giggled and yelled until he was released.

Colt cocked an eyebrow at him as he folded his big arms across his chest. "Let that be a lesson to you," he told Brody. "Every action has a reaction. Run me over with that skateboard again and pay the price."

Brody was grinning, staying out of arm's reach. "Eh, it didn't hurt you, you big...."

Colt was trying not to laugh. "Big *what*?"

"Big... man."

Colt started laughing then. "That's not the point."

"What's the point?"

Colt snorted as Casey shooed her son out of the kitchen. "The point is that you should apologize for running into Colt," she said. "And another point is that you know you're not supposed to ride that thing in the house."

Brody just smiled at his mother, who shook her head reproachfully at him. He scooted out of the kitchen, running into to his brother and some friends who had just come in the front door. All six boys settled down in the family room to play alien war games as Colt and Casey slipped upstairs for the evening.

Casey went into her bedroom and kicked off her shoes. "Ugh," she said as she fell back on the bed, staring up at the ceiling. "I'm so exhausted."

Colt closed the bedroom door and sat down on the bed, unlacing his shoes as well. "I know you are," he said softly, putting his hand on her gently rounded belly. "How's my boy today?"

She smiled up at him. "He's doing fine," she said, her smile fading. "You know, it's going to be more difficult for me to keep this from the boys as my belly gets bigger. My clothes are already pretty tight."

Colt rubbed her belly. "I know," he said. "It's becoming pretty obvious, at least to me. Have you told anyone at all?"

"I told Riley, but only because I had to. She saw me get out of the shower one day and nearly had a heart attack. She was upset at first but she's come to terms with it. I think she's pretty happy about it now."

"Good," he said. "I don't want to have to live in fear of her ambushing me in the hallway and shoving me down the stairs in vengeance for her sister's honor."

Casey giggled. "She wouldn't do that," she said. "But I think we need to make some decisions, soon, about what we're going to do."

Colt shrugged, kicked off his shoes, and lay down next to her. "Get married."

She lay on her side, facing him as he lay on his side facing her. "I don't want anything splashy," she said softly. "I just want you there, and the boys and Riley. Maybe my parents and your parents. Do you think the Cleburnes and the Sheridans can stay peaceful for the wedding? It won't turn out like the Hatfields and McCoys, will it?"

He grinned, reaching out to tuck hair behind her ear. "My parents will be fine," he said. "What about yours?"

She shifted so she was snuggled up against him. "My dad will probably wear a rebel flag t-shirt, but other than that, things should be fine," she giggled when he did. "Do you think we can do it this weekend? Is that too soon?"

His smile faded. "It's not too soon," he whispered. "But before we go into that, I need to talk to you about something."

"What about?"

He was quiet a moment as he organized his thoughts, thinking of what he had to say and wanting to phrase it carefully so she wouldn't implode. He'd been gearing up for this since his meeting with Meade, knowing what was coming and trying to ignore the grief it provoked until he could ignore it no longer. His task was set and tomorrow, he was leaving. Casey still didn't know but he'd meant it that way. He was genuinely afraid of her reaction.

He stopped playing with her hair and wrapped his arms around her. "We need to discuss everything you and the President and I talked about the other day," he confided, watching her features tighten. "We haven't talked about it since it happened, but we need to. It's not going to go away."

Casey's smile faded completely as she gazed at him. "I was really hoping it would," she said softly. "I still don't think I'm over the fact that you told the President everything."

"I didn't have a choice.

"I know."

He kissed her forehead and tucked her head against his chest. "I had a long talk with Mr. Meade about it," he continued. "I explained everything to him and he saw my point."

"Did he really? Or did you force him to?"

"Either way, he saw my point. I'm leaving for Bogota in the morning."

Her head shot up, the violet eyes wide. "What?" she gasped. "*You're* going to Bogota?"

He nodded, seeing that she was not going to be calm about this but the truth was that he didn't expect her to. He could only do his best to help her through what had to come.

"Yes," he whispered firmly. "Angel, this is my job. This is what

I do. I can't trust this to anyone else, not when your life hangs in the balance."

She stared at him with big eyes and he could see that they were already filling with tears. "Why not?"

"I told you why. This is the most important mission of my life. I have to see it through."

Casey stared at him, shocked to realize that he was deadly serious. Since their meeting with the President, Colt hadn't said another word and she'd been lulled into a false sense of security by it. Everything in their life had gone on like normal, including the family dinner tonight. She had cooked, Colt had helped. It had been sweet and wonderful and normal. She was looking forward to the rest of her life being like that, every day spent with the man she loved more than life. Now....

"But...," she shook her head and the tears spilled over. "I don't want you to go. You promised I wouldn't have to raise the baby on my own. Colt, you *promised*."

She was starting to sob, pulling away from him as he tried to hold her. "You won't," he sat up and pulled her against him even as she struggled. "I'll be back, I promise. But I just can't trust this job to anyone else. Your life and my baby's life hang in the balance. I have to do this myself to make sure it gets done, to make sure you're safe. A very bad man has to die in order to eliminate the threat against you and against the President. This has huge implications, Casey. Do you understand that?"

She was weeping deeply by the time he was finished. She just wrapped her arms around his neck and held him tightly.

"Please don't go," she begged. "Please don't leave me."

He held her close, lying back on the bed with her in his arms. A big hand stroked her hair, trying to give her some comfort.

"I will never, ever leave you," he promised. "I will always be with you, no matter where I am or what I'm doing, because my thoughts will be with you."

Casey didn't hear him. She was emotional and hormonal,

translating into volatile moods. She sobbed painfully against him as he tried to soothe her.

"Please," she whispered. "Please don't go."

He could feel a lump in his throat at her anguish-filled weeping. He held her tightly, rocking her, thinking of what lay ahead. He wasn't about to tell her how dangerous it was going to be or the hazards he would face. That would only make her more upset. But there was little time and much had to be said. For his own peace of mind, he had to.

Colt pulled Casey from the crook of his neck, his big hands cupping her face as he gazed steadily into her eyes.

"Casey, listen to me," he said as evenly and as gently as he could. "It's very important that you do. Please?"

She was still wallowing in great misery, shaking her head. "I... I don't want to," she sobbed. "I don't want you to go but you...."

He kissed her to shut her up. "Listen to me."

"I...."

He kissed her again, cutting her off firmly. When he pulled away, she had to catch her breath because he had kissed her so hard. "I can do this all night but I'd rather have a meaningful conversation with you," he whispered. "I want you to be calm and listen very carefully to me. Please?"

By this time, she was starting to come around, realizing that he wasn't going to give her time to have a temper tantrum. Colt was serious and level-headed, and she wasn't. Her violet eyes were wet with tears.

"I don't want to listen to you," she hissed. "I don't want you to go and I want you to stay here with me. There has to be something else that can be done that doesn't involve you going to Colombia to assassinate the drug lord that's blackmailing Russ. You're too important to risk your life like that. There are others who can do the job."

"I don't want to trust the job to anyone else."

"That's your ego talking. You have to be the big hero."

She was pitching a good fit; he had to give her credit. Colt tried not to grin as she did everything but stomp her feet.

"Angel," he cooed, knowing it wouldn't do any good to butt heads with her. "Baby, there are a couple of things we need to settle before I go for my own peace of mind. First of all, I want you to keep on with your life as it is. Go to work, take the boys to school, and come home and make plans for our wedding. I've put you on my bank account, so you'll have access to my money. You're going to need to buy things for the baby and I want you to be able to do whatever you want to do. Word at the White House will be that I've been reassigned to the European Bureau as a temporary promotion overseeing the operations for Western Europe. If anyone asks, that's all you know. As far as you're concerned, I'm fine, I'm busy, and I miss you. That's all anyone needs to know."

By this time, she was still in pouting mode but at least she'd stopped sobbing. She watched him, a frown on her lush lips.

"What can I say that will convince you not to go?" she begged softly.

His dark eyes glimmered. "Nothing," he kissed her. "This is something I have to do and no amount of begging or crying is going to change it."

Casey didn't like that answer in the least but she nodded stiffly, as if to let him know she was losing this argument kicking and screaming. Colt wiped the last of her tears from her temple.

"I'm not sure how long this is going to take," he murmured. "It could take a week, it could take a year. I just don't know. But I want you to know that I will think of you every minute of every day, and I will try to contact you from time to time to let you know I'm okay."

She was starting to tear up again. "If you're gone a year, you'll miss the birth of the baby. You *can't* miss it."

He shushed her softly. "I'm not going to miss anything," he assured her. "The baby's due date is August 3rd. I *will* be here, Casey, one way or another. Even if it's just for an hour to see you both, I'll be here. This baby means more to me than you can ever imagine. Please believe me."

She was struggling against the tears again. "I do."

He knew she didn't but he gave her credit for the brave lie. While she was marginally focused, he continued with what he needed to say. For both their sakes, he had to.

"I want you to listen to me carefully," his thumbs stroked her damp cheeks. "I will try to check in regularly with you so you know I'm alive and also so I can find out how you are. But if my calls or emails stop for longer than six months, you're going to have to assume something has happened to me and I'm not coming home. If that happens, I...."

She burst into tears, interrupting him, and he moved quickly to get through what he needed to say. She had to know.

"I want you to know how much I love you," he whispered, feeling a lump in his throat at the thought of not returning to her. "I also want you to raise this baby in the manner you see fit. You're a wonderful mother and I trust you completely with any decisions regarding our child. All I ask is that, if it's a boy, you let him fulfill his destiny as Philip Henry Sheridan VI. I would also ask that you maintain close contact with my parents and seek out my dad's advice for any critical decisions regarding him. And if it's a girl... well, I really *would* like to name her Adelaide after my grandmother and if she wants to go into the military, then she has my blessing. In fact, she has my blessing whatever she wants to do. I... I really hope you'll tell the baby about me and tell him or her how much I love him. That would mean the world to me."

Casey could only nod, far gone with tears, and collapsed against his chest. Colt held her tightly, knowing their conversation was over but also knowing he'd said what he needed to say. He was comforted with that. He remained awake for the rest of the night even after she fell into a fitful sleep, not wanting to relinquish his last moments with her to something as mundane as sleep. He wanted to remember her feel, her scent, the feel of her flesh against his.

By the time morning broke, tears were streaming down his face as he thought of leaving her and the unknown task ahead. Maybe it would be better for him to forget about the President, the Secret Service, the Colombians, The Core, and everything else, and just take Casey and the boys and go live on his grandparents' ranch in Montana. Maybe he would have blown a brilliant career, but at least he'd have Casey and they'd be together.

The eastern sky was turning shades of pink. He could see it through the blinds. He knew he had to make up his mind, to stay or go, and for several minutes he actually thought he would stay. His resolve was weakening. But the shadows of his heritage began to drift over his mind and he realized his sense of commitment, his sense of honor, meant more than anything else. It would be the one thing he left to his child that no one could ever take away from him. He had to see it through. He knew that.

Casey awoke to Colt making love to her, one last time, as dawn broke over the eastern seaboard. When they finally parted, it was with quiet tears and kisses, and Casey thought she was all right until an hour after he left. Then, she crumbled.

She took to bed and stayed there for three straight days.

SIXTEEN
EARLY JULY

RUSS WAS STANDING in the doorway to the Oval Office, speaking to his aide, Jason. They were discussing the assassination of a major drug lord in Colombia, something that had been plastered all over the news and the news outlets wanted a comment from the President. The drug lord had been very popular, a good friend of the Colombian President, and the Colombians were throwing all sorts of accusations at the United States. But Russ couldn't have cared less.

All he knew was that he felt more relief than he had ever felt in his life. Somehow, someway, Sheridan had orchestrated what he had promised. He had taken care of the man who had been menacing the President for over ten years.

Russ felt complete and utter elation except when he looked over at Casey, seated behind her desk and concentrating on her work. Then, his elation took a hit. The cost for his freedom had been her heart and soul. For the past six months, she had been a truly miserable person. His heart hurt every day that he saw her, knowing what she was going through and the sacrifices she had made. He felt guilty.

When Jason went off to talk to the Press Secretary, Russ

wandered over to Casey's desk. She was working on a spreadsheet, focused and pale, as he cleared his throat softly.

"Can I see you a minute?" he asked.

Casey looked up from her computer and forced a smile. Standing up, she collected her steno pad and pen and followed him into the Oval Office. Russ eyed her as he sat down at his desk and she took the chair opposite; there was no spring in her step these days. It was as if she was just going through the motions, efficient as always, but there was no joy or humor in her face.

More than that, it was apparent that her belly was growing. She had surprisingly been able to camouflage her rounded stomach with sweaters and jackets and layers of clothing or scarves, but Russ was concerned about the pregnancy and eventually broke down to tell his wife. Tracy had been particularly emotional about it but Russ wouldn't let her talk to Casey. As far as Casey knew, it was still a secret with only Russ and Peter in the know. But it was a secret she wouldn't be able to keep much longer because at almost eight months pregnant, she just couldn't deny the obvious any more. Anyone with half a brain would see that she was with child if they got a good look at her waistline.

Today, she camouflaged it in a pale yellow summer dress with an empire waistline. It was elegant and sophisticated. She sat down on the couch opposite the President and crossed her great legs, still wearing the five inch heels these days. Russ cleared his throat softly.

"Don't you think...," he was pointing at her shoes, "that, uh, those shoes are a little high?"

Casey looked down at the sexy nude-colored pumps on her feet. She shrugged. "I'm comfortable in them."

"What does your doctor say?"

She cocked an eyebrow. "The same thing you say," she replied. "She's not telling me not to wear them, but she doesn't think they're a good idea."

"Neither do I," Russ insisted with a grin.

Casey smiled weakly. "Is that why you called me in here?"

He shook his head. "No," his smile faded. "I wanted you to talk about the story on the news about the assassination of Gael Rodriguez Noestra. Have you seen the story yet?"

Casey's humor, as weak as it had been, fled and she averted her gaze, looking at her steno pad.

"Yes," she said softly. "I saw it last night."

"You know that Colt did his job, Casey."

She simply nodded and he continued. "When was the last time you heard from him?" he asked softly.

She took a deep breath for courage. "About three months ago. He left a message on my cell phone that he'd call back but he never did. He's been using burner phones, you know. Disposable things. I can never call him back."

Russ nodded, eyeing her, sensing her turbulent emotions. "That's smart," he said softly. "But now that his assignment's over, I'm sure he'll be home soon."

She nodded. Then she burst into quiet tears. Stricken, Russ leapt off his couch, grabbed a box of tissues, and sat down beside her.

"Don't cry," he told her quietly. "Please don't cry. Everything is going to be all right now."

Casey took a tissue and dabbed at her eyes. "I hope so," she whispered. "I just want him home."

Russ put his hand on her shoulder in a comforting gesture. "Come and have dinner with Tracy and me tonight," he said. "I know Tracy would like to see you. Can you bring the boys?"

Casey nodded, forcing herself to be brave. So much of her life was in turmoil right now and she struggled to stay above it.

"Sure," she said. "Thank you for the offer. The boys will be thrilled."

"Good," he eyed her as she wiped her nose. "What do they know about Colt?"

Casey took a deep breath, composing herself. "What everyone

else knows," she replied. "I've told them he's in Europe. Somehow, someway, he arranged to send Hunter a game station for his birthday last month. I don't know how he did it, but Hunter got a very expensive console from Colt. He's thrilled with it."

Russ grinned. "He thinks a lot of those boys, doesn't he?"

"They think a lot of him, too."

"Good," he stood up from the couch, watching her laboriously push herself up. "Uh... I hate to say this, Casey, but you move like a pregnant woman."

She gave him a lopsided smile. "I guess it's stupid of me to keep trying to hide it," she rubbed her belly through the flowing dress and Russ got a good look at just how big she really was. "I suppose if anyone asks me from now on, there's no use in denying it."

"And if they ask me?"

"Tell them Luke Skywalker is the father."

He laughed. "It's nobody's business who the father is but yours."

"Thank you." Casey paused by the door leading back to her desk, turning to Russ and extending her hand. "For everything you've done for Colt and me, I really want to thank you. You're a pretty good guy."

Russ shook her soft, warm hand. "I'm going to use that as my campaign slogan for my re-election," he said, letting her hand go. "But you're very welcome."

With a smile, a genuine one this time, Casey returned to her desk and sat down. She was about to launch into another project when she noticed that it was nearing lunchtime. Hungry, she knew she had to eat before she started feeling sick so she collected her purse and prepared to move out. As she stood up from her chair, Peter emerged from Colt's old office.

Peter had taken over as Special Agent in Charge in the absence of Colt Sheridan. He and Casey had shared a strained relationship, mostly because Casey didn't trust him anymore. She was afraid he might try to take her back to Mr. Meade and there would be no

Colt to save her. However, she never divulged to Russ that Peter was also an agent for The Core. She should have ratted him out but she couldn't bring herself to do it. Somehow, Peter reminded her of Colt and she didn't want to cut her ties to any reminders of him, good or bad.

"Hi Casey," Peter said, treating her very carefully as he always did. "Do you have a minute?"

Casey looked at him warily, purse clutched up against her belly as if protecting herself from him. "What about?"

Peter could see how guarded she was; she had been for months. Not that he blamed her.

"Please," he said softly, gesturing towards the front of the West Wing. "Can... will you please just give me a few minutes and go for a walk? It's important."

Casey's first instinct was to refuse. "I'm not getting in a car with you."

"No cars, I promise."

"I'm not going any place private with you, either."

It was good that Chris Eckart wasn't in the office. Peter felt more comfortable speaking of secretive things as he struggled to convince Casey he meant her no harm.

"Casey, I swear I'm not going to abduct you or take you to Mr. Meade," he whispered. "I really need to talk to you. It's really important."

Brow furrowed, she was indecisive for a few moments before reluctantly nodding her head. Then she began to walk out with Peter following. She passed by Lisanne's desk and the young receptionist waved to her while she was on the phone. Casey waved back, passing by Maggie's office and catching a glimpse of the woman at her desk. Maggie saw her and quickly hung up the phone.

"Casey!" she called, rushing out from behind her desk. "I was just calling you to see if you wanted to go to lunch."

Casey came to a halt with Peter beside her. "I'd love to, but

Special Agent Harrios and I have some business. I'll talk to you later."

Maggie smiled and waved her off, watching her walk down the hall with the handsome African-American Secret Service agent. Her smile faded as Casey disappeared from view. Turning back for her desk, she was startled to find Lisanne standing behind her.

"Oh!" Maggie jumped. Then she frowned. "Stop sneaking up like that."

Lisanne grinned. "I didn't mean to," she said. "I wanted to talk to Casey."

Maggie sighed heavily. "She doesn't talk much these days, you know that," she said softly. "She's been keeping to herself."

Lisanne's smile faded. "Poor baby," she whispered, looking around to make sure no one was listening. "Have you heard anyone say anything about her pregnancy?"

Maggie frowned at her. "No," she hissed. "And you need to keep your mouth shut, too."

Lisanne shook her head innocently. "I haven't said a word!" she insisted. "But I heard a couple of the Vice President's aides talking about her the other day. They were wondering who the father was."

Maggie just shook her head. "I'm sure it's Sheridan," she whispered angrily. "It has to be. Those two were dating and then he just disappeared. If I ever see that bastard again, I'm going to give him a piece of my mind."

Lisanne shrugged. "Poor Casey," she murmured. "She's so unhappy these days."

"I know."

"What should we do?"

Maggie shook her head. "I don't know," she shrugged. "Protect her as best we can. Make sure rumors don't get out of hand, I guess. And if I hear Chris Eckart gossip about her one more time, I'm going to plaster that guy."

Lisanne nodded as she turned back for her desk. She knew Maggie meant it, too.

304 KAT LE VEQUE

It was hot and humid outside, as July in Washington usually was. Casey began fanning herself furiously, her cheeks pink and her face glistening with sweat as they walked down the driveway away from the White House. There was a slight breeze, plastering her dress against her torso and showcasing her belly quite nicely. Peter noticed it but he didn't say anything. He kept silent as they walked down the hot asphalt driveway towards Pennsylvania Avenue. As they reached the sidewalk, Casey came to a halt.

"Okay," she said. "So no one's around. What did you want to talk about?"

Peter stopped and faced her. He could see she wasn't in a mood for foolish conversation so he got straight to the point. He'd been trying to figure out for the past several minutes how to broach the difficult subject.

"I thought you'd like to know about Colt," he said quietly.

Casey went from suspicious to apprehensive in a split second. Her violet eyes widened. "What about him?" she demanded. "Where is he? Is he okay?"

Peter was careful in his reply. "You know that I have refrained from talking to you about any of this," he said. "Even when you asked, I told you I didn't know anything. Remember?"

She was quickly verging on tears. "Of course I remember," she whispered, wiping at her eyes before they spilled over. "For the first three months, I asked you every day. Then I just stopped. I got tired of being disappointed every day."

He nodded. "The truth is that I really didn't know much," he admitted. "Whatever was going on with Colt was kept between him and Mr. Meade. But I did hear pieces of conversation between Meade and some of The Core members at times. They spoke of our contacts down in Bogota and how Colt had been sucked up into their network. From what I could gather, he went into deep hiding."

Casey's tears were forgotten as she listened closely. "But that's good, right?" she asked eagerly. "That's what he was supposed to do."

"Yes, it was," Peter agreed. "But three months ago, even our contacts lost track of him. No one knew where he was or what he was doing. It was like he just vanished. And then yesterday when Noestra was assassinated...."

"But that was his job," Casey cut him off insistently. "That's what he was sent down there to do, what forced him to choose between staying here with me and going off doing his spy stuff. He did what that old man told him to do!"

Peter sighed faintly and reached out, grasping her arm as she grew agitated. "Casey, I spoke with Mr. Meade about an hour ago," he confided. "He says that they're not entirely sure Colt was responsible for Noestra's death. Another rival cartel has taken responsibility for it and our intelligence in Bogota seems to confirm it. We can't find Colt to see what's really happened. We just don't know...."

He trailed off and Casey began to get panicky. "You don't know what?"

Peter tried to be gentle. "We just don't know where he is. No one has heard from him in almost four months and none of our contacts can locate him."

Casey stared at him a moment before yanking her hand away from him. "What are you telling me?"

"I'm telling you that we don't know what's happened to him."

"Is he dead?"

Peter looked pained. "Baby girl, I just don't know. He's vanished. That's all I can tell you."

"You're lying."

"No, I'm not. I swear I'm not."

"He wouldn't just leave me like this.'"

"You're right. He wouldn't if he could help it. But he may not be able to help it. We just don't know."

Casey stared at him, her growing apprehension evident. "So why are you telling me this? You didn't have to tell me anything."

"Because I thought you should know. If he... well, if he doesn't come back, I just thought you should know."

Surprisingly, Casey didn't burst into hysterics. She just stared at him like he had two heads. Peter gazed at her apprehensively, waiting for the explosion, but nothing happened. She just stared at him. She took a step back from him and then another. Then, she suddenly turned around and started walking. He trailed after her.

"Where are you going?" he demanded.

Casey's composure was holding together by a thread. She waved a vicious hand at him. "Leave me alone," she roared. "Get away from me and leave me alone."

"Casey, I can't," Peter was behind her, pleading. "You know I can't."

Casey swung a fist at him, barely missing him. "If you don't get away from me, I'll scream. Go away, Peter. Just... just leave me alone. I swear to God you'll be sorry if you don't."

They had reached the corner of Pennsylvania Avenue and 17th Street. Peter came to a halt at the corner, watching Casey as she turned south on 17th Street and continued walking.

"Casey!" he called after her. "Please don't walk off. Please!"

Casey didn't respond to him. She just kept walking, storming off blindly in ninety degree heat with one hundred percent humidity. Peter couldn't follow her. He had to get back to the White House. Breaking into a dead run, he sprinted his way back to the West Wing. From there, he sent out four uniformed Secret Service officers to bring her back. He figured she might return with someone other than him, someone she wasn't desperately angry with.

Two hours later, they still hadn't found her. When the President found out she was missing, and why, he yelled at Peter for a solid hour.

———

Scott had been to Charlie Palmer Steak House a dozen times in as many weeks. It was right across the street from the Capitol Building and a hip joint to drink and discuss politics after hours, only tonight, he wasn't here to discuss politics. He had come over to the restaurant because his aide had called him earlier in the evening, sounding rather concerned, and asked him to stop by because there was a problem. Kurt really wouldn't say much more than that so, intrigued, yet slightly impatient, Scott obliged and swung by before heading back to Georgetown. His son was expecting him and he was irritated at the delay. Leaving his Jaguar with the valet, he entered the busy, dimly-lit establishment.

It was crowded with people as he pushed through the clusters in the lobby, looking over towards the bar area in hopes of locating Kurt. As his gaze scanned the crowd, someone suddenly grasped him by the elbow.

"Senator," Kurt was standing beside him. "Thank God you're here. I didn't know who else to call."

Scott was perplexed. "Call about what? What's going on?"

Kurt crooked a finger at him and pulled him away from the hostess stand and a large group of patrons. When they were moderately alone in a corner of the plush waiting area, he turned to him.

"I came here a couple of hours ago and found Casey Cleburne sitting in the bar," he said in a low voice. "She... she's despondent or something. She was sitting there, drinking hot tea and just staring off into space. Senator, did you know she's pregnant?"

Scott looked at him, shocked. "No," he replied. "But what's the problem? Why did you...?"

"She's spacey and out of it," Kurt interrupted him. "Look, I know she's a big girl and all that, but I've known Casey for a little while and that woman is never anything other than completely together. I've been sitting with her for the past two hours and she's barely said five words to me. She just sits there and stares at her hands. Something's wrong and I just can't leave her like that. I didn't know who else to call."

Scott still wasn't over the pregnant part. He stared at Kurt as his mind absorbed the news. After several long moments, he sighed heavily and began to look around, as if he could spot Casey in all of the bustle.

"I don't know what I can do," he said honestly. "Where is she?"

Kurt silently motioned him to follow. They moved through the bar area and into a corner where a woman sat, all tucked up into the corner of the booth. Scott's gaze fell on Casey's lowered head and he felt his heart jump, just like it always did when he saw her. She was staring at a half-full cup of lukewarm tea.

"Casey?" Scott said softly.

Her head came up, the violet eyes fixing on him, and he smiled. "Fancy seeing you here," he tried to be light about it. "I just stopped by after work and Kurt said he'd found you here. How are you?"

Casey just looked at him. She was pale, with most of her makeup gone, but she was still the most beautiful woman in the room. Her luscious caramel-colored hair was messy, the signature bangs pushed aside and stuck together. She didn't look anything like her usual self, which put Scott on immediate edge.

"Hello, Senator," she said dully. "I'm okay."

Scott watched her closely, eventually sliding into the booth opposite her. "Have you eaten?" he asked. "Maybe you'd like to eat with Kurt and me. We haven't...."

Casey was shaking her head before he even got the invitation out of his mouth. "No, thank you," she said. "I should be going home, anyway."

"Why?" Scott wanted to know. "What's your rush? Kurt and I would love to have dinner with you."

Casey was back to looking at her tea again. As Scott and Kurt watched, tears began to rain from her eyes into her tepid tea water. Kurt slipped into the booth next to her as Scott reached across the table to gently grasp the fingers holding the tea cup.

"What's the matter, Casey?" he asked gently. "Can we help?"

Casey shook her head and the sobs began to come. Then she

seemed a little panicked, trapped by Kurt as he sat next to her and blocked her swift exit.

"I really need to go home," she wept softly. "Please... just let me go."

"Casey, we just want to help," Kurt insisted. "Please tell us what's wrong. I'm sure there's something we can do."

"You can't," she choked and shoved at him, pushing him out of the booth. "I really have to go. Thank you very much for your concern, but I really have to go."

Kurt reluctantly stood up and they both got a look at Casey's round pregnant belly as she climbed out of the seat. Without another word, she picked up her purse and scurried from the restaurant. Scott told Kurt to hang back while he went after her. He caught up to her as she moved for the taxi stand outside.

"Casey," he came up behind her. "Please, honey, don't run off. I'm not trying to be a bother, but I'm really concerned about you. Kurt said he's been sitting in the restaurant with you for a couple of hours. How long were you in there before he showed up?"

Casey took a deep breath, struggling to stop the tears. "I don't even know," she said after a moment. She wiped at her cheeks, composing herself as she turned to look at him. "I'm really sorry. I'm not trying to be difficult or a drama queen, but there's just a lot going on with me right now. No one can help. Thank you for your offer, though. I appreciate it."

Scott's gaze remained calm and warm upon her. "Congratulations on the baby," he said softly. "I guess now I understand why you didn't want to go out with me."

Casey instinctively put her hand on her belly. "I...," she stammered, looking sorrowful and torn. "The baby had nothing to do with it, honestly. It's what I told you. I was already seeing someone. I mean I *am* seeing someone."

"Sheridan."

She looked him in the eye. "Yes. But you already know that."

"Is he the father?"

Casey almost told him it wasn't any of his business, a natural response to the query. But she relented. It didn't really matter if he knew or not.

"Of course he is," she murmured, averting her gaze.

Scott took a step closer and lowered his voice. He was attempting to be comforting but in his own way, he was probing her also.

"I heard he was reassigned to the European Secret Service Bureau," he said. "At least, that's what I heard. But that's not the truth, is it?"

Her head snapped. "Why do you say that?"

He sighed faintly. "Casey, I know he's not in Paris," he confessed. "Colt walked out of his assignment as the President's Special Agent in Charge six months ago and no one knows what's happened to him. You and I have had discussions about him, Casey. I... I just don't want to see you wasting your life over the man."

She hardened. "I'm not wasting my life," she snapped. "Look, I appreciate your concern, but it's really not necessary. I can take care of myself."

She started to walk away from him but he would let her go so easily. "Who's going to take care of the baby?" he wanted to know. "You're a young, single, beautiful woman with two young children and another on the way. Who's going to take care of the baby, Casey? Not Sheridan. He's nowhere to be found."

She stopped in her tracks and turned to him. "So... what?" she was irritable and snappish. "You want to take care of me and a baby that isn't yours? What in the hell are you driving at, Scott? You've spent so much time trying to woo me away from Colt but the reality is that these attempts make you look desperate and manipulative. I love Colt, he loves me, and when he returns, we're getting married and raising this baby together. End of story."

Scott didn't rise to her emotion. "If that's true, then why were you in the bar wallowing in misery?"

She stomped her foot. "Because it's *my* misery to wallow in and it's none of your business."

He could see how fired up she was getting but he remained cool. "You know he's not coming back," he whispered firmly. "You know that you're going to raise this baby alone, right? Colt Sheridan is as shady as they come, Casey. I've told you that. You *know* that. Why do you insist on thinking well of the man when all he's done is lie to you, get you pregnant, and run off?"

She shook her head and turned away from him, telling the valet to call her a cab. Scott walked up behind her.

"I'm not trying to be manipulative," he whispered. "I just want to treat you the way you deserve to be treated. I want to put you on a pedestal and keep you there. I told you once that the first moment I saw you was the first moment I had felt alive in over twelve years. It just kills me to see you wasting your life over someone like Colt Sheridan."

She turned to look at him. "Talking disparagingly about him isn't going to get me to change my mind," she hissed. "It's only going to infuriate me. Although I appreciate your concern, Senator, I really have nothing else to say to you on the subject so I'd appreciate it if you'd just let it go. Nothing you can say is going to turn me against Colt."

Scott could only acknowledge that he understood her, not that he agreed with her. He had no intention of giving up. As Casey returned her attention to the taxi stand, she suddenly lost her balance and tumbled back into Scott. He caught her so she wouldn't fall to the ground but as he tried to put her back on her feet, he realized she was doubled over.

"What's wrong?" he demanded softly.

Casey couldn't help the grunt that escaped her lips. "I... I don't know," she was trying to stand up and pull herself away from him. "I just got a sharp pain in my gut, like someone stabbed me with an ice pick."

"Are you okay?" he asked with concern.

Casey tried to stand but the pain was intense. "I... I just need to get home," she gasped. "I need to lie down."

"Are you sure?"

"I'm sure," she said, then suddenly grunted again and grabbed her belly. "Oh... my, God...."

It was apparent that something was happening to her and Scott was on the move. He emitted a piercing whistle between his teeth, waving over the nearest cab as he practically carried Casey to the car. He firmly, gently, pushed her inside and climbed in after her.

"Walter Reed," he boomed to the cabbie. "*Go.*"

The cabbie floored it.

SEVENTEEN

"SHE'S GOT SOME COMPLICATIONS," the doctor said. "Maybe we should all sit down and discuss it."

It was well into the night on the sultry July day. Although the doctor had been speaking to Riley, there was also a collection of other people standing around her, listening to the doctor's words. Russ, Tracy, Scott and Peter were standing in a nervous bunch as they went to sit on a pair of blue cloth couches in the waiting room of the Perinatal Unit at Walter Reed Medical Center.

Riley should have been in awe that she was surrounded by the President of the United States as well as Arizona Senator Scott Dane, but she just couldn't spare the energy. She was completely focused on her sister and she had been since receiving a call from Senator Dane's aide, Kurt Isaacson, that her sister and the senator were on their way to Walter Reed Medical Center.

When Riley had arrived at the hospital, it had taken several minutes to get through the Secret Service because the President had also apparently been informed of his personal assistant's health crisis and had arrived earlier. The hospital was now like a fortress.

The President's wife was the most visibly upset. Tracy sat next to her husband on the older blue couch, a tissue at her nose. Riley didn't know Mrs. Talbot but she had heard a lot of good things about her from Casey. Still, Riley was focused on her sister and her current state of health. It was all she cared about at the moment.

"So what's going on with my sister?" she asked the doctor. "Is she okay?"

The doctor was an older man with a receding hairline. He sat down next to Riley as he spoke.

"First of all, she's extremely dehydrated," he said. "I'm pumping fluids back into her and she's feeling better, but there are still issues."

"What issues?" Riley demanded. "She's been perfectly healthy for the duration of the pregnancy."

The doctor nodded. "I know," he replied. "I talked to her regular doctor. She's on her way over here, in fact. She says that Casey has sailed through this pregnancy so far. But here's the issue; the last time she saw the doctor was three weeks ago and since that time, the placenta has moved to the base of the uterus and is covering the cervix. That's caused the baby to shift so he's sitting very low in her pelvis. With the dehydration and the fact that she's so exhausted, it's brought on pre-term labor and because of the position of the placenta, she's bleeding fairly heavily. We're trying to get it under control."

Riley looked stricken, her hand flying to her mouth in shock. "Oh, my God," she breathed. "She's not going to die, is she? What about the baby?"

The doctor held out a hand as if to forcibly calm everyone. "Right now, the baby's heartbeat is steady, so he's doing fine," he assured them. "It's the mother I'm worried about. I have to be honest and tell you that I'm very concerned about the bleeding. If we can't stop it in the next hour or so, we'll have to do an emergency caesarean."

Tears filled Riley's eyes. "She's not due for another four weeks."

"I know," the doctor was trying to be kind and optimistic. "The baby should do fine. Like I said, it's the mother I'm worried about right now."

Riley was struggling not to cry. "Can I see her?"

The doctor nodded and stood up, pulling Riley with him as he moved down the corridor. As they disappeared around a corner, Scott turned to Russ.

"Christ," he hissed. "I feel like... oh, God, I feel like somehow I had a hand in this. I shouldn't have...."

He trailed off and Russ lifted his eyebrows. "Why? What did you do?" he looked around, spying Kurt standing several feet away with a host of Secret Service agents. "I was told you brought her to the hospital. You probably saved her life, Scott."

Scott hung his head. "We were talking about... oh, hell, it doesn't matter. She told me to leave her alone and I didn't. I should have."

Russ wasn't oblivious to what was going on. He'd known that the widowed senator was very attracted to Casey and had even gone so far as to try and win Casey away from Colt. He'd seen the man in his offices, speaking with Casey, going out of his way to greet her, sending her flowers, so he wasn't entirely oblivious to the rumors that had been going around.

"Look," he leaned in Scott's direction and lowered his voice. "She's been upset all day. She left for lunch and never came back, and no one could find her, so whatever you think you did, it started well before you. Don't give yourself so much credit."

Scott was staring at his hands. "I know she's been seeing Sheridan," he said softly. "I've been trying to get her away from that guy from nearly the moment I met her. She doesn't need to be with someone like that. Here she is, in the hospital, and where in the hell is he? The guy's shady and she doesn't need that in her life. No one does."

Russ glanced at Tracy, who was looking rather angry about it. He put his hand on his wife's knee, silently shaking his head at her not to say anything.

"Whatever you think about Colt Sheridan, I can tell you from experience that he's a man of character and integrity," he said quietly. "Scott, the only reason you think Colt is shady is because you want his girlfriend. You need to come to grips with the fact that the woman is spoken for. She's pregnant with his child, for God's sake. What more proof do you need?"

Scott looked up from his hands. "Do you know about the man's record, Mr. President?" he asked. "He's got a...."

Russ held up a hand to quiet him. "I know all about Colt Sheridan," he cut him off. "He's my Special Agent in Charge and, yes, I know about his record. Mark Miller, Colt's boss, and I have had many conversations about it. My suggestion to you would be to forget about Casey Cleburne. She and Colt are made for each other and there's no chance for you. You'd save yourself a lot of heartache if you were to move on."

Scott didn't flare. In fact, he looked back at his hands again. He seemed pensive and quiet for a moment, perhaps reflecting on how he'd conducted himself with Casey since he met her.

"Maybe," he finally said. "I guess... well, I guess I've been lonely since Carol died but I didn't really realize it until I met Casey. I don't know what it was about her that lit me up, but everything about Casey just sets me on fire. I just want to be with her and take care of her and... hell, it sounds stupid, I guess. I just looked at Sheridan as a competition. I thought I could beat him."

"He's already won the competition, Scott."

Scott looked up at Russ again. "If that's really true, where is he? I'm here and he's not."

Russ sighed faintly and averted his gaze. He knew that Scott had been checking up on Sheridan; he'd known it for a while. Word like that got around. After a moment, he stood up and wandered over to where Peter and some of the other Secret Service agents were positioned. He caught Peter's eye and waved the man over.

"Mr. President?" Peter greeted him.

Russ looked at the handsome man. He had heard, from Mark Miller, that Intel thought Harrios was a double-agent for the CIA.

Russ knew that Peter and Colt were rather close and he further knew that they worked closely together. Maybe too closely. If Colt was an agent for The Core, then it might stand to reason that Harrios wasn't a double-agent for the CIA after all. Perhaps he was a Core operative as well. Colt had mentioned there were others in the President's security detail that were more than just Secret Service agents. Russ was willing to believe Harrios was one of them.

"I want you to listen very closely to me, Peter, because this is important," Russ lowered his voice. "Let me preface this by saying I'm not looking for a confession from you. What I'm about to say is my belief and my belief only. I think you know more about Colt than you let on, and this whole episode with Casey running off earlier today has solidified that belief. You said she ran off because you were talking to her about Colt. Just *what* were you saying about him?"

Peter's expression remained even. "We were speaking of his absence, among other things, Mr. President."

"What, in particular, about his absence?"

Peter drew in a deep breath. "That he'd been gone for a long time and she hadn't heard anything from him in a while. As I told you earlier today, she got upset about it and ran off."

Russ digested that statement, gazing steadily at Peter, before finally shaking his head.

"Look," he murmured. "I don't know what kind of monkey business you're in to, Harrios, but I've got a pretty good idea. I think you know more about Colt than you're letting on so I'm going to tell you this; I don't care who you have to call, or write to, or send smoke signals to, but I want you to get the message to Colt that Casey is very ill and he needs to come home. Is that clear? You get him back here. I don't care how you do it, but you get him back here. That's an order from your Commander in Chief and other than God himself, my word is obeyed above all else. Do you understand?"

Peter's dark eyes were intense. "Yes, Mr. President."

"You do it now."

"Yes, Mr. President."

Russ turned away from him, heading back to the couch and praying that somehow, someway, Colt would get the message. He knew that Peter understood the urgency. For Casey's sake, he sincerely hoped so.

Casey had been given a tranquilizer that knocked her out for two days. Her exhaustion, her health, made her very susceptible to the numbing effects and even though she'd tried to pull out of it a couple of times, for the most part, she slept heavily for two days.

Her doctor, an older woman who had delivered a lot of politician's babies in Washington, was with her about every hour. The woman's office was close by so she would head over to the hospital in between patients, checking on Casey to make sure she was holding her own and that the baby was stable. Dr. Carrie Steele was well regarded, well liked, and the best around. She kept a very close eye on Casey.

Riley hadn't spent much time at the hospital because she needed to stay with Hunter and Brody. Nick and Janice Cleburne had flown in the morning of the second day and went straight to the hospital, spending the entire day with Casey as she slept the day away. Casey's mother was particularly devastated about the situation, while Nick eventually went back to Casey's house to hang out with his grandsons so Riley could go over the hospital with her mother. The whole Cleburne clan was struggling to keep going through this crisis.

The next week was uneventful for the most part. Janice sat with her daughter all day and into the evening, reading to her, watching television with her, or even playing cards with her. Riley was in and out and towards the end of the week, and Brody and Hunter were allowed to visit their mother. Hunter pretended he was okay about the whole thing while Brody dissolved into tears more than once. Casey assured her boys that she would be fine after a little stay in the hospital. She was feeling a little stronger and was in better spirits, so the boys were comforted by what they saw. Still, Brody was having a hard time with it and nine days after his mother went into the hospital, his grandparents allowed him to take the day off of school to spend it with his mother. He didn't even bring his skateboard. He sat next to his mom on the big hospital bed and watched game shows with her all day.

Scott came every day to visit. He would always bring something with him, like flowers or a plant or a stuffed animal, and soon enough Casey's room looked like a florist shop. Casey's mom wasn't sure who the man was at first, then was impressed that her daughter had a senator taking interest in her. Janice knew about Colt, as she and her husband had had several conversations about him with Casey since the Thanksgiving holiday, but Casey wouldn't tell her where he was or even why he hadn't come to the hospital. She wouldn't talk about him at all, leading Janice to believe that the pair had broken up. Devastated for her pregnant and single daughter, Janice thought that the senator was perhaps a welcome substitution.

Casey didn't, however. She didn't particularly want to see Scott at all. Every time he came into her room, her heart rate would go up out of sheer stress and the nurse would eventually ask him to leave. It happened almost every time, but he kept coming back, even when Casey finally told him not to. He just couldn't stay away.

Into the eighth and ninth day of her infirmary, Scott just came to the hospital to sit in the waiting room simply to be near her. He didn't try to go into her room anymore, not even when Janice came out into the waiting area and invited him. He politely declined, asked how Casey was doing, and left. It was a sad thing to witness.

For Casey, the days passed slowly and the nights were excruciating. She was glad that the baby seemed okay but unconcerned that her life was in jeopardy. Without Colt, nothing seemed to matter anymore and her depression was a black, bottomless hole. She'd virtually stopped eating, so much so that they put her on I.V. nutrients simply to keep her strength up. Peter had come by to see her a couple of times but, much like Scott, any sight of him raised her blood pressure and the nurses would chase him away. He didn't have anything to tell her, anyway, and seeing him just reinforced the fact that Colt was missing.

Two weeks after entering the hospital and more than two weeks after the assassination of Noestra, Colt still hadn't made an appearance. Casey was coming to think that maybe he really was never coming home. Dazed and shattered, she just couldn't take it anymore.

The night was late and she wasn't sleeping, anyway. Quietly, she got out of bed and unhooked the fetal monitor from around her belly. She also pulled her I.V.s out. Her mother had brought her some warm pajamas and a robe, which she hadn't worn yet, so she went to the closet and put them all on. It was the only thing she had to wear. Her purse was hanging up in the closet and she took the money and credit cards out of it, shoving them in the pocket of her robe. Putting on her slippers, she went to her room door.

The hallway was dim and quiet outside due to the late hour. Casey could see the nurse's station off to her left and she even saw a nurse at the station, focused on the computer screen. With her eyes on the nurse to make sure she didn't catch the woman's attention, Casey slipped out of the ward.

She took the elevator down to the bottom floor. There were a few people in the lobby, mostly hospital personnel, but no one said a word to her as she walked out of the lobby and into the night beyond. Near the big, circular entrance were a few taxis idling beneath the mercury lamps and she found one, slipping inside and asking the driver to take her to the White House.

The taxi dropped her off at Lafayette Park. It was nearly midnight as Casey stood at the edge of the square, thinking of the time that she and Colt had spent there. She could see them walking hand in hand near the fountain or, in the earlier part of their relationship, standing about three feet apart and trying not to look as if they were in love with one another. The square reminded her of Colt almost as much as the White House did, and she turned around to face the enormous structure as the moon shined brightly above. Thankfully, the evening was warm so she was comfortable in her pajamas and robe. But the more she stared at the White House, reminding her of Colt with every breath she took, the more despondent she became.

Colt had told her that if she didn't hear from him for more than six months, then she needed to face the possibility that he was never returning. Although she understood his words, the reality was much different. She thought on his strong, warm hands, his beautiful body and handsome face. She closed her eyes and heard his silky-deep voice and the roll of his laughter. If she thought hard enough, she could smell his skin and feel the texture of his hair. She could remember everything about him, a man she loved more than anything on earth. She couldn't stomach the thought of never seeing him again, of never hearing his voice or touching his face.

The baby kicked and she put her hand on her belly, thinking of the child she carried, something that was part of her and part of Colt. She wasn't sure if she could look at the baby and not feel overpowering grief. Every day he would remind her of what she had lost. She wasn't sure she was strong enough to face it. She didn't want to face life without Colt.

Off to her right and across 17th Street was the parking structure where she and Colt would always park. On the third level, side by side, they had their parking stalls. More than anything, the parking structure reminded her of Colt, as strange as it was. Her violet gaze beheld the concrete building, remembering, pondering. In the dead of night, she began to walk towards it.

EIGHTEEN

RIOHACHA WAS a port city hugging the northern coast of Colombia along the Caribbean Sea. It used to be an important port back in the day, but now it appeared every inch a third world berg. Roads were rocky, the shanty areas dirty and populated, and the entire city reeked of depression and greed.

Summers were hot here this close to the equator and the humidity was the stuff that legends were born from. Big bugs, little bugs, and everything in between lived amongst the city dwellers who struggled day to day to survive. Poverty was rampant.

It was a lazy day, this day of days, as a very large man in dirty jeans, flip-flops made from old tire treads, and a stained t-shirt made his way from the nearby marketplace with a bag heavy with food. He passed buildings whitewashed with bright red trim, slowly decaying in the heavy, salt air. The man sported a beard, a heavy mustache, and a shaved head upon darkly tanned skin, keeping vigilant watch as he passed the deteriorating buildings. As he passed a group of children playing in the gutter near a local bar, he called out to the group.

"Hola, usted monstruos pequeños," he teased.

The children giggled and laughed, some of them throwing rocks at him but it was all in fun. They knew the man was their friend. One of the little boys ran at him, holding out his hands because he knew the man had food in his bag. The man paused, reaching into his bag and pulling out a green banana. Handing it over to the little boy, he grinned at the thrilled child.

"Ahora usted me posee dinero para eso," he told the kid. *You owe me money for that.*

The child giggled, ripped off the skin, and tore into the unripe banana. Then he tried to hand it back with a bite taken out of it. The man waved him off.

"Manténgalo." *Keep it.*

He could hear the children giggling as he made his way down the small street and turned into an even smaller alley. Off of this smaller alley was another walkway, and he turned into it as he headed for his small shack buried deep in the shanty town. But the moment he made the turn, he caught sight of a man lingering down the alley. He came to a halt and dropped the bag, preparing for a fight.

The man lingering down the alley heard the footsteps and the bag drop, turning around to see the enormous man standing at the mouth of the walkway. He recognized the man, the fighting stance, and held up his hands in supplication.

"¡Soy!" he hissed. "¡No me duela!"

The big man suddenly relaxed, recognizing the man in the smelly, dark walkway. He picked up his grocery bag and charged to the end, grabbing the man by the shoulder and yanking him into his dark, dusty, one-room shack and locking the door behind them. There was a single light socket hanging from the ceiling with a single bulb and he turned it on as he put his groceries on the worn and leaning table. He faced his visitor with displeasure.

"What are you doing here?" he asked in English. "Were you followed?"

The visitor was scrubby, fat and dark, smelling like mold. Dressed in slobby clothing that was torn and dirty, he looked like a drunken bum.

"I wasn't followed," he replied in heavily-accented English. "I have traveled by bus and bicycle to find you. I had to come. I have been given a message for you."

Colt's brow furrowed. "A message?" he looked perplexed. "From whom? Who in the hell knows where I am except for you and my contact at the Embassy?"

"The Marine *capitán* has sent me."

"Why?" Colt suddenly didn't look so displeased anymore. He began to get excited. "Do I finally have safe passage home?"

The Colombian messenger wasn't very good with English but he tried. "He say you must go home," he told him. "Your wife is *morirse*. Death. He say you must go home right away. There is a boat coming for you tonight at Malecon and you must go."

Colt was slapped with information he hadn't expected. It took a moment to sink in and when it did, he suddenly couldn't breathe. He grabbed at the rickety, old table as if it would keep him from falling over.

"*What?*" he gasped. "Casey's dead?"

The messenger shook his head. "No," he couldn't find the right word. "Not dead. *Duela. Enfermo.*"

Colt found his breath and his feet. He pushed himself off the table and grabbed the man by the arms.

"Sick?" he roared. "Hurt? Which is it?"

The messenger tried to peel his hands off of him but it was like trying to move iron. Colt had him in a death grip, emotions bleeding from the usually emotionless man.

"She at Walter Reed," the messenger was trying to remain calm. "You must go home now. The President say so."

Colt stared at the messenger for a long, painful moment before letting the man go. His hands flew to his mouth as if to hold in the terror that threatened. He could feel tears springing to his eyes and his legs were like water, but he forced himself to hold it together. He couldn't fall apart, not now; he had to get home to Casey.

"Oh, my God," he breathed. "The baby... it's too early. Is it the baby?"

"Yo no sé."

Colt swallowed hard, struggling to keep himself on an even keel. But he eventually broke down, unable to keep the tears of fright away. "Oh, Angel," he whispered. "I'm so sorry. I'm coming, I promise. Be strong, baby, just a little while longer. I'm coming."

The messenger knew that Colt wasn't talking to him. He watched the big man wipe tears off his face with a shaking hand. He felt sorry for him.

"I am sorry I do not know more," he said softly. "That was all I was told."

Colt nodded vaguely. "What time is the boat coming?" he asked, his voice trembling.

"When the moon rises," the messenger said. "By the rocks. You be there?"

"I'll be there."

"I will tell the *capitán.*"

"Later. For now, you're going to wait with me until the boat comes. I may need your help."

The messenger could see that Colt was pale and trembling. Colt turned away from him, fumbling aimlessly with the grocery bag before moving to the tiny rope bed in the corner and going through the motion of packing up his meager possessions. But he only got half way through that before he reached under the mattress and pulled out a semi-automatic weapon. Then he moved back to the table and sat heavily on the only chair to wait it out until moonrise.

The messenger had been wrong about being followed, but it was the last mistake he would ever make. He and Colt were caught boarding the boat by two groups of men who had followed the messenger from Bogota, lost him in the shanty town, and then found him again purely by chance. The big man with him was someone they'd been searching for. It was quite a fortuitous happening and when the surprise wore off, the bullets began to fly.

Colt made it on the boat alive but the messenger did not.

———

"The cops found her," Dr. Steele was walking very quickly. "She was in a parking structure at Pennsylvania and 17th Street, and it took them three hours to talk her down from the ledge on the top of the structure. She was just sitting there but they thought she was going to jump. Then they took her over to George Washington University Hospital, but I had already contacted all of the hospitals in the area about her so they knew her when she came in. I had her transferred back here."

Riley and Janice were practically running after Dr. Steele. The woman had met them in the lobby when they arrived at the hospital and now they were heading to Labor and Delivery in a hurry. There was panic in the air.

"How is she?" Riley wanted to know.

Dr. Steele took a sharp corner. "She's in labor," she said, not sounding pleased in the least. "Her water broke but that's about all I can tell you. She won't let me do anything to help her."

Janice was stricken. "What do you mean?"

Dr. Steele came to an abrupt halt and faced the Cleburne women. Her expression was grim.

"Look," she said softly. "I know about her boyfriend. All she's done is cry about him for the past six months. I don't know where the guy is, but I would strongly suggest that you find him and at least tell him what's going on. She's in a labor and delivery room, but she won't let us hook her up to anything – no fetal monitors, no drugs for the labor, nothing. She won't even let me check her to see if she dilating. She just lays there and cries, and unless she passes out, I can't touch her. She's refusing treatment and I can't legally go against her wishes."

Riley looked ill. "Oh, my God," she breathed, looking at her mother. "You go in there and see what you can do. I need to make a phone call."

Janice didn't argue or ask questions. She charged into Casey's labor room and Riley could hear her mother pleading with Casey to let the doctor examine her. She was high risk as it was and if something went wrong, with the placenta previa, she could bleed out in minutes. As Riley dialed the phone and put it to her ear, she could hear her mother crying.

Time was ticking.

———

By morning, Casey was in trouble.

Exhausted and weakening, her labor was in full-force by the time dawn broke. She still wouldn't let anyone touch her or hook her up to any monitors, screaming at them when they tried. Dr. Steele tried to convince her that everything would be all right if she would only let them help her, but Casey was far gone with hormones and agony and grief. It was a devastating combination putting her in an unsteady frame of mind. She told Dr. Steele that she didn't care what happened to her. She told the woman she just wanted to die.

Russ and Tracy came over in the pre-dawn hours to try and talk some sense in to her. Riley had called the President and gave him the update, which had the man and his wife driving over to Walter Reed with their entire Secret Service detail at an ungodly hour. Every Secret Service agent knew that Casey was pregnant with Colt Sheridan's baby and because of that, they all felt a certain connection to her and to the child. This touched them all on a personal level.

Russ was shattered by her attitude, feeling as if everything was his fault, and Tracy cried steadily as Casey moaned her way through hard labor. It was a horrific situation. So many people wanted to help her, but Casey was numb to it. Life, to her, was ending. Without Colt, she just didn't care, not about anything.

As dawn lit up the eastern sky, what they feared the most finally happened. Casey suffered through a big contraction and a tide of blood erupted from her. Dr. Steele swung into action and an entire trauma team went to work on Casey, who quickly passed out from the loss of blood. As a huddle of terrified people collected in the waiting room, Casey managed to naturally deliver a nine pound baby boy, who screamed lustily the moment he emerged.

The Neonatal team whisked the baby away as Dr. Steele and the surgical team went to work on Casey, who was quickly bleeding out. They were pumping blood into her as fast as she was losing it, and Dr. Steele cut Casey open in an emergency caesarean even though the baby had already been delivered. She had to get to the placenta which, now ruptured, was draining Casey of her blood and her life. She had to seal it off.

As the doctors struggled to save Casey's life, the neonatologist discovered that the baby was a very healthy specimen. At nine pounds and two ounces, he was twenty two inches long and had a crown of blond hair. He screamed furiously while he was weighed and checked out, but he quieted soon enough when his grandmother sat in a rocking chair in the Neonatal unit and fed him.

Janice wept over her new grandson, so torn between grief and happiness as her daughter fought for her life. She wanted to stay with the baby because she couldn't do any good for Casey worrying out in the waiting room. If Casey passed, then Janice wanted to be with the baby, a piece of her daughter that was still alive and vibrant. The baby had to know he was loved.

As life and death went on upstairs, down in the lobby of the hospital, the morning sun was just starting to trickle in through the big glass doors. There were six Secret Service agents spread out in the lobby, four of them near the elevators. They were quiet and subdued, listening to updates from Harrios through their radios. People were arriving at work for their shift and there was general bustle going on around them as they kept a sharp eye out.

One of the agents was standing near the lobby doors and he noticed a taxi pull up, spitting out a very tall and very big man. He was dressed in jeans, a worn white shirt, and his hair was shorn very close to his head. He was very nearly bald. As the man entered the lobby, the Secret Service agent took a closer look at him because something odd rang familiar about him. The man had piercing dark eyes and a big, dark mustache that merged with a trimmed beard on his chin. He was very tanned, swarthy, and rather scary looking. But something about him was very familiar, a feeling that grew stronger as the man approached.

"Sheridan!"

Steven Case was one of the agents back by the elevator bays. He nearly shouted the name, causing all of the agents to look at him in shock. Colt kept walking in spite of the surprise of his fellow agents, marching up to Steven as the man stood next to the elevators with his jaw hanging open.

"Colt?" Steven still wasn't entirely sure. Sheridan didn't look anything like himself. "Is it...?"

"Where's Casey?" he demanded.

Steven smacked the elevator button. "Third floor," he told him. "She's in labor and delivery. The President got the call this morning that...."

The elevator door opened and Colt pushed his way in. Steven followed as the lift doors closed behind them.

"We escorted the President and Mrs. Talbot here about three hours ago," Steven was looking at Colt, who was staring up at the display as they rose between levels. He still could hardly believe he was actually looking at the man. "She gave birth about twenty minutes ago."

Colt looked at him, then, and something of deep shock registered in the intense eyes. But he didn't say anything. When the elevator doors opened, the first person he saw was Peter, looking at him as if he were seeing a ghost. Colt looked at him but blew right by him. Peter had to run after him to catch up.

"It *is* you," Peter hissed. "I thought the guys downstairs were smoking crack. I can't believe you actually came. I wouldn't have recognized you if I passed you on the street, other than you're still the biggest man I've ever seen."

Colt still didn't say anything. He didn't trust himself to. He was frazzled, strung out on caffeine, and so emotionally volatile that he was truly afraid what he would do if he snapped. He'd been

330 KAT LE VEQUE

traveling non-stop for almost three days. All he wanted to do was see Casey.

Russ saw him coming from his position in the lobby. He leapt out of his seat as Tracy gasped, which caused Riley to turn around to see what the commotion was about. Spying Colt, Riley flew at him with open palms.

Colt grabbed her hand before she could smack him, but another hand came up just as swiftly and he barely missed being decked. He grabbed both of Riley's flying fists as she snarled.

"You bastard," she seethed. "You did this, you goddamn bastard. You left her and she was pregnant and... and you *left* her! I hope you rot in hell, you asshole!"

Colt pinned Riley up as Russ and Tracy tried to prevent her from fighting him. Russ actually put himself in between Riley and Colt.

"Riley, listen to me," Russ hissed. "Honey, it's not his fault. He didn't go away because he wanted to. He went because he *had* to. Don't blame him for leaving. It couldn't be helped. The important thing is that he's here now, isn't it?"

Riley was still struggling but she burst into tears. Distraught, she turned away from Colt and he let her go. He watched her collapse on Tracy as he turned to the President.

"I received your message," he said hoarsely. "Please... what happened? Where is she?"

Russ was still in shock over Colt's appearance. The man looked like a bandito from the Old Wild West. He was still big and chiseled and handsome, but he didn't look anything like the clean-cut All-American hero that Russ had come to know. The transformation was astonishing.

"I didn't really think you'd show up," he said honestly. "You dropped off the face of the earth, Colt. No one heard from you and no one could find you. I honestly thought you were dead. It's really... astonishing."

Colt didn't want to explain what drove him into hiding, not now. He was only concerned with Casey.

"Please tell me what's going on with Casey," he begged.

Russ grasped his elbow and pulled him away from Tracy and Riley. He struggled for the words.

"I don't even know where to start," he said softly. "I never thought I'd actually see you to explain all of this to you, so I'm sorry if I'm blunt. Casey's pregnancy went well until about two weeks ago. She went into pre-term labor and the doctor discovered that the placenta was blocking the birth canal. The risk there is that it can tear during the labor process and she can bleed to death. So her doctor put her on bed rest here at the hospital but for some reason, she left the hospital last night and disappeared. The cops found her on the roof of a parking structure near the White House. They thought she was trying to jump but they managed to get her off and get her back to the hospital. By the time she got back here, she was in full-blown labor but she refused to let anyone help her. She just kept saying she had nothing to live for. We all tried to talk to her, but she was despondent. About a half hour ago, she gave birth to your son."

By this time, Colt was looking at him with tears in his eyes. "A boy," he murmured. "Is the baby okay?"

"He's fine," Russ assured him. "Big and healthy."

"And Casey?"

Russ sighed faintly, his hand on Colt's shoulder. "Last we heard, they were performing emergency surgery on her," he said softly. "She was bleeding badly, Colt. They were trying to stop it."

Colt blinked and the tears ran down his face. "Oh, my God," he whispered, hanging his head. "I... I have to see her."

"You can't, son. She's in surgery."

Colt acted like he hadn't heard him. "I have to talk to her," he murmured, tears dripping off his chin. "I didn't want her to... I know I stopped contacting her but I didn't have a choice. She has to understand that. I've thought of her every minute of every day in the one hundred and seventy-eight days that we've been separated. She's all I've thought of."

"Then why did you stop contacting her?" Russ whispered. "What happened?"

Colt didn't even bother wiping at his face. He let the tears fall. "Because I'm a marked man," he replied in a murmured. "I pulled off Noestra's assassination, but the entire Norte del Valle Cartel is looking for me because one of my contacts flipped and told them who I was before I could even get close to Noestra. So I went into hiding. I couldn't take the chance of being seen or recognized, so I've been hiding out on the Caribbean coast. I couldn't even chance going into town, for any reason, not even to make a call. I had to stay out of sight, do my job, and then go back into hiding until the heat died down."

"But you're here now."

Colt looked at him, then. "I had to come," he muttered. "Casey's worth more than my life. I had to take the chance and try to get back here."

Russ could see how exhausted and tense the man was. He was still in hunted mode, that transition into something almost inhuman because his life was on the line every second of the day. Russ had heard about agents getting this way but he'd never seen it. Colt wasn't the Colt they all knew at the moment, but he was getting there. Slowly but surely, he was returning to normal. He was coming back to the world.

"Do you think they followed you here?" Russ asked.

Colt half-nodded, half-shrugged. "I was smuggled out of Riohacha," he muttered. "But the cartel wasn't far behind. They never are. They've got eyes and ears everywhere. It was a running gun battle on the boat until I reached a Navy destroyer in the gulf. After that, I had to wait for the destroyer to get within helicopter range of the coast and from there, I took a plane from Galveston to Dulles. It's been three days of hell and it's not over yet."

Russ wasn't sure what more he could say to that. Colt was being hunted because of what he had done for him with the Norte del Valle. Russ knew that group. He'd known them for twenty years. He knew what they were capable of. His guilt returned.

"Thank you," he whispered. "For everything you've done for me, thank you. It doesn't seem like enough to say that, but it's the truth."

Colt sighed heavily and wiped at his wet face. "I need to see Casey," he began to look around, as if he were looking for her. "Please... can you just ask someone how she is? Can you ask them if I can see her?"

Russ could see he was starting to get agitated. "They'll tell us something as soon as they know anything," he promised. "You have to let them do their job, Colt. She'll be okay. Meanwhile, come along with me. There's someone I think you should meet."

Colt let Russ pull him down the hallway with a half-dozen Secret Service agents in tow. Colt could hear babies crying and suddenly, they were standing in front of the nursery with big, wide windows opening to the incubators beyond. Russ knocked on a security door and a nurse opened it. She allowed the President and Colt to enter but made the Secret Service agents stay outside, which freaked them out a little bit. But Russ assured them that he was safe with Colt, so they backed down.

Russ explained why they were there and the nurse made Colt and Russ wash their hands and put on surgical gowns. Once they were properly scrubbed, they were allowed to go into a small nursery area with several incubators and a few bassinets. There were CPAP and other machines all over the place, looking odd and threatening amidst the puppy and kitten wallpaper.

Sitting over against the wall to their left was a woman in a rocking chair, draped in a surgical gown and singing softly to an infant in her arms. Colt had no idea who she was until Russ walked up to her.

"Ms. Cleburne," Russ said softly, watching the woman turn around. "This is Colt Sheridan. He'd like to meet his son."

Janice looked up at Colt with big, wide eyes. Colt gazed back at the woman who looked vaguely like Casey, torn between the awkwardness of their introduction and then huge desire to see his child. He wasn't sure who to look at, Janice or the baby, but the baby won over. He just stared at the perfect little face, feeling as if every fear, every care or every sorrow he'd ever had just washed away. The tears came again and he didn't even notice.

"Oh, my God," he breathed. "He's beautiful."

Janice didn't even know the man, but she'd heard plenty about him. She felt like she knew him but, unlike Riley, didn't feel the same animosity. She didn't know why not, but maybe it had something to do with the way Casey had talked about the man, and the way the boys had described him. Clearly, he was adored, and although he had been gone for about six months, Casey would only say that it was because of his job. She never seemed angry about it up until the last few weeks when despair overtook her. Therefore, Janice found no animosity as she gazed at him. She was just glad to see him.

"It's nice to finally meet you," she said after a moment, swallowing down her shock at his appearance. "Sit down and you can hold him."

Colt moved to the rocking chair and sat, holding his arms up awkwardly for the baby as Janice deposited the child neatly into the crook of his elbow. The moment Colt got a close look at the little face all wrapped up in his big arms, it was as if the sun suddenly came out from behind the storm clouds. His face lit up as the tears streamed.

"Hey, buddy," Colt spoke to his son for the first time. "Look at you; you're a monster. I'm so glad you're here."

Janice smiled over at Russ, who was struggling with his own emotions. It took him back to the time when he had been presented with his sons, boys that were no longer with him. But he managed to return Janice's smile, turning for the door of the nursery because he really couldn't take it. He had to leave. Janice watched him go before returning her attention to Colt.

"He's nine pounds, two ounces," she told him. "He's four weeks early but perfectly healthy. I'm kind of glad Casey didn't carry him to term. He would have been enormous and she's not that big of a woman."

Colt just stared at the baby. "He's got her lips," he said, snorting through his tears. "She's got the most beautiful lips."

Janice smiled faintly. "I think so."

Colt tore his eyes away from the baby long enough to look at Casey's mother. "Ms. Cleburne, no matter what you've heard or what's happened, I want you to know how much I love your daughter," he said hoarsely. "She means the world to me."

Janice's smile faded. "You mean the world to her, too," she whispered. "Colt, I don't know you but I feel like I do. You mean so much to Casey and Hunter and Brody. I don't know where you've been or why you had to go; Casey would never tell me. She never seemed bitter about it but it was very apparent how much she missed you. All I ask... all I ask is that you not hurt my daughter or my grandsons, okay? If you really love them, you'll stay with them, no matter what, but if you're not sure how you feel...."

She trailed off and Colt looked at her seriously. "I'm very sure how I feel," he told her. "I always have. I want to make a life with Casey and the boys, and now that I'm back, we're going to get married as soon as she's feeling better. Please believe me when I tell you I didn't go away because I wanted to. It was all in the line of duty, but that duty is done. I'm back to stay."

Janice patted his broad shoulder. "I hope so."

She turned and left the room, leaving him alone with the baby, who was sleeping like an angel. Colt held his son close, drinking in that perfect, little face.

"You already had a name before you were born," he whispered. "You come from a long, proud line and you'll carry the same name we all have, Philip Henry Sheridan. Someday I'll tell you all about your great-great-great-great-great grandpa. He was a very famous man."

The baby made little sucking noises in his sleep and Colt grinned, falling more deeply in love with the child by the second. He began to rock slowly in the chair, cuddling the baby, watching his little face as he slept. All of the grief and terror was gone for the moment as he focused on something he never truly thought he'd have; a son. Somehow, it made his whole life worthwhile just to look at that sleeping infant. It was the best feeling in the world.

He lost track of time as he sat there and rocked, his gaze on the baby as if nothing else in the world existed. Then he heard the nursery door open behind him and he caught a glimpse of someone in scrubs entering the nursery. Glancing up to see who it was, the smile vanished from his face.

Scott was gazing steadily at him. There was instant tension in the air, thick and uncertain. Seeing the man here, it began to occur to Colt that perhaps Scott had made his presence known to Casey during his absence. Not that Colt didn't trust Casey; he did without question. But Dane had been trying to pull her away from Colt since nearly the beginning. Feeling extremely territorial, Colt struggled not to lash out.

"I heard you'd come back," Scott said after a moment. "I'm honestly surprised to see you."

Colt regarded him coldly. "What are you doing here?"

"I've been here every day since Casey entered the hospital," he told him steadily. "Unlike you, I came to see how she was and if she needed anything. I care about her."

Colt struggled with his composure but he realized he couldn't get too angry with the baby sleeping in his arms. He labored to remain calm.

"Look, Senator," he said quietly. "I appreciate that you've shown concern towards Casey. But that's going to stop now, is that clear? I'm back and I hope you understand when I say that I don't need or want your concern or interference. Casey and I are going to get married and that'll be the end of it."

Scott didn't rise to the challenge. He was, if nothing else, persuasive and cunning. He put that talent to work.

"I'm wondering what Mr. Meade thinks about that," he said quietly. "He wasn't too pleased with your relationship with Casey in the first place."

Colt lifted an eyebrow. "I'm not sure what you mean."

Scott smiled thinly. "Yes, you do," he said, "but your training demands you deny association or knowledge. I get that. But you should know that I've been responsible for making sure The Core received funding through the Ways and Means Committee for the past eight years. One little line item that feeds into the Defense budget, which in turn feeds into the Scientific Endeavors and Research budget. Difficult to trace the funds or find a trail. I've known Mr. Meade for about fifteen years and, as such, I know all about you. I know about your trip to Colombia. Congratulations on your success."

Colt remained stone-faced but his mind was whirling. Having been in survival mode for the past six months, all he could think about was snapping Dane's neck. There was a threat against him and he had to do away with it. He struggled to stay on an even keel.

"Casey said you told her about my past," he rumbled. "I should have known there was more to it. The things you told her were things no one but inner Core members would have known and still you were unable to turn her against me. I'm not sure how much clearer I can be; Casey and I love each other and nothing you do or say is going to change that. Back off or you'll be very sorry."

Scott watched him, refusing to admit that perhaps the man was right in some respects. In Colt's arms, the baby stirred and mewed, and both men turned to look at him as he settled back down. Scott looked at the child, wishing with all his heart that it was his baby and not Colt's. He began to wonder if it was because he really loved Casey or if it was more a competition between him and Colt to see who could capture the prize of Casey's heart. He was competitive, that was true, but somewhere along the line, he wasn't sure if his motives got twisted up. Still, he couldn't give up. Not yet.

"I want you to think about something, Colt, and then I'll leave you alone." He began to back up in the direction of the nursery door. "I know that the Norte del Valle has its sights on you. You're a wanted man and they'll stop at nothing to get to you. Even if you resume your life as the President's Special Agent in Charge, they'll be gunning for you and you know it. That will put everyone around you in danger, including the President, Casey and the baby. Is that what you want? Would you really be so selfish that you would knowingly jeopardize Casey and your son? The fact is, Colt, that you can never have a normal life with her and the baby. You'll always be looking over your shoulder for an assassin. What happens if they go after Casey? Could you live with yourself if they killed her and not you? Stop being so damn selfish and let the woman have a normal life. Let your son grow up without the threat of a Colombian assassin lurking around every corner. When you went to Colombia, you signed your death warrant. You did it to save the President but you ended up killing yourself. You're dead already only you don't know it. If you love her as much as you say you do, you'll leave this hospital and disappear. That's the best thing you can do for Casey and your son."

Colt sat there looking at the baby, listening to the senator's words and feeling more despair by the moment. Nothing the man said was untrue. Colt had thought the same things himself only he didn't want to verbalize it. To speak the words made them real. As he sat there, staring at his sleeping son, the nursery door opened and Janice appeared.

"Colt," she said, looking nervously between Scott and Colt. "Casey's out of surgery. You need to come."

Colt stood up immediately and very carefully put the baby back in his bassinet. A nurse wandered in to take over at that point and, without a glance to Scott, Colt followed Janice out of the room. He pulled off his scrubs before exiting the nursery on Janice's heels, following the woman back through the waiting room that was still crowded with the President and others, and into another antiseptic smelling corridor.

Janice and Colt were about halfway down the hallway when a woman in scrubs emerged from a pair of big double doors. Janice headed straight for her.

"How is she?" Janice asked.

Dr. Steele sighed as she pulled the surgical mask off her neck. "Lucky," she said frankly. "We were able to stop the bleeding but she's still lost a huge amount of blood. Honestly, I'm surprised she's still alive. The next few hours should tell us which direction she's going to take. She's stable right now and that's the best I can hope for."

Janice reached out and took Colt by the hand. "This is Colt," she told Dr. Steele. "This is the father of the baby. He needs to see my daughter."

Dr. Steele looked at Colt with some shock, the enormous man with piercing, dark eyes. After a moment's surprise, she shook her head. "So you're Colt?"

Colt nodded. "Yes, ma'am."

Dr. Steele continued to shake her head, looking him up and down. "I don't know whether to slap you or hug you. You caused her a lot of grief, you know."

Colt sighed faintly. He didn't know what to say to that. "Can I please see her?"

Dr. Steele nodded wearily. "Come on," she pushed her way back through the double doors. "It may do her some good to hear your voice. She wanted to die because you weren't around, so maybe hearing you will give her the will to live. Let's give it a shot."

The recovery room was beyond the double doors. It was dimly lit, very quiet, with several bays, sectioned off with curtains. A few were occupied but most were empty. As a nurse brought out another surgical gown and helped Colt put it on, Dr. Steele proceeded into one of the recovery bays.

Colt followed the woman, hesitantly, seeing a myriad of machines and I.V. stands before his gaze came to rest on a very pale woman lying on the gurney. Casey looked like she was dead already. Her beautiful face was devoid of color and her luscious caramel-colored hair was pulled back and tied up with a surgical mask.

Colt's eyes filled with tears and his jaw dropped with shock. He had to make a conscious effort to close his mouth, so very startled at the sight of her. As Dr. Steele motioned him to the edge of the gurney as she backed away, Colt couldn't help the tears that began to flow with a vengeance.

Colt took a good, long look at Casey and the sobs began to come. She was so ashen and unmoving. He dropped to his knees, collecting her right hand as he did so. Pressing her fingers to his lips, he wept deeply.

"Oh, my God," he sobbed against her flesh. "Casey, can you hear me? Wake up, Angel. It's me. I'm here now. Everything's going to be all right."

He barely got the words out through his sobs. He was at eye-level with the gurney and he began to stroke her face, touching her soft skin, feeling her warmth. In spite of everything, she was more beautiful than he had remembered.

"I saw the baby," he whispered. "He's perfect, Casey. I'm so proud and thankful. I can't even tell you how much I love him and how much I love you."

Casey remained still and unmoving, which fed Colt's tears. Perhaps he'd foolishly believed she would hear his voice and emerge from her dreamless sleep. He'd had hope. But the reality was harsh; she was far gone, perhaps too far gone and he couldn't bring her back. He laid his head on her arm, simply to be close to her, as the tears streamed from his face onto her flesh.

"I'm so sorry I was away for so long," he murmured. "I thought of you every second of every day, wondering how you were and what you were doing. There was so much going on... I'm sorry I had to stop calling you, but it couldn't be helped. God, do I have stories about bugs and weird food. You wouldn't believe it. I thought about bringing some of the bugs home to the boys but, well, those plans kind of fell through. I thought Brody would have gotten a kick out of this caterpillar with a turquoise-colored head and a fuzzy green body. Creepy."

His tears were fading as he spoke, focusing more on the conversation and less on her dire state. He stroked her arm as he spoke, feeling her tender flesh beneath his fingers.

"I know how you are about strange food," he continued. "I

don't think you would have liked it very much. They eat whatever they can for the most part; birds, reptiles, that kind of thing. I don't see you eating that much. You would have had to subsist on beans. They eat a lot of those."

He lifted his head to see if there was any sign of movement but Casey remained deathly still. Colt could feel his eyes stinging with tears again as he touched her face again. Rising wearily to his feet, he leaned over and kissed her sweet lips.

"I love you, Angel," he said, his hands on her face. "I'm going to stay right here until you feel like waking up. I won't leave you, I promise. I'll be right here. Come back to me, Casey. Please come back."

He kissed her again as a nurse brought in a plastic chair, which he gratefully took. Laying his head on her arm again, he put his right arm across her body as if to hold her. It was a protective and comforting gesture, hugging her even though he couldn't really get a grip on her. As he lay there with his eyes closed and tears streaming down his temples, he felt a soft hand on his shoulder.

Lifting his head, he saw Riley standing next to him, her free hand over her mouth to hold back the sobs as she gazed at her sister. Her teary eyes moved to Colt's face.

"I'm sorry," she mouthed.

Colt stood up and pulled her into a warm hug, rocking her gently as she cried. The nurse pulled in another chair and the two of them sat down, Colt resuming his position with his head on Casey's arm and his arm draped over her body. Eventually, he fell asleep, awakened a few hours later when they decided to move Casey into ICU.

Colt moved with her, so exhausted that he was at the point of collapse, but nothing was going to deter him from staying with her. Casey still hadn't regained consciousness by the time they hooked her up in the ICU, but Colt stayed right next to her, resuming his watchdog position a chair he'd pulled up next to the bed.

Riley had moved with her sister, too, and stayed in ICU a little while but her exhaustion had the better of her, so she left with her mother to go home and get a few hours of sleep. Colt simply lay his head on the bed next to Casey's arm and went back to sleep.

All they could do was wait.

Footsteps woke Colt some time later. Startled, swiftly awake, he glanced at his watch and saw that it was early morning. Turning around, he saw the President standing in the doorway.

Russ was dressed casually in a sweater and jeans, unlike the usually dapper President. He looked particularly pale and sorrowful as he gazed at Casey, still unconscious on the bed. Timidly, he took a few steps into the room.

"How is she?" he asked softly.

Colt glanced up at Casey's still face, at the monitors she was hooked up to. "Still stable," he said. "She hasn't moved all night."

Russ stood at the end of the bed, his gaze moving to Colt. "What about you?" he asked. "Did you sleep here all night?"

Colt nodded, rubbing at his eyes. "I promised her I wouldn't leave her ever again," he said. "I'm going to stay right here until she wakes up."

Russ sighed faintly, shoving his hands in his pockets as he contemplated his next sentence. He wasn't quite sure how to deliver the information; information he had received in bits and pieces for most of the night. He eventually pulled up another plastic chair and sat next to Colt.

"I got a call from Naval Criminal Investigative Services this morning," he said softly. "It seems that they had a dead Marine on their hands last night, a murder, and as they were piecing things together, they came across a dossier in an apartment out in McLean, Virginia that was about you. It seems that this Marine was moonlighting as a hired assassin, and someone assassinated *him*. They were able to trace deposits to the Marine's bank account from a Cayman Island account registered to Maria Esperanza Diego Villa. If that doesn't mean anything to you, it should; she's part of the Noestra clan."

Colt sighed faintly, looking at him. "I'm not surprised. They've put a contract out on me."

THE SECRET HOUR 343

Russ nodded grimly. "It's all happened in a matter of hours. The cartel knows you're back in the States."

"I know."

Russ eyed him reluctantly. "Colt, I hate to say this, but maybe you should consider going back into hiding until all this is over. It's the only safe thing for you to do. If they're hiring rogue Marines to kill you, then we have no way of knowing who will be out to get you. It could be anyone."

Colt shook his head before the President was finished with his sentence. "I'm not leaving Casey, not again."

"You're not thinking clearly about this," Russ insisted. "You can't come back to work for me, not at the moment, because every assassin on the eastern seaboard is going to be gunning for you. More than that, they'll kill anyone who gets in their way and consider it collateral damage. I'm talking about Casey."

Colt's dark eyes fixed on him, somewhat suspiciously. "Have you been talking to Dane?"

"No," Russ replied. "Did he say the same thing?"

Colt nodded, his gaze drifting back to Casey. "He came into the nursery last night after I got here," he told Russ. "He tried to tell me what you just told me. He said I needed to get out of Washington for everyone's safety, especially Casey's."

Russ was quiet a moment. "Think of it this way," he said softly. "If someone else was in this situation, what would you say to them? What if it was Peter, a marked man who refused to leave the woman he loved even though he knew she could very well be killed by those who were targeting him? Worse yet, there's a baby involved now. How would you feel if some hired assassin took out your six-month-old son?"

Colt was starting to lose his composure. What the President said made perfect sense but he didn't want to admit it. He'd had the same thoughts himself but chased them away, convincing himself that the most important thing was that he and Casey were together, no matter what. Now he was starting to struggle because someone he greatly respected was telling him what he didn't want to hear.

"Obviously, I wouldn't like it," he muttered, looking at Casey's sleeping face. "I guess the truth is that it would kill me."

The President could see the pain in Colt's expression. "What if one of those bullets took out Casey?" he asked grimly.

Colt stared at Casey for a long moment before closing his eyes and hanging his head.

"How do you think I would feel?" he hissed. "It would eat me alive, destroy me, make me crazy bent on vengeance. I would wipe out whoever did it and everyone associated with him; mother, father, brothers, grandfathers... I would take them all out. I wouldn't stop until everyone who ever knew the person was dead. Revenge would consume me."

Russ watched him seriously. "Colt, I know you don't want to hear this," he continued. "I don't want to say it; believe me. I've spent the past six months watching Casey slowly die. I don't mean literally, but figuratively. She wasn't the same person after you left. She had changed so much. She was so miserable without you. But you have to think of her and the baby in this case and stop thinking about yourself. What would be better for her and little Philip? To be looking over their shoulder every minute of every day, waiting for that bullet to come flying at you, at them, maybe even at Casey's other boys? Or would it be better for them to miss you terribly but to be safe? You really have to ask yourself that question. When you do, I think you'll know the answer."

Colt was staring at Casey's arm, limp and pale on the bed next to her. As Russ watched, Colt's eyes filled with tears and spilled over onto his face. Then he reached up, touching Casey's arm, feeling her flesh beneath his fingers as he carefully stroked her wrist.

"Oh, God," he breathed. "I just can't... I really don't want to leave her."

"I know."

Colt continued stroking her arm. "Put yourself in my shoes," he whispered. "What would you do?"

Russ sighed heavily. "I *am* in your shoes," he said softly. "Every hour of every day, I'm a walking target. My wife got shot because of me and if you don't think that was the worst moment of my life, think again. I lost two sons, Colt. That was bad enough, but watching Tracy take a bullet meant... it was all kinds of horrible, son. Take it from me. You don't want to put your family in the line of fire if you can at all help it."

Colt was looking at him by the time he finished. "But you continue on," he said. "You continue to hold the most visible public office in the world. You didn't send Tracy into hiding just to keep her safe."

Russ cocked an eyebrow. "No, I didn't," he agreed, "but I've got an army of guys like you to keep Tracy and me safe. I have the most advanced security force in the world. You don't have your own personal security force, Colt. It's just you against contract killers who are going to view your family as collateral damage as they try to get to you. There's a world of difference there."

"So what are you telling me?"

"I'm telling you that if I were in you, I'd go hide someplace where they could never find me. I would rather have my wife alive and miserable because she missed me than dead from a bullet that was meant for me."

Colt had finished stroking Casey's arm and now held her fingers. He pulled her hand to his lips, pensively, kissing her fingers as the tears continued to roll down his face. He made no attempt to wipe them away.

"You really think it's what I should do?" he asked.

"I do," Russ replied firmly. "I'm sorry, but I do. Where do you think you'll go?"

Colt sighed, thinking of something he didn't want to think about but forcing himself. Russ was right and he knew it. Already, it was killing him.

"I know of three thousand acres in Montana where it would be pretty difficult to find me," he whispered. "How long do I stay?"

"However long it takes."

Colt finally wiped at his face, drying up the tears, although his gaze was on Casey's sleeping face.

"What... what do I tell her?"

"Nothing,"

Colt looked at him, shocked. "What?"

Russ remained firm. "She hasn't seen you in six months," he said. "I think in her own way, she's been resigning herself to the fact that she may never see you again. If she sees you now and you have to leave her again... you'll just undo what has been trying to heal within her. It's like ripping the scab off a wound that's just starting to heal. The damage will be worse the second time around."

Colt stared at him a moment before returning his gaze to Casey one last time. He was starting to choke up again.

"I really want to tell her that I love her," he whispered. "I want her to know."

Russ stood up. "Then you tell her now," he said, having a hard time looking at Colt and the despair on the man's face. "Tell her while she's sleeping. She'll hear you in her dreams. And then you get the hell out of here and don't look back."

"But she's going to know I was here," Colt pointed out. "Everyone has seen me. What's she going to think of me coming to the hospital and then leaving before we had a chance to talk?"

Russ took a few steps towards the door, his hands shoved deep into his pockets and his features lined with stress and sorrow. "I'll tell her why," he finally promised. "I'll tell her about this conversation and I'll tell her why you had to go."

"And if she asks where I've gone?"

"I'm not going to tell her. It's better that way."

Russ quit the room, leaving Colt sitting next to Casey, gazing at the woman's face and seriously wondering if he'd die of a broken heart before all was said and done. But he knew Russ was right;

God help him, he knew it. With tears streaming down his face, he wearily rose to his feet and bent over Casey, kissing her sweetly as his tears wetted her soft cheeks.

"I'm so sorry, Angel," he whispered, trying very hard not to sob. "I guess... I guess it just wasn't meant to be this time. But I want you to know how much I love you, okay? That will never change, not ever. There have been a lot of love stories over the centuries and millions of people in love, but I don't think any man has loved a woman as much as I love you. Maybe someday we'll be happy again, but that time isn't now. I'm so sorry."

A sob escaped his lips as he kissed her again, staring at her, memorizing her features for the weeks and months and years to come. It would have to sustain him. It was tearing him apart.

"Take good care of yourself," he murmured. "Tell the baby how much I love him. I'll see you both in my dreams."

Scott Dane was coming into the hospital just as Colt was leaving. For a moment, they looked at each other, unsure what to say or do. There was suspicion, jealousy and friction, but neither one said a word. Colt was the first to break away, lowering his gaze and moving out into the parking lot.

Scott stood there and watched the man fade away into the asphalt and trees, wondering where he was going and further wondering if that would be the last he ever saw of him. He sincerely hoped so.

When Scott appeared in the maternity ward several minutes later, Russ punched him right in the face.

NINETEEN

A STORM WAS ROLLING IN.

Colt threw the last bale of hay into the trailer that was tethered to his grandfather's old Chevy pickup. The thing ran like a workhorse but it wasn't much to look at. Farm life had seen to that. Bundled up against the cold in a heavy suede coat with a fur lining and a cowboy hat that he had picked up in town about six months before, he glanced up at the sky that was beginning to darken with clouds.

Across the plains of Montana, the storms could get bad. Colt climbed into the pickup and removed his leather gloves, putting the truck in gear and heading back to the barn about two miles away. His grandparents had a big herd of Angus cattle, one of the largest herds in Montana, and Colt had to get the hay back to the barn before the weather broke. Wet hay was no good to anyone and he didn't want to waste nearly forty bales of it.

The dusty road wound down from the fields to the north of his grandparents' spread, cutting a path through the high plains and the softly rolling hills until he could see the homestead in the distance. His grandfather had built the house back in the nineteen forties, just about the time Colt's mother was born.

As he drew closer, he could see the long, rambling house and the big porch that wrapped all the way around the structure. His grandfather had originally built it as a dog-trot house, with four rooms and a big, central, open hallway dividing the rooms into two and two, but over the years he had added on and now the house had four bedrooms and a host of bathrooms and other living spaces. It was a place that Colt had called home for the past year.

Pulling into the barnyard less than a quarter of a mile from the house, he drove the pickup right into the enormous barn to protect the hay. Turning the truck off, he climbed out just as the rain began to trickle from the sky.

Putting the leather gloves back on, he began to unload the hay into the neat pile of stacks his grandfather had all around the walls. His grandparents mostly grew their own hay to satisfy the black cattle who munched at it, animals whose meat was in high demand. Those little black cows had made his grandparents fairly wealthy.

As Colt unloaded, he thought it was odd that his grandfather wasn't there to help him. Usually, old Mike McCulloch worked right alongside his grandson, especially since he had been the one to send him to bring the hay in before it rained. But Colt didn't think too much of his grandfather's absence as he continued to off load the bales. They were heavy and he grunted as he stacked them up.

Finished with the last one, he removed his gloves, removed his hat and wiped the sweat off his brow. As he turned back for the pickup, he suddenly froze in his tracks.

A toddler was standing just inside the barn door. All bundled up against the weather in jeans and a jacket and a big warm hat, the child looked at Colt with big brown eyes, chewed on his fingers, and began to toddle off into the barn. Startled, curious, Colt rounded the hay trailer and watched the little boy squat down and pick up a handful of fallen hay.

"Hey," Colt didn't know what else to say. "How'd you get here, little guy?"

The little boy looked at him, standing up with a big wad of hay in his hand. He was too little to talk; in fact, he was barely walking but he was making a good stab at it. When he threw the hay down, he lost his balance and fell onto his bum. Undeterred, he rolled onto his knees and stood up. Then he took off again.

"Hey!" Colt followed the little boy. "Where are you going?"

The little boy looked over his shoulder to see the big man following him. He giggled, thinking he was being chased, and tried to run. He ended up tripping and falling, only to giggle with delight again and get right back up. Colt, watching all of this, was completely baffled.

"Grandma?" he called, turning in the direction of the open barn door and thinking that surely his grandmother or some other adult was nearby. Little kids don't just appear out of thin air. "Hey, Grandma? There's a little kid in the barn."

No one answered him and Colt turned to watch the little boy trip up again in the big pile of hay. Instead of standing up again, he just sat there and played with it. Perplexed, yet charmed by the cute little kid, Colt went over to boy and crouched down a few feet away.

"Who are you, little guy?" he asked softly, watching the little boy inspect the pile of hay. "Where's your mom?"

"His mom is right here."

Colt heard the reply, but it didn't come from the child. In fact, it came from the direction of the barn door and he turned to see who had spoken. He was still crouched down as a figure came around the rear of the hay trailer, heading in his direction.

Casey came to a halt by the rear of the truck. Bundled up against the cold weather, she looked radiant and gorgeous in a white wool coat and jeans.

It took Colt a moment to grasp what he was seeing and when realization finally dawned, he slowly rose to his full height, his dark eyes wide with shock and astonishment. His entire body began to shake as he turned in her direction, his heart pounding so hard that he was afraid it was about to burst from his chest.

"Oh, my God," he breathed. "Casey?"

"Yes."

"You... are you real?"

Casey couldn't help the tears that were filling her eyes. She nodded. "Yes," she whispered. "Are you?"

He could only nod. Then he turned, rather haltingly, to the baby playing a few feet away and pointed.

"Is that...?"

Casey nodded, and tears splashed down her cheeks. "Yes," she murmured. "I thought for sure you'd see the resemblance."

Colt swallowed hard, looking at the baby who was now rolling around in the dry hay and having a marvelous time. He stuck a piece in his mouth and chewed happily, grinning up at Colt. Realization struck like a hammer and Colt's hand flew to his mouth, tears popping from his eyes.

"Oh, my God," he breathed. "He's... he's so big. He looks just like my dad."

Colt's tears brought on Casey's as she watched her son eat hay. "He looks just like *you*," she whispered, wiping at her eyes. "He's smart and handsome and funny as hell. Hunter and Brody adore him. You should see them with him; they're so good with him. They called him Jack when he was born because they didn't like Philip, so he goes by Jack."

Colt was trying not to sob as he watched the baby get hay in his dark blond hair. Tears were muddling his vision but he could see the child clearly enough. He took his hand away from his mouth and looked at Casey.

"He's the most beautiful baby I've ever seen," he whispered, his eyes drinking in the sight of her. "God, I've missed you."

Casey's features crumpled a little but she fought it. She began wiping at the tears dripping off her chin. "I've missed you, too," she agreed, lower lip trembling. "Colt, I know what happened. I know why you went away. Russ told me everything."

Colt was struggling with his composure. "I told him not to," he said. "I did it to protect you and the kids. I can't...."

Casey shushed him softly as she began to move in his direction.

"I know all of that," she said. "Colt, it doesn't matter. None of it matters. I still love you as much as I ever did; that hasn't changed."

He began to move towards her, too. His gaze moved over her gorgeous face, looking more beautiful that he remembered.

"The last I saw you, you were in a hospital bed," he murmured. "Please... please understand that I didn't want to leave you. That's the last thing I wanted to do. But there's a price on my head and I just couldn't jeopardize you and the boys that way. I had to leave so you'd be safe."

She nodded patiently. "I know," she stopped when she came to within arm's length of him. "I understand you did what you thought was right, but the truth is that you never asked me what *I* wanted. You never asked me to come with you. Why?"

His tears were fading as he thought on her question. "Because you would have wanted to come. I couldn't let you do that to yourself. I couldn't let you put the boys in danger like that."

She lifted an eyebrow. "You know," she said slowly, "I always swore that when I saw you again, I'd really let you have it for not letting me make that choice. But now that I'm here, I can't bring myself to do it. I know you made the best decision you could. Did you think I would just forget about you and leave it at that?"

He wiped the tears off his chin, sighing faintly. "I'd hoped you would."

"Really?"

He looked into her violet eyes, eyes he loved so much, and eventually shook his head. "No," he whispered. "I didn't hope that."

"But you left me to the mercy of Scott Dane."

His sigh grew heavier. "He could take care of you and the baby and give you everything you needed. Your lives wouldn't be in danger."

"But I don't love him."

Colt just looked at her, unsure of what he could say to that. "Why did you come?"

"To tell you that I love you more than ever. You have a family, Colt, and we all need to be together."

Outside, thunder began to roll as they gazed at one another. There was a maelstrom of emotion swirling between them – hope, fear, uncertainty, joy, and pure adoration. It was everywhere. Colt couldn't take his eyes off her as he sighed faintly.

"Every day," he told her, "every single day since I left, all I've thought of is you and the baby. I would wake up in the morning, wondering how you were and then go to bed at night saying a prayer for you. I can't even tell you how much I love you because the word hasn't been invented yet to describe what I feel. Even as I stand here looking at you, I can't even put into words what I'm feeling. Joy doesn't quite encompass it."

Casey took another few steps towards him, her gaze open and honest. "I've talked it over with Hunter and Brody," she said softly. "We all want to be together and we all want to be with you, whether it's in Washington D. C. or out here in the wilds of Montana. I know you came here to hide out, so if that's the case, then we want to hide out with you. Don't you get it? You won us all over, Colt. We all love you. And Jack deserves the opportunity to know his father, who is a truly amazing and selfless individual. Would you deny him that?"

Colt was pale, tears lingering in his eyes, as he looked over at the baby, who was now crawling around in the hay. He was trying not to weep again at the sight.

"God, no," he whispered. "But what I did, I did to protect him. I did it to protect all of you."

"I get that. But we're willing to take the risk with you, so long as we're all together." When he didn't reply, she went for the jugular. "Would you rather that Scott raise Jack as his son? Would you rather that Scott is the only father he knows? And would you like to open the newspaper one day and see that Senator Scott Dane has married a woman named Casey Cleburne, knowing that he's now her husband and doing everything to her that a husband does? As much as you think you're doing us all a favor by dropping out of our lives, the truth is that you haven't. We love you and we want to be with you, through the good times or the bad."

Colt had turned away from the baby and was watching her intensely. Then he slumped, dragging a weary hand over his forehead. He made his way over to the hood of the old Chevy and leaned against the car hood as if he could no longer support his own weight. He was a man with a good deal on his mind.

Casey watched him, sensing his reluctance, his determination that he was doing the right thing for them all. She was starting to feel desperate.

"Please don't make me beg," Casey was starting to cry again. "Please don't tell me that you don't want me, that you don't want us."

He shook his head firmly, turning to look at her. "Angel, that's not it at all," he murmured. "I... I guess I'm just overwhelmed. When I left you at Walter Reed last year, it was the worst day of my life. I'm still not over it. But I truly believed I was doing what was best for you and the boys. But now... now I look at you, at the baby, and I've never wanted anything so badly in my entire life. But I still don't know if it's fair to you."

She walked up to the truck and leaned on the hood next to him, brushing against him, feeling his body heat and her heart racing as a result. It was enough to make her quiver.

"What's not fair to me is to not let me be with the man I love, the father of my child," she whispered, gazing into his dark eyes. "You know that there have been a lot of changes to the Norte del Valle cartel, right?"

He nodded knowingly. "I've heard it on the news."

"Hasn't anyone called you to talk about it?"

He shook his head. "I don't have a forwarding number or even an email address. For all intents and purposes, I died the day I left Washington D.C. I haven't had any contact with anyone."

She was careful in her reply. She didn't want to shock him anymore than he already was.

"Russ told me to tell you that those people who were out to kill you have been killed themselves, or have run off," she said softly. "A whole new regime has taken over that doesn't give a damn about you. If anything, you did them a favor by removing their predecessor and allowing them to come into power. They don't even care about you anymore, Colt. Russ wants to talk to you. He wants you back with him in D.C. He says you were the best damn Secret Service agent he ever had."

Colt looked at her seriously, glancing over at the baby as the kid continued to roll around in the hay. "I'd really like to believe that."

"Call Russ. He'll tell you the truth. He says you can have your old job back if you want it."

Colt was terrified to believe that it all might be true, afraid to get his hopes up. The fact that Russ had told Casey everything was now starting to make sense. There was no longer any reason to keep the secret. His expression was wrought with uncertainty, with excitement.

"Casey, it's not that easy," he said softly. "These people don't give up just like that."

"Russ seems to think so. Peter does, too."

He digested the possibility, feeling his hope rise. It was nearly too good to believe.

"And if it's really true?" he questioned. "Do we go back to the life we had before? What about you and me?"

She smiled, holding up her left hand and removing the glove. The big diamond engagement ring that Colt gave her glimmered in the weak light.

"Do you want this back?" she asked.

He gazed at the ring. "Of course not," he whispered. "It's yours. I gave it to you."

"Do you still want to marry me?"

"More than anything in the world."

"Then you come home and we get married. I haven't taken this ring off since you gave it to me. You promised me a wedding and I'm going to hold you to it."

"Even though I've been gone... nothing has changed with you? With us?"

She shook her head slowly, firmly. "Nothing."

"What about Scott?"

She shrugged. "He gave up trying to convince me to marry him months ago. I just wasn't interested. You are the only man I will ever love and he knows it."

Colt pushed himself off of the hood and just stared at her. After a moment, his hands came up, daring to touch her for the first time since she entered the barn. He cupped her face in his big hands and gazed steadily into the violet eyes. He watched as Casey dissolved into tears at his touch. Colt shushed her softly, kissing her forehead, her cheeks.

"No tears, Angel," he whispered. "I'm so sorry for what I did. I never wanted to hurt you."

She was sobbing softly. "Then please tell me that we'll never be apart again."

"We'll never be apart again."

"Swear it?"

He nodded, kissing her nose gently before moving on to her lips. "I swear," he promised, kissing her salty lips tenderly. "You are my life, Casey Cleburne. I love you very, very much."

"Then you'll call Russ?" she wept. "You'll come back to us?"

"I will. I swear, I will."

She threw her arms around his neck as he swallowed her up in his enormous embrace. As they hugged tightly, Jack let out a squeal and they both looked over to see that he had apparently spotted one of the many barn cats. He stood up unsteadily and began to run after one. Laughing, crying, Colt and Casey watched him approach a little cat that wasn't afraid of him. The kitty wanted to be petted, rubbing up against the little boy as the child grabbed for the cat's tail.

"Be nice," Casey admonished the baby. "Be gentle, Jack. Pet the kitty nicely."

Jack looked at his parents, grinning, as he patted the cat as carefully as a toddler could. Colt watched the baby, shaking his head with wonder.

"I still can't believe it," he whispered. "You're here. He's here. I'm stunned."

Casey wiped at the remaining tears on her cheeks, gazing up into his handsome face. "It's over, Colt," she murmured. "Everything that kept us apart is over."

He smiled at her, lowering his head to capture her lips in his. The passion that had been dormant these long months roared to life and Casey wrapped her arms around his neck as he pulled her into his powerful embrace, tasting her, reacquainting himself with her. Colt knew, no matter what, that he'd never be separated from her again. Come what may, they would face it together. He'd been a fool to leave in the first place.

"Come on," his mouth left hers, his eyes full of longing and adoration. "I guess I need to go give the President a call."

Casey smiled at him, thrilled beyond words. "You sure do," she replied, looking to Jack who was still petting the kitty. "Jack, baby, let's go. Leave the kitty there."

Unfortunately, Jack didn't want to leave the cat. He continued petting the animal until Colt swooped down and picked him up. Jack fussed for a moment at the strange man but he stopped soon enough when Colt promised him a dog to pet inside Grandma's house.

Intrigued, Jack went peacefully with his father and mother into the softly blowing rain outside.

TWENTY

"SERIOUSLY?" Casey sat at her desk on a warm July day, frustrated with the person on the other end. "Maybe you didn't hear me the first time. I'm talking about the President of the United States, and you're telling me you can't accommodate him at your restaurant? Are you really that dumb?"

Chris sat across from Casey, snickering at the conversation he was overhearing. Usually it was him yelling at people over the phone, but today it was her. As Casey continued to argue, they could hear a group approaching the Oval Office from the hallway. Casey was still entrenched in the phone call, but Chris glanced up to see Colt and Peter enter the office, followed by Russ and a few other agents. Russ was talking to his aide, Barbara, as they walked through Casey's office and on into the Oval Office beyond.

There was a lot of conversation and activity filling the office area. Colt and Peter went into Colt's office and had a brief conversation before Peter turned around and left the office as Colt sat down behind his desk. Phones were ringing and more agents went into Sheridan's office. He had a phone receiver in his hand as he issued directives to the two new agents and sent them on their way. Then he got on the phone just about the time his wife hung up.

"Morons!" Casey hissed as she began to type something into

Russ' calendar. "You would think that if the freaking President of the freaking United States is visiting your city and specifically requested to have dinner at your four star restaurant, you would move heaven and earth to accommodate him."

Chris snickered as Colt, hearing his wife's tone of voice, peered at her from his desk even though he was still on the phone call. As Casey typed furiously, Colt got off his call and got up from his desk.

"Keep your cool, Mrs. Sheridan." He fought off a grin as he made his way to her desk. "The President is up for re-election in November and you don't want to piss anybody off."

Casey glanced up at her husband of one year. It had been the best year of her life. Just the sight of him was enough to lighten her heart, and she smiled sweetly at him. Then she suddenly glanced at her watch.

"Are you going to be able to pick up Jack?" she wanted to know. "I have to finish this for Russ and Jack's out of school in a half hour."

Colt shook his head. "I can't," he told her. "The President wants to make a run over to that rally they're having over by the Vietnam Veteran's Memorial."

Casey glanced at the President's laminated schedule on her desk. "Oh, right," she lifted an eyebrow. "If he had enough time when he got back from his meeting on the hill, he was going to try and go."

Colt nodded, leaning over and bracing his big arms on her desk. "Have Riley pick the baby up."

Casey wriggled her eyebrows and picked up the phone. "I don't have a choice."

Colt winked at her and headed into the Oval Office. Casey got a hold of her sister and coerced the woman into picking up her nephew from nursery school. Then she continued making adjustments to Russ' calendar.

Casey could hear the voices in Russ' office as she typed, the day itself an ordinary day just like most of them. The President had been on the re-election trail for the past nine months and Colt had been with him, traveling like crazy, in and out of Washington, to points all over the nation. Casey had mostly stayed at home with the kids, her duties as personal assistant to the President having shifted slightly since Colt was doing so much traveling. They had decided one of them needed to stay home with their growing family and that choice was, logically, Casey.

So she stayed home at their residence in Falls Church, a home that had once belonged to the Cleburne/Nantz Clan but one that now belonged to three Sheridans and two Nantzs. Riley had moved out when Colt and Casey married, deciding she needed to have her own space, so Colt sold her his townhome and he now parked his flashy Audi next to Casey's Cadillac in the driveway of the two-story brick home. He went to soccer games and baseball games when his schedule allowed, cheering on Brody and Hunter in the stands along with Dennis, Casey and Riley.

Oddly enough, Colt and Dennis had become good friends, which benefitted the boys when their dad and step-dad took them to Washington Nationals games or some other event. Colt had become part of their lives, the step-dad who the boys thought was pretty cool. But wherever Colt was when he was home, it was never far from Jack.

The three-year-old had pretty much taken over the entire household. He was a very big boy, like his father, with dark blond hair and intense dark eyes. He was vocal, intelligent, sweet and hilarious, always wanting to be with his brothers, toddling along after them and trying to do big boy things. Colt was so proud of the kid that he could burst, very attentive to the point of nearly pushing Casey out of the way. He fed the boy, changed him, bathed him, and generally made himself a fixture in his son's life. He'd spent the first year of his young life away from him and was determined to make up for lost time.

Casey thought it all rather sweet when he would lay his enormous body on Jack's toddler bed and read stories to him at bedtime. Brody and Hunter would usually join in, all of them trying to cram onto Jack's little, red racecar bed in spite of the fact that the older boys were too old for storytime. They just wanted to be part of the huddle. She would stand in the doorway and watch her boys; it was the time of the day she loved best.

Over the past few months, Colt had been dropping hints about having another baby but Casey would change the subject. She was busy enough with three boys, and with Hunter now in high school, her time was limited. She was just happy to be Mrs. Colt Sheridan and if they happened to have another baby, it would just have to work itself out. Life, at the moment, was amazing as it was. She didn't think another baby could or would make it any better.

So the days, like today, were precious and normal, and Casey was already thinking about what she was going to make for dinner. She finished adjusting Russ' calendar, pausing as she listened to the conversation coming out of Russ' office. She could tell that they were preparing to head out to the Mall and the Vietnam Veteran's Memorial rally. Soon enough, Colt appeared, talking into his radio as he headed out of the office. He gave his wife a wink as he passed by and she watched him walk out, admiring his big frame and sleek dark suit. The man only grew more handsome by the day.

Russ, Barbara, and more aides followed Colt, along with several more Secret Service agents. As Russ passed Casey's desk, he came to an abrupt halt.

"Can you come along, Casey?" he asked, motioning to her. "We can take care of some things on the drive over."

Casey nodded, picking up her usual equipment – the iPad, purse and two cell phones. She ended up walking out with Peter, waving to Lisanne as she exited the West Wing to the waiting motorcade in the newly paved driveway outside. It was a sunny day, slightly humid, as Casey followed Russ to the Presidential limousine.

Colt was standing next to the car, directing the agents over the radio, when he realized that one of his agents had been displaced from one of the big black Escalades because of some equipment they had stored in the car. Colt pulled Peter out of the chase car, put him in the front of the Presidential limousine, while Colt climbed into the rear of the car after Casey. The leftover agent took charge of the chase car.

Russ was talking to Barbara when the limousine pulled out, realizing that Colt and Casey were in the cab with him. He grinned at Colt.

"I don't think I've ever seen you back here," he said.

"No, sir," Colt grinned. "So this is how the other half lives."

Russ snorted. "I have a mini-bar," he taunted. "If you're real nice, I might let you have a look."

Colt's grin grew as he answered some chatter on the radio. Casey was smiling as well as she pulled out her iPad and prepared to go to work.

"Don't tease him with that stuff," she told the President. "He'll sneak in after hours and drink all the good bourbon."

Russ laughed at Colt's expense. "Your wife is ratting you out, Sheridan."

Colt just shook his head, pretending to be exasperated. "It wouldn't be the first time, Mr. President."

Russ sat back in his seat, glancing to the sidewalk and scenery outside when they stopped at a red light.

"Speaking of a Sheridan," he said thoughtfully, "Tracy wants to know what she can get Jack for his birthday. It's coming up here pretty quick."

Casey looked at Colt, who shrugged. "He's got everything he could possibly need or want," he replied, "but he likes those big metal dump trucks. He's been into digging in the dirt lately."

"Perfect," Russ replied decisively. "I'll have her get him one of those dump trucks that kids can drive around in. You've seen those things. They're pretty cool."

Casey was still looking at Colt, this time reluctantly. Colt took the hint but he tried to be tactful.

"I think he's a little young for a driving truck," he replied. "A toy truck will make him just as happy."

Russ looked defiant. "I'm his godfather," he pointed out. "I can get him whatever I want and you can't stop me."

Colt grunted softly, with resistance, looking to his wife with a faint grin on his face. Silent words passed between the two, knowing there would be no discouraging the President from spoiling the child he felt that he was responsible for. Jack Sheridan wouldn't exist had Russ not introduced Casey to Colt, so in that respect, Russ wasn't too far off. He treated the boy as if he were his own, with gifts and little toys and other goodies.

Jack had even spent the night at the White House once when Colt and Casey went away for a weekend, simply because Russ and Tracy had begged to watch him. It had been hard to say no. Russ cleared out his calendar for the entire weekend and every moment had been dedicated to hanging out with little Jack Sheridan. Russ still talked about it.

Colt gave up trying to discourage the man and Casey went back to her iPad as the Presidential motorcade neared the Vietnam Veteran's Memorial. Security was tight and there was quite a crowd on hand. Colt scanned the crowd as Russ and Casey began to go over a few points for his speech for the rally. It was a big operation, one that had both the Secret Service and the D.C. police scrambling because the President's appearance hadn't been confirmed. Now that he was here, security was massive.

Colt paid close attention to where they were going to stop the limousine, coordinating with other agents who were already on-site. When the big black car finally pulled to a halt by the Lincoln Memorial, Colt swiftly kissed his wife and opened up the back door.

"Off to work," he murmured as he exited the vehicle. "Love you."

"Be careful," she whispered as he brushed by. "Love you, too."

Colt gave her a smile and a wink before he put his sunglasses on and went to work. Casey climbed out, followed by Barbara, and finally Russ. The crowd cheered when they saw the President and Russ smiled broadly, working the crowd as he followed Colt and

Peter across the parking area and on towards the memorial several dozen yards away. The Mall was nearly half-full with people, spilling out in into the drive, and there were even people in the reflecting pool on this warm summer day.

Casey was lingering towards the rear of the entourage, still within the scope of the Secret Service agents, as she followed Russ' movements. She could see Colt up at the front of the pack, at least a head taller than everyone else around him, and she smiled as she watched him directed his agents. He was always a model of efficiency to watch. She even watched him push back some photographers who got too close. One guy ended up on his ass. But the procession moved through, heading towards the Vietnam Veteran's Memorial as it resided within green parklands.

The crowd was cheering Russ as he walked the path towards the memorial. Colt had moved to mid-pack now, shadowing the President closely as they walked, mostly because there were trees and trees could hide or hold gunmen. As they neared the memorial and the crowd was held back by ropes and police officers, Colt turned around to look for his wife. He caught sight of her towards the back with Steven Case following a few feet behind her, and he removed his glasses so she could see that he was looking at her.

Casey saw him, the faint smile on his face, and she smiled at him, giving him a brief wave. Colt smiled back, never realizing that her beautiful face would be the last thing he ever saw. He heard the gunshot shortly before everything went black.

... and then there was silence.

TWENTY-ONE

"THEY NEVER FOUND out where the shot came from," Mother was whispering softly. "One minute he was there and in the next... well, he never knew what hit him. I guess I should have been grateful for small mercies."

Jack lay against his mother, stunned. When his mother had opened her mouth an hour ago, he'd never expected anything like this. It went beyond what his imagination could have ever dreamed up and he was struggling to process it.

"So... you were really the personal assistant to President Russell Talbot?" he asked with disbelief.

"Yes," Mother replied.

Jack just shook his head. "And he was my godfather? Why didn't I know that?"

Mother shrugged weakly. "Because with everything that happened surrounding Colt's death, I pretty much cut out that part of my life, Russ included. I just couldn't handle it. I think he understood. He still sent you birthday cards every year with a check. I put the money in your college fund."

Jack thought on that for a moment. "What you've told me... that's not stuff you'll find in history books. It's a pretty amazing story."

"Better than me being a prostitute or being a spy?"

Jack grinned, a gesture that looked very much like his father. "Definitely." He fell silent for a moment, focusing on the more important issue. "So I'm descended from General Philip Sheridan on my father's side?"

Mother nodded slowly. "You are the product of two great American families," she murmured. "Your birth name was Philip Henry Sheridan VI, but when I married Scott, we legally changed it on your birth certificate to Philip Henry Dane. I thought it would be better that way, especially if the Norte del Valle was behind Colt's death. I didn't want them to find you."

"That makes sense."

"Your kids carry Sheridan and Cleburne blood as well. It's a proud thing."

Jack sat up and climbed off the bed, turning to look at his mother with an expression between bewilderment and excitement. "That's an understatement," he responded ironically. "I really can't believe you never told me all of this before. I'm almost offended."

Mother was watching him with her soft violet eyes. "Don't be," she whispered. "I guess... I guess I just couldn't bring myself to talk about it. You have to understand, Jack, how much your father meant to me. We had that love that people hope for but seldom have. I've missed him desperately every day of my life for the past forty-three years. It's been grief like you can't imagine, and you look so much like him that, at times, it's been difficult to look at you and not feel the pain."

Jack thought on the man who had been revealed to be his father. He had so many questions he didn't know where to start.

"Hunter and Brody knew him," he said softly. "They never said a word to me about him, not ever."

Mother watched Jack struggle with his feelings. "Probably because his death was painful for us all," she confessed. "They knew how hard it was for me. I would never speak of him and I think they just learned not to speak of him, either. They assumed I'd tell you the truth, someday."

Jack began to pace. "Colt Sheridan," he said, repeating the name as if to make it all the more real to him. "Do they think it was the cartel who took him out, then?"

Mother shrugged weakly. "It was one of the theories," she said. "They could never prove it. The most prevalent theory was that someone was aiming for President Talbot and hit Colt instead. They did all kinds of investigations. There was even a senate committee investigation about it. From the trajectory of the bullet, they think the shooter came from Henry Bacon Drive, but they never found anyone or anything. It was very strange; as if whoever did it just... vanished."

Jack was listening intently. "What about The Core?" he wanted to know. "From what you said, those guys had the ability to assassinate someone and then just disappear, just like Colt did when he assassinated Noestra. If Sheridan stopped working for The Core like you said, maybe they wanted to eliminate him. He knew too much about them."

Again, Mother shrugged. "Another one of the theories."

Jack's FBI training began to kick in as he tried to gather information on a forty-year-old mystery. "Did you ever ask Agent Harrios?" he asked. "He was part of The Core. Did you ever rat him out to the President?"

Mother thought on the African-American agent who had been both enemy and friend.

"No," she answered. "There wasn't much point. When Colt was killed, Peter was devastated, so I really don't think he was a part of any greater conspiracy. He requested a transfer after Colt's death, in fact. After Colt's funeral, I never saw him again."

Jack scratched his head, pondering that information. "What about the funeral?" he said. "If the Core faction had assassinated him, wouldn't that make you a target, too? Did you think about that?"

"I never thought about it," Mother said quietly. "To be honest, I don't remember much from that time. But I do remember there were a lot of people at his funeral, including a group of men who identified themselves as old friends. One man in particular was very distraught about his death. His name is Nash Aury and he was once the governor of Louisiana, among other political posts. He was a good friend to your father and Colt used to talk about him. Though I didn't know him well, Nash told me to let him know if I ever needed anything, but I never did. If he tried to reach out to me again after that, I wouldn't know. I just shut everything out."

Jack could see that even talking about that time brought her some distress, all over again, but he needed answers. "What about that Mr. Meade character? Did you ever see him again?"

Mother shook her head. "No," she replied. "I don't know what happened to him. To be honest, I didn't care. After Colt died, I didn't care about much of anything. He was dead and no amount of investigations or prosecutions could bring him back. All of that just didn't seem to matter anymore."

Jack looked at her. "So his death remains a big mystery?"

Mother sighed. "We'll never know if Colt was the intended target or just happened to be in the wrong place at the wrong time," she said. "All I know is that I was looking right at him when he was shot. I remember running towards him while the Secret Service was trying to get the President back into the limousine and, much like Jackie Kennedy, I held Colt's bloody head in my lap until they physically separated us. I remember clinging to him and refusing to let go. He was buried at Arlington with complete military honors, if you should ever want to go and visit his grave sometime. But, as I said, I don't remember much after that. The President gave me as much time off as I needed, but I was so grief-stricken that I ended up taking almost six months off. Every time I went near the West Wing, I'd have anxiety attacks. Finally, I just quit my job because I couldn't go near the White House. Too many memories."

Jack was subdued as he thought on his mother's heartbreaking horror. "And Senator Dane?"

Mother simply shrugged. "He waited a nominal amount of time after Colt's death before he came around again, trying to convince me to marry him." She sighed heavily. "I just didn't have the strength to fight him off anymore."

"So you gave in."

"I gave in to a man who I knew would be good to you and your brothers."

"You gave up."

"Yes, I did. I admit it. I never loved Scott and he knew it, but he married me anyway. It's rather sad if you think about it."

"But he remained a senator until his death," Jack stated. "You lived in Washington all that time and you never saw the President again?"

"No," Mother shook her head. "He tried to contact me a few times. So did Tracy. But I just couldn't talk to them. They both reminded me too much of Colt."

"And then Scott died in a plane crash."

"By thirty-nine years old, I had been widowed twice. Not such a good record."

Jack continued to pace, thoughtfully, perhaps with a little agitation now that all of the news was setting in.

"I had every right to know who my real father was," he said after a time. "You always told me it was Dane but, somehow, I knew that wasn't the truth."

Mother didn't seem particularly remorseful. "You weren't quite three when Colt was killed. I'm surprised you don't remember him, at least in some small way. You two were very attached to one another."

Jack thought hard. "It's possible that I do," he said thoughtfully. "I seem to have very early memories of a red racecar bed and a man lying with me in it, reading books. You always said it was Dane but based on the pictures I've seen of the man, it wasn't him. It was someone else."

Mother smiled faintly. "It was Colt," she confirmed. "Oh, how he doted on you. You were absolutely the apple of his eye."

Jack lingered on the faint memories of his racecar bed. "I wish I'd known him."

"I wish you had, too."

Jack sighed, becoming resigned to what he'd been told. There was no use in scolding Mother for withholding the information for so long. It really didn't matter and she'd had her reasons.

"Well," he said after a moment. "Thanks for telling me."

"You be sure and tell your children someday, okay? Tell them what a great man their grandfather was. Colt deserves that."

Jack simply nodded. Exhausted from all of the talking, Mother faded off to sleep after that and Jack stood at the foot of her bed, thinking on the earliest memories of his childhood and trying to recall what he could of Colt Sheridan. He couldn't remember much, really, but there were phantom images in his mind of a warm smile and deep, soft voice. He remembered someone tickling him. The more he thought on it, the more depressed he became.

A glance over at Mother showed her to be sleeping soundly, so Jack quietly left the room to ponder the revelations from the past.

———

When Mother opened her eyes again, it was very late and very quiet. Soft rain pelted the windows of her hospital room and she lay there a moment, watching the rain, recalling a dream where she had been standing in Lafayette Square on a warm summer's day. A soft breeze blew and she pushed stray pieces of hair from her eyes, watching Colt approach from Pennsylvania Avenue as he crossed the street and waved at her. She just stood there and watched him, waving in return, seeing his handsome features as they loomed closer and closer. And then, she woke up to soft rain on the windows and the cold reality of a hospital room.

With a sigh, she brought up a hand to rub her eyes, disappointed that she had not been allowed to remain in her dream. She dreamt of Colt regularly, and had for forty-three years, but tonight's dream had been different. She almost got to touch him. As she rubbed her eyes, she drew her hand back and happened to glance at it.

Her flesh wasn't wrinkled and tissue-paper thin any longer. It was soft and creamy, as it had been in her youth. Confused, she looked at her other hand and noticed that it, too, was young and supple. Startled, she sat up, purely a reaction to her surprise when she realized that she hadn't been able to sit up in weeks. Shocked, she looked at her hands and arms, noticing how young and soft they were, so she climbed out of bed. She hadn't been able to stand on her own in months, either.

The bathroom was to her left and she caught a glimpse of herself. The violet eyes widened as she saw herself as she had been in her youth, a startling beauty with full lips and luminous eyes, staring back in the reflection. Mouth agape, Mother went to the bathroom mirror and turned on the light, seeing herself as she had looked in her mid-thirties, the height of her beauty and the time in her life when she had met Colt. It had been the happiest time of her life.

Casey touched her face, feeling the smooth warm skin beneath her fingers. She hadn't touched that kind of skin in decades. Then she noticed her hair; the sleek, caramel color with the heavy fringe of bangs. She laughed a little, with shock and glee, as she hadn't had that hairstyle in over thirty years. She realized that she missed it. Running her fingers through her hair, she recognized the soft texture from years past. Thinking she was dreaming, she was more than happy to linger in this wonderful dream.

Exiting the bathroom, she noticed that she was dressed in a long white gown that showed off her ample figure. She had no idea how she got into the gown because she didn't remember putting it on. As she inspected the feather-soft garment, a soft voice came from the hospital room door.

"Hello, Angel."

Startled, she looked up to see Colt standing in the doorway. He looked the same way she always remembered him; enormously tall and strong, his dark blond hair stylishly cut short, his dark eyes glimmering at her from his exquisitely handsome face. He was dressed in a sleek, dark suit, the expression on his face nothing short of adoring. He was worshiping her as he stared at her. A smile spread across Casey's face as she met his gaze.

"I must be dreaming," she murmured. "Please, I don't want to wake up."

His smile broadened as he stepped into the room. "Don't worry," he assured her. "You won't."

He was reaching out a hand to her and Casey swiped at it, grabbing it, holding his big hand firmly in both of hers as if afraid he were going to dissolve away and she would be left with only a painful memory again. She held him tightly.

"Oh, my God," she whispered, realizing that she was actually touching him. "I... I can feel you. I've dreamed about you so much but I have never been able to actually feel you. Every time I get close, I either wake up or you fade away."

Colt put both arms around her and pulled her into a crushing embrace. "Not this time," he whispered. "God, I've missed you. I love you so much."

Casey threw her arms around his neck, holding him with a death grip and terrified of letting go. She could smell his distinctive scent and feel the texture of his hair. Euphoria swamped her.

"I've missed you, too," she whispered, closing her eyes tightly. "The last time I held you, your brains were bleeding out into my lap and the Secret Service was trying to separate us. I wouldn't let them take you, though. I don't know why. I knew you were dead. I guess I just didn't want to let you go."

Colt released her long enough to cup her beautiful face and kiss her soft lips. "I know," he murmured. "I watched it all. I tried to tell you it would be all right but you didn't hear me."

Casey looked at him, her euphoria now being clouded by curiosity and confusion. "What do you mean that you watched it? You were dead."

He shrugged. "I guess I didn't realize it for a few minutes. It took me that long to look at my feet and see myself lying there with my head in your lap. Then it made sense as to why no one was responding on the radio, or ignoring me as they ran to protect the

President. Once I saw myself on the ground and you crying, I figured out what had happened."

Casey had her hands on his face. "But here you are...," she grasped for words. "I can't let you go, Colt. I can't wake up from this. It'll just kill me."

He smiled gently at her, grasped her by the shoulders, and turned her around to the bed that was in the room. Casey was confused until she looked at the bed and saw a very old woman lying there. She peered closer as her expression loosened with recognition.

"That's *me*," she hissed, startled when a couple of nurses suddenly ran in to the room and began going through the check list of resuscitation. Confused, she looked up at Colt. "What's going on?"

Colt wrapped her up in his big arms and hugged her. "I've been waiting forty-three years, two months, eighteen days and sixteen hours for you," he murmured. "I was supposed to cross over a long time ago but I couldn't do it. I couldn't leave you."

She still wasn't clear on what he was saying. "Couldn't *leave* me? What do you mean?"

He put his arm around her shoulders and began to lead her towards the door of the room as more nurses came in and began CPR on the old woman on the bed. Monitors were going off and people were buzzing in on the intercom, creating some chaos in the darkened room.

"Just what I said," Colt replied softly. "I wouldn't leave you. So I've been hanging around, waiting for your time to come. I knew it would come soon so I've been waiting in this hospital until you were ready."

"Ready for what?"

"To die."

Casey didn't react for a moment. Then her eyes got wide and she paused in the doorway, grasping his big hands. "Is that why I can touch you?" she asked, shocked. "I'm *dead*? This isn't a dream?"

He shook his head and kissed her forehead, leading her out of the room. "It's not a dream," he assured her. "It's time for you and me to move on to the next adventure."

Casey gazed up at him, choking up. "Are you serious, Colt?" she begged softly. "I'm really dead?"

"Yes."

"And you've been waiting for me all this time to *die*?"

"All this time," he confirmed. "There was no way I could leave you, Casey. I've watched you go through hell and then some over the years. I've watched you remarry, knowing you had other husbands, but still, I hung around because I knew that what you and I shared was special above everything else. Maybe that was arrogant of me, but I don't think so. I knew you felt the same way."

She touched his face, blinking back the tears. "Of course I did," she whispered. "I married Kevin because he reminded me a lot of you. But I married Scott because I was so emotionally crippled at the time that I just couldn't fight him off. Besides, he took good care of the boys and set up trust funds for their college. He never lived long enough to see them use it, though."

"I know."

Casey looked around, spookily. "You haven't seen him around here, have you?"

Colt laughed softly. "No," he told her. "He passed over a long time ago. He told me that you never got over me."

"I didn't."

"I never got over you, either."

They paused as they reached the waiting area near the elevator banks. Colt glanced over, seeing Jack sitting on the sofa with his head in his hands as a nurse spoke softly to him. Casey saw him, too, and the tears came.

"My poor baby," she whispered. "He's not ready for this."

Colt watched his son as the man came to grips with his mother's passing. His gaze was soft, warm, perhaps wistful.

"You've done such a wonderful job with him, Casey," he

murmured. "He grew up into such a fine man. I'm very proud of him and of you."

Casey sniffled, her head against his chest as his big arms went around her. "Could... could you see him? As he grew up, I mean?"

Colt nodded. "I could," he whispered. "There were times I would enter his dreams, too, just to talk to him. But the older he got, the more he didn't really remember me, so it became harder and harder for me to fill his dreams until one day, it just stopped. But I could still see him and see how he was doing. You, on the other hand, always kept my memory alive, so I was always able to enter your dreams to be with you, if only for a short while."

Strangely, the confusion and surprise over her death faded quickly and Casey realized she was accustomed to the idea that she had passed away. Everything he said made perfect sense. The truth was that she wasn't frightened at all because Colt was here, waiting for her, and she knew they would never be apart again. Whatever came, they would remain together for eternity. Already, she knew she had reached heaven because they were together again. That was all that mattered.

"I could never forget you." She turned to him. "You are the love of my life, Colt Sheridan, in this life or the next. Whatever comes, as long as we are together, I can take it."

He smiled at her. "I'm told it's pretty great on the other side."

Casey looked over at Jack one last time, reconciling herself to the fact that she was moving on and leaving him behind. Hunter, Brody and the daughter she'd had in later years... she was leaving them all behind. Tears threatened but she fought them.

"We'll see the kids again one day, right?" she asked softly.

Colt kissed the top of her head. "Absolutely."

With a lingering glance at Jack, who was now being escorted by the nurse into Mother's room to see the body, she turned to Colt.

"Then I'm ready if you are," she said. "Let's see what's waiting for us on the other side."

Colt cupped her face tenderly, gazing into the eyes he knew so well. "I love you, Angel."

"I love you, too. Always and forever."

Colt kissed her deeply before taking her hand and leading her from the waiting area into another hallway that seemed to be very bright. Casey held his hand tightly, following him into a brilliant, white light that beckoned them both. As long as they were together, nothing else mattered. Their love transcended time and space and death, only to be continued with the coming of the dawn.

For them, the next adventure had begun.

THE END

ABOUT THE AUTHOR

ABOUT KAT LE VEQUE

KATHRYN LE VEQUE is a critically acclaimed, USA TODAY Bestselling author (having hit the list over 30 times), an Indie Reader bestseller, a charter Amazon All-Star author, and a #1 best-selling, award-winning, multi-published author in Medieval Historical Romance with over 150 published novels. Kathryn also writes Romantic Suspense as Kat Le Veque.

Kathryn has received praise for her writing and has won several awards for her work, including two nominations for the Holt Medallion. Her books have topped bestseller lists, and she has gained a loyal fan base that eagerly anticipates each new release.

Kathryn is a talented author who has made a significant impact on the world of historical romance fiction. Through her captivating storytelling and meticulous research, she has enchanted readers with her tales of love, adventure, and the enduring power of the human spirit.

Kathryn loves to hear from her readers. Please find Kathryn on Facebook at Kathryn Le Veque, Author, or join her on Twitter @kathrynleveque, and don't forget to visit her website at www.kathrynleveque.com.

ALSO BY KAT LE VEQUE

The Unholy Angels

Hour of Surrender

Trent Chronicles

Valley of Shadow

The Eden Factor

Canyon of the Sphinx

The Eagle Brotherhood

The Sunset Hour

The Killing Hour

The Secret Hour

The Unholy Hour

The Burning Hour

The Ancient Hour

The Devils Hour